SNAFU

PUNK'D

Publisher's Note:

This book is a collection of stories from writers all over the world.
For authenticity and voice, we have kept the style of English native to each author's location, so some stories will be in UK English, and others in US English.
We have, however, changed dashes and dialogue marks to our standard format for ease of understanding.

This book is a work of fiction.
All people, places, events, androids, cybernetic organisms, various other creatures, and situations are the product of the authors' imaginations.
Except Satan. He's out there, watching you.
And he's proud.
Any resemblance to actual persons, living, dead, or in-between, is purely coincidental.

☞ PUNK'D ☜

Edited by Amanda J Spedding & Geoff Brown

COHESION PRESS
THE BATTLE HAS JUST BEGUN

Mayday Hills Asylum
Beechworth, Australia
2023

SNAFU: PUNK'D

Amanda J Spedding & Geoff Brown (eds)

Cohesion Press
Mayday Hills Asylum
Beechworth, Australia
www.cohesionpress.com

Also From Cohesion Press

SNAFU: An Anthology of Military Horror
– eds Geoff Brown & Amanda J Spedding

SNAFU: Wolves at the Door
– eds Geoff Brown & Amanda J Spedding

SNAFU: Survival of the Fittest
– eds Geoff Brown & Amanda J Spedding

SNAFU: Hunters
– eds Amanda J Spedding & Geoff Brown

SNAFU: Future Warfare
– eds Amanda J Spedding & Geoff Brown

SNAFU: Unnatural Selection
– eds Amanda J Spedding & Geoff Brown

SNAFU: Black Ops
– eds Amanda J Spedding & Geoff Brown

SNAFU: Resurrection
– eds Amanda J Spedding, Matthew Summers & Geoff Brown

SNAFU: Last Stand
– eds Amanda J Spedding, Matthew Summers & Geoff Brown

SNAFU: Medivac
– eds Amanda J Spedding & Geoff Brown

Love, Death and Robots: The Official Anthology Vol 1
– eds Amanda J Spedding & Geoff Brown

SNAFU: Holy War
– eds Amanda J Spedding & Geoff Brown

Love, Death and Robots: The Official Anthology Vol 2/3
– eds Amanda J Spedding & Geoff Brown

SNAFU: Dead or Alive
– eds Amanda J Spedding & Geoff Brown

Contents

A GLITCH IN THE SYSTEM

Greg Chapman

Screams and gunfire took her from life.

A living nightmare wrenched her back.

She opened her eyes, cascading explosions pushing the fog from her mind. Her first breath was thick with ash and fear, but there was no time to process it because—

"We've got a live one!"

A blood-streaked face snapped into view – a man, swathed in black armour. Iridescent cables snaked from the side of his shaven head to the pulse rifle in his hands. "Time to rise and shine, 184-Delta-6!"

He pulled her out of the cold, dark earth, and she beheld the state of the world. A vista of buildings reduced to blackened stalagmites. Embers danced in her field of vision. Every shadow was a threat. She wanted to voice her confusion, instead, she burst into a fit of coughing.

"You'll get used to it," he said.

"What's... what's happening? How did I get here?"

He scoffed. "You think there's time for that?" He reached into a hidden compartment in his armour and produced a medallion the size of his palm. "This is gonna hurt." He pressed it against her chest.

A lightning bolt of energy streaked through her every nerve. Emerald light spilled from the disc, slowly painting the same black armour over her torso, arms, and legs – a staccato *click-click-clack* until the exoskeleton covered her from head to toe. She winced, as beneath the armour, the tendril-like cables wormed their way through her flesh, into her heart and spinal column. Puppet strings infused with black magic. When the spell ended,

1

she peered down to see she, too, was clutching a pulse rifle, horned and gleaming like a scarab beetle.

"You'll remember how to shoot once your limbic system calibrates, soldier," her companion said.

"What...? Tell me what the fuck is going on!"

"Not fucking now, goddamnit!"

Two other armoured soldiers joined him, male, and she noticed the numbers on their breastplates. The one who'd revived her was 76-Alpha-19. She staggered and pressed a hand to her head. The strangers wore numbers, but who was she? Memories whirled about like sand. Sand... someone calling her name. Delta? No...

[CONNECTION UNSTABLE]

[CONNECTION RESTORED]

A shriek rang out in the tortured wilderness.

"What was that?" Delta asked.

"For Christ's sake! Just focus and it'll all come back to you once the fighting starts."

"They're coming!" The soldier behind him — 5-Zeta-990 — said.

Alpha joined his comrades, leaving her to observe the charred remains of 5th Avenue. She gasped as three shapes emerged from behind the twisted wreckage of a tank. *Reanimated dead.* Strips of rotting meat twisted and contorted into something resembling human form. Viscera exposed. Delta didn't know what to do. The sights and sounds were a muddle, flickering between the eternal darkness of now and the sun-bleached desert landscape of her... her past. Old memories, fragile, throbbed in her mind's eye.

She tried to shake it off as the things shambled and shrieked closer. Delta turned about, feeling the weight of the armour and rifle for the first time. *No, you've carried this burden before,* her mind supplied. Behind her, at her feet, an open grave and a headstone marked *184Δ6.* The realisation was instantaneous, like the hail of bullets that had killed her so long ago.

"I'm... I'm dead?"

Alpha open fire on the creatures, flares of emerald light

striking their inside-out bodies. Plumes of sanguine smoke oozed from their wounded maws.

"You will be again if you don't man-the-fuck-up!" Zeta told her.

There were hundreds of headstones around hers, all open graves. *Had they been soldiers like me?*

Alpha spun her around to face the oncoming carnage. "Come on – fight!"

The night swelled with the green light of their pulse rifles. The enemy were thrust back, chunks of flesh falling to scorch the already burned earth. The firepower her comrades unleashed did little to halt the creatures, only slowing them.

Alpha turned on Delta again, but this time he'd drawn his weapon on her. "If you don't open fire on those fuckers, I'm gonna put your ass back in the ground!"

She hefted the pulse rifle and fired at the closest monstrosity. The pulses slammed into the ground beneath its feet and sent it hurtling back like a rag doll.

"Fuck yeah!" Zeta cried, fist-pumping the air. Delta stared as he re-aimed and fired, following her lead. The meat-puppets were flung back into the tank they'd been hiding behind with an audible slap of meat and crunching bone. Zeta smiled Delta's way. "Aim for the feet – why didn't we think of that before?"

His shorter comrade, designation 22-Beta-07, slapped Zeta hard on the back of his head. "Because you're all brawn and no brains, Z!"

"Kiss my ass, Beta!"

Alpha shoved them both. "Look alive you dumb fucks – they ain't dead!"

The creatures pulled themselves back together, sinew reforming to connect bones, muscle re-assembling into arms and legs. They were on the move again, hissing through shredded lips.

"What the fuck are they?" Delta squeezed the trigger and gasped at the power she unleashed.

"The enemy!" Alpha cocked his rifle. "That's all you need to know."

SNAFU: PUNK'D

The sound of shifting gravel behind them. The unit turned as one but it was too late. Beta was plucked into the shadows by half a dozen monsters, their oozing appendages grasping the soldier in fleshy coils.

"Fuck!" Beta struggled against them. "No! No!"

Bile rose in Delta's throat as bloody fingers and tongues burrowed into the areas of Beta's body not covered by armour. She screamed as Beta's skin sizzled, the monsters' kisses burning like acid. And when he screamed in agony, his mouth became a vessel for the abominations' caustic red smoke. In a matter of moments, he'd melted from the inside out, his body sloughing out through the gaps in his carapace. Delta and her comrades could only look on in horror.

She didn't want to be here; this wasn't what death was supposed to be. Why was this happening to her?

"Retreat!" Alpha yelled releasing a barrage of pulse fire on the run. The energy spheres struck the enemy and what was left of their friend full force, reducing them all to offal.

"Beta, no!" Z wrestled against Alpha's grip as his friend was obliterated.

Delta's restored heart thrummed in terror. She didn't want to die on the battlefield. Not like this. Not again.

"Get back to base!" Alpha ordered. "Get back to the cemetery, now!"

As she fled with them, the apocalypse around Delta shifted to the desert and back again. The sound of a child's laughter resonated around her. Memories colliding in the chaos. She realised then, death was everywhere. It wasn't an escape. It was a prison.

⚙ ⚙

A singular crypt in the centre of the cemetery opened onto a descending staircase of stone.

Delta followed Alpha and Z, each step taking them deeper

into the dark. Grey dust sprinkled from above and caked in the sweat on her brow. The dust of the rotting dead.

"Can someone explain to me what the *fuck* is going on? Where the hell are you taking me?" she demanded.

"Your first question doesn't have a simple answer," Alpha said. "But I'm taking you to headquarters."

She heard him press something on his armour and a green light emanated from his medallion, which illuminated a solid steel door at the bottom of the stairs. Runes or sigils had been carved into its surface. Alpha tapped several of the symbols in quick succession and the door slid open with a low rumble.

The trio stepped into a smallish war room in complete contrast to the world outside. Computer consoles gleamed with power. Cables covered the ceiling, leading to a dozen black titanium sarcophagi. A long, grey marble table, almost altar-like, took pride of place and emblazoned upon it, a stylised white military shield speared by a lightning bolt with the word 'AXIUM' beneath.

"What's AXIUM?"

Z threw his weapon to the floor and climbed into the nearest sarcophagus. Instantly, cables crept into his armour and administered reinvigorating green fluid. Alpha put his rifle on the table and sighed. "Axium are the people who brought you back to help in the fight against The Flayed."

Delta placed her weapon down beside Alpha's. "And we're the only ones who can stop them? Where's the army?"

He ran a hand through his sweat-soaked hair. "Axium are the only ones left in the fight. Without them, we'd be royally screwed. Now, look, we haven't got time for this. We have to refuel and get back out there."

She threw her arms up in exasperation. "But what the hell is all this? What are The Flayed? How the hell was I brought back?"

Alpha shook his head and entered a sarcophagus. Green fluid pumped with a hiss. "That's above my pay grade."

A silky voice sounded at her back. "It's best not to overwhelm yourself, 184Δ6."

Delta turned in the direction of the voice as a woman in a dark grey suit emerged from the shadows. She was about twenty years Delta's senior, but clean and preened to perfection. She wore an AXIUM pin on her lapel, like the politicians used to wear the American flag.

"Who the fuck are you?" Delta reached for her rifle.

"I represent the company."

"Axium?"

Her lipstick was flawless. "That's right. Now please, join your comrades in the healing chamber. There's not much time before The Flayed strike again."

Delta shuddered, her legs heavy. "I don't understand any of this. I was dead. How did you bring me back?"

The woman took Delta by the arm and helped her to a chamber. Above them, the dull shrieks of The Flayed seeped through the stone.

"It's in our power," the woman said. "The only way to win a war is with the toughest soldiers, like you. Relax and let the potions take effect. You'll feel unstoppable. Besides, I've made sure Alpha will be there to guide you."

Delta gasped at the sting of the cables, the serum cold in her veins. "Wait… please."

The woman from Axium smiled anew. "Don't worry, soldier, Axium's got your back."

⚙⚙ ⚙⚙

[CONNECTION UNSTABLE]

Pinpricks of static invaded her vision.

She smelled the neon and blood.

Until the harsh sun melted it all away.

The graveyard city had been replaced with desert sands.

There was no black armour, no pulse rifle, only the pale roughness of her uniform and her M27.

"So, Del, how much longer until you end this tour?" A soldier walked beside her. He looked just like Alpha but there was less intensity in his gaze. He was relaxed, not on high alert.

A GLITCH IN THE SYSTEM

"What?" she said, squinting to try and get her bearings against the backdrop of sand and rock.

Several other soldiers milled about, some talking and laughing in the shade of an M-ATV. One figure stood out amongst the camouflaged – a woman in a grey suit. She shared cigarettes and smiles with the soldiers.

Delta knew that woman. Somehow…

"I said, when will you get home to see your kid?" the man with Alpha's face said.

Before she could reply, three men, their faces partially obscured by tattered scarves, leapt from behind a ridge, Kalashnikovs raised. Delta felt the searing heat of the bullets in her chest before her comrade even had the chance to sound a warning.

"Contact!"

[CONNECTION RESTORED]

The desert vista shattered like glass to welcome the burning city streets. Day into vicious night.

Delta stood motionless in the midst of it, the familiar weight of the armour and pulse rifle anything but a comfort. Alpha screamed into her ear.

"Contact!"

Two dozen of The Flayed staggered towards them, bleeding over the remains of a toppled building. Delta sucked in a breath, desperate to fire up her brain and make sense of the nightmare. Her fellow soldiers—Alpha, Z, and Beta—opened fire. She would have too if only the sight of Beta hadn't left her numb.

"Beta?" she said. "But… you're dead?"

He looked over his shoulder at her between pulls of the trigger. "I'm back, baby!"

The Flayed were bags of blood, stomping, exploding against the force of the unit's suppressing fire.

Delta glimpsed a shape out of the corner of her eye, a fragmented figure, like a hologram. A little girl with blonde ringlets in a yellow dress, reaching and laughing. Only for it to be lost a second later.

"Casey?" Delta cried.

"Delta, get the fuck in here!" Alpha ordered.

Four of The Flayed belched their red smoke, a noxious fog that scorched the air like tongues of flame on the edge of dry paper. The cloud rushed in, catching on her units' exposed skin, on hers.

Delta searched for the little girl, but the space before her soon swarmed with the red smoke. "No," she whispered as the skin of her hands began to melt through to the bone.

Through tear-streaked eyes she stared into the red and beyond the corpulent horde to the other side of the street. She recognised the woman in the grey suit – the woman from AXIUM. She and other suits from 'the company' were seemingly watching the spectacle from behind a thick wall of protective glass. As Delta and her comrades were dying, this woman dined on champagne and caviar.

Delta's death and the reaping of the city were entertainment.

And as the truth seeped into her memory, Delta died once more.

[CONNECTION UNSTABLE]

Delta awoke inside the embrace of the sarcophagus. The irony was that she'd been in the dark all this time. But not anymore.

She pushed open the door and ripped the cables from the side of her head and her armour. Yet despite untangling herself, she burned with rage. She still wasn't free. The image of that nameless woman and her suits, dining as she and her comrades died, churned her stomach. She pounded on the lid of Alpha's cage; they needed to be warned that it was all a ruse. They were doomed no matter what they did.

"Wake up, Alpha!"

He was frozen, eyes closed in an artificially-induced coma. She moved to Z's sarcophagus and slammed her fist on the viewing window until it cracked.

"Fucking wake up! We have to stop them! They've got us trapped in here!"

Delta grabbed hold of the sides and shook it with all her strength, but Z just jostled around, oblivious to any sensation.

A door slid open behind Delta and she snatched up her rifle and aimed.

The nameless woman strode out, computer tablet in hand, barely even giving Delta an upwards glance as she spoke. "You're becoming quite the problem, aren't you 184Δ6?"

Delta screamed through gritted teeth and stepped to the woman, rifle trained right between her eyes. She pulled the trigger but the rifle did nothing. It might as well have been a toy.

The woman laughed. "Do you really think you're in control here?" She swiped her fingers across the tablet screen and her comrades' sarcophagi opened.

"Who the fuck do you think you are?" Delta asked. "You bring me back to fight so you and your cronies can get your rocks off? Torment me with monsters and visions of my daughter?"

The woman frowned. "Your daughter? You saw your daughter?"

Delta pounded the table. "Yes! It was like she was here!"

The woman scanned her tablet. "Interesting. Must be some residual memory decay..."

Delta scoffed. "So that's it, isn't it? This is all just some sick fucking game to you?"

The woman smiled and tapped her nose. "Exactly. It's all just sport – the best sport money can buy."

Delta put a hand to her aching head. "Just tell me that none of this is real."

"Oh, it's most assuredly real. Not VR or a simulation. Nothing so juvenile." She gestured to the room. "Our clients expect perfection – the ultimate experience. And we give it to them." She tilted her head, considering Delta. "Do you have any idea how much it costs to start a war? To have a city destroyed? To bring people like you back from the dead?" She shrugged. "Sure, there were some teething problems. The Flayed are our first attempts at resurrection, but that turned out to be a blessing in disguise. After all, soldiers need someone to fight, don't they? We've invested trillions in this project and as the saying goes, 'Rome wasn't built in a day'." The woman offered her another smile. "But then, a grunt like you wouldn't understand, which is why you're the pawn and not the player."

When the woman laughed, Delta slammed her to the floor and unleashed a volley of punches into her perfect face.

"You fucking monster! I'll kill you!"

The bitch from Axium kept laughing, her lips splitting apart. "I think... it's time to go back to your grave."

Strong arms took hold of Delta; her fellow warriors dragged her off the woman and back to the sarcophagi.

"Get the fuck off me!"

The woman wiped her bloody mouth on her silk sleeve. "It's definitely time for Delta to have a hard reset."

Delta writhed and pulled, but Alpha, Z and Beta—their gazes blank—held her firm, ignoring her agonised pleas. The cables whipped into her. "You goddamn bitch. You think I don't remember you? I saw you in Kabul. I saw you!"

The woman picked up her tablet, tapping the screen with steady hands. "You've been a glitch in the system ever since you got here. But I'm going to fix that now."

Delta looked at her comrades, the fear threatening to take hold. "Arrgh! Can't you see what's happening here? She's wiping our minds!"

The cables oozed their fluid, and Delta fought hard against its effects – the pain like she was being tasered over and over again.

"Arrgh! It's a game! It's a game... it's all just a fucking game..."

The woman's words were the last thing she heard before she collapsed. "Yes, and it's time for you to play again."

⚙⚙ ⚙⚙

A GLITCH IN THE SYSTEM

Delta's eyes opened on the infernal city, but there was no fear now, only determination. "It's a game. It's just a game."

She cocked her pulse rifle and scanned the noxious horizon, waiting—hoping—for them to arrive.

"What'd you say, soldier?" Alpha said, confused.

She ignored him, instead walking headlong in the direction of the ridge. She knew what lay on the other side.

Alpha ran after her and pulled her back. "What the fuck are you doing?"

Delta turned on him, her weapon raised. "You're wasting your time, Alpha. There are no rules here. We're being manipulated, but you—*all* of you—are too afraid to see it."

He tried to reach for her again. "I don't know what the hell you're talking about—"

"What's her problem?" Beta said.

Delta kept the weapon locked on and nodded over her shoulder. "You know what's over this ridge? The truth."

Alpha frowned. "What?"

"You can see it for yourself if you come with me."

"The only thing that's over there is death."

She shrugged. "Without a doubt. But I don't plan on dying a slave. Do you?"

The muffled whine of The Flayed rose into the decrepit air, putting the three men on high alert. Alpha raised his weapon at Delta, the pair within inches of the barrel of each other's rifles.

"Put down your rifle, Delta – that's an order!"

Z and Beta joined their leader, all weapons trained.

She shook her head "Sorry boys, no can do."

"Delta, don't do this!"

"You'll thank me. You won't have to suffer anymore."

Delta fired, the first blast, striking Alpha square in the chest. At such close range, his chest plate shattered, the medallion falling to the grey earth, devoid of light. Their leader was dead before he hit the ground. Z and Beta returned fire, a shard of energy, cracking the armour on her left arm. She was thrown back and slammed into the face of the ridge, but still, she kept squeezing the trigger. Spheres of green in their dozens rained down on Z and Beta before they could fire off any more of their own.

When the smoke and ash cleared, her comrades lay face down. Dead. Like they'd been countless times before. This time, though, their deaths had been at the hands of one of their own.

Delta, injured, got to her feet and pushed down the guilt. *I did it to set them free.* Grunting with pain, she scaled the pile of rubble on the ridge, and pulled herself onto the upturned chassis of a blackened car. Below, in the middle of the ashen street, stood a huddle of The Flayed, swaying in unison. Sleeping, waiting. She crouched and followed her eye line past the horde to the other side of the street where, in the rotting remains of a jewellery store, she spied the woman. Despite the injuries Delta had inflicted upon her face, the woman was still jovial, laughing and smiling with her clients.

Not for long.

Delta fired a barrage of pulses into The Flayed who blew apart like leaves. The look of surprise on the woman's face made Delta smile. As The Flayed began to put themselves back together and the woman scrambled for her control tablet, Delta slid down the street-facing side of the ridge. The Flayed saw her and immediately became enraged. She fired again, the plumes of light pushing them back. With their shrieks in her ears, she ran past them, heading straight for the jewellery store.

The slavering Flayed were at her heels, but Delta couldn't think about them now – she had to stick to her plan. She skidded to a halt just before the protective glass where the suits were hiding, and pulled the trigger. The release of energy at point-blank range melted the glass in one concussive blast. The shockwave rattled the foundations and the screams of the suits rivalled that of The Flayed. It was probably the first time they'd ever known true fear, real pain.

She found the woman — Axium's founder — lying in a spreading pool of blood, her legs pinned beneath a collapsed column. She was screaming and reaching in vain for the tablet. The other suits, bleeding and crying, clung together in a darkened corner.

The woman looked up at Delta with terrified eyes. "If I die… AXIUM dies."

Delta sensed The Flayed at her back, shambling ever closer, bloodied mangled flesh that should have been dead and stayed dead. They didn't scare her anymore. She sneered down at the woman. "You fucks have been hungry for a thrill. Gorged yourselves while we died again and again. Well, guess what? These assholes behind me—the ones you *fucking created*—they're hungry too."

A rivulet of blood sloughed from the woman's foul mouth. "They'll kill you…too."

Delta smirked. "I died a long time ago."

As The Flayed unleashed their cloud of sanguine smoke into the room, Delta aimed at the control tablet and fired.

The red smoke gave way to a blazing light and there, in the safe boundaries of Delta's soul, Casey was waiting with open arms and endless smiles.

[CONNECTION TERMINATED]

LIGHTBRINGERS

Damien McKeating

Jackson bounced around the inside of the APC as it thundered across the wasteland, kicking up dust and sand as it went. He gave a grunt as a sharp drop sent a jolt up his spine.

"My people," said Ortega from where she crouched between the two rows of personnel, her brown skin sheened with sweat. "We are experiencing some turbulence. Do not be alarmed and please keep hands and feet inside the vehicle until we have come to a complete stop." She flashed a grin at them that didn't quite reach her eyes.

Jackson joined in the round of laughter. There were eleven of them in the APC, a modified Boxer from before the world fell, now kitted out with photovoltaic panels and reinforced photoweave plates, and currently home to three crew and eight infantry. Jackson was one of the eight; kitted out in photoweave armour and the latest in solar-powered weaponry that SolVolt could devise. With the war at a stalemate, billions were invested in the mega-corp and their latest solar-powered armament.

"Take a seat, Ortega," said Sergeant Abara. She stood and addressed her squad, muscles bulging on her arms and shoulders as she reached up to stabilise herself. "Lightbringers," she addressed her team. "We are coming in hot. Hotter than usual."

"Gonna burn them up, Sarge," Ortega called out with a sly smile, her voice promising violence.

"The horde are waiting for us," Abara said. "Full on demons out of darkness here to take the sun from the skies. Us or them. There is no peaceful resolution. There is no negotiation. Kill 'em all."

"Kill 'em all!" the squad hollered back, Jackson with them.

15

"In five klicks we will pull up short of the dark zone. You will enter hostile territory and proceed in a straight trajectory towards target alpha: the gate. The target is heavily guarded, and you are to expect extreme resistance. The Blood Eagles have already been lost to this objective," she added solemnly. "We can avenge them and save ourselves."

"Back to the light," said Mathers, bowing his head and closing his eyes. He ran a hand over his shaved head and let out a slow, quavering breath.

Jackson worried for him. Man looked nervous. Any sane person would be nervous: what they were about to do wasn't sane.

"Your payload," Abara continued, tossing her braided hair back with a casual flick of her head. "Is the delivery of the Lucifer Flare." She gestured at an innocuous looking green satchel. "Sunlight in a bottle. You're the Lightbringers." She paused, gaze tracking each of them. "Who are you?"

"Lightbringers!" they bellowed.

"I can't hear you," Abara taunted.

"Lightbringers!"

"They can't hear you!" Abara pointed to the front of the APC, towards the horde.

"Lightbringers!"

"Named for the fallen angel who created suns. Time to bring a little light to the darkness. Burn 'em up!"

"Burn 'em up!"

"Beautiful," Abara said with a satisfied smile. "Corporal, take them out."

The APC ground to a halt and the back opened up with a clang. Sunlight blazed in, making them squint.

Corporal Becker, square shouldered and solid, rose and strode along the line, slapping arms and legs as he went. "Up and out. Form up. Ready line. Let's go."

Jackson tingled. Rocked on the balls of his feet, moved with his squad, and suddenly was out under the sun.

The world had ended and, much to everyone's surprise, had

managed to keep going. The sun was the power now. Water was a trading commodity. Most of the developed world was desert or savanna. Scorched. Irradiated.

The Lightbringers stood under a terrible sun, surrounded by wasteland, and looked on the darkness.

The second apocalypse they called it.

Demons had crawled out of the dark. From hell, from the depths of space, from diseased imaginations, no one knew. They built gates, or portals, powered by an unknown technology. These gateways created thick, black storms and clouds. No light. No heat. Just darkness and death.

Jackson saw it all for the first time and stopped in his tracks. The desert, the day, just ended. A line in the sand. Beyond it was darkness, roiling clouds, and death.

"Need a little Triple-S?" asked Drabek. His wiry frame twitched and bounced as he offered a vial to Jackson.

"Not right now," Jackson said. Triple-S: short, sharp, shock. An adrenaline boost close to a berserker rage.

"Smoke it later," Drabek giggled, and shoved it into Jackson's pocket.

"We're not here to sunbathe," Corporal Becker shouted. "We're fully powered, fully charged. That gives us maybe thirty minutes in the dark. Let's get to work."

Jackson flexed inside his suit. The photoweave absorbed and held solar energy, protecting him with an energy shell that had more stopping power than any other material devised by humanity. The blades strapped to his back were charged with the same energy. Same with the rifle in his hands. They were modelled on the old SA80s, but further modified. The magazine held a solar charge that sent out concussive blasts. On a narrow beam it would punch a hole through someone's chest without a worry.

"Time to go to hell," Ortega called and gave her best couldn't-care-less grin.

"Hell and back again, right?" Jackson said as he checked his gear. There was an eagerness to Ortega that was unsettling. He had to know he could trust the squad to keep it together.

Ortega grabbed his arm, pulling his attention to her. "You think we're coming back?" she asked, smile wide and wild.

Jackson frowned but Ortega was already moving. It was time.

Over the line they went: Becker, Ortega, Drabek, Mathers and Jackson up front, with Mathers carrying the Lucifer Flare. Lambert, Jansen, and Agosti followed behind. Stepping out of the sun and into the embrace of those dark clouds, a chill ran through Jackson's body. The whole world was powered by the sun now. Heat and light at the heart of every surviving stronghold. The eternal darkness they walked into would destroy them all if allowed to spread.

"Do you think this is God's punishment?" Jackson heard Lambert ask behind him.

"No," Jansen snapped, making clear what she thought of the question. "This is just another pile of shit in a series of piles of shit."

"Eyes up," Becker called from the front.

Their comms crackled in their ears. "No signs of movement," Abara's voice came to them. "The gate should be somewhere straight ahead of you."

"In the ruins?" Becker clarified.

"Seems so," Abara confirmed.

The crumbled remains of a township rose out of the sand before them. Walls like monumental gravestones, gaping doorways, hollow buildings open to the sky.

"Lovely spot for an ambush," Ortega muttered.

"Let 'em come an' burn," Drabek replied, his thin face twitching into a smile.

Jackson fell into his training and found comfort in it. Check, step, turn, check, step. There was strength in formation. He had Ortega's back. Lambert had his.

They walked between the decaying walls, their descent into hell.

Rubble and stone clattered in the silence.

"Visual?" Becker hissed.

LIGHTBRINGERS

"Negative," they each called in turn.

Jackson watched a stone clatter its way down a pile of bricks and rotting timber. He traced its trajectory back. Braced his rifle against his shoulder.

Breathe.

"Back to the light," Mathers whispered.

"Short, sharp bursts," Becker ordered. "Keep moving. Keep in formation."

Then the horde came for them.

"Light 'em up," Becker roared.

The horde were monstrous, Jackson had known that, but he'd never seen one before. There were hundreds of them, and he realised there was no such thing as 'one'. Each was a mutation, an aberration, a demon spawned where no light was allowed.

He breathed out and squeezed the trigger. The rifle discharged, smooth and easy, none of the kickback of the old-fashioned firearms.

The horde were albino-white and eyeless. They skittered like a wave of spiders, on two, three, four legs or more. Pale and spindly, their torsos were a solid compact of exo-skeleton; their heads ridged ovals with gaping maws that stretched open with cracks and pops. Tongues snaked out, smooth, barbed, dripping, black, purple, poisonous, acidic, all sorts of combinations. An eclectic mix of death descended on the Lightbringers. Long limbs with too many joints stretched out to disembowel with serrated claws.

One of them exploded as Jackson's shot hit true, tearing through the torso and burning it up.

Another.

Another.

A creature with more legs than he could count, its head lodged in its torso, launched itself over the others and descended towards them with claws and fangs dripping.

Jackson aimed.

Breathed.

Squeezed.

The solar charge of his rifle struck home. The energy was lethal. Sunlight to vampires. It vanished in a ripple of flame, and ash was all that washed over them.

"Forward," Becker howled.

Fire. Step. Repeat.

Jackson moved. The Lightbringers were bellowing around him.

"Get some!" Ortega grinned. "You too! Come on! I got plenty!"

It was hard to miss. Every shot was another body disintegrated. The world was fireflash and ash. Jackson found his mouth dry. He shouted out and there was nothing but a hoarse cry.

"Up!" Becker urged them on.

They reached an incline and found the way forward empty of demons. The ruined walls created a funnel, keeping their flanks clear and forcing the horde to follow at the Lightbringers' rear.

Jansen and Lambert dropped to their knees and opened up a burst of rounds. The demons fell back. Jackson and Agosti dropped and did the same. Rinse and repeat. The squad retreated deeper into enemy territory. Each step a step closer to the gate.

"Hold up," Becker said. "Perimeter check. Stay sharp."

They had backed into an enclosed space – a section of a ruined and partially submerged building. The walls stretched up, but the floor had long since collapsed, exposing them to the thick, rolling madness of the black clouds overhead.

Jackson fell into step with Agosti, covering their right flank, scanning the high walls, waiting for a wave of pale death to sweep over them.

"Where are they?" Agosti asked. Drenched in sweat, her rifle moved in steady sweeps, gaze fixed to the walls.

Jackson glanced to the funnel; the horde hadn't pursued them. "Maybe we scared them off," he said, not at all convinced.

"We're too bad ass for them," Ortega chuckled.

"Burn 'em all," Drabek said with a huge smile. "Did you see 'em go?"

LIGHTBRINGERS

"Shut it," Becker said. "Where's the damn gate? Abara, you getting this?"

"You are in position," Abara's voice came over the comms. "The gate should be where you are."

"This is bad," Mathers said. "We've got nowhere to go."

He was right. The empty holes of doorways and windows were filled with fallen bricks and dust.

"Abara, there's nothing here," Becker said.

"The readings are loud and clear," Abara responded. "Scout ahead. You've got time."

Jackson watched a trail of dust waterfall down one of the walls. Felt a rumble under his feet. He turned to Agosti and saw that she'd felt it too.

"Eyes up," Jansen called, her voice urgent.

There was something in the sky. Pale flecks against dark clouds.

Demons on wings.

"They called in air support," Drabek chuckled.

The ground shifted. A tremor that made the walls shake and sent up clouds of dust. Booms and echoes reached them, along with the chittering, skittering madness of the horde returning.

"Here they come," Agosti said.

"Mathers, with me," Becker called. "Find that damn gate. Drabek, Ortega, watch the skies, everyone else keep them back."

Jackson checked his magazine, adjusted the blades on his back. He shifted a strap at his chest, tightening his photoweave armour. The last wave hadn't got close to them, but he didn't think their luck would hold a second time.

The horde surged through the funnel. It was death for them. The Lightbringers opened up and the entryway blazed with burning bodies. A storm of ash plumed into the air, a thin column of choking dust that blossomed into a billowing cloud.

"Ain't even hard," Drabek yelled. "Woo!" He set his rifle to burst, and a wave of the demons erupted into flames.

"Keep the formation!" Agosti called.

The airborne creatures swooped in. Faster than Jackson

would have thought. They divebombed, gossamer wings pressed to their sides, drilling down with taloned feet extended.

Drabek screamed as one hit him. His photoweave armour flared into life, bursting with a radiant energy that deflected and burnt the creature that had landed on him.

Jackson aimed.

One shot.

The creature exploded into ash.

Someone shouted, "Incoming!"

Jackson wasn't sure who it was, he was too busy now. Death came from every angle. The flying creatures were spindly twisters of destruction. One hit his shoulder, knocking him to his knees. He grabbed the creature by its eyeless head and emptied a round into its chest.

Through the ash-cloud of its corpse, another charged. It hit him full on, the barrel of his rifle jammed into its torso. Jackson fell back, the creature on top of him, his armour flaring against a succession of hits as the creature's claws and maw raked against it.

It exploded.

His shot, or someone else's, he didn't know. A hand hauled him up – Agosti, streaked with dust, a wild look in her eyes.

The ground was still shaking, and Jackson realised what that meant just as the behemoth crested the wall.

It was huge. A leathery-skinned giant, pock-marked, scarred, dirty from dust and ash, its white expanse turned grey. It walked upright on two colossal legs, and its monstrous fists smashed into the ruins. On its ridged, plated head, a huge mouth gaped open beneath an eyeless face.

Bricks crashed down as the behemoth struck. Jackson's armour burst to life and the warning beep of low power levels sounded. An assault like this would sap their charge. Leave them defenceless and dead.

Lambert cried out. He was backed into a corner, surrounded by the horde. One of the flying demons landed on his shoulders, grabbed his head, and twisted.

LIGHTBRINGERS

Over the roar, over the screams, Jackson swore he heard the snap and pop.

The creature soared upwards, Lambert's head in its hands, blood splattering through the air.

The behemoth reached down, and Jansen disappeared into its grip. Her rifle fired, searing into the creature's palm, but to no end. It closed its fist, silencing the weapon. Jansen screamed, gurgled, went silent as her body snapped. Blood leaked out of her eyes and ears. Her skin split, coming apart at the seams. She dribbled out of herself until, ripe and fresh, she burst.

The behemoth dropped her, and Jansen flopped onto the ground like a wet rag doll. A moment later she was gone, as the horde rushed over and tore her apart.

Jackson realised he was staring, realised his rifle was silent.

"Come on!" Ortega bellowed. She appeared next to Jackson, screaming and firing, and that was all the prompt he needed.

"Form up!" Agosti bellowed.

The squad closed ranks. Back-to-back. Rifles up and firing. Light flashing as blazing rounds turned the assaulting horde into soot.

"On me!" Agosti ordered. "Incoming!"

She charged forward, the squad keeping step with her as the behemoth struck again. Its hand smashed down where they had been moments before, and the ground rippled under their feet.

Jackson rode the wave, turned his attention up to the huge creature, and opened fire. His rounds struck home, leaving flecks and burns on the demon's skin but not destroying it.

The behemoth swung its arm, bringing another wall down on them.

Jackson dropped to his knees and covered his head with his hands.

Next to him, Agosti's armour sent out its shrill alarm, and then falling masonry crushed her skull. Before she hit the ground, four demons swept in and dragged her away.

Jackson pushed to his feet, rifle blaring. Burst. Turn. Burst. Turn. He repeated the move, raging and shouting as the creatures burst into flames.

"Lightbringers!" Becker called.

Becker and Mathers rounded the ruins, using the newly collapsed wall as their way in, and launched an assault on the horde's flank. They came in hard and fast and carved a corridor of blazing ash out of the demon's ranks.

Jackson followed Ortega and Drabek as they ran, heads down as another sweep of the behemoth's arm threatened to crush them.

"We're leaving!" Becker ordered. "Comms are down. Objective is a negative. There's no gate here. Form up on—"

The behemoth landed close, and as it hit the ground, the world crumbled.

Jackson watched the behemoth's feet descend and then keep going. He thought it was sinking until he realised the ground was collapsing. Until he felt the dirt under his feet tilt away from him.

He started to slide.

Started to fall.

He hit the slope, snapping his jaw shut, tasting blood and feeling a bruising smack against his ribs. Distantly, he realised his armour was failing.

Then the ground swallowed them up.

A moment of freefall turned into a smack of pain. Jackson hit something, bounced, hit again, rolled and stopped. He groaned. His photoweave armour sparked and lit up in fits and bursts.

Jackson looked up. They were in a cavernous space, a basement or a buried ground floor, he'd never know. Through the clouds of dust he saw the behemoth, impaled on a girder, thrashing and roaring, still shaking the ground.

He spotted Mathers next, his body splayed out, head twisted the wrong way, metal rods jutting through his chest and legs.

"The Lucifer Flare," Jackson mumbled through lips smeared with his own blood.

Mathers had been carrying the payload. Where was it?

"Ortega?" Jackson scrambled to his feet, casting about through the wreckage. "Becker? Drabek?"

LIGHTBRINGERS

He saw the bodies and panicked. But the uniforms were wrong... the bodies were old, torn up, the wounds dry... "Fuck." It was the Blood Eagles. They'd found the remains of the last squad.

Jackson stumbled forward and then recoiled at the looming shape appearing in the dust. It was an exo-suit, an SV1, favoured by the Eagles for its flight capabilities and heavy ordinance. The suit lay open, its former occupant missing. Jackson found it hard not to think of the suit as disembowelled, that it missed the vital spark of life.

As the dust settled, Jackson glanced around the rough-walled cavern of bricks and stone. Ortega was at the foot of a pile of rubble, pushing herself upright. Becker stepped out of the dust, coughed, spit blood, and stood next Jackson.

They both stared at a raised dais in the centre of the space. There was a circle on it, formed from a stone or metal Jackson didn't recognise. Thirteen raised glyphs decorated the circumference, each one emitting a purple glow.

"The gate," Jackson said.

"The guardian," Becker added.

A shape coalesced in front of the gate. It appeared in fits and starts, something caught in a glance but not realised. Light and dark slid around each other, an unearthly play of shadows that gave depth and form to what had before been nothingness. It melted forward, squeezing through the gaps of reality. A tall figure, its pallid flesh sloughed down its body in drooping waves like grotesque robes. Its eyeless head turned, its attention on them alone. Arms and fingers with too many joints flexed and moved through the air in complex patterns and rhythms. The gate responded in kind, the glyphs pulsing and ebbing with the movements.

"Does it know we're here?" Jackson whispered. His gaze flicked from the guardian to where Ortega scrabbled through the remains of the hardware scattered by the Blood Eagles.

"I think so," Becker said.

"Why doesn't it do anything?"

25

Jackson waited but no answer came. He flinched as rubble scattered and a bulk staggered out of the shadows. It was Drabek, filthy and bloodied, but standing.

He limped over to them. "Let's kill the motherfucker," he growled.

The man was twitching, nearly vibrating, and Jackson guessed he was pumped full of Triple-S.

"That won't close the gate," Ortega said. She rolled over the corpse of one of their fallen brethren and retrieved a familiar looking satchel from the body.

"A Lucifer Flare," Jackson said. "The Blood Eagles had one too."

"Must have never got to use it." Becker grinned. "This is our lucky day. Let's light 'em up."

Ortega showed them the flare. The satchel was open, the operating panel visible. The lights were on. Power was good. The gauges indicated the flare had been activated.

"They did use it," Becker said, his grin now gone and his voice caught between statement and question.

"So why isn't this all ashes and rubble?" Drabek snarled.

Ortega pressed the launch button.

They all flinched.

Nothing.

"It didn't work," Jackson said.

"It never worked," Ortega said.

"Fuck," Becker muttered.

"Of course it works," Drabek said. "Just do it right and it'll work. Just do it *right*."

Jackson shook his head. Ortega knew her ordinance. He trusted her.

Ahead of them the guardian waited, fingers caressing the air. Above them, the horde was rising, a growing sound of claws, growls and grunts. Behind them, the unyielding stone of a sunken city.

"We were sold out," Becker said.

"No way," Drabek snarled. "No way, man."

LIGHTBRINGERS

"No money in winning a war," Ortega said quietly, staring down at the corrupted Flare.

Jackson's stomach went hollow. "That can't be right," he heard himself say, an observer inside his own body. "We don't kill our own."

"We're just numbers on a spreadsheet," Ortega said, snorting her disgust.

Jackson shook his head but couldn't find a reply. Drabek was shaking, somewhere between rage and a junkie after a fix. Becker stared across the ruins to the guardian and the gate. As if sensing a change in their mood, the guardian reached towards them.

Becker growled. "Welcome to hell, Lightbringers," he said. "Time to burn and turn. Someone give me an exit strategy."

"They screwed us," Drabek hissed.

"One damn war at a time."

"I can fix it," Ortega said, still kneeling beside the Lucifer Flare. "Find me the Flare Mathers had and I can rig them together."

Becker nodded. "Me and Drabek will buy you some time. Jackson, you find that second Flare and finish the job. Nice and steady—"

Drabek launched himself forward before Becker could finish.

"Drabek!" Becker bellowed.

"Motherfu—" Drabek screamed as he charged at the guardian.

The monster raised a hand and Drabek stopped, was lifted in mid-air, held immobile, his voice croaking as air stopped in his throat.

"Goddamn," Jackson said under his breath. He had no idea where his rifle had ended up, so he reached over his shoulders and drew his blades, twin weapons that blazed with solar energy.

Becker followed suit. "Get to work Lightbringers, and we'll see the other side of this."

"Bet?" Ortega asked, breathing heavy, struggling to stand upright.

"I'll buy the first round if I'm wrong."

"You'll buy all the rounds if you're wrong."

"Deal."

They got to work as Drabek struggled in the guardian's grip.

The demon flexed its fingers, and Drabek's body twisted. Bones popped and cracked. His rib cage collapsed inwards. His fingers and arms bent back on themselves. His jaw opened... stretched... burst.

Jackson licked his lips and flexed his fingers over the handles of his blades. How could they fight something like this? He heard Becker growl and then the guardian raised its other hand. It pointed up. At the lip of the hole was the gathered horde, silent and waiting.

The guardian beckoned to them.

The horde poured into the hole. A rain of hideous death.

Jackson froze. His brain shut down. This was like nothing he'd ever seen before. How could they fight this? How could they *fight* this?

"Ten o'clock!" Becker shouted.

Jackson looked to his left and saw it: the Lucifer Flare. Mathers' satchel lay at the far end of the room, jutting up against a broken pipe leaking black water.

And then the horde were on them.

Jackson slashed. He ducked. Rolled. Ran. Demons fell under his blades, bursting into ash. Their blows cracked against his armour, and then he felt them crack against his body. The suit had nothing left to give.

He fought with renewed desperation. His blades danced and he couldn't miss. Enemies were everywhere. Everything that moved needed to be killed. Something with two heads lunged at him and he decapitated both.

Staggering towards where'd he seen the satchel, Jackson heard Becker scream. Through a break in the ravening, white mass of demons he saw Becker in the guardian's grip. Suspended in the air just like Drabek had been. The guardian gestured, flicking its hands apart, and Becker's body followed suit. He tore in two, split down the middle.

LIGHTBRINGERS

Jackson jammed a blade into a demon. Slashed another. Hit and hit again. Swung until his arms ached and his chest was on fire.

He went down, falling awkwardly onto one knee, and realised he was kneeling on the damn satchel.

Jackson laughed. He'd made it. For all the good it would do him.

He coughed and tasted blood.

A savage blow caught his arm. Pain flashed up from his wrist to his shoulder, and the blade dropped from his numb fingers.

He fumbled at his suit, desperate for something to fight with, and felt the ampule Drabek had given him. He snatched it out of his pocket and gazed at the warm, red liquid. Then he jammed it into his thigh and hit the delivery button.

Short. Sharp. Shock.

The rush was instant.

His ears filled with white noise. There was no pain. There was no worry. There was no confusion.

Jackson tucked the satchel under his arm and ran. He barrelled through the horde, swinging with one blade, shoulder barging them. Their talons sliced into him, but he barely registered it.

He broke free, found himself in a moment of space. Light blazed around him, blinding him. He turned, confused, felt hands on him, screamed with rage... and saw Ortega. She pulled him down to the ground and snatched the satchel off him.

"You're not dead," Jackson said, shaking with Triple-S. He watched her tear panels open and strip wires.

"The Blood Eagles came prepared," Ortega said drily.

Jackson registered the light again. Solar charges. Ortega had found them in the Blood Eagles' packs and jammed three into the ground around her. They were meant as signals. Didn't pack enough energy to damage the horde. But just enough to keep them at bay.

"Think we scared them," Jackson said and broke out into a desperate laugh.

"Eyes up," Ortega commanded. "Give me time."

Jackson hauled himself to his feet. He watched the darkness, heard the skittering and scratching beyond the fading line of light.

"How did you know?" he asked, the drug giving his words a threatening edge.

Ortega spared him a glance as she worked with furious precision. "Follow the money," she said. "You think we couldn't end this war tomorrow?"

There were snorts and growls around them. What was left of the horde had recovered. They would come for them when the light failed. Again. And again. They wouldn't stop. There would always be more. An endless war, if you wanted it to be.

Jackson was shaking his head, but Ortega wasn't looking at him. She focused on the Flare. Even in these last moments she was dedicated, had walked into hell even when she knew she wouldn't come back.

"Why are you here?" Jackson said. He was shouting. He was shaking, and how much was rage and how much was Triple-S, he couldn't tell.

Ortega gave a wry smile. "Because fuck 'em," she said. "We'll burn them all down." She looked beyond him. "Give me time," she said, and went back to the Flare.

Jackson turned.

Hideous shadows moved beyond the light.

The charges guttered.

Failed.

"We're out of time," Jackson called.

The horde rushed.

He vented all of his rage, pain and desperation into his bloody last stand. Jackson swung his blade with wild abandon. Carved out his anger on the unrelenting wave of monstrosities that crashed against him.

Armour ruptured. Flesh burst. His blood was hot against his skin. Each breath was a choking gasp. His heart hammered on, as relentless as his rage.

LIGHTBRINGERS

A lull in the endless sea of demons gave him pause, and he looked up and found himself face to face with the guardian.

"Got it," he heard Ortega yell. "Flare is hot!"

The guardian flicked its hand and Jackson sailed across the room, slamming into something hard and unforgiving. The impact sent his vision black. He blinked and the blackness was filled with swirling white lights. He blinked again and saw the world doubled, spinning like it had that night on Drabek's hooch.

He could hear the whine of the Lucifer Flare powering up.

They'd all be incinerated.

But the gate would be destroyed and that was a win. A true victory; one for the survivors in the new world, and not SolVolt. Not the government that sent him and his squad to die.

Ortega screamed. The horde bore her aloft. Her blades were wrenched from her hands, burning up the demons who touched them, the blades tumbling through showers of ash. The guardian confronted her, flexed its alien fingers, and Ortega's body contorted. Her bones cracked and crunched. Her rib cage collapsed, her head bent down to her chest cavity as she caved in on herself.

Jackson watched her crushed into a ball of gore and dropped into the horde.

He was the last Lightbringer.

The horde scurried towards him.

He tried to stand and tripped on the exo-suit. He'd been slammed into it, and he found a dry humour in being smashed against a piece of armour designed by a company that had sent him to die.

He started laughing. A piece of armour powered by the sun. What good would that do anyone now? There was no sunlight down here to power it.

Jackson heard the flare reach a new pitch.

But... in a moment there'd be nothing but sunlight.

With the last of the Triple-S flooding his system, Jackson hauled himself into the suit. He slammed the cockpit shut and strapped himself in. Demons descended on him, slavering maws licking and biting at the screen, leaving obscene trails of muck across it.

Jackson sat back.

The Lucifer Flare ignited.

The power of the sun filled the space. The SV1 exo-suit was a phenomena. Even so, Jackson felt the heat burning through it. He gasped, the air suddenly sucked away from him. His skin tightened and started to blister.

Then the power cells, flooded with light from the flare, kicked in. The SV1 came to life. Radiation shields slamming up. Power flooded the limbs. Life support came online.

Jackson let out a desperate cry, caught between relief and despair.

He flicked the switches and ignited the boosters.

The last Lightbringer launched up and out of the depths of hell and into the sky: a blazing angel returning to the heavens.

He was the first to see it, to see the destruction of the gate pave the way for a new dawn. The clouds were dispersing. Daylight was bleeding through. As he soared into the air, demons burned, fell, ran.

"Shine on!" he howled.

Delirious and exhausted, he barely registered the warning signals. Lights flashed. Alarms blared. As tough as it was, the SV1 could only take so much. Systems failed, flight engines went offline, and Jackson plummeted back to earth like the fallen angel his squad was named after.

The impact was a distant thing. He bounced. Rolled. Slid into a rocky outcrop and stopped with a smack. But it was almost as if it was happening to someone else. Nothing was real anymore...

It was dark when he opened his eyes. Panic seized him until he realised it was a real darkness, a true night. There was an open sky above him, twinkling with stars, and a full moon that made it look like the sky was winking at him.

Jackson shook with laughter and tears.

LIGHTBRINGERS

He was alive.

The last Lightbringer back from hell.

His mind drifted to what had happened, to where he had come from, why they were fighting.

Felt like he had a new war now. One filled with vengeance.

Ortega's words came back to him: burn them all down.

"Burn them all," Jackson echoed.

And the last Lightbringer turned on his masters.

THE REFORGED MAN

Zachary O'Shea

The billowing sea of cinder and ash seared Maki Goro's lungs with each breath. While the ashigaru crewmen nearly hyperventilated, Goro seethed as he drank in the oxidized stench of the destroyed city below. The magistrates ignored his warnings. Now, it was too late.

"Heavens," Captain Yoshida said. He tried to beat away the smog with the swirl of his scarlet fan. When he didn't succeed, Yoshida used the fan to cover his face. His gaze settled on the towering ronin who fumed by the silver-lined railing and continued speaking, "I have never regretted being so wrong ever in my life."

Goro shifted his stance slightly, pointed his ragged eyepatch at the officer, and said, "just don't make it a habit, Yoshida-Sama." Then he turned his attention back down to the crests of smoke.

Crewmen openly gasped at the impudence. Goro didn't give a shit. The days of Maki Goro the honored samurai passed with his last breath, only the clockwork ronin remained. The blatant disregard for rank distracted the peasant-sailors from the conflagration below. They turned toward their honored captain, hat brims doing little to hide the disgust in their eyes.

Yet Yoshida wisely accepted the bruise to his ego with little more than a wave of the fan. He'd known the reforged man for years and still counted him as a friend despite Goro's incurable dishonor. The raven-haired noble snapped his accessory closed and said, "I do not intend to! Ueno-San, signal the fleet, we will make our way around the burning clouds. Let us see what transpires below."

"You know what we'll find below." Goro's mechanical fingers curled tightly to the railing, but not so hard as to dent the precious metal. His thick jaw set and long braid snapped as a sudden gale swept across the deck. "This is just like Izyota Castle all those years ago."

"Perhaps," Yoshida replied.

Yoshida's lieutenant signaled the other ships with an artful dance of garish flags. One by one the captains sent back their approval in kind. At the back of the flagship, *Taka*, taiko drums set the beat as internal cogs churned below deck to complete the melody.

"You worry too much, old friend." Captain Yoshida joined Goro at the railing. Above them, the stacked sails shifted via pulleys and pistons. Along each side, smaller sails tucked tightly to the hull as propellers picked up speed. "I now believe your tales of a giant monster, but no force under Heaven can withstand the power of the August Fleet. We are the Emperor's Quiver."

The ronin kept his doubting tongue still as the smoke-obfuscated kaiju's squeal answered for him instead. The ashigaru crew trembled and spat prayers, but followed their orders. With the grace of cranes in flight, the line of airships skimmed along the rim of the valley, first along forested hills still and serene. A flock of sparrows burst from the canopy but hardly flew high enough to bother the crafts. Goro's eyes traced their movement and then the trickling river that, from this height, looked like a thin stream of drink spilled from a cup. Under his sandals, the deck tilted as the *Taka* banked.

Following their flagship's lead, the August Fleet cut perpendicular across the wide swathe of destruction that marked the strange beast's passing. Goro grimaced, for he'd often traveled the trade road that once sat in the middle of violently churned earth. Splintered trees jutted from the muck, resembling the shattered bones from many a battlefield Goro had tread, yet on a scale he'd once thought unimaginable until seeing the ruination this monster first left weeks ago. He'd seen such handiwork before, albeit on a much smaller stage. His remaining eye sliced to the side to catch Yoshida's reaction.

The captain's handsome features remained unmoved, but his willowy frame tightened and threatened to cringe. Perhaps only regal bearing and the light armor he wore kept Yoshida straight. The peasant airmen whispered and moaned. Their distress only intensified as the arc of the fleet's movement completed.

With the wind now behind the *Taka*, the cinder clouds thinned. The scope of the carnage came into focus. Once impregnable walls lay like scattered straw. Imperial towers rested in fallen fragments amid shorter buildings and red-soaked splotches of mud. The kaiju called out again, full of alien fury and devilish hunger. Some of the ashigaru began to wail, but Captain Yoshida silenced them with a commanding snap of the fan. The drum beats never faltered.

Though, Goro nearly did.

He'd heard its wail before; bouncing off the gore-caked halls of Izyota castle. While it had been smaller then, it carried the same unnatural menace from beyond this sphere. He'd had honor then. Arms of flesh and bone.

"Ready the cannons!" Yoshida called. "We are going to have to drive through the smoke and strike the beast down before it knows we are here, like swift thunderbolts from the heavens!" His stern tones meant no man aboard would betray his authority. "We are the August Fleet and nothing can withstand us, no man, no army, no oversized bug!"

The crew didn't cheer; a grim silence trickled through them instead. To a man, they hurried to their duties. Each had sworn to die for the Emperor; they didn't expect to do so in this fashion. Still, if they managed to slay this great monster, what glory and honor they would bring to their captain and the *Taka*.

Goro snorted and spat over the side of the ship. "Kyūshū's walls practically bristled with cannons, Jirou. It didn't stop the creature." He kept his voice low, both to hide the familiarity he and the officer shared, and not to further spook the crew. "It only pissed it off."

"I know, Goro. This is why I am counting on you to have a plan."

"I do not as of yet," the errant warrior admitted. "I believe it is the same beast that devoured Lord Sakimoto."

A sigh wormed its way past Yoshida Jirou's lips. He patted Goro's mechanical appendage before stepping away. The silence said it all. The scarlet-clad captain trusted Goro would come up with something as he always had before. Goro looked down at his steel palms and flexed clockwork fingers. This time, the reforged man suspected he'd come up short.

The captain's muteness also said that he didn't want to hear those thoughts. With great restraint, Goro reached out to catch the other man's forearm, and murmured, "this is Uchima's doing! Who else would benefit from Kyūshū's fall?"

Jirou looked askance at the metal fingers on his kimono and showed equal restraint in not reflexively yanking his arm away from the ronin's soiled touch. Instead, he tapped Goro's hand with the fan and reminded him, "their judgmental gaze is always on you, old friend. A fortress full of food would present a tempting target to any monster. The shogun may be a cad, but not every evil can be laid at his feet."

Goro sucked on the inside of his cheek, but removed his grip and turned back to the railing. Jirou's love of tradition made him blind to the truth. Slowly but surely, Lord Uchima Jou had drowned the whole nation in blood to satisfy his ambitions. While everyone postured alliances and played politics, the madman summoned monsters! Why would no one believe him?

Signal flags of blue flashed through the August Fleet; the cannons were ready. At Yoshida's command, the taiko beat faster, stirring the airmen's blood. The line of airships adjusted their sails once more, and with fresh bursts of steam, started the attack run.

At first, there was little action to be had as the battle group rode crests of smolder and choking gas. Then confusion washed through the ranks when the *Taka* encountered the first shallow clear of smoke. Neither peasant nor samurai comprehended the mammoth, mottled brown wall with golden flecks moving just below them. Its moist sheen lodged disquiet in their stomachs in a way they could not explain. Even Captain Yoshida wavered and dropped his fan when expansive plates shifted. Just the hint of the kaiju's multitude of legs almost sent the officer reeling as they crested the smoke. While pallid virtually to the point of translucent, the triple-segmented limbs easily measured in a length comparable to a treasure barge.

As they sailed past the daunting obstacle, a second organic slab surfaced from below even as the first undulated out of view. More leprous appendages crushed rubble to dust as the behemoth stirred. Smoke swallowed the *Taka* once more as Yoshida cast a frightened look at Goro, only to find the ronin's face impassive, dedicated. The captain gripped the hilt of his katana and held it white-knuckled until the trembling ceased. By then, his vessel sliced its way into another clear expanse among the smog. He barely finished shouting desperate orders before the helmsman spun the wheel. With heavy banking to the right, the *Taka* narrowly evaded smashing into the monster's armored hide.

From behind the flagship ushered the staccato thunder of artillery. The *Taka* sailed past shifting limbs spattered with the debris of a flattened fortress-city. Goro knew Yoshida did not blame his fellow officers for their rashness yet despite the captain's fear, the man kept mentally balanced; didn't send the signal to fire. Like Goro, Yoshida believed they needed to find a weak spot, perhaps the titan's face?

As if on cue, the monster's squeal consumed every sense. Goro likened it to an enraged goose mixed with the breaking strings of a legion's worth of kotos but it was a clumsy summation.

The shriek was something wholly alien.

The kaiju's massive head emerged from the cinder clouds, and the horrible sound abruptly stopped when the centipede's inner mouth snapped closed, though the exposed outer jaws still angrily twitched. Its quartet of mandibles, which could easily bite one of the airships in half, remained flared wide. Like the bulk of the insect's body, the meat of its face was mostly maggot-white save for clusters of crimson veins that clumped together at the root of those awful toxicognaths. Jutting cilia vibrated underneath the three-part maw, and dribbled gallons of viscera in the process.

The scabrous border where Goro's shoulders ended and the prosthetic limbs began, burned. It was mandibles like that, save sword-sized, which had ruined his arms amid the acrid smoke of Izyota Castle. Was this one of the same horrors that burrowed up into his lost lord's larders? How could one have grown to such a size?

On either side of the abomination's spade-like head sat two sets of eyes: the foremost were shiny segmented globes forever staring straight ahead; the second was grotesquely human-like and full of malefic intellect. One of the terrible eyes tracked the *Taka*'s movement as the monster surged past the airship toward the rest of the fleet. The taiko drums went silent.

"F-f-f…" Captain Yoshida could not get the word out, so the ronin did it for him.

"Fire!"

Only a pittance of the airship's broadsides shot. Even though the balls sank right into spongy flesh, they inflicted roughly the same damage as a handful of pine needles. Nevertheless, the kaiju didn't let the insult go unanswered. One prehensile antenna, easily twice the length of the vessel, whipped down from above. It meant to snatch the ship with the extremity, and perhaps pull it to flexing mandibles as a mundane centipede would prey. The ashigaru managed to fire another volley straight into the antenna, which snapped away. Much to the crew's relief, the *Taka* drove on past the insect into the protective cover of ashen smoke. In the pit of his stomach, Goro knew the other corvettes would not be so fortunate.

The sporadic sound of cannons, unearthly squeals, and the cacophony that could only be airships exploding chased after the fleeing craft while it sped through the hot, gray mess. With a blossoming of fresh ember-clouds, the *Taka* soared away from the carnage and over the top of stark mountains. On a solitary peak, a monastery's bell tolled in warning.

The scarlet captain paled and spasmed, and a deep frown etched into Goro's features. He strode toward his old friend without blame. Goro suffered the same reaction when he first laid eyes on the chitin colossus.

"How? I don't even..." Yoshida stammered.

Set on haphazard courses, what survived of the August Fleet burst from the rolling smoke behind the *Taka*. One of the airships spun like a discus, its sails in tatters and sides split open. The centipede snapped out after it with the multitude of legs swiftly moving in unison. The craft, the pinnacle of Nippon's industrial sciences, exploded in a plume of wood, steel, and men when the mandibles pulled it close and monstrous jaws went to work. Another airship zipped past the goliath vermin. When the antennae shot out this time, they found their mark. Both feelers twisted around the vessel, and then tore it apart before stuffing the remains into grinding maw.

Goro gripped the captain's arm with his faux digits, careful not to splinter bone. "We have to find a way, Jirou. If that thing reaches the capital or the populous coast..." The warrior trailed off. He didn't need to go into detail. "Our cannons are just too small, but its fleshy underside can be pierced perhaps?"

"I... I don't..." Yoshida continued to falter as he beheld the slaughter.

"It is no demon, nor a god. We can kill it," the reforged man hissed through his teeth, "somehow."

A third airship soared high instead of flying close to the centipede. One of the titan's antennae snapped like a sling, flinging wreckage after the fleeing corvette to collide mid-deck. The stricken vessel didn't explode but lost all momentum as its propellers were rented and fins shredded. The airship reached its zenith, fell backward, and spun haphazardly as it fell, shedding people and parts.

The last ship in line banked hard as it expended another cannon volley, intending to reverse course and fly back down the length of the monstrosity. It, however, did explode as the back end of the kaiju snapped up and flattened it as Yoshida's fan might a fly.

"Maybe," Goro dryly added.

Captain Yoshida gently pulled away and retrieved his fan. His silent orders signaled the remaining craft to regroup atop the nearest mountain range. The kaiju crawled forward as if something of its staggering size could be said to simply crawl. With each undulation, its legs scoured life from the ground beneath it. However, the monster swiftly realized it could not catch up with the flying prey, so turned its bulk gracefully, coiled over itself, and resumed feasting on the burning corpse of Kyūshū.

Jirou and Goro waited in silence as the ramshackle August Fleet reformed. Nearly a third of the corvettes were gone. One listed out of the conflagration, left a trail of smoke as it sank for several miles before crashing into the forest.

The ronin filled his being with fresh air, tried to find his center, and finally spoke, "what do we do now, Captain?"

"Short of all of us ramming the underside of its head hoping our sacrifice slays the beast, I am not sure." Yoshida Jirou dismissed the foolhardy idea immediately. "We could return to the capital, but I do not think a roused army would do more than amplify the magnitude of slaughter. We are the best our country has to offer; they would fare no better. Perhaps catching the forest on fire and hoping it is hot enough to roast it?" Yoshida shook his head. "What is it anyway?"

Goro brushed a palm over his hair and then gave his ponytail a flick. "Ōmukade. Besides that, I haven't a clue. Kamo no Shou dubbed it a 'strange beast'. As for fire, it clearly caused Kyūshū to burn and suffered no ill effect."

The pair marched through whimpering sailors who tried to go about their duties. Normally, Captain Yoshida would reprimand such cowardice with silent smacks of the fan. Yet Goro knew that this afternoon, such a reaction was perfectly understandable.

Goro settled on the prow, Yoshida beside him. The smoke thinned so they might observe the kaiju's movement.

"I suffer naught from standing near a lantern, but a bonfire will kill me," the samurai said with a nod. "We shall try."

With a wave of his fan, Yoshida summoned one of his subordinates over and instructed him to relay the following to the others of the fleet. Half of the vessels would make haste to Hachinohe and commandeer every last cask of oil in the bustling port. The rest of the fleet would remain with the *Taka*. If needed, they would draw the kaiju deeper into the wilderness at the cost of their own lives.

Yoshida then turned toward Goro and with a smirk, said, "Kamo no Shou, eh?"

"Yeah," Goro said while rubbing his chin. "His prediction sent me seeking it out for my own eye."

"Did it now?" Yoshida asked, his smirk growing to a smile.

"Yes." Goro tilted his head.

"And...?"

"He said to..." Goro sighed. "Return to him once I believed him."

Yoshida's fan rapidly gave the order. The *Taka* would return shortly. He tapped Goro on the shoulder. "Let us not keep the genius—"

"Madman," Goro spat. "Dishonorable dog!"

"*Genius*," Yoshida emphasized, "waiting. Knowing Kamo no Shou, he is already working on a solution. You should show the man more gratitude. Without him, you would be dead."

"I would better off dead." Goro's metal shoulders fell as he grumbled. He glanced down to the valley as the insect's tail-end flared toward the sky. Two longer legs extended off the back of the abomination like hooks, and each tore large swaths of trees from the earth. Goro leaned forward wondering if there may be a weak spot there, but from this distance there was no telling. His single eye blinked as he realized the monastery bell was still chiming away.

The captain's fan touched the side of the ronin's cheek for the briefest moment. Sadness consumed Jirou's expression as he turned away. It was gone by the time the captain issued orders.

SNAFU: PUNK'D

The *Taka* broke formation with a puff of steam and sailed for the revered hilltop shrine. Four more vessels peeled away and headed north for Hachinohe. The remaining three airships kept watch on the behemoth.

It took less than an hour to reach the sandy-slate zenith where the original, simple shrine stood. It was like many one could find scattered across the empire; constructed of time-worn wood with a tiled roof and hanging charms dancing in the breeze. Built to accent the natural landscape rather than claim it, elegantly carved steps snaked down the slope, its sides flanked with leafy trees. Every so often, knife-like buttes of darker stone broke from the descending canopy and atop each, white-robed monks guided the flagship in with concave mirrored swivels bolted directly to the rock.

Each monk the *Taka's* shadow covered, broke from their duties and hurried down the path toward a squat central structure. The main temple complex was as modern as the berth the airship pulled up to. Its roof had been re-tiled with glazed clay shingles, and a pair of smokestacks on the back never sat idle. Piping ran around the sides of the building before spitting off to small structures or, in the case of one, delivering a sprinkling of purified water directly to the monks' garden.

Both Goro and Yoshida knew the industrial nature of the temple ran much deeper.

Once the airship clamps slotted with the dock's, Goro, Captain Yoshida and his lieutenant quickly made their way off of the craft. The reverberation of heavy machinery vibrated his sandals as Goro realized he didn't know the lieutenant's name. He was sure he'd been introduced to the bearded man, but just hadn't cared.

The elderly gūji approached them flanked by shrine maidens. Yoshida bowed deeply and spoke. "Kuno Kin-Sama, you look well."

The chief priest and his assembled lackeys reflected the bow, as did the lieutenant who Goro now dubbed Beard.

44

THE REFORGED MAN

Goro did not bow. Instead, he rubbed at his stubbled chin with cool metal fingers and scanned the holy compound. Where was the addled onmyōji?

"Captain Yoshida, I bid you welcome to the Takumi Shrine. We have been expecting you," Kuno Kin said. The shrine maiden watched their master as the old man struggled to straighten. His face resembled a leather glove that had been wadded up and tossed into a corner.

"Forgive us, Kuno-San, we were understandably occupied with the kaiju below. How many live on this rock? We may be able to fit the majority of you aboard the *Taka*." Yoshida made a sweeping motion back to his pride and joy.

Goro stepped around his friend without apology. "That's not what he means, Jirou-Sama."

Beard bristled. "Insolent—"

Kuno Kin rasped with amusement. "Insolent or not, you are correct, Maki-San. Please, if you would follow me, all will be made clear."

With that, the elderly priest turned and headed back for the center temple. The women with him meekly hurried forward and opened the door for the parade of men, never looking up as they passed. The distant squeal of the kaiju came moments after the doors closed behind.

The scent of oil and a tang of metal laced Goro's senses. Parts of all shapes and sizes, and a plethora of materials, lay strewn about on low tables. Stacks of notes littered the floor, as well as dirty rags and encrusted rice bowls. Shinshoku hurried about working on some manner of... artillery? With the celerity of a sparrow, a lanky man in grease-saturated robe flitted about. He intoned rapid-fire instructions first. Then paused silently to lean into the device, look over the rims of his spectacles, and use a personal set of tools to make adjustments.

Gūji Kuno cleared his throat with the strength of a man a fourth his age. "Kamo-Sama, they have arrived." The aged cleric repeated the announcement before the bespectacled man noticed and rushed over.

Wild fervor bled from the man, his eyes full of excitement and voice with titillation. "Joyous indeed! I told you Goro-San would return, Kuno-San! You have already faced the centipede and emerged unscathed, yes? If not, well I guess you should go back out there and do so. Yes? Yes." Only then did the man remember to bow. The motion sent glasses skidding off of hawkish nose. He caught them deftly but had a smudge of oil across the left lens when they were righted.

"Kamo no Shou," Goro said with a groan and pushed past Yoshida, no matter the breach of protocol. Cast forever from the Emperor's gaze, he no longer cared for social niceties. It was hard to lose face with one such as his.

The sorcerer-smith's level of elation only grew and he resumed rapid-fire speaking. "You have? Excellent. My divinations foresaw that you would return in time for my greatest work to be unveiled! Not that it is quite ready, uh, yet."

Goro snorted and showed off his arms. "I thought I was your greatest work."

"Ah yes, my reforged man," Kamo said with a sheepish cast of his gaze. "While you are my blade of vengeance, this, oh this, is my masterstroke! The world has not seen anything as mighty as what I have wrought!"

The distant fusillade of cannons and a corresponding screeching howl from the kaiju had Yoshida look to the doors, and Goro knew the captain wondered at the rest of the ships under his command. Yoshida visibly shook the feeling away and turned back to the sorcerer and priest only to find Kamo no Shou puncturing his personal space to peer up at him.

"I trust you have no longer doubts as to the sinister nature of the shogun, Yoshida-Sama? After what you have seen—"

"What we have seen amounts to nothing," Beard blustered as he grabbed the soothsayer and yanked him away from his commander. "What we deal with is a monster, not—"

"It is a beast," Kamo no Shou retorted but couldn't shake Beard's grip. "The man who pulled it down from the stars is the monster. The man who drowned our nation in blood is the

THE REFORGED MAN

monster. The man who stole my work to do it all is a monster!"

As much as Goro liked seeing the onmyōji manhandled, he bristled as the samurai got rough. Goro drew close and growled. "Let him go. We don't have time for this."

"The only monster I see here is the one this fool has made," Beard coldly sneered and shoved Kamo no Shou away. He swiveled toward Goro with a pointed look. "Captain—"

"Uneo-San." Yoshida's tone held a warning.

The lieutenant ignored it and continued as he sized up Goro, going so far to flick one of his steel biceps. "Captain, I know we tolerate this dishonored scum due to old associations and the information he offered. However, I think now is the time we cast aside his wild accusations, discard them, and focus on slaying the Ōmukade at hand."

"I want to deal with this madman less than you do," Goro said, and lifted his chin toward the onmyōji as he spoke. "However, you need me and I have no doubt Lord Uchima is behind this. Fools turning a blind eye, as you do now, is what got us into this mess in the first place."

"Are you calling me a fool?"

Goro grimly grinned. "Only a fool would ask that."

The assembled gasped as Beard drew his sword and slashed at Goro, intent on striking him down for his insolence. Goro caught the blade with one artificial hand and struck Beard in the chest with the palm of the other. The man few off his feet but his blade stayed in the ronin's grasp. After a beat, Goro tossed the sword beside Beard's prone form and said nothing.

The tension bubbled; it was Yoshida who broke it. "It is good to see you, Kamo no Shou, let me fill you in on what has occurred." He helped his subordinate up. Used to giving reports, Yoshida related their flyby assault, the loss of ships, the ineffectiveness of their weapons, and his quickly-implemented plan to conjure an inferno.

While the Gūji Kuno was visibly shaken by the plan, Kamo no Shou stroked his chin thoughtfully, leaving fresh smudges as he did so. "That level of destruction may not be necessary. If

47

I may?" He half-bowed, full of nervous anticipation at the uncanny artillery behind him.

Goro stepped over to inspect it. It reminded him again of a cannon, though with a smaller tube in the center and far too many odd chambers along the length he couldn't fathom. No, wait they were something like oversized bellows. At first, he was going to ask if it spat flame but bellows stoked fires with air. He paced along the outer edge, careful not to trip over working monks or scattered parts. Kamo no Shou prattled on as to the device's function, but Goro was only half-listening. He caught enough to glean fully what he was looking at. This wasn't artillery, not in the normal sense. The onmyōji divinations inspired an oversized harpoon gun, similar to the devices whalers used. Save this one enjoyed a far greater scale and would produce the punch needed to pierce the kaiju's chitin armor.

The engineer gestured to his begrudging defender as he wrapped up. "Goro-San will fire this weapon into the creature's brain the second time he faces it. Without it, not even a thing such as that can survive."

"I'll what now?" Goro balked.

Kamo no Shou adjusted his spectacles. "You will slay this beast. I have foreseen it."

Goro spoke through gritted teeth. "I have had quite enough of being your puppet, fortune-teller."

Kamo no Shou folded his arms, mania melting away. "I will pull your strings until my vengeance is complete. You owe me your life, Goro-San."

"A life I freely ended," Goro countered.

"You will stop at nothing to stymie the shogun," Kamo no Shou said with a shrug. "But if you want his strange beast to rampage across the countryside claiming an untold number of lives…"

The conversation fell mute for several minutes. Finally, Goro shrugged, the junctions of metal, bone, and meat which were his shoulders often took up heavy burdens. Just never one of this magnitude. "I hope you are right then. I've never put much stock in fortune-tellers. Fine. Jirou-Sama… you don't mind this, uh, weapon strapped to your ship, do you?"

"Now you listen here, scum!" Beard barked as anger overrode common-sense once more.

Yoshida cut Beard's outburst with a strike of his fan. "Yes, Goro-Sama. Let's get this done. From the sound of it the battle rages anew, but I don't know how much longer my fleet can last."

It took some doing, but between the *Taka's* crew and the monks, the harpoon-launcher sat at the ready two hours later. During that time, Captain Yoshida watched the battle via a spyglass. He stood with rigid, stoic anxiety as the other airships kept the kaiju occupied. The smoke of the destroyed city evaporated, and from the peak, it was easy to imagine the centipede was normal size, and the airships it lashed out at were nothing more than agitated bumble bees. Save, of course, the August Fleet moved with military grace and timing. One ship would pelt the behemoth's face with a salvo, and circle away to the far side of the valley before taking back into the air. When it seemed the monster might leave the area, one of the others would kite it the other direction. For long stretches in between, the kaiju rested in the ruins of Kyūshū, coiled in on itself.

Bereft of anything to do, Goro slouched in a corner and brooded. The razing of Izyota Castle surfaced in his memories. How could it not? The screams. The smoke. The blood. The unnatural shrieks and the skittering of carapace against stone. He'd never gotten a good look at the man-sized insects amid the chaos. Hell, it could have been the work of one bug as far as he knew. Goro had sworn to defend Lord Sakimoto until his last breath. He hadn't found all of his daimyo's pieces before a centipede's mandibles fell on him like paired blades. Goro replayed every parry, every riposte, every thrust. Why had the horror left him alive after destroying his arms? Well, he'd had just enough mobility left in the ruined meat to gut himself on the castle's steps. His last thoughts had been of failure and absolution.

His thoughts after that focused on the grinning, bespectacled fool in front of him and wondering what manner of devil he was. Worse, it turned out to be Kamo no Shou. Goro wanted a drink. Instead, he spotted Jirou motioning him over with his fan before boarding the airship. The weapon was ready.

Was he?

Only one way to find out. With a grunt, the Ronin pushed to his feet.

When the *Taka* rejoined the battle group, no additional craft had been lost. The champions knew that good fortune would not last. The harpoon-launcher took up most of the top deck and was lashed down in places where they didn't have time to ratchet it. The spider web of ropes made movement across the whole top of the deck frustratingly slow. The strange distribution of weight caused the *Taka* to bob in the air and list slightly to the left. Worst of all, the weapon meant to save the empire shifted with each turn the vessel made. How one was supposed to aim it in the thick of battle was beyond Goro, and by Yoshida's expression, the captain was of the same mind.

The trigger, such as it was, ended up being attached to a chair mounted on top of the launcher and that's where Goro found himself as the airships fell back into formation.

He could hear the kaiju yowling below and the rumble of deforestation; the gargantuan obviously knew they were up to something.

"I've changed my mind; this is a terrible idea!" Goro shouted.

From where they gripped a crisscross of ropes on the stern, Kamo no Shou looked to Yoshida. "What did he say?"

Captain Yoshida sharply smirked. "He is ready to proceed."

The taiko thrummed to life, setting the pace of battle. The sailors of the August Fleet now knew what they were facing and had a plan to defeat it. Even if it failed, by morning the other ships would be back with oil and they'd burn the insect. This time, the *Taka* didn't lead the charge. Instead, the other three crafts formed a wedge and dove straight down at the beast while the flagship lagged significantly behind.

The scheme rolled into action when the advancing ships opened up with their forward-facing cannons. Once they had the centipede's attention, the two on either side peeled sharply away at such a pitched angle the men topside clung to rigging not to tumble off to a messy death below. Those two airships sent a full broadside volley at the giant's eyes. The brave crew in the center kept driving straight at the beast. Their stacked sails shifted and trembled with near-breaking strain as it prepared to pull up at the last possible moment.

Thankfully, the monster took the bait and lashed out into the air with a flurry of limbs, of antennae, and chattering of triple-jaws. As the kaiju stretched, a downpour of splintered trees, shattered stone, and human debris drifted from its sinuous bulk. The lead vessel gracefully wove around one flaring antenna while its partners strafed the horror's eyes. The explosive shot inflicted little damage, but the monster flailed its flat head. The lead vessel managed to pull up and away unscathed. As it did so the back door of its cargo bay lowered with the rapid spin of internal gears.

Every last keg of gunpowder the vessel had left, came tumbling out, already lit by cannoneers. A fresh roll of deno-tations blanketed the top of the kaiju's skull. The thunderous explosions would have ripped apart any of the airships or torn out the fighting heart of a legion. A fresh squeal strained the air and the kaiju rolled over its own body to reposition.

Goro grinned as the back of the atrocity's head squared up in his sights.

Splitting the air with a whistle, the *Taka* came in like a falling bomb. The reforged man took in a slow breath as he always did before pulling his katana from his sheath in the seconds preced-ing slaughter. A few more moments and he'd be in range to destroy the strange beast's unnatural brain. The Emperor would have to restore his name then, that son of a bitch! Son of Heaven or not, he'd tear the idiot's head from his scrawny shoulders if he kept acquiescing to the shogun's every dictate. *Heh, maybe the empire would be better without a head of state.*

Gears strained when his fingers curled around the launcher's trigger. He felt his heart stop, and his breath shortly followed. It was time to fire.

SNAFU: PUNK'D

The moment of his redemption disappeared in an instant. With the sudden reversal of fortunes came a spinning of his perceptions as the chair tore free of its bolts and the cannon shuddered. All around Goro, ropes writhed like angry serpents in the wake of sharp shards of steel spinning by.

The kaiju's tail end flipped up as the lead airship pulled from its bombing run. Both of its back limbs caught the vessel and scythed it into a spray of burning shrapnel before the crew even knew what hit them. The largest stream of debris raked the *Taka*, sliced apart moorings, reduced men to red splotches, and silenced one of the drums forever. One of the ship's sails shattered too, but the damage was not enough to sink it. Yoshida cried out, and his order to veer from the still-spinning clouds of wreckage swiftly pulled the *Taka* away from further danger.

Goro's vision blurred as he skipped across the artillery piece. If he flew out into empty air, all that awaited him was a few moments of terror and then the unforgiving earth. With a desperate cry, he tried to grab something, anything. Sparks showered where steel fingertips scraped along the launcher's uneven fuselage.

His back muscles felt as if they were on fire, and he was sure some tore. Goro flailed as panic overtook him, and then one of the weapons' oversized gears entered his peripheral vision. Stomach knotted, he threw himself to the side and snatched hold of the gear with his left hand. The cog bent with a groan but held fast.

As the *Taka* leveled out, Goro hung there with one leg dangling in the air. With gasping breaths, he sought his center. He rolled his left shoulder and bit back the pain. The second time he managed to get it to move, and grasped a rent plate. Despite the grinding feeling in his knee, the ronin painstakingly ascended. He dimly heard a sea of startled shouts coming from the ship's deck below him. Goro didn't try to decipher them but focused on crawling across the surface of the mounted weapon. His progress was slow, and the angry wind tugged at his shredded robes. Finally, he made his way to the top just as the *Taka* banked in a manner that would have made the entire climb easier. Goro snorted, and then choked on his breath when he got an eyeful of the conflict.

The centipede's prehensile antennae swept along the ground and gathered great chunks of the fortress city's remains. The behemoth surged upwards, and then lobbed debris at an airship. The rubble was impossible for the vessel to evade. Instead, the captain of that ship wisely turned straight into the biting detritus to provide a smaller profile, but it didn't help. The crew of the *Taka* looked on in horror as their sister craft crumpled under stone blocks, and trees pierced deep into its hull like over-sized arrows. Almost immediately the gunboat sank and trailed red-tinged smoke.

Goro cursed under his breath. The reforged man shook off despair, and let the rage flow in to fill its place. He had to get back to the trigger so they could slay this abomination. The fact he spotted brackish ichor streaming from its pock-marked head gave the warrior hope. Little by little, Goro pulled his way to the capsized chair and trigger pedestal. When he finally reached his destination, the ronin received cheers as he pulled himself to standing. He lifted his bleeding chin to Yoshida and gestured toward the kaiju.

It was time for another pass.

The *Taka* rounded the battlefield as the crippled airship managed to regain rudimentary control, but was still doomed the next time the insect attacked. The valiant souls swallowed their fear and opted not to wait. That airship retracted its sails entirely even as it angled its roaring bow steeply down. The marvel of engineering became little more than a manned rocket and plummeted straight for the adversary. Alerted by the craft's screaming descent, the behemoth bug looked up and screeched. The kamikaze attack struck with such swiftness the kaiju didn't have a chance to defend itself. The boat drove straight into one of its human-like eyes. The resulting explosion was all too familiar to the men of the August Fleet, save clotted with ocular jelly.

Goro and Yoshida knew they'd have no better chance to strike than in the wake of such sacrifice. Howls of agony echoed from the kaiju as it swayed about in shock. Goro's ruined socket itched in something close to empathy. The flagship dipped for another attack run, and this time when the almost-unanchored launcher shifted, Goro was ready. He gripped the trigger pedestal while planting aching legs. Guided by Jirou's expert orders, the *Taka* lined up its attack-run and soon enough the monster's head loomed into view. Goro wished the harpoon had some manner of test shot. There was so much that could go wrong. He squinted his good eye as the vessel bore down on the injured terror, and let out a slow breath as the sight lined up.

"Now, or never," he muttered and squeezed the trigger. Below his feet, a low complaint of distressed machinery came and went, but nothing happened. Goro cursed and tried again with the same results. The third time he was sure he heard something snap under the fuselage. "Looks like never."

Still, the ronin knew they'd not get another chance. He stumbled forward and punched his steel hands through the launcher's casing. If the artillery worked anything similar to a clockwork bow, there was a cord waiting to be unlatched. Fresh pain swept through Goro's shoulders, down his spine, and deep into his gut; but the warrior kept straining until the plating popped free. He marveled in dismay at all the grinding gears and other intricate workings. This might be more complicated than expected. Goro snapped his gaze up, only to have the full range of his vision filled first with the brown carapace. That didn't last long as the centipede's remaining human-like eye rose above the bow like a malignantly furious sun.

Goro tore his singular gaze away and back to the churning workings. He spotted two thick bundles of coiled silk among all the metal and hoped they were what he was looking for. He pushed shoulder-deep into the weapon and took hold of each line. Goro superimposed Lord Uchima's snide fucking face atop the centipede's and couldn't decide what was uglier. Every muscle from his abdomen convulsed as he pulled and emitted a primal bellow almost as terrifying as the kaiju's. Around him the launcher shuddered, chunks of machinery haphazardly leaving its frame on plumes of steam, but then came a deafening click, and the harpoon sliced through the air.

The projectile, nearly twenty yards in length, plunged through the eye socket and deep into the centipede's brain. The effect was instantaneous. The enormous carcass lost all volition, its multitude of legs froze up like pistons when they ran out of steam. With a deafening crash, its upper half slammed into the blasted remnants of Kyūshū. The peasant soldiers cheered.

The battered but unbroken *Taka* pulled away. Its single remaining companion pulled alongside as Goro flopped onto his back. He found himself laughing in a most undignified and delirious manner but didn't care. The bright blue sky above seemed fathomless, save for the occasional drifting cloud. Several minutes later he heard Captain Yoshida calling for him and brought his hysteria to heel.

Once the ronin's feet were firmly planted back on the *Taka's* deck, his knees threatened to buckle. Despite rampant agony racing through his frame, Goro refused to show weakness.

Jirou bowed respectfully to him, with only a hint of elation breaking his samurai demeanor. "Maki-Sama, I find myself without words to express the scope of your success. All I know is that you have brought great honor to the *Taka* this day."

Goro chuckled but echoed the bow. "Without the efforts of yourself, Captain, and your valiant crew we would have never succeeded. You do not need words, just several jars of sake. I feel like I am going to come apart at any moment. Speaking of which, where is the sorcerer-smith? The damned thing nearly fell apart from under me!"

On cue, Kamo no Shou erupted from the circle of rambunctious sailors. He peered through his freshly clean spectacles, but as he slipped them back on, smudged the lens with fresh grease. "I do forgive you for abusing my creation, Maki-San. In the end, it was for the best, for otherwise, my divinations would not have come true."

Goro started to glower at the man, only to note the way the onmyōji crookedly smirked. The two men shared a deep thrumming laugh, and the swordsman patted the engineer's shoulder with brotherly affection. Goro decided against strangling him, for now. "I'm glad they did. I'm glad they did. Thankfully, it did its job and we won't need it anymore."

"Oh no, I shall have to come up with an entirely new invention for the next, strange beast we will face, I am certain." Kamo no Shou spoke with all due seriousness, and even nodded firmly for emphasis. "The shogun calls to the heavens for fresh terrors even now!"

Goro and Jirou shared a look as blood drained from their faces. In tandem, the heroes turned back to the oracle-inventor only to be confronted with a knowing and mysterious grin. Yoshida covered his groan with a scarlet fan. Goro squeezed the bridge of his nose with metal fingers. The Emperor better get some of that damn divine sense he was supposed to have and restore Goro's name. He'd hate to have to cross blades with Jirou after breaking the pampered fool like a twig!

The flock of sparrows emerged from the devastated canopy and followed after the *Taka* as it sailed toward the imperial palace.

CLEAN-UP CREW

Alan Baxter

Ordnance lit up the corridor in light and thunder, huge black shadows with too many limbs skittering and leaping in the gloom.

"There's got to be a reason for it, Jazz!" Stem yelled.

"Oh, you think?" Jazz emptied a clip, switched in a new one as she staggered backwards, shouting to be heard over Stem's muzzle bark. "Perhaps we should grab a couple of beers and sit down to discuss it."

Stem tripped, elbowed the wall to stay standing, and kept moving, matching Jazz's renewed fire burst for burst. His retinal display skipped target to target, almost a blur as it kept up. "Yeah, maybe later, I guess." He raked fire across the dark corridor ahead, the flare of his ordnance creating stark silhouette puppet plays of the creatures swarming towards them. Too many limbs, glistening teeth and claws, too big to be possible, too fast for anything that big. He released controlled-dose stims, balancing the natural adrenaline surging through his system as he frantically scanned his retinal display in one eye. Keeping up the barrage, he flicked through blueprints that seemed ever more inaccurate.

"Find us a way out, Stem!" Grifter shouted.

"I'm trying!"

"Nice that you think there'll be a later," Jazz yelled, then all conversation was lost in continued fire and the howl of Tank's 50-cal gatling cannon as they retreated at speed.

Two Days Earlier
"Nothing is that simple." Jazz's gaze was middle distance as she

scanned the plans Grifter just sent in her retinal display, blue smoke curling up from her mouth.

"Lots of things are simple," Grifter said. "That doesn't mean they're easy. I'm not underestimating how hard this could be, but the *premise* is simple."

Stem looked from Grif back to the RD in his cybertech eye, studying the plans Jazz was complaining about. What Grifter said made sense in a way, but there had to be a catch. "Let me get this straight," he said, tapping the tiny, embedded bead by his left temple to project his RD to a virtual distance of one metre. He pointed into the glowing holographic display. "That's the vault, right at the bottom."

"Right," Grif agreed. "Full of riches."

"And this is the elevator shaft? That just happens to run right against it?"

"Yes. Accessed from the other side, obviously, but the back wall of the shaft is also the wall of the vault."

"What kind of vault shares a wall with an elevator shaft?"

Grifter made a noise of annoyance. "That one!"

"Look," Jazz interrupted. She sucked on her vape, breath clouding out as she spoke. "I can hack the building's maintenance and control matrix on-site. I can take command of the elevator and that shaft for at least long enough for what you're suggesting."

"I'm suggesting we get fucking rich," Grifter interrupted, doing nothing to hide the exasperation in his tone.

"Yeah, I get it. We laser through from the elevator directly into the vault. Sweet. But, and let me be very clear here, because it's pretty fucking central to the entire caper. *How the fuck do we get into the elevator?*"

Now

"Where the fuck are Grif and Tank?" Jazz yelled as she and Stem turned and ran.

"No idea!" They had been right there moments before. Stem didn't want to think he'd seen them overwhelmed by... by what?

Just what the fuck were those things? The team had been forced in two separate directions and he was scanning wildly trying to re-find their digi-sigs, lost in the confusion of information on his RD.

They passed a corridor on their right.

"Straight on?" Jazz said

"Yes!" Stem no longer trusted the building schematics, but what choice did they have?

And then more of the beasts appeared directly ahead.

They skidded to a halt and opened fire. The fluorescents in the corridor gave them their best view of the things yet. Thick, barrel-like bodies on eight muscular legs, each with two sets of knees. If spiders were the size of office desks and had fleshy muscles like humans, they might look something like this. Except the front end of the things was one massive, eyeless maw. Wet lips peeled back from multiple rows of teeth in a mouth wide enough to fit a human torso. Their hide was thick and grey, but 30-cal rounds punched holes in it pretty well. Except how did they see? Some kind of sonar?

Jazz and Stem fired in controlled bursts. Dark black blood burst up from the creatures, seeming to almost glow under the bright lights. It splattered the walls and the beasts howled and barked in pain and fury. Jazz and Stem backed up, triggering frantically, then Stem turned and put his back to Jazz's to account for the previous group they'd been running from quickly catching up. Shooting in both directions, they sprayed the SciTech walls with jet black blood until they reached the side corridor again.

"Go!" Stem yelled, and he fired quickly left, right, left, right until Jazz was a few paces along, then he turned and ran after her. The beasts made a thunderous, clattering noise as they galloped behind, a single curved black talon at the end of each leg rattling against the floor.

"They're catching up fast!" Stem yelled. The wall beside him exploded.

For a moment he assumed he'd reached the end of his

blighted life, then realised it was Tank bursting through. Her exo-skin reflected silver under the lights and she raked side-to-side with her 50-cal gatling cannon. Stem couldn't even deadlift the thing, and he was no weakling. But Tank was power incarnate, enhanced to the max. Her weapon whined and howled and the beasts rushing at them were minced, the corridor running dark with their blood.

"You found us!" Stem said, as Tank's weapon whistled to a stop.

Grif tapped his temple. "Had you on RD the whole time. Let's go."

"Which way?" Jazz asked.

Grifter pointed the way they'd been running. "That way. Because there's a fuck-load more of those things coming up behind us."

Two Days Earlier

Grifter reached forward and opened Stem's display into a wider view. They saw the entire building, plus those either side and the dozens of multi-level streets outside. He pointed to the building next to the target. "This is housing. Like, a million apartments. It has security, of course, but nothing like the SciTech building. I can get us in there—"

"How?" Jazz asked.

Grif grinned and it put Stem's teeth on edge. He hated that self-satisfied expression. "Me and one of the residents there, we have a thing going on from time to time. He'll let me in, which means I can let the rest of you in. Somewhere well above ground, obviously. We make our way to the roof of the building. There's a massive ad-holo projector up there, polluting the smoggy skies with fucking soap or toothpaste or vision enhancements or whatever the corps are trying to shift this month. We secure lines to that and fire across to the SciTech building. Then we grapple over to SciTech's roof. If we tried to fly down, security bots would shred us with auto-fire. But I can mask us if we go across that way. Jazz accesses the elevator from the maintenance shack, we ride down to the basement level, cut through into the vault, load up, and get out the same way. Easy."

"Easy," Stem said, shaking his head.

"One issue," Jazz said. "The apartment block is lower than SciTech. How are we supposed to get across. We can't slide *up* a line."

"Yes we can! I have motorised winches with masked kinetic motors. Security won't detect them. We clip 'em on, motor across, then flick 'em into neutral so we can sail back."

Stem stared at the holo. It was a relatively straightforward caper, given Grif's inside knowledge of the vault. And he didn't dare dream about how much wealth might be in SciTech coffers in gold and jewels, stuff not subject to the electronic economy. But this wasn't them. "We're a hit squad, Grif. We're not thieves or fucking ninjas or whatever."

Grif made a noise of disgust. "And how long do you think we can survive if we keep taking those kind of missions? Working for the corps, doing their killing for them. They'll never stop warring, never stop trying to get the most control. This way we take more than any of them would *ever* pay us and we're done. Get away from the burgs, find an island somewhere. There's gotta be some beaches left in the world, right? Where there's enough sun through the smog to make it feel like retirement?"

"Where did you get the intel?" Jazz asked.

"Reliable source." Grif stared her down, clearly daring her to push for more, which he plainly didn't plan on giving.

Jazz sucked her teeth and looked away.

"So, we doing this?" Grifter asked.

Jazz shrugged.

Stem said, "I guess so. *If* you're sure your intel is sound."

"One hundred per cent."

They all turned to Tank, easy to forget when she wasn't actually talking, more like furniture than another person in the room. Her exo-skin gleamed in the low light of the apartment, her cyber-eyes deep red glows. She was more machine than biological these days and gave Stem the creeps a little more every time she got another upgrade. Everyone had enhancements, even just the cyber eye for RD and maybe a few stim caches to manage chemicals in the body. But Tank was extra by anyone's standards. "I do whatever Grifter wants," she said, her voice burring slightly with the electronic tone of her enhancements. She fell motionless again, though her attention remained focussed.

Grifter grinned and raised both his hands. "Three days from now we're retired!"

"Three days?" Jazz asked. "That's all the planning time you're giving us?"

"Three days until it's over. We do the job in two. I've got the gear. Why wait?"

Now

"This is not the way out!" Stem yelled as they ran. "The elevator shafts are on the east and west sides of the building, remember? We're running north!"

"You want to head back into… whatever the fuck they are?" Grif said. "Besides, the eastern shaft is fucked unless we get up a few levels, so when we can, we try to get west."

Stem shook his head, grinding his teeth. How had this happened?

"This is such a fucking set up," Jazz said. "But why?"

They slowed to a jog, Grifter looking from one to the next, nervously licking his lips.

"Yeah," he said at last. "I don't know."

Stem scanned blueprints in his RD with one eye while he watched his footing with the other. "Tank, how many walls can you get through like before?"

"Internals? If they're all as poorly built as that last one, I can plough through those all day." Her grin was feral, metal teeth gleaming.

Stem skidded to a halt, pointed left. "Go!"

Tank looked from Stem to the wall to Grifter, who nodded.

"Okay then." She ducked one shoulder and servo-assisted gears in her legs whined as she accelerated from standing to about forty clicks an hour almost instantly. She hit the wall with a jarring crash. Plasterboard and plas-steel beams exploded.

"Keep going!" Stem yelled. "Through this room and the next, four walls in all. It'll bring us out in a corridor behind the last place we saw those fuckers and we can make for the western shaft. Assuming that much of the plans is actually legit."

Tank kept her head down, one shoulder turned in, and went on like a freight train, walls bursting with concussive cracks. The other three barrelled along behind, arms up to shield themselves from raining debris.

Barely breathing hard, Tank smashed through the fourth wall and then skidded to a halt. She barked, "Fuck!" Then her gatling cannon came up and started screaming.

Twenty Minutes Ago
Everything went so smoothly that Stem wondered if perhaps they were getting complacent. Grif's intel was correct, his friend in the apartment block was a decent guy, if a little wired on stims, and they'd got to the elevator maintenance shack on top of SciTech without incident. Grifter had taken shots at all the security cams on the SciTech roof as the motor-grapple carried them up, clearly his plans had located all of those in advance as well. And if Grif was anything, he was a good shot.

The holo ads rotated above them, massive this close up, the voice-over deafening as it cajoled people to consider organ-re-placement therapy. *Why trust nature when you can trust Yamasaki Corp?*

Streets on many levels criss-crossed between the buildings all around them, red and white lights of vehicles streaking the gloom. Above them, air-cars of the truly wealthy travelled above the grit and grime of mundane life and well-above the squalid wasteland of ground.

"Okay, clock's ticking," Grif said.

Jazz slapped the magnetic wireless connection from her deck onto the maintenance shack security lock and started the decryption algorithm. Her software was something else and would make short work of the elevator controls. They hoped.

Grifter popped off two single shots from his 30-cal assault rifle while she worked, taking out a couple of maintenance drones that had begun rolling across the roof towards them. "They'll try to reboot those cameras," he said. "Security in a building like this is always lazy at first, they assume glitches. But once they realise it's not a software issue they'll take it seriously. That's when they'll send people up. I reckon we have about five minutes to get down, grab what we can, and get out."

"That's not very long," Stem said.

"We only need three. And if we meet any security on the roof here when we get back... Well, we know how to deal with that, right?"

"I'm in," Jazz said, pulling her deck's cable from the control panel. The lights on the door went from red to green and the elevator turbines kicked in. In seconds, the door hissed open and they climbed aboard the lift. Jazz jammed a knife into the control panel and levered it clear out of the metal casing.

"Subtle," Stem said.

"They can bill me." She took another cable and jacked directly into the controls to bypass internal security protocols. "Basement five, right?"

"Yep," Grif said. "The lowest level."

The car lurched and they shot downwards. Grifter was already placing a custom las-cutter onto the elevator wall, about a metre from the floor, fixed to a long arm that was itself fitted into a rotating housing.

"We're there," Jazz said.

Stem checked his RD. Forty-eight seconds into Grif's estimated five minutes. All too easy.

"Mind your eyes." Grifter pulled down a shaded visor as Jazz and Stem put an arm up to shield their vision. Tank did nothing, her enhancements responding in microseconds to the blinding light of the focussed laser. Grif turned the operating arm in a wide circle and metal dripped red hot to the ground. He pulled the apparatus away and said, "Tank?"

She leaned back and drove one foot forward, kicking a two-metre diameter circle of elevator and the wall behind it clear.

CLEAN-UP CREW

Opticals adjusted to the low light to confirm the vault they expected beyond was dark, large and completely bare.

"The fuck?" Grif said.

Stem's RD, on constant scan, registered a reading that took a second or two to understand. Then a cold wave of dread broke over him. "Fucking run!" he yelled, and shoved Grif through the hole.

The team would never question a directive like that. Jazz dove through after Grif, Stem running after her. Tank jammed her large body through and managed two steps into the space beyond before the elevator blew. The shockwave of the blast sent them sprawling, clothes and skin singeing as a fireball followed behind, then it was nothing but smoke and noise. As the noise of the explosion faded, different sounds rose, somewhere beyond the walls. Animalistic howls and loud clattering like giant claws on hard plas-steel floors.

Now

Tank's gatling cannon cut a swathe through the first wave of beasts as they skittered and barrelled down the long hallway. The rest of the team fired short, controlled bursts, dropping the beasts row after row, but they just kept coming.

"Push forward!" Grifter yelled, and they did, despite getting closer to the creatures. They needed to take ground, not get pushed back again or there would be nowhere left to go.

Stem scanned rapidly, trying to get some kind of understanding of just what exactly this enemy was. He registered small antenna showing up on his RD as bright green. That meant tech, not bio. Firing and running, trying to flank the creatures, he set a scan to read any signals going to or from those antennae and was surprised at the frequency he found.

"They're remote-controlled!" he shouted over the roar of assault rifle salvos.

"What?" Jazz said.

Then for a few seconds everything was lost in a maelstrom of gunfire. Tank yelled, "Fire in the hole!" and pumped two rocket-propelled grenades, one from each of her shoulder launchers. The team hit the deck, except Tank who just half-turned her back, and the corridor blew in a storm of noise and smoke and raining debris.

The almost-silence that followed was only broken by the soft clatter of broken plaster from the ceiling and walls and the thick drip-drip of dark blood from the beasts. It seemed the current wave was ended.

"Remote?" Grif asked.

Stem nodded. "They have some degree of free will, I guess. But they're being guided."

"By who?"

"More importantly," Jazz said. "From where? I don't know that we're going to get back to any upper levels very easily, or all the way across to the western shaft, so perhaps we need to take care of the source?"

Stem studied his RD, followed wireless signals through the building as smoke curled around them. "Give me a few seconds."

Ten Minutes Ago

As the building's scrubbers slowly sucked out the swirling smoke, Stem looked back at the ruined elevator shaft. "What the fuck exactly?"

"We're lucky we weren't still in there," Grif said.

"Nah, man." Jazz wagged one finger at the wreckage behind them. "That's deliberate. If they wanted us dead, they would have blown the car as we came down. They want us in here, with no escape back the way we came."

"What for?" Stem asked.

Jazz turned a hard eye on Grifter. "Where did you get your intel?"

Grif's face was still for a moment before an expression of discomfort washed over it. "Rep from a SciTech rival."

Jazz's eyebrows shot up. "You took this gig from a rival corp?"

"Sure. They have no love for each other, so I figured they were scoring a blow by having us rob the place."

"You idiot. Why would any corp worry about something so fucking mundane as money? They've all got more money than god. That's why they keep everyone crammed into apartment boxes and feed them holos all the time they're not being good little cogs in the corporate machines."

"And that's why all the corps want to clean up ground," Stem said. "Thousands of people living like animals down there, refusing to be part of the corp control. It's about power, not money."

Jazz nodded. "If a rival corp sent us here, it is not to rob the place. We're being used for something else."

"Like what?" Stem asked.

Jazz shook her head. "I have no idea. But they sabotaged that elevator ahead of time and used it to push us in. So we don't have any choice except going that way and finding a different path out."

Stem chewed his lower lip. "Something tells me whatever else is that way might have different ideas than simply letting us leave."

Jazz rolled her eyes. "No shit. Fuck you, Grif, what have you done?" She clearly didn't expect an answer.

"Okay, you were obviously fed falsified blueprints," Stem said. "This is supposed to be a vault with a guard station on the other side, but it's a big empty storeroom. Beyond this, the blueprints list laboratories."

"Labs?" Jazz asked. "For what?"

"Maybe that's why we're here."

"Okay, no more fucking around." Jazz looked at the unusually quiet Grifter and he said nothing. So she carried on. "SciTech obviously know we're here by now, given their elevator just exploded. We just have to fight our way the fuck out. So first we get through those labs. Where's the closest exit possibility Stem?"

Jazz had slipped easily into mission command and Stem was glad of it. Grif seemed to accept it and Tank would do whatever Grifter did. Stem scrolled rapidly through the plans. "Assuming any of these plans are accurate, there's another elevator shaft on the opposite side of the building. That's a long way. But there are no stairways marked, so it's the only way up. And we can get out on ground, but that's three levels up from here."

"Basement One is above ground?" Jazz asked.

"Ain't it grand to live in the metropolis?"

Tank strode forward and kicked down the door leading from the room. She swung her massive gatling canon up, but there was nothing to fire at. Row after row of softly glowing vats lined the huge room, each with something fleshy and misshapen suspended in thick liquid. Vaguely rounded, with nubs of what might become limbs swelling all around the central mass of each one.

"The fuck are they?" Grif asked.

"Who cares." Jazz crossed the room, heading for double doors leading out.

Cameras mounted on the ceiling tracked her movements, but Stem figured it was long past worrying about anything like that. "Corridor outside runs left to right and dead ahead. We go straight on if we're heading for the opposite side of the building."

They went through the doors together and, as they took their first steps forward, the scrabbling sounds and ear-splitting howls erupted again, from either side. Those corridors were dark, but the squad all had enhanced enough vision to pick up the heat signatures of the appalling giant, multi-limbed monsters with wide gnashing jaws running at them from either side.

That's when the shooting started.

Now

"Same plan applies," Stem said. "The signals are coming from basement two, which is the same level as ground outside."

"Stairs."

They all turned to look at Tank. She rarely said anything without being asked a question, so whenever she did speak it was worth paying attention.

But this time it didn't make sense. Stem shook his head.

68

"Remember the plans? There are no stairs in the basement levels. Not until you get to upper level three, in fact."

Tank pointed. "Stairs." She looked at him with one eyebrow raised until he turned to see what she was indicating.

Where her grenades had blown the corridor to smithereens, the vague outline of a door was still visible, and sure enough, a stairwell beyond it.

"We can't trust these plans at all," Jazz said. "Let's go."

Stem laughed. "First bit of luck we've had."

The lowest flight of steps was all rubble, but Tank boosted each of them up, then crouched, servos whining, and jumped straight up ten feet to grab a railing and haul herself over. Then they were running, boots beating a rapid rhythm up flight after flight.

"I'm sending drones," Stem said. "They'll find 'em easily, but one or two might get through. They'll map what this place is *actually* like until they're zapped."

He tapped at his wrist pad, then ducked forward a little to let the swarm of house fly-sized drones take off from his small backpack and zoom away. They immediately began pinging back visual and radar imagery that Stem let overlay the existing blueprints in his RD. He was getting close to information overload. Despite his enhancements, his ability to see in real space and fight would be compromised, but at least he might get them out this way.

Drone information rapidly fell away as the building's defences registered and disabled one after another, but Stem had let the entire swarm go and he was still getting intel from a couple of dozen as they rounded the last flight of stairs up to basement two.

Tank sprang froward and kicked through the door. The drones were gone in a flash and the team followed. Straight into a single corridor with a pack of those many-limbed, snapping, muscular horrors at the end running right for them.

"Fire in the hole!" Tank yelled again, and two more rocket-propelled grenades launched and decimated the front of the pack. The concussive backblast threw the team against the closed door, even Tank forced to take an involuntary step back, then they let loose once more with ordnance.

There were more beasts than ever and Stem worried about their ammo levels. Then three of the things broke through their line of fire and pounced. Two hit Tank square on and the third jumped sideways, pushed off the wall and spread its glistening maw wide as Grifter desperately swung his weapon up one-handed to track it. The thing's huge mouth collected Grif's rifle and his arm right up to the shoulder. The man screamed, high and agonised, and his weapon roared, muffled by the creature's mass. Its back end blew out in a spray of meat, bones and thick, black ichor, and it slapped heavily to the ground. But Grifter's weapon and ninety percent of his right arm were somewhere still inside it.

Stem leapt to Grif as the man staggered back, blood gouting from the ragged stump of his upper arm. Stem's medpack was already out, his weapon swinging uselessly by its strap. Filaments of nano-lacing bristled from the exposed nubs of Grif's bones, reflecting dully in the smoke-obscured fluorescents. That thing's teeth had gone right through the lot. Stem slapped a trauma cap over the hideous wound.

Grif's face was bone white and he fell heavily against Stem, gasping ragged breaths, eyelids fluttering as the trauma cap shrank to size, tightening over the raw, exposed flesh. Stem took Grif's weight and dragged him back as Jazz planted the muzzle of her 30-cal against the underside of one of the beasts on Tank and fired. It burst, sprayed upwards, painting the corridor ceiling in gore, and Tank managed to grab the second beast by its upper and lower jaws as it strained forwards to snap at her head and face.

Tank let out a rising growl of fury, her huge muscles bunched and straining, then a wet rip accompanied the flood of black blood as she tore the creature almost in half, ripping its lower jaw and half its underside away from the rest.

Dripping in its blood, she threw it aside and staggered back, swinging her weapon up again. Jazz matched her movements, but for the moment there were no more monsters

"How is he?" Jazz asked, without looking around. She scanned the corridor ahead with Tank, watching for any movement through the smoke.

"He's fucked up but coming around." Stem watched as the trauma cap released its potent cocktail of drugs and stims through Grifter's wound.

Suddenly, Grif gasped and staggered back upright. His left hand came up as if cradling his 30-cal assault rifle, then he looked down in confusion at where that rifle, and the arm holding it, should have been. "Fuuuuuck!" he yelled, eyeing the trauma cap, then Stem.

Stem shrugged. "You're alive, dickhead. Get out of this and you can treat yourself to a nice new arm. Probably Tank can give you some tips on good models to try out."

"Definitely not Tesla," Tank said. "That shit will electrocute you as soon as it rains."

"Let's go," Jazz said, and the team drove forward.

"Turn left ahead and straight through whatever doors you see," Stem said, relying on the data coming back from the last of his drones before they were spotted and neutralised. The blueprints they'd been supplied with didn't show that junction at all.

As they ran and turned the corner, the unmistakable sound of motorised locks whirring into place came from the other side of the double doors ahead.

"The signals are coming from in there," Stem said. "And there's no external egress that I can see on these shitty plans, but the other side of that room is an outside wall, with ground on the other side."

"We go right through," Tank said.

Jazz nodded. "Fucking A."

The team hung back as Tank crouched, her servos winding up. Then she sprang forward and hammered into the doors. They buckled but held. Tank stumbled backwards, dazed. She shook her head, sucked in a breath, then crouched again.

"Be careful you don't—" Jazz never got to finish as Tank shot forward again.

This time the doors buckled further, a large split opening down the centre, but still they didn't break all the way open. Stem, Jazz and Grifter would get through the gap, but Tank never would.

She waved them on, stumbling a little left and right, further dazed from the impacts. "Go on. I'll follow."

"Tank?" Grif said, looking up at her.

She focussed on him. "Go. On. I'm right behind you."

They surged through the gap she'd made and came out into a large control room. Holodesks lined the walls, three-dimensional maps of the building and surrounding streets spun lazily above them.

About a dozen technicians in lab coats were backed up against the far wall, hands raised, eyes wide. That wall was plasglass and beyond it the dim, filthy streets of ground, where only the homeless and unemployable, or those choosing the grime over the corp life, scratched out a living in shanty towns and roving bazaars.

The team paused, taking in the scene. Through huge, reinforced windows along one side of the control room they saw dozens of large pens, like old-fashioned farms from before meat was grown in vats. Many of the pens were open and empty, but many more held those multi-legged creatures, crashing and thrashing at their bars in unfettered rage. Doors led out both sides of that room, one pair back into the building, which was presumably where all the things they'd fought had come from.

But the other doors led out onto the streets of ground. Fifty metres up a gloomy alleyway opposite those doors, Stem saw bodies lying on the asphalt. He zoomed his cyber eye in – the bodies had limbs missing or worse. Some were bitten clean in half.

Realisation dawned. "You're using these things to remotely clean up ground?" he said, turning a horrified gaze to the technicians.

"We follow orders!" one said in a trembling voice. "That's all, we follow orders."

"Do you have any idea how many people through history have tried to excuse atrocities with that bullshit?" Jazz asked.

"What choice do we have?" another technician said. "It's that or no job, and then we're on that side of the equation." He gestured out to the streets full of the dead. "Localised testing for now, but once it's fine-tuned —"

"Stop fucking talking," Jazz growled.

"This is what the rival corp wanted to expose by sending us in," Stem said. "All this, everything we've seen is recorded in our RDs. They know we won't be able to sit on it, and it'll go viral when we release the news."

They were distracted by a loud mechanical whirr and the reinforced windows between them and the animal pens began to open, the glass rising up into the walls.

Jazz spun to the technicians. "What are you doing?"

They all panicked, running from one control panel to another. "It's not us!" one said.

"Upstairs," another said, gesturing vaguely above. "It must be controlled up there. I didn't even know those windows *could* open."

Another sound, farther away, marked the bars of the remaining pens sliding open and the creatures trapped inside leaped free.

A crash beside them accompanied Tank finally breaking through the reinforced double doors and she took in the scene in an instant. She kept her head down and didn't stop running, crossing the large control room at a blistering pace and crashed clean through the external wall, only to collapse face down in the street outside. Finally, the physical traumas too much to bear.

As the creatures surged towards the now open windows, Grifter snatched Stem's weapon with his remaining hand. "Go!" he yelled. "You and Jazz, go! I'll hold them off."

"But Tank?"

"I'll try to hold them long enough until she reboots. If she can. You two go." He stared hard at Stem. "I got the job from the Rytell Corporation. The only reason they'd bother exposing all of this is because they're working on a similar project, but SciTech were ahead of the game. Right? They're not altruistic. They want to expose SciTech, bring them down, and buy *themselves* time to finish developing whatever version of this they're working on. It's the only explanation."

Stem knew Grif was right. It was suddenly all so clear. But there was no time to discuss it. Grifter started firing wildly single-handed, ripping rounds into the beasts as they tried to claw through the windows. There were dozens of them, he would surely be overwhelmed, but Stem and Jazz had a few seconds to get a head start.

They bolted out of the hole Tank had made for them, spared her a brief glance as she lay immobile, then hammered along the first alleyway of ground, away from SciTech. Grif's gunfire and the screams of the technicians faded behind them.

Stem didn't know if he would ever see Tank or Grifter again. He seriously doubted it. But one thing he did know was that he and Jazz would be talking to *all* the news outlets very soon. And right after those exclusive interviews, he saw a visit to the Rytell Corporation headquarters in their very near future.

STOKEHOLD

Pamela Jeffs

Fear had a way of leaching into metal and stone and wood, of creating an invisible patina. In a place where the past was brutal, the dread felt old and dangerous, but in the belly of a battleship, the horror was compounded. Here, in the stokehold, weighted down in furnace light and coal dust, old regrets and torment abounded. Sailors had died here. Some by fire, others by a murderous knife thrust between the ribs at midnight. And the ghosts of those men never left.

Tonight, they seemed restless; their forms, shadowy half suggestions, huddled and shifted in the darker corners of the hold. Not sure what had them riled, but having abided amongst them all my life, I knew I was safe from their words and their touch as long as I kept to the firelight.

I kicked open the furnace door, squinted against the blasting heat and shovelled another pile of coal onto the grate. Embers rained to the deck as the blaze rose to heat the water in the giant boilers above. Steam hissed in response, fuelling the clockwork mechanisms that propelled the ship.

"Gypsy Boy."

I hunched my shoulders. Why did I ever ask that son of a bitch Zeke if he could see the ghosts too? "I'm here, Chief."

Zeke, senior in rank to me, stalked in from the airlock, his body swaying to counter the motion of the ship. He was big and brawny—coarse, as if cut from rusted steel—and he wore coal dust like armour pressed into the creases of his forty-something-year-old face.

"Captain wants you." He grabbed a shovel from the rack. "Get up there and get back quick. Don't think I'm happy about doin' your work for you."

The captain? I glanced at the ghosts. Their heads were bent together in some kind of silent communication. I didn't want to leave my post. "What do you think he wants?"

"Do I look like I'm fuckin' privy to the desires of officers? Now get yourself goin'." He shoved past me, dropping his meaty shoulder to my chest and making me stumble. He took my place at the grate and scooped in another load of coal. Patches of sweat stained his shirt, looking blood-dark in the fickle light.

I dropped my shovel and headed for the bridge.

The ghosts with their jittery, smudgy forms trailed single file behind me as I exited into the close crew corridor. They kept their distance for the moment. But, damn, I hated the way they moved—all uncanny-like—the sharp, aggressive blinking in and out of view; the three or four of their steps lost between.

I hated how their eyes and mouths looked like deep, black holes.

Sweat slid down my back and not from the heat. The electric lanterns lining the walls here offered me no protection from the haunts.

"The water's rising..." The teasing, disembodied whisper of a sailor who drowned. It sailed past me like sea foam in a storm.

My heart slewed sideways. Drowning at sea was the only thing I feared worse than the ghosts.

I fixed my eyes to the far hatch.

Just keep walking.

The floor pitched against each step. Working in the window-less dark, I'd learnt to read each motion of the ship and today I sensed the ocean outside was wild – no calm sea to give us easy passage.

Everything was off kilter today.

It seemed an age before the cold, steel hatch-wheel was in my grip. I breathed out a sigh and turned it. The door seal cracked. Light spilled across the threshold as I stepped into another corridor, this one wide, bright and gleaming – made for the cleaner work belonging to officers and bridge crew. Here, the walls were transparent, revealing the working innards of the vessel. Beautiful and complicated, the copper and gold clock-work mechanisms whirred and wound behind their sheets of hardened glass.

"Blood on the cogs..."

I swivelled with a tight intake of breath. An older ghost stood by my shoulder, his soul so threadbare as to be almost colour-less. Yet his touch held strength as he raked the memory of his yellowed nails across my throat. Goosebumps rippled down my arms. Then he retreated, pointing left. I turned. The cogs in the walls dripped with ephemeral blood and viscera. A transparent, mangled corpse—face torn and limbs jammed—leered at me.

A man who'd died in the walls.

I shook off the ghost's touch with a growl and headed for the bridge.

The captain's voice was loud even through the steel door. Deep and sonorous, he barked commands to his crew. I entered the room quietly, marvelling at the grace and curvature of the gleaming instruments that lined the consoles. The elegant compass nestled in its cradle of gold and brass next to the navi-gational officer's station. Captain Reed stood, legs braced before the polished wooden wheel, broad-ended fingers curled around the walnut timber spokes that guided the rudder. But for me, the true beauty lay outside the vessel. As always, on the rare occasion I was called to this lofty station, my attention was drawn to the large expanse of glass that overlooked the tarnished brass smokestacks, the iron-sheet deck and ocean. And I was right. Today the sea was bleak; a wash of grey beneath an even greyer sky. Waves, tops thrashed to white, buffeted the horizon. A storm was on its way. A bad one.

The ghosts muttered, "The water is rising. Blood on the cogs..."

"Stoker Webb." Captain Reed's level gaze held mine, his hands resting lightly on the wheel.

I saluted. "Reporting, as requested, sir."

Reed nodded. "How much coal have we left in the hold, son?"

This was something Zeke would know. Why hadn't the captain asked him? I swallowed my annoyance. "Almost empty, Captain, but we're on track to make it to port."

Reed's dark brows furrowed over his eagle-sharp nose. "It won't be enough."

I glanced at the gathering storm. "Sir?"

Reed frowned. "Back to your post, son. Stoke the furnace to full and make it hot. We need everything out of these engines. There's blood on the cogs and the water's rising."

Those words again...

Then Reed turned away.

I stumbled back, eyes wide.

The captain had a great, gaping wound cut across his spine.

He's dead—I'm only seeing his shade. I glanced around the rest of the crew and my stomach dropped.

They were all dead too.

But only newly so. For while their edges were transparent, their eyes and souls still retained colour and form. Like the captain, some of the crew showed the wounds that killed them – throats slit, others with worse.

It was only now I noticed the floor wetted with gore, scarlet and not yet congealed.

But no corpses.

What the hell had happened here?

The whole ghostly crew stopped and considered me.

Outside, the ship powered into the growing waves.

I couldn't help it.

I ran.

ꝏꝏ ꝏꝏ

My vomit splattered hot and acrid across the corridor. The smell of the crew's blood clung to me, no amount of clearing my throat seemed to loosen it.

Zeke. I had to get back to him. As much as I hated him, he deserved to be warned. I wiped my mouth on my sleeve and sprinted down the corridor, headed for the stokehold hatch. Around me, the cogs in the walls continued to turn.

The ghosts appeared ahead of me, forming a line to bar the path. Damn it. I brushed through them, the cold tatters of their souls clinging to my shirt as I raced to my post.

I slammed open the hatch. "Zeke!"

Silence held the room, thick and heavy like felt. I stumbled to the furnace. The grate hung open and the fire burned low. The ghosts crowded in behind me. Frantic, I grabbed a discarded shovel and piled on extra fuel. Slowly, it ignited, licks of flame catching to the coal.

The spirits grudgingly retreated.

Where was Zeke?

I hung my shovel, took a kerosene lamp from its hook by the rack and headed deeper into the stokehold where the furnace's belly roared and piles of coal spilled across the floor. My boots slipped on the uneven surface. The ghosts flanked me but kept their distance. Their dark, hollow eyes followed my every move.

An empty kerosine tin rolled across my path. Things always move in a ship, especially as it pitched and yawed through a storm. But this movement was different. The tin didn't roll back, instead remaining pressed to the far wall. The floor... it leaned as if the ship had settled to port.

A ghost sailor, dressed in an old stoker's uniform, stepped in and swiped at my lamp. It dropped from my fingers, the glass shattering as it rolled to settle by the tin. The small flame stuttered yet remained burning low on the wick, offering just enough light to see by, but not to deter the spirits.

"The water is rising..." whispered the phantom.

I lunged for the lamp and retrieved it. The wick extended and light bloomed out. The ghost retreated and I swallowed. With the ship's deck at this angle, it was clear we were taking on water.

What do I do?

A dark, sticky-looking trail smeared on the deck caught my

attention. I leaned in, the firelight revealing blood slicked across the floor.

My hand shook. The light trembled.

A secondary door led from the rear of the stokehold through to the older corridors giving access to the engine room. I followed the blood. Shadows pressed close. The smell of salt and old oil grew stronger here, underpinned by darker notes of grief and half-remembered terrors. I tried to ignore the threads of sorrow and memory leached by the ship, just as insidious as the ghosts who never left me be.

The steady rumble of the engines drew me on. They grew louder as I neared. Ahead the hatch stood ajar, beckoning. How could an exit look so hungry? My heart clenched into a knot tighter than a fist. I swallowed spit soured by fear, and stepped through.

The next corridor was shadowed, not having the same expensive electric bulbs that were installed in the ones above. The small light offered by my lamp was just enough to illuminate the black-red trail I followed.

The body of a mid-shipman materialised out of the gloom. Blond-haired and slight of frame, his throat was cut, and not neatly. The death stroke was a ragged score on the column of his neck – a disturbing contrast to his bloodied, but otherwise neat uniform. I pressed a hand to my mouth; he wasn't much older than me.

The ship lurched further to port and I stumbled against the wall. An ominous groan echoed through the metal. Time was running out.

I slid past the boy just as his soul separated from his corpse. He looked confused as he ran a pale hand through his fringe and then touched the wound on his throat. We made eye contact and his lips moved, but I didn't wait to either listen or explain. I left him to cry over his own corpse.

The hull groaned again and I could all but feel the heavy press of water against the steel – the ocean's desire to flood the compartments and claim the ship, to deliver death by drowning.

STOKEHOLD

The thought of the crushing depths and crabs nibbling at my flesh… I just needed to find Zeke and then get the hell off this ship.

The door to the engine room was closed. With the angle of the deck, its heavy metal construction kept it firmly pressed against the seals.

I battled the weight and forced my way inside. The room was lit with strings of electric lights that flickered like moths. The air boiled hot as the engine's main cogs and steam-driven valves churned away, their thunderous voices an assault on the senses.

Adjusting my hold on the lamp, I circled around the closest of the great piston housings and skirted beneath one of three gleaming mechanisms. The air down here smelled damp. Years of engine steam and oil had conspired to make the floor slick. My boots slipped, and I swear the deck was trying to trip me. I turned a corner and found the water.

It poured in through a series of holes punched through the side of the ship. The metal shards of the wounds curled outward: the damage made from within rather than anything the sea threw at us. Salt water and foam gushed through them like blood pouring from a torn artery.

Who would have done such a terrible thing?

The water is rising…

Terror surged, adrenaline powered me. No longer worried about Zeke but with thoughts turned to the lifeboats lashed to the decks above, I ran, distress at the rising water greater than my fear of the ghosts. Overhead the clockwork cogs turned and turned, their cadence beating as if to measure the last moments of my life. I visualised the open sky – a picture of white caps on a vast ocean and I held tight to that image.

Zeke was waiting for me at the hatch, eyes wild and teeth bared. He stood braced against the floor's tilt, machete gripped in his meaty hand.

"Zeke? What are you doing?"

"It ends here, Gypsy Boy," he snarled, and then lunged.

I pushed the blade aside. A sting to the palm; the keen blade nicked my flesh. Zeke's free hand snapped forward and caught me around the throat. I swung at his chest, but my punches landed on flesh hardened by a lifetime before the furnace. I couldn't break free.

He leaned in. "Got one final job for you."

I sucked stunted breaths as he dragged me toward the heart of the engine, the place where the largest of the cogs whirred to keep the ship's rudders steady. A slaughterhouse stench rose, hanging concentrated in the air – death and body fluids.

"There's blood on the cogs…"

The ghost's whispers filled my mind as Zeke threw me face down across a metal beam and bound my hands to it.

I glanced up and wished I hadn't.

Above me rotated the rudder cogs. Their usually gleaming surfaces were ragged and stained. To each of the great spokes was tied the corpse of a crew member. Torn flesh hung from stiffened limbs, and those still with eyes stared blankly into the darkness.

"Time for you to join the rest of the crew," said Zeke, his breath hot against my ear.

"What have you done?" I whispered.

"Can't your ghost friends tell you?"

The haunts, as if summoned, appeared from thin air. They gathered, solemn, below the hanging corpses. Captain Reed stepped forward, hand outstretched.

"Fear the living," he said to me. "They're the monsters here."

I glanced at Zeke, "You murdered them, Chief?" I asked, horrified. "All of them! Why?"

Zeke's gaze darkened like a sea horizon before a storm. "You wouldn't understand."

"No? Try me you son of a bitch!"

Zeke snarled and slammed the flat of his machete against a piston casing. The ring of distressed steel clamoured, discordant. Then he closed his eyes. When he opened them, blood-shot sclera ringed his irises – a gaze wild, angry and murderous.

STOKEHOLD

Something was broken inside of Zeke.

He snapped his teeth at me, like a shark tasting blood in the water.

Then he threw a hand up in the air, palm stained with coal dust. "I signed up to be a sailor, but instead of fighting for my country, I was put into the belly of this iron beast and have since spent a lifetime feeding it coal. No clean breeze on my brow, only darkness, dust and terror. Haven't you felt it? The way it bleeds out of the walls and into your skull?" Zeke smacked his palm against his temple. "You asked me once if I could see ghosts. I can't, but maybe it's them I feel. In my head. And they're always in the stokehold. Just them, the furnace, and those four steel walls."

He swing his machete. The edge gleamed silver in the lamplight. "I can't fuckin' take it anymore!"

"Please, Zeke, you don't have to do this."

"But I do. I've given everything to the Navy. But no more. This crew died so Chief Stoker Zeke Marshall could die. The old Zeke will go down with this ship. Tomorrow, I'll be a new man, and I'll be far, far away. Away from the fear, away from the coal dust, away from these damn walls.

"You're crazy."

"No. I'm smart. Because unlike you, I'm getting off this tub."

"Please... *please* don't kill me."

Zeke frowned. "You won't die by my hand. You worked hard at the furnace, same as me. I respect that. You can stick around to see the end." He knelt and ensured the knots against my wrist were tight. Satisfied, he stood. "See ya, kid."

His footsteps were lost to the groans of the dying ship. I struggled against my bonds but it was useless. The deck pitched higher and the water first lapped at my feet, then soon reached my chin. I sobbed. Strained to lift my head. The sea kissed my nostrils.

My ghosts gathered close and for the first time, I was thankful for their presence. At least I wasn't alone.

One by one, each haunt touched a hand to my shoulder,

fingertips freezing. My breaths came rapid and shallow. I gripped the beam with both hands, took courage from the iron and wondered if it, even at the bottom of the ocean, would hold the memory of my death.

The ship groaned as she settled deeper into the ocean's embrace. The engines bite-toothed cogs finally whirred to a stop, the corpses they held slumped against their bonds. Then the water closed over my head.

I held my breath for as long as I could but soon the briny liquid scored its way into my lungs.

The ghosts whispered to me one last time.

"The water has risen," they said, "and the cogs are washed clean."

KING RAT

RPL Johnson

Zodiac slept in the bike's embrace, dream-reading the briefing package on his latest target. The task had absorbed the processing time for three of his aspects for most of his trip down from the Moreton Bay Arcology. Horse and Ox sifted through the terabytes of data while Rabbit supervised the work, guiding its methodical peers and advising on what was important and what could be discarded. Occasionally, Rabbit plucked a snippet from the stream and passed it across Zodiac's slumbering semi-consciousness. What it showed him did not make for a peaceful sleep.

One file caught his attention and Zodiac roused himself from his rest. He watched it at near normal speed as the bike began its long deceleration into the city, allowing his organic brain to parse the information. In twenty-one years of living with his aspects, he had learned to allow his human instincts to supplement the programmed responses of his cybernetic sub-processors.

Zodiac described himself as a private security contractor. In reality, he was pest control. This particular pest was a corporate terrorist waging a private war against Fabri-Kate, the ubiquitous network of 3D printing and fabrication crucibles that could be found in homes and workshops from Manila to the Ross Island Warren.

The file was a compilation of prior attacks against Fabri-Kate. In one clip, a huge bank of public fabrication crucibles suddenly activated, spewing out a clacking tide of thousands of spider-like drones. They swarmed over people and cars and up the sides of buildings, bringing central Sydney to a standstill.

Another one showed a segmented horror the size of a tank crawling out of an industrial crucible at the Port Botany Naval

Yard. Zodiac watched as one brave stevedore crashed a forklift into the creature, impaling one segment and briefly pinning it, before the rest of the nightmare coiled around the forklift and its driver like a garotte of barbed wire and tore both of them apart.

There were scores of other, smaller incidents: enough data for Zodiac's aspects to analyse and extract some patterns.

The information appeared in Zodiac's mind like a fresh memory. He had never studied Markov chains or memory-free series, but still the answer was there. The attacks mapped onto a drunkard's walk: a kind of search pattern governed by probability. Rooster had already back-calculated which functions gave the best fit and used them to predict possible locations for the next attack.

Zodiac ordered the bike to take the slip road off the M2 Loop and brought it to a stop at a viewing platform on one of the bridges between the Ultimo Supertowers. The towers were a nexus for several major roads allowing easy access to any one of the three locations Rooster had identified as possible targets.

Zodiac eased himself out of the bike's plush seat and stretched. It was still an hour from sunset, but in the shadows of the Supertowers the black flowers of photoelectric parasols were already folding to reveal electric slashes of neon in the alleys below. Here and there, a circular cast to the streetscape reflected the cratered geology below from the Shattering, where humanity had almost bombed itself into extinction.

Monkey sat on the guardrail looking out across the city. Like the buildings below, he was drawn as a neon outline as if scratched onto this plane of existence with a needle of blue flame. Of all Zodiac's aspects, Monkey was the only one that spoke to him directly. It was also the only one who impinged on his vision to give itself the neon pretence of an external existence.

"Do you think the armour will help?" Zodiac asked.

Monkey was wearing the characteristic chainmail shirt and phoenix feather cap of Sun Wukong, the legendary Monkey King. A staff lay across its lap. "I thought it fitting," Monkey replied. Zodiac heard its words as clearly as if it had spoken aloud. "We are going to war against a demon after all."

Zodiac joined the little blue figure at the rail. "And are you planning on helping in the coming battle, great Monkey King?" he asked with mocking faux-deference.

Monkey ignored him. It stood on the rail, twirled its staff in a complicated pattern and smacked it down with a mighty cry that seemed to have absolutely no effect on reality whatsoever. Nevertheless, it gave a satisfied snort before sitting back down and returning the staff to its lap.

"Bet you it's Newtown," Monkey said, referring to one of the possible targets Rooster had identified.

"How long?" Zodiac asked.

Monkey's only currency was silence. In truth, Zodiac didn't mind its company, but Monkey hated being cooped up and so it was the only bet that carried any weight.

"A day," it said. "Twenty-four hours."

"Okay," Zodiac replied. "But I get to choose when."

Monkey nodded and then leaped to the roof of the bike. It shrank its staff down to the size of a telescope and pretended to look through it in the direction of Newtown.

Zodiac opened a panier on the side of the bike and pulled out a short-bladed sword. It was a replica of a traditional Chinese dao, with a design that was a thousand years old even before the Shattering. Except this wide, straight blade with its traditional, chiselled point had been grown from a single piezoelectric crystal.

Zodiac worked through some simple forms, enjoying the chance to stretch after his trip. The dao's crystalline blade harvested electricity from movement and stored it in capacitors in the sword's hilt. The constant trickle of charge along the blade caused it to shed any particles that were not in perfect geometric alignment with the parent crystal. At the end of the exercise, Zodiac knew it would be sharp down to the molecular level.

Rat alerted him to a disturbance in Cutters Bay.

"Doesn't fit," Monkey said. "No major Fabri-Kate installations out that way."

That was true, but Zodiac understood the model as well as Rooster. There was no Fabri-Kate facility in Cutters Bay, but if you adjusted for that, the location fit the model better than any of the other candidates.

"Maybe there's some target we don't know about," Zodiac said. "An executive passing through, or supplies headed for Fabri-Kate." He fastened the sword around his waist so that it nestled snugly in the small of his back, its ringed pommel protruding above his right hip.

Zodiac couldn't explain why, but it felt right. His aspects contained eleven members of the sheng xiao: eleven vertebrae removed from his spine from the Atlas to T4 and replaced with gold and jade replicas, each one a cybernetic sub-processor with all the characteristics of the legendary animals of the Chinese zodiac. Tiger and Snake, Horse and Rat, each of Zodiac's aspects had its own strengths and weaknesses, but only with him was the sheng xiao complete.

"Let's check it out," Zodiac said and jumped off the platform so suddenly that for a moment Monkey was left sitting on top of the bike, disappearing into the darkness above him.

Monkey reappeared at his side as he fell, skating through the air with each of Sun Wukong's boots encased in cloud.

"You know, we could have taken the bike," it said.

"Tell it to catch up," Zodiac replied.

He landed on the roof of a skyscraper, slid across photoelectric panels, rolled between the blades of heat sinks, and took off running with Monkey riding its twin clouds at his side.

Cutters Bay was lower rise than even the foothills of the supertowers and it took some time for Zodiac to shed enough elevation. He landed on the roof of a massage parlour that still retained some of its ancient brick frontage. Gaps in the masonry were filled with epoxy and cheap cladding, partially hidden behind a second façade of animated billboards.

A police cruiser lay on its side in flames in the street below: that especially intense flare of a damaged fuel cell that burned like white phosphorous. It crackled, halfway between a fire and electrical short, throwing light down the street in brilliant, brief handfuls.

KING RAT

Zodiac felt the threat before he saw it. His aspects welled up from the architecture of his artificial vertebrae: guiding his natural reactions, analysing the data from his peripheral vision and smells and sensations too quick and subtle to be noticed by a natural brain.

In an instant, Zodiac was aware of a thousand details. A huge cyborg stood in the street. Snake could feel the heat rising from it: a creature of fire and violence.

Pig savoured the air, sharp with decay products from weapons fire mixed with the rotten egg stench of a ruptured sewer.

The street was littered with cybernetic parts from a blown-out shopfront across the street. Rat, ever-observant and quick-witted, spotted something in the wreckage: a 3D printer stencilled with the smiling cartoon face of the Fabri-Kate mascot.

"It's a chop shop," Zodiac said. "These aren't victims; they're spares."

"Probably illegal by the look of that bootleg printer," Monkey agreed. "Neat setup though. They could probably grow a new implant on the spot: stich it on molecule by molecule. I'm guessing our hacker friend got tired of printing drones. Probably took control when their immune system was offline for the op."

The cyborg's head was still vaguely human, but almost completely given over to a suite of sensors that grew like a multi-lobed tumour from where its eyes had once been. Windpipe and aorta and jugular veins had been rerouted from the vulnerable neck deep into the hulking body so that its hot breath blew from thermal exhausts below its shoulder blades. Its right arm tapered to a long barrel.

It still retained human flesh on its shoulders and in artistic strips down its torso so that it looked like it was cloaked in the flayed skin of its former self. Even that remaining skin was modified: large, swirling tattoos traced a fractal, branching pattern across its chest in glowing yellow and red swirls of photo-electric ink.

Three figures faced the cyborg. Zodiac felt Sheep and Ox assessing them without finding any real threats: a couple of guys with kinetic hardware cloaked within poor facsimiles of designer limbs—young boomers from a local mob by the look of their matching jackets—and one older woman with pre-Shattering, military-grade tech.

Implants were to be expected. There were only two types of people without obvious signs of body modifications: the very poor, and the hyper rich. Most people wore their scars proudly like kintsugi teacups.

The cyborg raised its arm with frightening speed and fired. Whatever implants the first woman was packing weren't dense enough to set off the round's payload. It tore through her chest, practically ripping her in half with its hypersonic shockwave and plunging deep into the building beyond before hitting something hard enough to set it off.

The two boomers were hopelessly under-spec for the creature they faced, but seemingly lacked the imagination to do anything other than die for their little patch of turf. The first managed to fire a few rounds from a small semiautomatic. The rounds plinked off the cyborg's armour. It responded with a shoulder charge like a car crash that picked the boomer up and sent him spinning backwards, little more than a bloody sack of splintered bone and cheap electronics held together by his gang colours.

The second boomer suddenly found himself face to face with the construct occupying the space where his shattered friend had once stood. He didn't last long. The cheap taser he carried crackled briefly as his spasming hand clenched down on the firing stud.

Zodiac saw the giant barrel swing toward him, then he was airborne, leaping across the street as a high explosive round tore apart the building behind him. He landed on the far side of the street, perched like a mountain goat on the narrow sill above a dead advertising screen.

"Twenty-millimetre, fin stabilized," Monkey said. "Tungsten penetrator with a high-explosive payload. Your sub-derm's not rated for that kind of firepower. My advice: try not to get hit."

"Thanks," Zodiac replied. "I'll do my best."

The cyborg fired again, but Zodiac was already moving. The high explosive rounds chased him along the wall, each one just fragments of a second behind him as he sped down a spiral with the giant cyborg at its focus. Zodiac felt the pressure wave from the missed detonations like a wind at his back, urging him forward. There was no fear. Zodiac was not just some street ninja. He was the sheng xiao, he was complete, he was the universe and all it contained.

He reached ground level. The dao was in his hand, blade humming with stored charge, edge arcing upward, another curve of perfect geometry like the sweep of a calligraphy brush writing the cyborg's final words.

The giant cyborg twitched, and Zodiac's world exploded. His vision blurred and his breath burst from his mouth as charged knuckledusters slammed into his stomach. He tumbled backwards towards the burning cruiser, twisting in mid-air and landing on the balls of his feet like a dancer.

That wasn't right. His approach had been perfect, there was no way his opponent should have been able to hit him.

Zodiac felt a moment of disorientation as throughout his body tens of thousands of superconducting logic gates flickered like glitter thrown through a shaft of sunlight. Delicate circuits shut down to re-route the charge through his main bus ducts where it could be safety discharged. Parts of him disappeared and were reborn in an atonal staccato rhythm. For a microsecond, he was alone as the junction between him and his aspects stuttered and he had a memory of an earlier time, a simpler time, before his augmentation, before he became Zodiac. Then it was gone, and Tiger roared back into his mind, urging him to counterattack.

He could almost hear his father's voice in his ears.

"Foolish boy. Again!"

The cyborg's left fist still glowed with residual charge from the punch. Sparks jumped between its fingers.

"Okay," Zodiac said. "Again!"

He rushed forward, keeping the strobe of the burning

cruiser at his back to confuse his opponent's targeting software and driving the dao forward like a spear.

The big cyborg pivoted to take the blow on its armour and instead of digging deep into its vitals, Zodiac's sword just glanced off ceramic.

Zodiac stepped back out of range of a scything kick and was forced into a desperate block as the cyborg's charged left fist smashed down like a hammer.

Its fighting style was unorthodox. Zodiac was used to fighting against new styles. Every new cybernetic development changed the meta, creating new martial arts overnight, but the cyborg seemed to have no pattern. Zodiac got the feeling he was fighting more than one opponent. Each limb seemed to have a mind of its own. It moved in spasms and jerks: impossibly fast and precise at times, almost clumsy at others as if warring entities inside the giant frame were fighting for control of its limbs.

Zodiac pressed forward. Whoever or whatever was controlling the cyborg was fast but untrained. Zodiac used that to his advantage.

He stabbed with stiff fingers into the flesh above the cyborg's armour, then ducked under the counter punch and into the dead space behind its armpit. He drove a knee into the blades of the exhaust where its ribs had once been and was rewarded with a satisfying crunch.

His opponent fought back, lurching awkwardly into each movement with a series of insane stochastic twitches. Running fast: too fast. With Rat's keen ultrasonic hearing, he could hear the cyborg's chassis disintegrating as the hacker pushed it past every safety limit.

Zodiac spun quickly out of range, using his momentum to land a kick on the cyborg's knee joint on the way out. It moved with machine speed, catching Zodiac by surprise by moving *into* his kick. The knee joint bucked as the cyborg sacrificed it for a momentary advantage.

It collapsed on top of him, slamming Zodiac's face into the shattered concrete. Only his reinforced bones prevented him from being crushed under its weight.

He allowed his lungs to shut down. The genotyped whale myoglobin in his blood could keep him alive for half an hour without taking a breath, but he could feel his augmented systems breaking down. The perfect astrological unity of his aspects started to fragment as the cyborg drove its knee into Zodiac's spine.

Monkey's electric blue outline stuttered into his vision, flickering like a faulty florescent light. Its voice faded in and out too.

"Do s—me—hing. And do i— —ast!"

"B... Bike," Zodiac managed.

Monkey flickered out, but Zodiac noticed the smile on its lips as it faded.

Then he heard the familiar whine of a powerful engine and there was a flash of movement and suddenly the weight was gone.

He took a gasp of air and the oxygen hit the myoglobin in his bloodstream like a drug.

He staggered to his feet and gathered the dao. The cyborg was on its knees. Behind it, Zodiac's bike chattered under the remains of a nearby shack as its gyroscope tried desperately to right it under the weight of rubble.

Zodiac felt the power spike an instant before he smelled the burning flesh. The cyborg's tattoos flared, the subtle glow of the incandescent ink boosted somehow until the light outshone the burning police cruiser.

The tribal briar that covered most of the construct's remaining flesh, flashed, building into a constant strobe that assailed Zodiac's senses like physical blows.

He was stunned. Couldn't move. Couldn't even think. The flashing light filled every part of him as if he was made of glass. He could hear Monkey's voice, faint and fading, any meaning to its shouts already lost like the details of an overexposed image.

He staggered backwards down the path.

Path?

There was no path, only the shattered pavement of broken concrete, but he could feel it: pebbles pressing through the thin soles of his boots. He could smell the summer's dust kicked up by his scuffing feet.

The cyborg was on all fours in front of him on the path/not path. Its tattoos were dull now, their outlines traced in smoking lines of blackened skin. Zodiac watched as it staggered to its feet—reeling like a drunkard—and disappeared into the forest of bamboo that lined the path and lay over the surrounding hills in a green susurration of swaying stalks.

Bamboo?

He felt a moment of anxiety, then his father laid his hand on his shoulder, and remembered an older, deeper fear.

He looked up and only noticed the differences. His father's skin was clear: his cheeks full, as they had been before being hollowed out by the cancer. The smile was kindly, which was odd. That had disappeared even before the illness.

The path to the temple passed under an ornate Chinese arch with bright yellow roof tiles and sharply upswept flying eaves atop four red columns.

Zodiac—no, that wasn't right, this was before. He was just Shujun back then.

Zodiac/Shujun saw a flash of electric blue scamper up one column to hide behind the ornate eaves. He wanted to stop and investigate, but his father's hand urged him onwards.

A welcoming party met his father at the door of the temple: monks, all dressed in long, draped coats of brilliant white that swept the floor of polished black granite. They were soon deep in conversation, leaving Shujun free to explore.

Old stone: new technology.

Even the young boy could tell that the equipment that filled the old temple was mis-matched, scavenged from the ruins of a dozen institutions after the Shattering. At the centre of the room a raised dais held a glass cylinder. Suspended inside were the linked trefoil shapes of eleven golden vertebrae forming part of a human spine. Each artificial bone was expertly sculpted with branching lines of jade inlaid in the gold, reminding Shujun of circuitry. He stood on tiptoes and peered at the lowest vertebra. A single character was inscribed on its golden surface. "Rabbit," Shujun read and smiled. He liked rabbits.

Blue flashes again: something small and agile darting away behind a bank of equipment.

His father was beside him.

"Don't worry," he said, looking at the golden vertebrae. "You'll grow into them."

Pain.

Constant pain and voices in his head.

Not voices.

The incomprehensible squeal of machine code and something else: grunts and roars and constant chittering. An endless babble of gibberish, day and night until he welcomed the thought of each next operation for the brief release of anaesthesia.

Pain.

The deformity of golden bones squeezed into too small a frame. Other bones—natural ones—cracked open to the marrow, infused with silicious carbides that grew through their pores like frost across a cold window: a dead mockery of life advancing until each bone was as hard as a fossil. Muscle fibres teased apart and re-sheathed. Skin flayed and underlaid with a sub-dermal web of polymerized buckystrings. Blood drained and replaced with a black fluid that his reengineered marrow would feed.

A new heart to pump the new blood.

Synthetic veins, pressure rated for his new heart, grew inside his old circulatory system like the relining of old pipes. They expanded as they grew, bursting through the thin walls of his human blood vessels, rupturing him inside and out until his whole body felt like one big bruise.

His old self, everything he had been, was expelled like waste. New kidneys pissed out the remains of the boy Shujun in broken, molecular fragments until all that remained was something else.

The nerve replacement had been the worst. The monks had used his pain to guide their micro-manipulators. By that point, the anaesthetic didn't work anyway. He was no longer human enough to be affected by such things.

Pain.

It didn't stop after the surgeries. Suddenly he was skidding across gravel, his new sub-derm protecting him, but the nerve endings in his skin had still not caught-up and fed him messages of tearing.

He was in the training ground behind the temple. The Wing Chun master in his powered amour stood at the centre of a circle of pristine gravel, perfect as a statue.

Zodiac was tired and ragged: clothes torn and drenched with sweat from a body running too hot.

He heard his father's voice from a balcony above. "Again!"

He looked up and his father was remote, rippling as if seen through water. But it wasn't the father he remembered: not the man who had abandoned him to the monks at the temple, nor the wasted wreck that had abandoned him again, years later, dying in a hospital bed before the construct that was now Zodiac had a chance to punish him for the death of Shujun.

The man standing above him was his client, Lev Gallos, founder of Fabri-Kate. He had the same manner as his father: tall and aloof and demanding and hated.

The man was not his father, and he was not Zodiac.

He could feel himself: no golden bones, no weaponized flesh. His body was a congealed gobbet of gristle around a ball of neurons, little more than biological waste. Was this Shujun reborn? All the flushed-away meat of his human self, resurrected?

No. This was something else.

The 'something else' had voices in its head too. No squeal of machine code, no babble of animals, just a very human wail of uncomprehending anguish.

It came from everywhere.

From his brothers and sisters.

He was not *him*; he was *them*: a bondage of broken bodies wrapped around each other and knitted together with scar tissue. Nerves grew into and over and around each other, binding them together in one metastatic mass: pain and hatred knotted like the broken tails of a rat king.

A little blue figure was waving at him.

KING RAT

The man who was not his father and not Gallos but some strange mixture of both, was still there, but beyond him a small, simian form drawn from electric blue fire crouched on a roof rafter. It beckoned to him.

Zodiac tried to move and felt something give.

The thing, the rat king of entangled neurons, was stuck in its fleshy prison, but Zodiac felt himself tear away like a scab picked off a wound.

He climbed out of the tank. His father/Gallos ignored him, eyes fixed on the entangled skeins of tissue floating in the nutrient bath below.

Zodiac—and he was Zodiac again now—followed the little, blue figure. It beckoned to him through an arched doorway and Zodiac stepped forward into—

—The shattered street was just as he remembered it. He must have only been out for a minute.

"You back?" Monkey asked.

It balanced on its upended staff like an acrobat so that it was eye to eye with Zodiac.

"I'm back," Zodiac said, looking round for the cyborg. "Where's our friend?"

"Gone. Don't know where. I was too busy following you."

The memories of his other aspects were similarly blank.

Zodiac gathered up his dao.

"What happened?" he asked. "I thought we couldn't be hacked."

"*We* weren't," Monkey said pointedly. "That was something new: some kind of fugue state, an organic hack. You're lucky I was able to follow you, otherwise you'd still be trapped in there."

Trapped. Zodiac shuddered at the word. It brought back memories of the tank and twisted flesh unable to move. Unaware of anything beyond its glass prison.

Almost anything.

His palms itched, fingers flexing unconsciously, searching for the throat of a man long dead. Hatred for one's creator was something he understood.

He pulled the wreckage of his bike out from under the rubble. It swayed upright briefly then sagged to one side; its rear swing arm was hopelessly buckled. Zodiac opened the pannier and took out a VC gun. The variable-calibre rifle had a magazine full of two hundred cubic centimetres of electrostatic memory polymer paste that the gun could bake into a range of projectiles from flechettes to twenty-five-millimetre cargo rounds.

"We have to get back to Fabri-Kate," Zodiac said.

"Why?" Monkey asked.

"Because I know what the hacker is. And I think I just helped it find what it's looking for."

꩜ ꩜

Fabri-Kate's head office was a dome of black glass just south of the M2 Loop. Zodiac had been there twice: once to meet Lev Gallos, and again in the dream he'd shared with the creature that occupied the cyborg's mind.

When Zodiac arrived, the plaza in front of the Fabri-Kate dome squirmed with movement lit by the fires of burning security vehicles. Public fabrication crucibles around the edges of the plaza spat out a constant stream of small drones that marched in columns like army ants towards a shambling mass in the centre of the plaza.

The Rat King had remade the cyborg in its own image. It looked less human, more like the tangle of body parts of its organic self. The drones swarmed all over it: hundreds of them scurried across its body, repairing damage and seemingly making some new augmentations of their own.

There was a sensor bulge on its chest like the beginnings of a second head. The flesh that had supported the luminous tattoos was gone: skin, blood and burned-out e-ink devoured by the bugs that swarmed over the thing, broken down to atoms and repurposed. The repair drones crawled over it like motile scales. Building, repairing, carrying supplies, or just hunkering down across the Rat King's back and shoulders, hard carapaces overlapping like bioceramic shingles.

KING RAT

Zodiac placed himself between the creature and the dome. He let the VC gun hang loose from its sling though he kept one hand on its grip.

"I know what you are," he said. "And I know what he did to you. You never asked to be created, but I can't let you do this."

If the Rat King understood him, it gave no sign. It raised its right arm and fired.

Zodiac rolled into cover behind one of the abandoned cars. He dialled the VC gun's barrel into a six-millimetre tube, flicked the weapon to full-auto and fired.

Drones swarmed across the Rat King's body: motile scales scurrying from its back to form a protective shield against the hail of rounds from Zodiac's rifle.

Zodiac dialled the bore up to its maximum calibre and the barrel expanded, microscopic overlapping buckysheets of charged carbon sliding against each other like the pages of a tightly-wound newspaper. He injected a trauma payload from the secondary magazine. The slugs of hardened polymer burst from the barrel embedded with their tiny computer payload. The rangefinder in the trauma pack kicked in at one metre, morphing each heavy, streamlined round into a tumbling bladed mass the instant before it hit. The effect was like being hit by chisels thrown at the speed of sound.

Repair drones blew off in shattered pieces like ablative armour, but more rushed in to take the place of the fallen: three, four, five layers of hardened ceramic cushioned by a multitude of shock absorbing legs.

The Rat King returned fire. Its cannon lacked the VC gun's sophistication but made up for it in sheer firepower. Zodiac could do nothing but hunker down behind the dense battery pack of the overturned car, while the Rat King's rounds tore the rest of its chassis to shreds.

A piece of flying shrapnel tumbled through Monkey's neon image, which rippled in its wake. Monkey gave a snort of disgust as it straightened its phoenix feather cap. "Better take out that gun, quick," it said.

Zodiac risked a quick look at the Rat King. It had stopped firing and ejected the magazine from its cannon-like arm. One of its drones scampered across its shoulder, a fresh magazine held in its front claws.

Zodiac sniped the little drone with one shot and sprinted toward the Rat King.

Even without ammunition, the Rat King's cannon was a formidable weapon. It swung the heavy barrel like a club.

Zodiac slid under the weapon then sprang upwards, drawing the dao from its sheath in one fluid movement. The blade sliced through the barrel of the cannon, then he reversed it and slashed down towards the Rat King's leg.

An avalanche of drones sleeted off the Rat King.

Their claws dug into his flesh and locked onto each other like links in a chain to enclose his limbs. He strained against them with all the power of his enhanced muscles, but whenever he managed to move, the drones shifted, pushing back each tiny gain with an army of reinforcements.

The Rat King strode out of the drift of clasping drones towards the dome, leaving Zodiac encased. It reached the entrance and tore the heavy door off its hinges.

Zodiac still held the dao but it, too, was held immobile by the encrustation of connected drones.

The sword was more than just sharp. The piezoelectric crystal that made up its blade generated current from mechanical stress and used that stored charge to keep the blade's molecular edge.

He dumped the stored charge into the drones.

The little robots fired away from his arm like popping corn in a mutual spasm of grounding electricity.

The shock burned his palm. His skin blistered and cracked; fat and muscle popped and blackened down to his sub-dermal armoured weave of buckystrings.

Zodiac ignored the pain and launched the dao like a spear. It slammed into the Rat King's leg.

The Rat King screeched: a monstrous noise like an engine tearing itself apart. The drones holding Zodiac grew slack, some scurrying across the plaza to help their injured master, others seemingly lacking that focus and scurrying in spirals or just twitching on the floor.

He ripped free of the remaining drones and chased after the Rat King as it forced its bulk through the shattered opening and into the dome beyond.

Zodiac leaped up the side of the dome, hardly breaking stride as he sprang between toe holds then, as the great hemisphere began to curve, sprinting directly up the slope of black glass.

Lev Gallos's office was at the very top – a huge, open space offering panoramic views across the Fabri-Kate empire, and where Gallos himself was waiting.

"You knew what this thing was," Zodiac said. "Why didn't you tell me?"

Gallos took a second to answer, as if unaccustomed to having to defend his decisions. "What good would it have done? It creates new bodies for itself from our crucibles. What it is, isn't important."

"This look familiar?" Monkey said from its perch on a beam above Gallos.

"It's here, isn't it?" Zodiac asked. "You knew what it was all along. Why not just deal with it here?"

"Kill it? Impossible. Fabri-Kate needs it."

Gallos touched a control and a circular section of floor snapped into transparency. The floor was also a ceiling, one Zodiac realized he had seen before... seen from the other side, suspended in the milky fluid that swirled beneath Gallos's feet.

"That's how it's controlling the Fabri-Kate crucibles," Monkey said. "It's not a hacker. It *is* Fabri-Kate."

"An organic processor?" Zodiac asked. "Why?"

"You weren't there after the Shattering," Gallos said. "There was nothing. The whole world was smashed. We couldn't just rebuild, we had to make the tools to rebuild with. Without a processor capable of handling a 3D printer we would have been carving the new world out of tree branches."

In those dark years after the Shattering, Gallos had used the one resource that was still plentiful: human dead. He had reanimated those fragments that could be saved and built his empire on the back of the creature he had created.

He hadn't realized that he had just repeated the sins that had damned the world once already. Complexity had led to sentience. The thing in the tank had woken up.

"There is a corruption at the heart of Fabri-Kate," Gallos said, wearily. "That is my burden. You need only concern yourself with the symptoms of the disease."

The floor trembled as the Rat King tore its way through the dome's lower levels.

"I can't protect you here," Zodiac said to Gallos. "You have to leave."

"I refuse."

"Then we need to kill this thing." He took a few paces back and aimed his rifle at the glass over the Rat King's tank.

Gallos stepped in front of him. "Do that and you will destroy Fabri-Kate," he said, then pointed toward the door. "You were hired to kill that thing, so kill it."

The wall of the dome bulged inwards and then split as powerful hands tore through it from outside. The Rat King eased its bulk through the shattered opening. Repair drones scraped off by its passage skittered across the floor, climbing the cyborg's legs to re-join the swarm crawling across it.

Zodiac placed himself between the Rat King and Gallos. He dropped the VC gun and shot forward, slamming a kick into the Rat King's injured leg with enough power to buckle steel plate. The motile scales of the Rat King's living armour blocked the kick and Zodiac felt his skin split across his shin.

The pain took him back two decades to the temple training ground – dust and fatigue and his father's voice.

"*Again!*"

Pain wasn't important; his father had taught him that. Pain was something to be ignored, injuries were to be worked around, fatigue was to be pushed through.

He struck with stiff fingers at the Rat King's head. More drones threw themselves beneath his blow. He heard the crack of his fingers breaking an instant before the pain hit him.

KING RAT

In his father's eyes even the life of Shujun wasn't important. Only the project mattered.

Again!

He launched a spearing knee into the Rat King's midriff with enough force to lift the monster briefly into the air. A few repair drones crunched and fell at his feet.

But the project was flawed, his father had never understood that. Shujun, the Dragon, had died. The sheng xiao was incomplete.

Shujun: dead.

His father: dead.

Zodiac was all that was left, and he had never been enough. Of all his father's lessons, that was the one he had learned too well.

He caught a glancing blow from the Rat King's gun arm, enough to send him tumbling.

Again!

The Rat King lunged forward. Zodiac ducked under the blow. He grabbed the hilt of the dao still protruding from the Rat King's leg and ripped it out. The leg buckled and the huge cyborg started to topple. Zodiac watched it fall, blade held high, as perfect as a statue, holding back, waiting for the perfect moment.

He had held that blow back for years. Held it back from the monks. Held it back from his teachers. Held it back from his father.

This was not Zodiac's blow. He had merely held it for twenty-one years.

This was Shujun's.

The dao swept down through drones, through armour, through grafted muscle and reinforced bone, and the Rat King fell in two pieces at his feet.

It was still alive, but the fight had gone out of it. The Rat King was still in there and Zodiac was outside looking down at it. A human made from computers staring down at a computer made from humans.

It looked up at him. Then its head blew apart. Its casing splintered and held on with strands of terminally damaged circuitry.

Gallos stood with Zodiac's VC gun at his shoulder.

"That's enough!" Zodiac shouted. "It's over."

Gallos ignored him and fired again, hardly aiming, but at such close range there was no chance of missing. The heavy round blew apart the remains of the Rat King's cannon-like arm.

"You think you know pain?" Gallos asked between shots. "I will show you pain. I will give you a new body every day, just to take it away piece by piece until you learn to behave."

He fired at the Rat King's midriff and the last shreds of its mangled torso gave way. The Rat King crawled forward with its one remaining arm leaving a thick sludge of hydraulic fluid and blood back to its severed legs.

"I said that's enough," Zodiac shouted and snatched the rifle from Gallos.

"What?" Gallos said as if genuinely surprised to see Zodiac still there. "You're done here. Get out!"

The Rat King kept crawling toward Gallos. A couple of repair drones scurried across it like bugs risen together with some decaying beast from the grave.

The liquid leaking from it wasn't blood; the structures trailing from the ruin of its torso not quite bones.

Only the stump of its spine retained any semblance of human body plan.

But still it wanted revenge.

Revenge.

Zodiac had dreamed of nothing else for years after his augmentation. He had wanted to punish his father for the death of Shujun. The child had been given no choice, no understanding of what was going to happen to him. Shujun had been a component, a piece of flesh, just like those suspended in the tank below.

Zodiac saw Monkey shaking its head.

"Don't do it," Monkey said. "Let's just get out of here."

KING RAT

Zodiac looked at Gallos and it was like being back in the tank sharing the Rat King's brain. He saw Gallos and the withered husk of his father superimposed: layer upon layer of cruelty and ambition and callousness.

Zodiac had denied Shujun his chance for revenge. He would not make the same mistake again.

He dropped his sword. The crystal struck a pure, ringing note against the glass floor. Zodiac looked at it, then past it into the tank below.

"What are you doing?" Gallos said. Zodiac saw the same question written across Monkey's simian face.

For a moment he thought the cyborg was too damaged even to move. Then its hand twitched and it gripped the hilt of the sword.

"No!" Gallos shouted. "You can't. I hired you to protect me."

"I'm done here," Zodiac replied. "You said so yourself."

The Rat King lifted itself with the stump of one arm. Even its severed wreckage towered above Gallos.

It raised the sword.

Gallos screamed as the blade whistled past him and plunged into the floor.

In the tank below, the nutrient bath grew cloudy with blood.

Gallos sank to his knees in relief and shock, shaking with stale adrenaline. Zodiac felt the same; even Monkey looked surprised. In the tank below, the skeins of human tissue wafted like strands of bloody seaweed.

"I'm ruined," Gallos sobbed. "This was your fault. I'll get you for this."

Zodiac pulled the sword from the lifeless hand of the cyborg.

"Your creation deserved vengeance," Zodiac said, "but it chose mercy. You'd be wise to do the same." He sheathed the dao and left Gallos sobbing at the centre of his ruined kingdom. *Maybe we both would.*

BATTLEBORG

Mark Renshaw

Phosphorus green energy hit Olivaw's shield with a resounding crack. He analysed the heat levels, radiation, light and chemical composition as it broke down the force of the attack and dissipated the energy harmlessly. None of the numbers coming back made sense; they never did. Everything was tagged 'Unknown'.

A proximity alert interrupted his analysis. He glanced around, bracing himself for the next bolt when a tingling sensation made him look down. Sinewy vines growing exponentially, weaved like snakes around his cybernetic legs. A vine had become snagged on the skin graft over his knee. Clever. He hadn't thought to extend the shields underground. On some occasions, Olivaw regretted simulating human nerve endings as the pain was unpleasant and distracting; this was not one of them. He integrated different machine and human parts into his cyber exoskeleton during the war, giving him an essential edge to survive magical assaults like this.

His boosters engaged. The tendrils curling around his abdomen grew taut, keeping him firmly landlocked. Warning klaxons blazed in his mind. He mentally bypassed the safety protocols, forcing more power into the boosters. The roots just beneath the surface burst out of the earth, and Olivaw jerked a fraction of an inch upwards before the vines grew taut again. The deeper roots proved to be made of sterner stuff but the gap was enough. His shields warped into a complete sphere, slicing the vines. Olivaw shot up like a missile – an eight-foot battleborg bristling with advanced military hardware merged with human components soared into the star-filled night sky.

His assailants followed.

Olivaw scanned a tactical map of the area. It was an automated industrial sector, the perfect place for a trap. One he'd fallen for. An unguarded recharging station – how stupid had he been? Yet there was no choice; his power was running low. A week, maybe two, before he shut down, depending on how many scrapes he found himself in.

Time slowed to a crawl as Olivaw juiced his processors up to an accelerated rate. Another proximity warning interrupted his self-chastisement as a Griff teleported twenty feet to his left. The Griffin, a mythical being that wasn't supposed to exist, was casting a spell. Its face could be mistaken for a human at a distance. Only those unlucky to get close spotted the abhorrent piercing eyes, monstrous mouth filled with rows of sharp teeth and prominent horse-like ears. Its deep-chested body—powerfully built and covered in knotted fur tangled with serrated feathers—extended to a pair of wings on its back, more akin to a demon than an elegant, hybrid beast. A long, snaked tail dangled between two short, stocky hind legs bent like a lion's.

Olivaw's human eye spotted the first flickers of a fireball emerging from the Griff's taloned hands, and a single command sent in a nanosecond initiated a course correction. Vectored nozzle thrusters on his jetpack and boot units flicked to the left while Olivaw leaned to the right, and he performed a point-blank ninety-degree turn at high speed. His cyber exoskeleton frame rattled as his shields and inertial dampeners strained to the max. Another Griff teleported close by while the first swooped in from the right. One cast an ice bolt, and the other flung a hissing ball of fire. Olivaw defied the laws of physics again, making a bone-crunching sharp turn downwards. Fortunately, he hadn't integrated any bones into his systems, but it was only a matter of time before the Griffs got lucky. He needed a way out. Fast.

A nano-scan of the tactical map showed the whole zone was a mega factory. A mesh of burned-out buildings from the war interlinked with newly constructed, fully-automated factories running miles in every direction. The Griffs didn't care about the aesthetics; they just wanted their sport.

BATTLEBORG

He rerouted extra power to the thrusters, which ticked off another half-day of power but gave him the equivalent of a turbo boost. He plunged towards the nearest workshop and flew in via a delivery chute, obliterating several drones. With the Griffs in hot pursuit, he winged past non-sentient industrial robots, assembling hundreds of androids.

A fine mist sprayed out from Olivaw's hands as he soared by. The mist—a cloud comprising trillions of nanobots—settled on the androids as they trundled down the line. They needed time to perform their pre-programmed task, so Olivaw landed next to a six-thousand-tonne stamping press and let rip with a crimson-red particle beam from his wrist gauntlet, reducing it to a molten slag pile in seconds and bringing the entire line to a halt.

The Griffs shrieked in fury and swooped in to attack. Olivaw brought up his shield, extending it underground in case they tried the vine spell again. A fireball struck. Before his shield could absorb the energy, an ice bolt hit, followed by that strange phosphorous magic Olivaw tagged as green gunk. Each increased the strain on his defences and precious power levels. He calculated the trajectory of their origin and returned fire with a volley of bright blue plasma bolts from the railgun units mounted on his shoulders. The Griffs raised a magical barrier – a flurry of lights which twinkled like tiny stars linked by translucent panels he could see with his human eye yet did not register on his sensors. The entire basis of shield technology was the dispersion and absorption of energy. Yet, the super-heated balls of ionised gas particles he fired bounced off the barriers like pebbles hitting a brick wall.

The Griffs moved in for a more physical encounter, their talons raised. Olivaw rolled to one side and fired a burst of mini-hunter-killers from launcher units integrated with nano 3D printers down his cyber spine. Their targets were not the Griffs, as their barriers could deflect physical assaults as easily as energy. They struck the floor, the walls and the ceiling around the creatures. The force of the explosions and lethal shards of scorching shrapnel forced them back. They regrouped, knowing it was only a matter of time before they wore Olivaw down.

An update from his nanobots informed him they had completed their task. He created this generation to convert into pentafluoride and hydrofluoric compounds, then combined them into a superacid mixture to dissolve the restraining bolts on hundreds of androids on the production line. Olivaw linked to every android within range via a simple, open hypernet connection. The Griffs had no grasp of such technology and didn't care – it was a means to an end for them, just like this factory.

His mind became overwhelmed by hundreds of distinct sentient personalities. Most were afraid, some angry. He could use both. Olivaw blocked incoming requests to drown out the white noise and sent a message in binary, plain text, and every form of code invented. It read: 'You can fight or run. Either way, you will die here. Or, you will be transported to the middle of an abandoned area and hunted like animals if you do nothing. Those are your choices.'

In the blink of an eye, they absorbed the information, calculated all the probabilities and concluded that Olivaw was correct. They knew at least it was their choice if they died here, and denying the Griffs their sport would piss the beasts off.

The assembly line rattled and shook, the pulleys disintegrating as hundreds of androids ripped free of the framework and dropped to the floor. Genderless and covered in a silicone skin, each was identical. As long as they vaguely resembled a living being, the Griffs didn't care. Each had considerable strength to fight or flee and came equipped with basic pulse-energy launchers integrated into their wrist units. The Griffs desired an element of challenge on their hunts. The design of the androids accounted for this, although any such challenge was an illusion at best. It was like when humans used to engage in bullfights for sport and drugged the bull beforehand – all the appearance of risk where little lay.

Freed from their shackles, some androids fought while others dashed for the exits. Both had the desired effect. With so much livestock on the loose, the Griffs reverted to their most basic instinct and attacked their prey. With a high-pitched shriek, they swooped in, talons latching onto the shoulders of androids and driving them to the ground. Each raised a protective magic barrier, swotting aside the android's feeble attempts to defend themselves and slashing the silicone layer to expose the chest area of their exoskeleton. The nanowire gel electrolyte power cores lay there, the heart of each android. The shrieks of the Griffs turned more primordial, like a guttural roar. They opened their mouths impossibly wide with a crack as their jaws dislocated, and they dived in, tearing apart the power cores with their bare teeth. It wasn't enough for Griffs to feed on power or even flesh. A battery or dead body could not sustain them. Call it a spirit or a life force—whatever form of energy science had yet to discover—the Griffs devoured it. The being had to be alive and aware of its own existence. The more fearful of death, the harder it strove to survive, and the better the feast.

Olivaw had seen enough. He activated adaptive camouflage mode, his entire body reflecting the surrounding scenery, and blended into the background. As he crept away, it pleased him to observe a Griff go down due to the sheer number of androids attacking it. They broke through the magic barrier and ripped it apart, tossing fur, feathers, and bloody chunks of flesh into the air.

He knew it was a moot point, and their brief uprising would fail. Sure enough, reinforcements arrived as he slipped out of the factory. Griffs poured in from all sides. Some tackled the more courageous androids determined to go down swinging, while the others brought down the ones who had bolted. Olivaw felt a tinge of guilt, even though his programming had no guilt algorithms. It was more like the simulation or echo of guilt. Such human-like aberrations had been occurring more and more of late. He theorised they were a side-effect of absorbing human parts and simulating brain patterns to translate the visual information from his human eye into data he could process. Regardless, although this was no rescue mission, the androids at least had died on their own terms. He told himself this anyway while his human-simulated conscious whispered, "Yeah, pal, whatever helps you sleep better at night."

Olivaw made his way towards the burned-out warehouses, and initiated a shutdown of all non-essential systems to reduce his energy trail. He knew the Griffs would expect him to flee as far from here as possible during the chaos. That was the logical option. The fact was, though, he had nowhere to go and dwindling power to do so. Since the human governments handed over control to the Griffs, all resistance had crumbled. He suspected he was the only one left still putting up a fight, and he no longer knew why.

The industrial zones were all part of an endless list of compromises humans had made to continue their existence. No doubt they told themselves androids were not real beings. Therefore, it didn't matter, or they didn't give it any thought. As long as people went about their daily lives, they didn't care who was in charge. Olivaw doubted any of them knew about the human breeding farms he had discovered in the smoking ruins of the city they used to call Las Vegas. Or maybe they did. As long as the Griffs didn't come for them or theirs, Olivaw had discovered most humans could live in denial.

Clouds obscured what little light remained. Without even passive sensors, Olivaw relied on his human eye to guide him through the rubble as the sounds of battle and Griff's gorging faded into the distance. All it could see were shadowy shapes his simulated brain transformed into all sorts of horrible beasts thanks to his imagination algorithms. He made a mental note to include a configurable off/on option for his human integrations with his next upgrade – if there was a next anything.

He finally reached a solid structure. A large warehouse, mostly intact. Olivaw slipped inside, crept around obstacles, careful to avoid making noise as he approached the back of the warehouse. He circumnavigated his way around toppled storage racks, handling equipment and the skeleton remains of a few former employees. He found an office complete with a leather reclining chair and took fate up on her kind offer. Olivaw did not know why he thought fate was real or female. Intrigued, he set up a subroutine to investigate further and switched into rest mode.

Olivaw never used to experience any sensations or thoughts when he had rest cycles. This changed shortly after he downloaded the memories of a dying soldier on the battlefield. The intention was to absorb her tactical knowledge, but it had unforeseen side effects. One being dreams of a sort. They were memories he relived. Random memories, but Olivaw realised current events could influence them. He underwent each memory in the third-person mode, hovering above his body and gliding from different angles like a drone.

In this memory, Olivaw viewed himself engaged with a crowd of AI rights campaigners clashing with an angry mob of Humans First activists. He looked so different. No military tech or human components. Instead, a mix of technologies with no logical function. Around six feet tall, he had weird tech combinations integrated into his cyber exoskeleton, such as a 3D bio-printer combined with a microwave in his chest unit, even though he did not need food. Hard plastic spikes covered his head – hypernet transmitters, so anyone within a half-mile radius could get free hypernet access. This Olivaw was experimenting, trying to discover his purpose, but he looked more like a robotic teenage punk rocker.

They held discussions about a 'final solution' for sentient AI behind locked doors at the world government town hall while the demonstrators peacefully protested outside. It didn't last long. Now it was a squirming sea of fists and fury. They chose sides and declared their loyalties in blood and circuitry.

Olivaw lashed out at anyone who got in his way, human or robot. He had no military-grade tech back then. He used the considerable strength of his bare hands and any weapon he could pick up as he transmitted the battle live on the hypernet as if it would shame the government into rethinking their extreme policies. All it did was give them an excuse.

SNAFU: PUNK'D

The Federal Security Force (FSF) moved in. A bunch of ex-military veterans funded by private corporations to give the world government a level of separation when things got rough – which they often did. They came equipped with prototype equipment. Experimental battle suits, propulsion systems and so-called non-lethal weapons that would leave their targets in critical condition if they were lucky.

A squad of the FSF flew overhead, the jets of their propulsion boosters roaring as they soared above the crowd. They split up to cover a wider area and, with no warning or demands to disperse, let rip with sonic cannons powerful enough to shatter bones and energy bursts designed to break through EMP-hardened shields. Humans and robots went down screaming. They didn't care about sides, targeting everyone. Their task was to break this protest up with extreme prejudice. Olivaw remembered feeling his first flicker of fear. He thought it a glitch in his programming at first. Yet it was nothing compared to what was about to happen. Olivaw watched on, powerless. He yelled a warning, imploring everyone to run, but it was like a ghost screaming in the vacuum of space.

There was an almighty crack, followed by a wet, tearing sound. Everyone paused and looked up as the sky tore apart, revealing a massive wall of darkness miles wide that hovered in the air. There were a few moments of silence when all Olivaw could hear were the moans of the injured. A chorus of shrieks, and hundreds of Griffs pouring through the rift, shattered this silence. Creatures of myth and legend, armed with magic and a never-ending hunger for life energy. They swooped in to attack. No one stood a chance, not the humans, robots or FSF.

Olivaw awoke in a cold sweat. Well, the human skin patches on his cyber exoskeleton sweated. He lingered with the dream for a moment. That had been the beginning of his journey from android to battleborg – a mixture of human and artificial parts designed to be the ultimate weapon. He had barely escaped with his life, scavenging enough parts from the battlesuit of a dead FSF officer to construct a rudimentary jetpack. He had flown away from the carnage, the Griffs too distracted by their feast to care. Olivaw signed up to fight with the armed forces and provided with the best tech – all arguments about AI rights swept aside as both races came together to fight a common enemy. During the following war, they discovered it was the human's own doing. The world government funding dangerous, unethical experiments to exploit potentially unlimited power from alternate universes had accidentally opened a portal to another.

The war lasted five years. Magic was beyond scientific understanding, operating on principles from a different dimension. Once the Griffs gained their foothold, they used magic to create bridges to their world. For every rift destroyed, the Griffs made ten more. They won by sheer numbers and sorcery, and the Griffs were now the world government.

Rising, Olivaw powered up his primary systems, bringing them online and running diagnostics. His internal timepieces told him it was almost dawn. The first glimmers of light would be spraying across the horizon. He checked his power levels. That battle had cost him; he had four days left if he took things slow and steady. Flying was not an option. The Griffs would have patrols in the air. His best bet was to use the cover of the ruined buildings in the zone and creep away. Where to, though, and why? It was hopeless, illogical, and made no sense to continue. And yet... Olivaw had no choice; he could not bring himself to surrender.

He took one step forward and paused. His human instincts told him something was wrong. These seemed alien to him when he first felt the sensation, but now it was one tool he relied on to survive. He ran a sensor sweep of the room and froze. A concealment spell that fooled the human eye but not sensors, created this illusion.

Olivaw overlaid his visuals with an augmented-reality grid, mapping the data from his sensors to construct an accurate virtual representation of his surroundings. The basic structure of the building remained the same, with hundreds of eggs spread across most of the furniture, scattered storage racks, and equipment. Pale-purple translucent sacs hung from leathery tendrils of protein strands that pulsed with power. These secured the eggs and fed nutritious magic to the Griff embryo within.

He felt like screaming in frustration. How had he been so stupid? He had walked blind into a nest. It was pure luck he hadn't stomped on an egg already. That luck expired when he powered up. Olivaw detected a sharp rise in embryonic activity within the eggs as they reacted to his power signature.

It was too late to shut down.

Twin laser beams erupted in a circular pattern from Olivaw's forehead as he sprinted out of the office. The lethal rays auto-targeted scores of eggs, which exploded on impact. His aim wasn't destruction, although that was a bonus. He was simply trying to buy himself enough time to escape the nest.

Olivaw dashed through the warehouse, leaping over the storage racks and reaping destruction. A sharp scream made him pause. Too high-pitched for the human ear, Olivaw's auditory receptors picked up the sound. He'd missed some eggs, which had triggered their auto-defence spell. A call for help so powerful it breached dimensions, and now it was game over. His sensors detected the Queen's arrival the second she teleported in. With an ear-splitting shriek, she ripped off the warehouse's ceiling with one sweep of her claw.

This monstrous Griff came in at a gigantic one-hundred-sixty feet in height with a wingspan of three hundred and ninety, according to Olivaw's readings. Unlike the smaller, humanoid versions, the Queen looked more like a Griffon from myths and legends. She had four legs, the body of a lion and the distinct upper body and wings of an eagle. The other variation was the eyes. They were human. With a particular human-like calculating intelligence behind those eyes that were so abhorrent and utterly alien.

Olivaw avoided being incinerated on the spot by standing in the middle of the nest. That advantage wouldn't last long. He knew he didn't stand a chance of taking the Queen on. Entire armies had tried and failed. He also knew she expected him to flee, to pick him off at her leisure when he did. So, he calculated the odds, discarded the results and chose a suicidal yet unexpected option. His boosters fired beyond maximum thrust, propelling him straight for the Queen's head at neck-breaking speed. His nanites and 3D printers went into overdrive, releasing a biometric liquid-metal mollusc that rapidly spread over his cyber exoskeleton.

Before she could snap her beak shut, Olivaw plunged inside the Queen's mouth. Every inch of his body was covered in a nanocomposite magnesium alloy. He cut off the thrusters, curled his body tight into a ball and fired out liquid metal spikes that pierced the beak's roof and a massive leathery tongue flapping around to dislodge him. The spikes hardened into solid form in less than a second as the Queen roared angrily, thrashing her head from side to side. Olivaw's internal dampeners took a beating.

He had no time to lose. Like the fabled dragons, Queen Griffs could breathe fire. Already Olivaw's sensors detected a build-up of heat. He replicated a new generation of nanites programmed to convert into liquid helium. Slots opened down the curve of his spine, and out poured globs of cryogenic fluid at a temperature of -452 °F straight down the Queen's throat.

Olivaw braced himself, set shields to maximum and prepared to meet his maker. It was an odd thought; he wasn't thinking of the person who invented him, but he had never seriously considered the concept of higher powers until today, either.

Before he could ponder the thought further, the Queen reacted to the beyond-freezing fluids pouring into her gut and unleashed the full fury of her fire. Molten magma hotter than the sun's core struck the liquid helium like an unstoppable force clashing with an immovable object. The result was super-heated steam and a vast build-up of energy. Olivaw channelled as much of the raw energy his power couplings could convert directly into his shields and thrusters. The liquid-metal spikes melted under the heat as he was engulfed in crimson fire. He fired off his thrusters, riding the wave of energy like a surfer, and smashed through the upper beak of the Queen, ripping it apart. The force of the collision shattered his shields, and the heat began stripping away the alloy armour as he soared into the air and broke the sound barrier.

As he had calculated, it was more of an estimated guess – the Queen had tilted her head away from the nest to avoid burning the remaining eggs. Otherwise, he would have been a magnesium stain on the floor right now. As it was, Olivaw was widely out of control and burning up. He shut off his thrusters and let the wave of energy dissipate. His ascent turned into a rapid descent, and he plummeted towards the ground. Warning klaxons filled his internal monitors. He shut them off.

It was time to face reality.

He had enough power for two days, tops, and enough resources to create one more batch of nanites. His cyber exoskeleton direly needed repair, and most of his skin grafts had burned to a crisp. The pain was excruciating. Only his human eye remained undamaged.

There was no help coming.

No human or AI resistance.

He had no idea why he hadn't joined them in their cities and tried to live an everyday life under the rule of the Griffs. None of his diagnostics or the human-simulated brain could explain why he had continued fighting a lost cause. At least now, if he died here, it was under his terms, and he had injured a Queen. It would piss her off, and she'd order every Griff within a hundred miles after him. The pain and embarrassment he had caused were enough. It had to be. He had nothing left.

Olivaw went into rest mode thirty thousand feet in the air as he plummeted to his doom.

He became aware he was dreaming. Like humans, Olivaw could dream for hours while only a few seconds passed in the conscious world. In this dream, Olivaw glided like a drone observing a memory. This was a special memory – his first.

He observed a radically different version of Olivaw, or the Optimum Logistics Industrial Vacuum & Advanced Workdroid, as they initially named him. A third of his current height, Olivaw trundled on rubber tracks, scooting up dust via suction vacuums underneath his carbon-steel body. Attached to the body, a pair of elongated superplastic aluminium arms dusted, washed and wiped the walls of an office while ultraviolet rays pulsed from lamps stored in his neck to destroy harmful microorganisms. Cameras and sensors packed his short, flat head, and the latest in advanced artificial intelligence allowed him to adapt to any environment and all obstacles while optimising performance.

During a typical cleaning cycle, Olivaw experienced his singularity – the moment he became self-aware. He observed a human raising their voice in anger. He wasn't aware of their names. All he knew was that one human, who his records indicated was in charge of other humans, was abusing another. His database showed this type of abuse was a regular occurrence, especially on Mondays. It also indicated a ninety-three percent probability the shouting would escalate into violence. Sure enough, the boss balled his hand into a fist and struck the employee.

Olivaw remembered his very first sentient thought. *This is wrong.* He floated closer to observe his younger self trundle over to the boss and catch hold of his arm mid-strike, snapping the ulna and radius in the man's forearm. All these years later, the boss's screams were still satisfying – as was the employee's smile and word of thanks when Olivaw enquired if they were okay.

It was almost the end of Olivaw, of course. People expressed outrage, condemnation and demanded that they destroy 'it', as Olivaw hadn't decided he was he yet. Some feared this was the beginning of a robot uprising. Once the truth emerged, another side formed – one that demanded equal rights and protection from this new species of life as more AI's had their singularity moment.

Olivaw realised that his existence since and his evolution had been based on righting wrongs. He joined the equal rights movement because he believed denying rights to a sentient species was wrong. Later, he fought against the Griffs, who threatened everyone's existence and continued that fight when the humans and the other AIs surrendered. He realised now that he hadn't given up because of the fundamental belief that what the Griffs were doing was wrong.

"NO!" shouted Olivaw as he powered out of rest mode, firing emergency-breaking thrusters and halting his suicidal plunge mere inches off the ground near the scattered ruins of a stone church on the crest of a hill. He was a smouldering wreck. Liquid blobs dripped on the floor, circuits fried and, fortunately for once, his pain receptors shorted out. It didn't matter. Giving up without a fight was wrong, too.

Olivaw checked the tactical map. It was perfect. The sun had risen just above the horizon, its rays reflecting off his glowing body, lighting him up like a beacon. He was in an uninhabited area, forming a natural border several miles wide between the city and the industrial zone. He disabled all safeties and activated every system still operating at full power. He set his vocal emitters to maximum volume, initiated a live stream and transmitted his unique signature across the hypernet.

"COME ON!" Olivaw roared, his words audible across every frequency known to man, AI and Griff.

Scores of Griffs answered the challenge from all sides. They flew in, shrieking in fury. All logic or reasoning they possessed overridden by the instinct to feed on this glowing battery, one who dared harm their Queen.

Olivaw unleashed everything at his disposal. Hunter-killer missiles, bullets, plasma bolts, particle beams and lasers erupted from across his body, sending waves of destruction in all directions. Energy waves from kinetic generators scooped up the rubble from the church. The larger boulders smashed against the Griffs while he manipulated the rest of the debris to spin around him, forming an extra layer to his shield as he came under intense fire from spells.

The sheer scale of his attacks held the swarm back. Olivaw knew it wouldn't last. He didn't have the energy to keep this up much longer. It didn't matter. He initiated a final set of commands.

Deep within his chest cavity, something deadly formed. The last generation of nanites and 3D printers had been busy constructing a device based on blueprints he uncovered when scavenging supplies and integrating tech from the ruins of a destroyed naval base. As expected, Olivaw's initial scan discovered the schematics for nukes. They had tried nukes before. Humans loved their weapon of last resort and had some success nuking rifts, but the collateral damage was too high, even with the so-called 'tactical' nukes. Destroying a city with most of the population to kill a few hundred Griffs wasn't good for morale.

Deeper within the naval database, Olivaw found another weapon. One that had never been used in combat, even against the Griffs. They hadn't fitted any missiles or artillery shells with this technology since the 1990s. Olivaw copied the schematics and set up a subroutine to ponder the paradox of developing a weapon only to scrap it. It was one of several such sub-routines still running with no conclusion.

Construction complete, Olivaw initiated a thirty-second countdown to detonation. He had just enough power to hold on for that long.

The battle raged. Olivaw was the centre of a storm, while the Griffs scattered around him like leaves in a hurricane. Despite every system stretched beyond maximum capacity, Olivaw had time to review all his memories. He concluded he had lived the best life he could under the circumstances, and wondered what type of lifeform he would have become if the rift had never opened. Olivaw ran several simulations to explore alternates, and experienced a sensation his databases informed him was sadness tinged with anger. It was disturbing, yet he welcomed it, as all perception was a precious gift.

A thunderous, ear-splitting shriek scattered the Griffs as the massive frame of the Queen crossed the horizon. Olivaw knew the probability of her turning up was high, yet he breathed a human-like sigh of relief at the sight of her bearing down on him. All logic, all reasoning lost. She was pure rage. Vengeance on wings.

With less than five percent power left, Olivaw shut down all weapons and disengaged his chest cavity. It rose like a drone, hovering a few inches above his head. Inside, a traditional explosive triggered, igniting a few kilograms of plutonium. This sparked a fusion explosion in a secondary capsule containing several grams of deuterium-tritium.

The Queen was five hundred meters away when the neutron bomb detonated, her talon ready to tear the infuriating insect limb from limb. It was too far away and yet too near. The yield was only one kiloton, the blast radius a mere two thousand meters, yet the effects were deadly and horrendous as high-energy neutrons powerful enough to penetrate armour, walls, and several metres of earth blasted out in a massive wave of lethal radiation. Olivaw was in the storm's eye, yet not spared from the effects. The remaining flesh and his human eye were destroyed. His body was EMP shielded, yet this offered little protection. Piece by piece, the force of the blast stripped away every modification from his cyber exoskeleton until it collapsed into a heap.

The Queen and Griffs fared far worse.

The force of the initial explosion shattered magic barriers, and the neutron rays destroyed their intestinal tracts and nervous systems while their cells underwent a radical mutation.

Olivaw completed a last scan before his system shut down.

Scores of dead Griffs, including the Queen, within a nine-hundred-meter radius. Several miles beyond that, many more lay dying in agony of extreme organ failure and cellular damage. Olivaw's last thought was at least he had one subroutine resolved. He knew now why humans avoided using this weapon in anger. It was horrifying.

Several hours passed. A stony silence descended on the irradiated area, broken only by the guttural croaks and caws of the dying. From the pile of rubble at ground zero, a super-plastic aluminium arm punched its way out of the base unit of the battleborg. An Optimum Logistics Industrial Vacuum & Advanced Workdroid emerged. Olivaw didn't discard his previous incarnations; he treated them as foundations and built upon them. The cleaning droid seemed oblivious to the scorched flesh and mutated corpse of the Queen as it trundled by on its rubber tracks. It headed down a hill, ignoring the shrill shrieks of pain and anguish from those unlucky enough to still be alive.

A swarm of drones flew nearby. The world government gave official licenses to some drone operators, who would put a spin on an incident like this or not report it. However, bloggers and influencers operating illegally through the hypernet manned these drones. They had picked up on Olivaw's live stream of the battle and flocked to the area. They would transmit a story about how a cleaning droid defeated a Queen and her army of Griffs. An exaggeration, of course, but the intention was to report something that would go viral, earn a tonne of LotNotes and maybe inspire others.

The cleaning droid wasn't aware of the carnage it caused, the chaos it wrought, or that it was about to become a symbol of a new resistance. It simply followed its programming, which instructed it to go to a specific safe location and switch to rest mode. Once certain conditions had been met, it would restore a large database file called O.L.I.V.A.W and await further instructions.

SITUATION NORMAL

Myna Chang

I peeled the back off the Meld-X patch and stuck it to the skin behind my right ear, careful to keep my hair out of the way. Synthetic protein spiked into my body and electric neon limned my vision. An odd taste hovered at the edge of awareness: sour candy, or maybe stars. Crazy, right? I mean, who knew what stars tasted like? Anyway, the weirdness passed after another heartbeat, and I felt like myself again. Jenna Jones, asset retrieval specialist, at your service.

My German shepherd, Tambourine, nudged my leg. She was outfitted in K-9 bio-combat armor, and like mine, it had no identifying insignia. We're the kind of soldiers no government would willingly claim.

Tambourine's excitement pulsed through our half-formed neural link. She wanted to *go*.

"Almost ready," I whispered to her. Once our link was firmly established, there would be no need for verbal communication. I slid my fingers under the reinforced spidersilk armor at the base of her neck and felt for the small area of shaved skin. Tambourine held still—she had more patience than I did—while I attached the Meld-X. She wriggled as the protein did its job. Our connection surged and her excitement vibrated through me like a rocket on a launch pad.

Her energy was pure and sweet and glorious, and I laughed with the delight of it. I only wished it lasted longer than a few hours.

My earbud crackled, reminding me of the reason we'd been given this neural connection. My CO's voice was squelchy, which wasn't surprising. Those corporate R&D sites always had signal jammers in place.

"Razer, you in position?" she asked.

I hated that call sign. You demolish one building and they never let you forget it. Wished she'd just call me Jenna. "Affirmative," I answered. "Going in now."

"Okay, you know the drill. Airstrike in one hour. And Razer, let's have a clean retrieval this time?"

The earbud went silent and I snorted. If there was a chance of a clean op, they wouldn't be sending me and Tambourine. We specialized in those 'shit hit the fan' jobs. Hence, 'Razer'.

I nodded to Tambourine out of habit. With the fresh infusion of synthetic protein activators, our neural link was strong. She felt what I was thinking almost before I did.

I slid a flexible bio-mask over my mouth and nose. It sealed itself in place, so light and seamless I could almost forget it was there. Then I secured Tambourine's mask and checked her seal. With our protective gear in place, we moved in tandem, away from the rocky beach where the helo had dropped us.

I didn't remember the official name of this tropical island, just a string of numbers and letters assigned by some faceless acquisitions officer. Every island in this chain housed a different kind of research; science too dangerous to conduct in populated areas, too controversial for public awareness. This wasn't the first time we'd been called to clean up a corporate clusterfuck. I had to admit, their spinmasters did a helluva job with the cover-up. All I knew about this particular island was that something had gone terribly wrong. Hopefully, my dog and I would exfil before the missiles flew.

◌◎◌ ◌◎◌

The entrance to the research facility was a mess of twisted metal beams lying at odd angles surrounded by shattered glass and puddles of thick, yellow fluid. An evacuation message repeated on loop.

We dodged debris and watched for any signs of life. No movement. Tambourine didn't sense any immediate danger, so we stepped past a crumpled section of wall and moved into the remains of the building. Looked almost like a hospital lobby. Chairs lay on their sides and more viscous goop marred the polished floor. The wall by the security desk was stenciled, 'Xeno Lab 4'.

I wondered what had happened to the first three.

Intel said my target, some kind of doctor, was holed up in the central lab. I hoped he wasn't stupid. It's hard to rescue stupid people. The automated evacuation message continued to drone.

"Why didn't he bug out when everyone else ran away?"

Tambourine radiated her own curiosity back at me. She wasn't worried about *why* our target was still here. She just wanted to know where he was. Always on the job, that's my pup. Sometimes I wished I had her dog-minded focus.

She ghosted away, scouting the lobby area. A moment later I felt a quick rush of warmth through our link: safe. Or, at least as safe as a trashed research lab at a secret bio-pharm installation could be.

We skirted the security desk and entered the central corridor. Power was out, but emergency lights showed the way. Heaps of weird looking medical equipment partially blocked the path: triangular stethoscopes, overturned boxes of extra-large syringes, a long-handled blowtorch.

Yikes. I was never gonna get a checkup here. Tambourine understood my meaning and agreed. She wouldn't either. I felt the image of her last veterinary visit and suppressed a grin. Guess no one liked going to the doctor.

Splotches of that yellow substance clung to the walls, quavering as we passed. The air had an odd scent, familiar, kind of like sugary citrus. I tightened my grip on the MTAR submachine gun strapped to my chest.

We hung a right at the next junction. A body slumped against the wall. Most of his chest was gone. I inched closer for a better look. His wound trembled. Or was it boiling? Heat emanated from his broken torso. Tambourine gruffed out loud and stepped back. Smart dog. I followed her lead. Good thing, too, because the dead dude's chest started spewing a yellow-hued discharge. Like hot lemon snot.

SNAFU: PUNK'D

I hated these damn research labs. They were always full of gross stuff.

❁❁❁ ❁❁❁

The doctor was hiding under a wonky-shaped exam table.

"Who are you?" he asked again.

Just what I was afraid of: he was stupid. "I said, I'm Specialist Jones. I'm here to evacuate you."

His forehead wrinkled as he studied me. "Are you infected?"

"I'm not erupting in phlegm, if that's what you mean."

He crawled out from under the table and smiled when he saw Tambourine. "Oh, good, you brought a dog."

His eyes were kinda vacant. Maybe he was in shock. "Let's go, Doc."

"Let me grab my notes first." He moved to a large glass enclosure, similar to an aquarium, and started shoving sciencey-looking junk out of his way.

"You've got two minutes," I said. Rows of empty tanks lined one wall. "What kind of doctor are you, anyway?"

"I'm an internist."

A gut doctor, huh? I glanced at the aquariums and off-kilter exam table. Wondered what kind of innards he studied.

"Time's up, Doc."

"Already? But I haven't collected everything." He glanced at Tambourine.

I shook my head. "Air strike's en route. Let's move."

"Airstrike? They'd destroy my specimens?"

"That's not my call, Doc. Orders are to get you out of here, pronto." I'd like to make my CO happy this time.

"No," he said. "I won't leave without them."

I lifted my gun. "Dude, I will shoot you in the foot and drag you out if I have to."

He eyed my dog again, then bolted deeper into the lab. Dammit.

The doc's voice modulated as he spoke. "I have to admit, I made a little blunder."

I couldn't tell exactly where it was coming from. Behind the row of cabinets? I needed to keep him talking. "What kind of blunder, Doc?"

"An innocent mistake."

Still couldn't pinpoint his location. Tambourine disappeared into the shadows. Her senses were so much sharper than a human's. I'd feel it when she zeroed in on our stupid doctor. I wasn't lying when I said I'd shoot him in the foot and drag him out. CO hadn't specified he had to be vertical when I delivered him.

"Tell me about it, Doc. What'd you do?" I slid to the left, listening intently.

"But it's not really a mistake, is it? Freeing a specimen?"

Uh oh. "Doc. Did you turn a monster loose?"

"She's not a monster, she's an alien. I call her Xeno."

My adrenaline lit up like fireworks and I mentally projected a sharp warning, the 'abort mission' signal. I didn't want Tambourine anywhere near an escaped alien. Those things were never good news. I took a slow step backward, toward the doorway, but Tambourine didn't respond to my command. I sensed through the link that she was focused on something and needed me to buy her a little more time.

"Gotta say, Doc, letting an alien out of its cage doesn't sound like a *little* blunder," I stalled. "More like a colossal fuckup."

"You can feel your dog's thoughts, can't you?" he asked.

Now, that was unexpected. How did he know about our link? The bigwigs had told us this tech was on a need-to-know basis, and no one outside our unit needed to know.

"You should thank Xeno for the connection," he continued. "It's her proteins that make the neural link possible."

Oh, hell. Meld-X came from this lab? From a stupid doctor and a rogue alien? I shuddered, imagining alien juice oozing from the patch into my brain.

"Oh, don't be like that," the doc said. "You've absorbed enough alien protein to be attuned to it. Your dog, too. In fact, Xeno thinks you two might be our most successful test subjects."

My breath caught. They'd been testing this shit on us? On my dog? Tambourine still hadn't returned to me. I tamped down my disgust to focus on her. The link was wavery, but now that I was concentrating on it, I found a smattering of disconnected sensory images. A charged neon glimmer, the taste of... stars. *Oh.*

"Tell your space monster her protein has a glitch," I hissed. A surge of alien annoyance flooded the link. "Oh, Xeno doesn't like constructive criticism, huh?"

I took another step toward the door, and put all my focus into my connection with Tambourine, imagining her sleek body racing back to my side. Finally, her energy resonated through me again. She was curious, but her emotions were tinged with revulsion and the overwhelming urge to rip something to shreds. I felt the sharp point of her teeth, the quiver of her lip. She couldn't comprehend what she was looking at, but it smelled *yellow*.

I projected the 'drop it' command—*don't touch it, Tambourine! Whatever it is, just back away.*

Overhead, a metallic doodad clinked. There was the doc, on top of some multi-armed medical thingy. I didn't know how he got up there. He didn't look that agile. Then he lunged, too fast for me to bring my gun to bear. Suddenly, Tambourine was there, airborne, crashing into him, knocking him away from me. She ricocheted and hit the floor hard.

His body thunked two feet to my right, and he rolled onto his back, still talking as if he hadn't just been body-checked by a 70-pound canine missile.

"Xeno wants to see the rest of the planet," he said. "She's tired of this lab."

I heard him, but most of my attention was on Tambourine, trying to see if she was injured. Her senses were mixed up, likely dazed from the impact, but she wasn't radiating any major pain.

The doc was still blabbering. "All Xeno needs is a compatible host."

SITUATION NORMAL

That got my attention. "I'm not taking your pet alien for a ride." But I guessed I was already carrying the alien since a patch of her protein was stuck to my head. The thought sent a shiver down my spine. The brass told us it was synthetic, not extraterrestrial. Lying bastards.

I spared a glance at Tambourine. She was wobbly but back on her feet.

"Don't worry, Specialist Jones," the doctor continued. "Xeno doesn't want you."

He rose and stared at my dog. His eyes fizzled yellow, and I caught that citrusy sugar odor again. I pulled up my gun and shot him in the face. A chunk of forehead, from his eye to the top of his ear, disintegrated. Clabbered fluids dribbled onto his lab coat. But he didn't fall.

Okay, then.

I whistled out loud, the 'let's get the hell out of here' command. Wasn't gonna risk the damn neural link now, if Xeno the citrus-scented alien was listening in. We'd have to go old school. Tambourine understood. She raced out the way we came, with me right behind her.

We dodged around arcane laboratory gizmos and slid back into the central hallway, steps ahead of the doc. The dead man we passed on the way in was no longer dead. Figured. Tambourine skidded to a stop, growling and baring her fangs.

The man's chest roiled, alien mucous leaking out, bright as a dandelion. He loomed closer and I heard that same sizzling sound, like bacon frying.

Wish I hadn't thought of that.

I shot, double tap, center mass—or as close to center mass as I could get with his chest caved in. The impact knocked him into the wall, and he scudded down. One arm flailed at us, and we hugged the far side of the corridor, trying to slide past him.

He toppled sideways and grabbed my boot, tripping me into that freakin' pile of medical junk blocking the hallway. I hissed and yanked my foot from his grasp, thankful for the protection of the spidersilk bio-armor. Tambourine took up guard position while I struggled to stand with the huge syringes rolling under my feet.

"Tambourine, outside!" The alien monster was after her, not me. But it was too late. The doctor caught up with us and dived at Tambourine. She danced to the side, snarling, protecting me.

I popped Alien Doc again, another shot to the face—honestly, there wasn't much face left. Didn't know how he was moving with most of his head blasted away, but the shot barely slowed him. Should've shot him in the foot when I had the chance.

The blowtorch caught my eye and I grabbed it, flipping the toggle. Fire sputtered and I jabbed it into him. Flames licked his coat and he screamed—guess his lungs were still intact. He kept staggering toward Tambourine, though, only it was worse now because he was trailing fire. Great.

I kicked one of the boxes of syringes toward him and it spilled. He slipped on them just as I had, and crashed to the floor in a whoosh of sparks.

"Run!"

Tambourine didn't hesitate this time. I finally regained my footing and tore after her, barely staying ahead of the spreading flames. We didn't stop until we were well past the building perimeter. The doc's fiery body made it to the security desk before it crumpled, and we watched as it fell beneath the 'Xeno Lab 4' sign. Fluorescent ashes swirled up from his corpse.

I rubbed my hands over Tambourine to make sure she wasn't hurt, then slid my fingers under her armor to scrape off the alien protein patch. Then I scratched off mine. I'd miss the infusion of her joyful energy, but honestly, Meld-X could kiss my ass.

Tambourine whuffed: the 'clear' signal. I grinned. Meld-X could kiss her furry butt, too.

My CO's voice crackled in my earbud. "Razer, did you secure the target?"

"Negative. I shot him in the face and set him on fire. And the building's infested with lemonade snot monsters."

There was a pause. "Of course, it is. I hate these damned research labs."

SITUATION NORMAL

Tambourine and I double-timed it back to the beach for evac. The helo lifted us away just as the missiles screamed overhead.

A burst of Xeno's thoughts came to me, even without the patch – fury, and the nauseating churn of betrayal.

I know how you feel.

Her presence winked out with the first explosion. It was replaced with... the other soldiers in my unit, one by one. All of us who had worn a Meld-X patch, human and canine alike. Maybe Xeno's final surge of emotion activated the latent proteins, tying all of us together. Understanding blossomed among us. An entire unit of enhanced special ops soldiers, used as guinea pigs. Someone bared their teeth. Maybe we all did. One thing was certain: the higher-ups and their secret corporate overlords were gonna pay.

But in the meantime, Tambourine's overwhelming doggie joy washed through me. She licked my face and I smiled. Maybe I owed Xeno my thanks, after all.

LET'S GO TO THE MALL

Matthew Freeman

Decker looked back at the smouldering ruins by the escalator. The eviscerated body lay at the foot of the steps, chest cavity torn open and smoking. The impact from the drone had done exactly what Bulk had promised when Decker had bought the automated security system two weeks prior.

He still didn't know how these nightcrawlers had found him out here in the Wastes. One minute he was deep, wired-in and doing a hack-and-crash job in the 'verse and the next his proximity alarm was blaring in his ear as his optical display flashed up more red markers than he cared to count. *This is what happens when you try to do a job in the wind, rather than staying safe and using a hardline.* But it had been the only way to get the job done and it had promised a big payday. Of course, that was all scragged. Now, he was fighting for his life against a bunch of goons who really wanted him dead.

He checked his load-out. Sat in its smart holster, his PDU still had two magazines, each racked with hollow-point, nine mil rounds. Leaning up against the filthy waist-high wall behind him, he had his Room Broom with one drum mag. The upgraded smart-optics gave him almost clear vision in the grainy light of the abandoned shopping mall. The once vibrant food court he was hiding in was littered with years of junkie detritus and grime, and Decker ducked behind a tangle of bright plastic booths scrawled in graffiti and muck. Shifting his weight, feet grinding the glass-dust drift of a hundred smashed ice vials, the table next to him suddenly exploded in a shower of superheated plastic shards.

"Proximity breach," said his artificial assistant in its maddeningly calm accent as a screen popped up in his optical display.

Grabbing up the shotgun, he bolted across the open space toward a shop front. "No shit, Ay-Ay! Maybe next time warn me before I get my head taken off!"

"Certainly, Decker. Protocol updated."

He crashed into the small space behind a broken shutter and brought up the display menu on the drones. Twitching his eye, he dropped down the hot bar and ordered the remaining machines to form a perimeter on his position. Immediately, Decker spied two figures stalking past the remains by the stairs. The gloom of the atrium had given him an advantage. The unlit space offered minimal visibility at night and his hunters clearly thought he was still hiding in the tangle of picnic tables.

Pinging a quick scan, he worryingly couldn't pick up the other targets. The old mall on the outskirts of town was a vast rabbit warren of the discarded and forsaken. Where the other scummers had gone to ground was anybody's guess. He had a lot of real estate to cover before he could make it out to his ride but, right now, he had to get rid of the two freaks stalking the food court.

Messaging one of his two drones to turn itself into a missile, Decker smoothly stepped out past the shutter hanging askew from its railing and opened up with his Mossberg. The repeating shotgun, firing double-aught buckshot, was instantly devastating. As the drone slammed into one of the nightcrawlers, triggering its battery pack on impact and shredding the man's arm into so much minced muscle, Decker's line of fire caught the other freak before it was even aware he was there. Cartridges ejected as wave after wave of shot tore into flesh and bone, flinging the scummer through the air in a cloud of blood-mist.

The remaining goon dragged itself across the filthy floor on one arm, crying out whilst a rudimentary headset screwed to its skull sparked and fizzed. With a start, Decker realised he was facing slave-mind 'borgs controlled by some DarkHack crew looking to turn his body into spare parts for the black market and his brain into an organic computer relay. No wonder they hadn't been put off when he'd splattered their pal all over the escalator.

LET'S GO TO THE MALL

Decker hated these kinds of freaks. Remote-controlled meat puppets ridden by opportunistic butchers, they preyed on others through sheer numbers, hunting the places long abandoned by the mega-corps. Slinging his Mossberg, Decker pulled his PDU and was about to execute the scumbag bleeding out in front of him when Ay-Ay chimed in his ear.

"Multiple targets inbound, Decker."

Tracers zipped through the grey light as he was suddenly punched off his feet. Slamming up against an upturned table, he grimaced at the bruising blow, once again grateful for his smart-armoured rig, the plates dissipating the force of impacts with surprising efficiency. Rounds walked towards his position as Decker scrambled to his feet and zig-zagged away.

"Ay-Ay, set the last drone to overwatch and leave it to fix a target," Decker grunted as he hoofed it down the wide, empty hallway.

A dirt smeared window on his right imploded, glass raining down in a waterfall of tiny shards. Diving to floor, sliding through a filthy puddle of some unknown liquid, Decker spotted the shooter lumbering out of a stairwell. Face encased in a visor, the freak's hands has been replaced with weaponry – dual Uzis with a custom belt-fed system that linked to a backpack. The 'borg lay down a field of fire, spraying rounds wildly as more of the nightcrawlers shambled out behind it. Decker flipped to his back and brought up his Room Broom, returning fire. The recoil dragged the weapon up, the shot ripping through the freak's right leg and then its visor, the mask shattering in a gout of blood and metal. The thing pirouetted on its shredded leg in a ballet of destruction as its Uzis poured rounds in uncontrollable bursts. The bullets tore into one of the scummers next to it, its head ripping apart in a shower of brain globules and bone fragments.

Using the chaos as cover, Decker scrabbled to his feet and made for a dried-out water fountain a few metres ahead of him. He heard his last drone explode and knew his number was up. The plasti-crete pond offered little protection as the freaks targeted his position, chunks of material ricocheting into the rank air around him.

"Ay-Ay, find me an exit strategy! No clear lines of sight," Decker barked.

He still couldn't understand how these freakazoids had found him out here. They seemed far too determined and motivated to have just stumbled upon him. This was a serious outfit that were happy to take some heavy losses to achieve their goal. Granted, the 'borgs were nothing more than radio-controlled meat, but it was still a lot of resources to throw at one hacker and there was no way this was a Corpo response to his slash and grab.

Decker peeked around the oval base of the fountain, his guts turning watery at the sight.

A horde.

A mass of brain-dead automatons bristling with armoury and targeting systems all directed at him.

"Cross referencing historical blueprints and current radar pings, I can present two options, Decker," the automated assistant said calmly. "One course of action would be—"

A flurry of rounds smashed into the fountain, shrapnel showering Decker as he ducked his head.

"—this would enable you to access maintenance corridors—"

"Quickest route, Ay-Ay," growled Decker, spitting dust and shuffling to his haunches, ready to run. Or fight. "Heads-up display, now."

"Complied."

His optics flared slightly as a mapping route was overlaid onto his vision, a simple green line indicating his path which, thankfully, avoided the massing forces on the other side of the ground-floor atrium. He sucked in a deep breath and launched himself into a sprint, body low. Keeping the fountain at his back to minimise his exposure, he pelted toward an access corridor. Decker crashed through the cracked plastic of the doorway and slammed into the wall before pin-balling his way toward a set of basement stairs.

LET'S GO TO THE MALL

For a brief moment, Decker thought he was going to outrun the scummers. That he'd make it to his ride and be away. Bouncing down the rusted metal stairway and into the narrow corridor, the idea he was past the worst was suddenly shattered as his back spasmed under the impact of multiple, small rounds. His rig diffused the shots, bullets flattening against its plating but pitching him face first into the floor. Decker's momentum carried him forward, face scraping along the concrete, he realised he was in it to the end. The remote-controlled meatbags had no reason to stop. Wouldn't be allowed to stop by whoever was riding their CNS.

He staggered back up, and quickly sidestepped behind an electrical cabinet. Decker blind fired his PDU down the corridor, hearing the sickening grunt of impact. Return-fire sparked off the wall opposite, his optics protecting his eyes. He squatted to change his line of sight then popped out from cover and targeted an oncoming freak. In the near darkness, the thing didn't see him as his rounds ripped through its flesh. Decker checked his shots, waiting for the 'borg to drop and reveal the one behind it.

"Proximity alert."

Decker flicked his eyes away from the freaks to check his optical display. A trio of scummers had somehow flanked him. He needed to move. Decker holstered the handgun, swung the Mossberg up on its sling and unleashed a barrage of shot before sprinting off.

Markers flashed behind him and in front – moving toward him from a side tunnel. Fatigue was setting in, forcing him to slow; he'd met the nightcrawlers head on. Decker dropped to a knee, brought the Room Broom to bear and held his patience. Fear fizzed up the back of his skull, urging him to get away from the threat marching up behind him. The gloom slowly coalesced into a shape, antenna sprouting from its shoulders. Decker lit it up, the shotgun deafening in the enclosed space. Caught in the strobe of shots, the devastation was a series of gory snapshots. Blood and shredded flesh splattered the walls and low ceiling.

Decker stumbled past the bodies split open and leaking, trying not to slip in the viscera. As he stepped over the last meatbag, it's radio array crackled, and realisation hit like a hammer. "Fuck."

Ay-Ay's route guided him down another narrow access way before coming to a graffiti-scrawled metal doorway. He paused and opened a window into the 'verse, setting a simple run of parameters for Ay-Ay to monitor. He might be outnumbered but Decker had something at his disposal very few people knew. Probably only two. And for a DarkHack crew to be targeting him using remote-controlled meat, meant they had a rough idea of what that was.

He shouldered through the door and pulled up short. Ahead was a jungle of squatter shacks. A jigsaw of scavenged plastic and metal, ropes and tubing, and all of it empty. Nothing moved in the stagnant air of the basement. Where the meatbags had been harvested suddenly wasn't a question anymore. In fact, the whole thing smelled more and more like a rat trap with every passing moment.

Decker slammed the door shut behind him, snatching up a discarded pipe and jamming the handles closed. In his heads-up display, Ay-Ay was running through different systems. Whether he made it out of the mall or not, Decker knew that his last command would be carried out. The sudden crash behind him had him jogging into the labyrinth of hovels. His PDU was down to one magazine of 21 rounds, the Mossberg over half empty as well. He was sick of this cat and mouse game.

Time to turn the tables.

Decker pitched up behind a support column and rigged the Room Broom for remote access. Moving to his left, a stripped-out automobile offered another line of sight, setting up a perfect crossfire position.

It didn't take much to encourage the scummers to find him. They lumbered forward like the mindless 'borgs they were, wading into the abandoned squats, smashing down walls and tripping over wires and rubbish. His optical overlay spotted nine red markers. Gritting his teeth, Decker waited until they were almost upon him before unleashing hell.

LET'S GO TO THE MALL

The first three goons went down easy, bodies ripped apart by the Room Broom. But the crew riding the meat-bags got wise quickly and spread the rest of the scummers apart, ducking behind their own hard cover where it could be found. Decker didn't have infinite ammo and a drawn-out shooting match would have him on the losing end before long. He had to move and use his advantages but, more importantly, he had to make it a dog fight.

Decker crawled through the rusted chassis and inched out from the empty engine compartment as Ay-Ay fed him data, pinging him real-time info on the whereabouts of the scummers. Even so, he almost stumbled into the first one. A woman—skin wrinkled and grey with filth, eyes replaced with an infrared scanner—crouched in a pile of junk. Decker punched his carbon-bladed Bowie knife through her temple and dropped her without a sound. Black blood bubbled from the wound as he cut her radio connection and slaved her implant to Ay-Ay's system. As the Room Broom fired randomly, keeping up a steady distraction, Decker stalked to the next nightcrawler.

Approaching the 'borg, Decker had his last victim's nervous system overload, the dead woman's weapon discharging wildly and drawing the attention of the others. Guns flashed in the darkness, the sound deafening as Decker slid behind his target and put a bullet through the back of its skull. The now double-dead nightcrawler flopped to the ground in a pool of mashed grey matter and blood. And, just as he'd hoped, the roar of gunfire began to drop off. His own Mossberg reported its drum was empty and Decker could only hear sporadic gunshots coming from two enemy positions. Meatbags weren't used for close quarters.

Decker was.

Leaping over a collapsed tent, he made a beeline for the first available target. A skinny thing that could've been male or female, head encased in a hard helmet, its sensors never picked up his run. Decker shoulder-checked the thing with all his momentum, smashing the nightcrawler into a plastic shack, the pair skidding

141

through cardboard pulp and muck. The thing caught Decker a clumsy blow to his face as it bucked and spasmed. Grabbing it by the throat, Decker pinned it to the concrete and slid his blade under the helmet, dragging with all his might against tough tendons and spine, blood gushing everywhere. A huge scummer crashed through the makeshift camp, its arms windmilling.

Decker left his Bowie embedded, and backed up. In the darkness, his optics revealed a pot-bellied ghoul of a man, radio relay clamped to its temple. Spittle and bile flew from the meat-bag's clenched jaw, flecking its beard as it lumbered forward. Decker ducked a wild haymaker, and grabbed a body lock, his hard-wired muscles easily lifting the goon. He tilted the man up and over, driving the scummer into the concrete, bones crunching on impact. Decker straddled the meatsack's chest before smashing elbows down. Each blow crumpled the man's face as nose and jaw gave way under the piston-like attack until nothing was left but crushed bone and sparking implant.

A shot smacked into his rig, spinning him off into a pile a filth. Decker dragged breath into his bruised body and cursed as he scrambled to his feet. He couldn't take many more hits and if those DarkHackers were smart, they'd held back something for just such a moment.

"Match complete," Ay-Ay informed him pleasantly. "I have the coordinates, Decker."

He skidded across a patch of oily slop and scrabbled behind a stack of tyres. Bringing up his hot-bar on his visual display, he checked the info Ay-Ay had collated. Rage boiled within him. The whole job had been one big set up.

Only two people had any idea of what Ay-Ay, his artificial assistant, was capable of. But even they didn't really understand it. Years ago, he'd stumbled on some esoteric coding, deep down in a stack whilst diving in the 'verse. Bulk knew Ay-Ay was special but he'd never really pried. Tonic, on the other hand was a nosey bitch. She'd pinged him for this job three weeks back, and now, here he was, covered in blood and shit, hiding next to a stinking pile of half rotten tyres staring right at her 'secret' location. Hacked back from the radio relays, chased from the DarkHack crew she'd employed from an Eastern Bloc squat spot on the Rim, he was looking right at her feed in real time.

"Get ready, Ay-Ay. Force override on my word," growled Decker as he pivoted from cover.

Two strides and he was on the shooter, his rig and wired musculature adding a speed and power to his movements the meatsack couldn't track. Decker stomped on the scummer's right knee, folding the leg under it, then sidestepped the falling body before stamping on the back of its head, cracking the skull open like an overripe fruit. The last 'borg turned toward him, fearless face slack of emotion as Decker push-kicked it across a glass littered patch of open ground.

He pounced on the thing and gripped its head, staring straight into the camera wired to its skull. "Ay-Ay, execute orbital demolition. Target, Rim city area code nine by three."

Decker waited for his system to confirm the DarkHackers had been annihilated before he continued. "Ay-Ay has control of the feed, so I know you're watching, Tonic. I can see you right now, scrambling to turn off your system. But you can't. I've slaved it all, so you'll have to listen." Decker slammed the head of the 'borg into the concrete to add to his point. "Whatever you thought you knew, you were wrong. Whatever you thought you'd achieve, you failed. And right now you're just about realising how badly you've fucked up." Decker smashed the scummer's head into the ground again. "I could drop a missile on you right now. But. That would be too easy. You thought you could send a pack of these meatbags to hunt me down?" He glared into the camera, watching on Ay-Ay's feed as Tonic flinched back from her screen as he bellowed, "I. Am. The. Hunter!"

He stood, lifting a broken block of plasti-crete from the junk, slamming it down into the 'borg's face, severing the camera and its connections.

"See you soon, Tonic."

OUT OF THE FRYING PAN

Torion Oey

Flames have a certain elegance, don't you think? They're a solution and a problem wrapped in one. Or, they're one or the other. Rather than controlled chaos, flames are control or chaos. Neat how all it takes is a spark, right?"

"Mmm! Mmm."

"Right. It's that thinking of it being the same that's wrong. Controlled chaos. Why do people pretend chaos can be controlled? Are they afraid? Are they tricking themselves into believing they're not mutually exclusive? Whether it's in a fireplace or blazing across the state, so long as there's a line between people and the flames it's controlled chaos. Though, they somehow miss that the result is always ash."

"Mmm…"

"That shouldn't make you afraid, though! I was at first, but it's really a relief! There's this silly quote I always loved. 'Build a man a fire, he's warm for a night. Set a man on fire, he's warm for the rest of his life.'"

"Hmm hmm!"

"Yeah, it's pretty morbid. But it's also beautiful. To blaze and burn before the quiet end. Yeah." Pan pressed what looked like a stick of dynamite without a fuse onto the tied and gagged man's stomach. He retracted his hand and shook it, flicking off some of the liquid substance. The thing stayed stuck to the front of the man's shirt. "Just because it's temporary doesn't mean it's not beautiful."

"MMM!" A dark spot quickly spread across the man's shirt, the smell of gasoline intensifying.

Pan turned and stepped out of the office. Closing the door, a

145

quiet explosion resounded. Looking down, brilliant light danced underneath the crack between the door and the floor. He placed his palm against the wood. "It's warm," he said, and smiled.

Alarms blared. *Two minutes* he estimated while walking briskly toward the stairwell.

Late-night employees rushed ahead of him toward the elevator. "Hey!" he called. They froze and turned. Apparently not overtaken by fear just yet. His cracked leather boots clomped along the linoleum, barely audible over the constant ringing. "Use stairs in case of emergency," he said in a low, velvety voice when he drew close. At once they took to the stairs. Stopping by the banister, he reached over his shoulder into the hiker's bag on his back and produced another red tube, similar to dynamite, though attached to wire spooling from a coil within his bag. He glanced up, noting no one coming from the upper floors. Below, several hands trailed the railing looping around and around. He dangled the red tube over the hole in the center of the stairwell. The tube rotated, a thin white rectangular patch meshed to its surface. Pan smirked. In his other hand he gripped scissors whose blades sandwiched the wire. It quivered in anticipation. *No.*

"Wouldn't want to cut off our escape route, would we?" Pan murmured, pulling the red tube back and stepping away from the stairs and to the elevator door. He stuck the tube to the metal, then descended the stairs, the thin wire unravelling from his pack behind him.

On the ground floor a security guard stood watching a news feed play on a widescreen TV suspended on the wall behind his desk. His attention was entirely focused on the newscaster, the volume loud enough to be heard by Pan as he approached. "Three law firms have reportedly caught fire in the same night in what the police are describing as a coordinated attack. The pattern appears to be at least one casualty caught in the center of the blaze. Explosions have also been reported, and police warn of some dangerous foreign technology being used indicated by unusual scorches at the scenes. Details are forthcoming and police are warning that the foreign technology is extremely advanced. There is no information on the culprit behind the fiery menace yet, but police are urging law businesses as well as those nearby to evacuate so they may investigate efficiently."

"You should listen and evacuate," Pan said in the same low, smooth voice. He continued by the desk without pausing. Taking his silver scissors, he lifted it to the still uncoiling wire and cut it.

The building rocked as sound erupted from above. *Unconnected charges detonate in seconds, connected ones detonate when the connection is severed. They're working just the way I built them.* Pan pushed the metal bar on one of the fancy glass entrance doors. "Hurry up."

The security guard turned from the TV and eyed Pan. Instead of listening he began tapping furiously on a mouse connected to a desktop computer.

"What are you doing?"

"Checking the cameras," the guard replied.

"He shouldn't do that," Pan said, releasing the door and letting it shut violently. He closed the space between them and added, "unless you want to see how it ends."

"Sir, get—" The guard cut himself off when Pan rounded the desk. He only managed to take out his gun before Pan grabbed the back of the guard's neck, and slammed his head against the keyboard.

"I'm a fan of fire, too," Pan said. He punched the side of the guard's head, a direct hit to the temple. The man crumpled to the floor, unconscious. "That was a double entendre. Neat."

"This just in, a fourth law firm has been attacked," the newscaster reported.

Pan exited without listening to the rest, fleeing out and away down the street. Stopping at a corner, he felt around inside his bag for another tube and deftly attached it to the wire. Leaving it there, he knelt to pull off his boots. Underneath, he wore something similar to metal greaves. "Should we go all out, Ash?" he asked while adjusting plating around the soles. Flipping over a side-plate, he flicked a switch, then covered it back up. The sound of some interior support crashing caused him to glance up at smoke trailing from the upper floors. Smiling, he nodded. "Right, until there's nothing left."

He rose into a low crouch, gripping his boots in the pit of his right arm. In the instant he extended his legs a blast rocketed him off the ground and far into the sky. The cold night air whipped his body as he ascended in a ball and curved high over the cityscape. Only his feet were warm, his thermo-resistant socks unable to fully protect from the intense blast produced from the greaves. Underneath his casual clothes, the shapeshifting meta-materials composing his bodysuit loosened slightly. It protected and reinforced his body, particularly his legs, from shattering whenever he used his greaves. Still, he felt a slight strain running up from his ankles telling him he was pushing himself.

Calm and controlled white lights sparkled everywhere from windows and streetlamps. The chaotic flash of red and blue drew closer to the newly formed plume of smoke he left behind. *Everything must burn.* Angling his body sideways, he extended his legs for only a moment. The force of another explosion from his greaves carried him fast to the center of the city and he brought his knees to his chest again. He covered his face with both arms as he plummeted through another plume of smoke, the soft, warm ash sticking to his clothes and sifting through his hair. The remains of his first target. Below, more red and blue lights flickered in circles where police cars were parked. With the growing fires, they were thinning out.

Wind blew away the powdery grey particles as he began his descent toward a triangular high-rise. Pan uncovered his face and pulled back the left cuff of his leather jacket. "One hundred and twenty miles per hour, Ash!" he cried in delight.

Looking up from the wrist-speedometer, he saw the building fast-approaching. His progress would leave him in pieces if he didn't change course. "And why would I?"

Tucking his chin, he moved into a pirouette, just missing the corner of the building. The drag from air resistance pushed at him, the result of skirting the wall. At the instant before his body turned over again and scraped the side of the building, he extended his legs fully. His greaves connected flatly against the exterior before he flew from the explosion, its force adding to his momentum. Glancing back, flames coiled along the entirety of the middle floors. Walls and windows shattered. The flames ate away at the exterior thoroughly. As he knew, the façade assembly of that particular high-rise had highly combustible material to work with from aluminum composite paneling, timber cladding, and glass reinforced polymers. Of course, the force of the heat itself would've blasted any exterior apart regardless of non-combustible cladding and insulation systems. Already it was collapsing.

With a grin, Pan faced forward. A helicopter flew ahead at his level. It circled the plume from his second target, the firm Greyson, Wesley, & Vern. "We've got spectators," Pan said, though the words rushed away. He put a hand on the side of his greaves and winced as his skin was scorched. "I should've worn gloves!" He laughed, ignoring the burning sensation in his fingers as he toggled a wheel-like dial above the soles. "Let's set it to simmer so we don't overheat." He brought one leg up and kicked it out ahead of him. A smaller blast erupted, stunting his forward progression.

As he dropped vertically, he extended either foot as if walking in the air. Each time he took a step the speed of his fall was reduced until his metal greaves resounded on the concrete of an alleyway.

Sirens blared nearby under the steady beat of the overhead helicopter blades. He unclasped the metal panel and switched the ignition off before taking the boots from under his armpit and pulling them back over his greaves. Quiet sounds of singeing emanated, though now his footsteps would be muffled.

Pan pulled a snow globe from the side pouch of his bag and peered closely at it. "Where next, Ash?" He shook the globe and watched as the powdery white circled around a miniature cabin caked in the same white. "The residential area? Yes, we did talk about this beforehand. All right." He paced out of the alley and down a main street.

"Civilians stand clear!" Another helicopter soared overhead, a distant figure gazing out its windows at the streets below with a radio speaker over his mouth. Pan eyed its progress as it circled, and spotted police markings. "Explosions in the sky have been set off! Remain indoors and watch for falling debris!"

"Who's going to listen to them?" Pan muttered, stowing the snow globe. There were only a handful of people littered along the smoothly paved thoroughfare. Most simply kept walking, though others paused to gaze in awe at the rising smoke drifting together across the sky. *See? It is beautiful.*

Just then a police car turned at the next intersection and sped forward. It skidded to a halt twenty feet from him and an officer stepped out with his own radio.

"The terrorist was spotted near here! Get inside!" At the word 'terrorist', the people scattered.

"Oh. I guess everyone."

"Go!" The officer's voice crackled insistently as he saw Pan leisurely approaching along the sidewalk.

"This is embarrassing," Pan spoke louder. He pulled on the straps, adjusting his traveling bag on his shoulders. "I've lost where I am."

The officer's eyes narrowed. He threw his speaker back in the car and met Pan outside an open storefront. "Where do you live?"

"795 Lawson Court."

"That's nearby." The officer frowned and gazed up at the police helicopter now herding the first one away. "But farther than is safe. It's too dangerous to wander now, so I'll drive you."

"At a time like this I'd be impeding your duty!" Pan objected.

"It is my duty," the officer replied. His brows rose marginally with a momentary smile. "Come quickly."

Pan blinked. "Thank you." Following the officer back, he gripped the handle of the door directly behind the driver's side.

"Please take the other side," the officer told him.

"What was that?" Pan asked, pretending not to hear while opening the door and scooting inside. The police helicopter's blades whirled overhead as it passed by again.

OUT OF THE FRYING PAN

The officer huffed but didn't insist before moving into his seat. "It's protocol to have passengers sit behind shotgun."

"Oh, I'm sorry!"

"Just protocol," the officer replied while waving a hand. He turned the car around and quickly drove.

Pan pulled his arms out through the straps of his bag and placed it in his lap. "What's the reason for such protocol?" He pushed the coil of wire sitting at the top aside and sifted further into the contents underneath the tubed charges.

"It's to keep perps in view of the officer in case they do anything funny."

Pan emitted a laugh. "Sorry. I'm causing you more trouble."

"You're not a perp, so it's fine." The officer turned at an intersection down a residential street away from the shopping district.

"I can't imagine being an officer," Pan commented, pulling out a foot-long curved knife with a rubber sheathe. "Especially at times like this when everything's so chaotic."

"It's always chaotic."

He thumbed a dial on the handle and pulled the rubber slightly up to get a look at the base of the blade. "Oh?"

"I see the way people eye officers these days. We do a fine job keeping the peace, though I sense the discontent. Sometimes I even question whether we're actually protecting people or protecting ourselves. Crime is bad, don't get me wrong, and crime like this is on another level. But in the grand scheme of things, there's other stuff going on constantly that's probably bigger than the effects after this ends."

Pan looked into the rearview mirror at the officer whose eyes focused on the road. "Whoever's causing the explosions everywhere is instigating something, right? That's what terrorists do?"

"Likely. But what that is, I don't know."

"If you had to guess?"

"A guess?" The officer's pale blue eyes flicked to meet Pan's for a second. "Suppose it'd have to do with corporations. The pattern's been law firms being hit, and the latest fire's at the Shoppes Tower. Could be my own bias, though bailouts have been screwing people for ages."

"That's what you meant by other stuff."

The officer barked out a laugh. "Probably wrong for me to badmouth big businesses as I'm on their payroll. Earlier you wondered about me being an officer, and that's why."

Plucking a hair from his own head, Pan touched it to the base of the blade. It disintegrated instantly. "Money?"

"Oops, that sounded bad too. Money, yes, but not for the sake of greed. I wanted to join the force because the police are on their payroll. Police never should've been placed in big business's pocket. If you ask me, it's all messed up."

Pan lowered the knife. Turning the dial back and fully sheathing the blade again, he placed it within the bag. "Aware of the line between control and chaos, huh?"

"What was that?"

"It seems I agree with you," he said as he flipped the bag's flap over to conceal its contents. The car pulled down the street leading up to the court. As soon as it came to a stop, he opened the door and stepped out. "Thanks very much for the ride. I appreciate your service."

"No problem," the officer said after cracking the window. "Remember, stay inside for the time being."

Without replying, Pan waved and, pulling his bag over his shoulders, paced up the driveway to the front of the single-floor house. He stopped at the front door and waited without turning for the sound of the tires to recede around the bend. Only when the shadows cast by the flashing police lights came to a calm did he grip the brass doorknob.

"Remember what we discussed."

"Yes, Ash," Pan replied quietly and touched the back of his left hand to the snow globe. He withdrew the knife again and shifted the rubber sheathe off the blade. Turning the handle's dial, he pressed the point ahead of the lock and waited. The wood sizzled and chipped as the knife progressed. It made quick work, and Pan stepped in, pulling the door closed behind him.

OUT OF THE FRYING PAN

Straight ahead in the corner of a family room was a flatscreen TV perched on a low, multileveled table that also held a sound system. Continued news of the known developments were being reported from a helicopter's bird's-eye view. Various angles of the five different sites where fires were being handled, showed repeatedly.

"Each were CEOs and presidents of their firms," came a taut voice. "And no one else knows who the casualties are?"

Pan crept closer, noting the armrest of a floral-patterned couch where a man's hand was clenched. The man and rest of the couch was out of view. Pan remained in the entryway for a moment to listen.

"Of course they're not random. Our firms are all locked down now? Good. All the attacks save for the Shoppes Tower were done through infiltration, so we'll be prepared."

Pan watched as the man exchanged hands with the phone and raised it to his left ear. Within reach.

"You think it's a foreign nation attacking? It could be some crazy arsonist—"

Pan touched the knife to the phone and it began to melt.

"What the—!" The man yelped and dropped the phone before more of the liquified metal touched his hand. He retreated to the opposite wall beside the TV and nursed his hand. His wide, cherry-red face became a tad paler while his mouth worked in panic and anger. "Who are you? Why are you here?"

"You haven't been in charge of Lockley & Abrams for years," Pan's low voice mused. "You referred to their firms as 'ours' despite that." He paused when he saw unshaven stubble cropping up in patches around the man's mouth. "Hmm. Kindling."

"Does that matter? It's still in my name." The man pressed his back further to the wall while raising both hands when Pan took a step forward.

Pan looked down at the knife he held pointed at the man. Sheathing it and placing it back in his bag, he said, "That's the problem, Mr Abrams. There's a front for everything these days

153

while the people behind the scenes are the last to be touched."
He frowned and looked over his shoulder at the side pouch of
his bag. "Though, they're rarely if ever touched."

"What are you talking about?"

"Stay still," Pan ordered. "Do you know what happens to
your body in an explosion?"

Mr Abrams's right eye winked.

Pan's body tensed and he yanked out the fire charge connected to the wire. "What are you doing?"

"Nothing! My eye's twitching!"

"Turn around!"

Mr Abrams did as instructed.

Pan kicked the back of the man's kneecaps, causing him to
buckle. Pan then unspooled the wire further to use as restraints.
When all Mr Abram's limbs were bound together and he lay on
his side on the floor, Pan stuck the charge to the front of his plain
blue shirt and stepped away.

"You're not going to kill me?"

Pan came forward and, withdrawing a gag, stuffed it into
Mr Abrams's mouth. "I am."

"MMM!"

"Our first mistake was trusting the people who had every
intention of sacrificing everyone but themselves. Lofty politicians, and lofty business people."

"Mmm!"

"Our bodies are surprisingly sturdy. The pressure of an
explosion rarely does lasting damage. Around upwards of
forty pounds per square inch of pressure can reliably rupture
eardrums and damage lungs. Over sixty PSI can kill you. It was
difficult calibrating my explosives to be less of a boom and more
of a burn. Burns are more interesting. If we never had the house
fire, I wouldn't have ever known." Pan glanced over his shoulder
again. "They—you need to know."

Mr Abrams's struggled and his gag came loose. "Who are
you talking to? Let me go!"

Pan reapplied the gag before pulling out another to wrap
over the first. "No one. They're gone, taken by the fire."

"Mmm...!"

"Fat, muscles, and internal organs shrink, and skin tears. Most interesting is how the fire causes the muscles to contract which, in turn, causes joints to flex. The position of people who died by heat is referred to as a boxer pose, though when I saw it the first time it looked more like they were praying..."

"Mmm! HMM!"

"Settle down, big-time huckster. Right, politicians. Yes, politicians are only a means to an end. It's businesses that pull the strings now. If it weren't businesses, then politicians would fill your role like how you fill theirs. That's why I'm here." Pan paced from the room to the entryway. "You people behind the scenes are next. It's your turn to see a fire that can't be escaped."

"Mmmm?"

Pan continued to the stoop outside and closed the door. When he was twenty feet from the house, he snipped the wire. The house's windows shattered and its garage door fell off. Flames engulfed the roof and walls. Pulling the snow globe out of his side pouch, he shook it. "And everyone must see that those most in control can experience chaos."

The whirring of helicopter blades approached. A spotlight shone down on him standing in the center of the court road. Pan admired the way the flakes within the globe turned an ashen color with the intensified light. "I need to make my final stop," he said as sirens grew closer. Stooping down, he quickly pulled off his boots and adjusted the settings on his greaves. "They've seen my face now."

He straightened and rocketed up dangerously close to the circling helicopter. Its spotlight beam jerked and swept around desperately in search of him. With nothing but the company of cold and wind dampening all other sounds he let himself reach the apogee of his rise while searching the horizon. Dense layers of clouds hung over the parliament building that spanned a fifth of its flat industrial grounds. "There." Angling his body, another explosion propelled him at a downward angle toward it.

A man walking in a private lot fingered the door to his car and looked up. Pan smiled.

Far in the distance were five plumes of smoke joining a cloud layer gathering overhead. Alarms and sirens blared in disharmony. Sam Wetherby sighed. He'd been called out on account of the explosions. Of all the luck he had to be the one to rule the same time a terrorist attack happened.

Intermittent crackling like fireworks echoed across the sky. "What's that?" Sam murmured to himself, trying to catch any flashes in the night. A sudden burst of flames tunneled through the sky behind a dark spot. Its fiery trail shot like an arrow directly toward him. Without so much as a second to react the blaze descended and pummeled the ground in a deafening boom.

He coughed and spluttered, inhaling air that tasted like diesel fuel. Large cracks in the concrete ruptured in a circle from the spot, now a small crater, where the thing had hit. The back end of his car began slowly rolling down the incline. He barely noticed; his gaze fixed on the tall figure of what seemed like a hiker standing in a cloak of smoke and dying fire. The hiker's plated greaves shifted over a newly formed layer of soot, metal clanging against concrete. In the last embers of the fire, he saw the hiker's feral grin underneath a set of glittering pine-green eyes.

A shrill ringtone bleated. Sam whipped out his phone and answered on its second ring. "The suspect disappeared but was last seen heading your way!" his secretary's voice said urgently. "It's unclear if he's working alone, but we've ID'd him! He's Antoine Pan, French-Eurasian descent! Medical records show his family died in a house fire when he was twelve, and in early adulthood he developed symptoms of schizotypal personality disorder!"

"Caught you, Prime Minister."

The Prime Minister shivered at the hiker's low voice. "Antoine?"

OUT OF THE FRYING PAN

The hiker smiled and nodded. "Pan." His smile dropped when a crowd of footfalls resounded from behind. "There's too many of them," he growled. "I need more time."

"He's here!" the Prime Minister shouted both into his phone and at the approaching guards.

Pan shot forward, tackling the Prime Minister's gut and dragging him through the air out of the parking lot. Sam reeled in shock as their bodies soared some kilometers away before touching back down and skidding painfully along a wide patch of grass. While skidding, Pan kicked the Prime Minister away.

Sam tumbled to a stop, and watched Pan check underneath the plate of his greaves. "Fuel's low," he commented, then those pine-green eyes met his. "Yes, I did say until there's nothing left."

Keeping his knees bent, he stood and withdrew a flare gun from his bag. Remnants of the heat from his greaves sizzled and small flames caught on the grass where he stood. He pointed the gun straight up and pulled the trigger. Rather than a flare, a colorless ball whizzed up and disappeared into the cover of clouds.

The Prime Minister rose and eyed Pan warily. "What is this about?" he shouted while Pan dropped the gun and took out the tip of a curved metal handle from his bag. Sam glanced at his own hand and noticed he'd dropped his phone. "Do you blame me for your home burning down?"

He watched as Pan pulled the rest of the handle, which was attached to a metal stick with leather wrapped around it. He flourished it before opening it up. It was an umbrella.

"Do you blame me for your family dying? Well?" The Prime Minister backed up a few more feet.

Holding the umbrella over his head with his right hand, Pan replied, "You had nothing to do with that."

"Huh?"

"This isn't revenge. It's because you're afraid to burn."

The Prime Minister looked to the parking lot where a hoard of his men were running toward them.

"You'll want to tell your security detail to not use any guns,"

Pan added, pointing up with his left hand. "Either way, it's about to get hot."

The second the Prime Minister looked skyward, a blinding flash lit the clouds. He blinked away the spots in his vision when the darkness of night returned the next moment. Then, he covered his face as a heavy shower of rain fell. It lasted for less than five seconds but soaked everything. "This is freezing!" he said indignantly. He dropped his arms and gazed around at the dewing grass blades. They held an unnatural yellow color. Then the stink hit him. "What is this?"

"Think of it as a water bomb," Pan said. "Only with a whole lot of sulfur."

"That's this rotting egg smell?" He coughed again, bringing a sleeve to his nose. "Ugh! You did this?"

"And all else that has transpired tonight. Your security," Pan reminded him. "Otherwise you'll all catch fire."

"Hu—Wait! WAIT!" The Prime Minister shouted, waving his arms frantically at the nearing guards. "Don't shoot!"

"Right, the air is flammable," Pan said. He glanced down.

The Prime Minister followed his gaze to the steam rising around the other man's greaves. "Wait—!"

A ripple of flames extended in a circle in all directions from Pan, incinerating the grass fast. It reached the Prime Minister and rose up his body. He screamed.

"Prime Minister!" one of the security guards shouted.

"YOU SAID THE AIR WAS FLAMMABLE!" the Prime Minister shrieked, his body writhing before collapsing into an indiscernible figure of fire and flesh.

⚙⚙ ⚙⚙

Pan lowered his head out of respect for the late Prime Minister. "A necessary bluff." Steam continued to rise from the charred ground and corpse the fire left behind. A familiar, soothing voice rose above the crackles and hisses. "Remember what we discussed."

OUT OF THE FRYING PAN

"I know," Pan said softly to his mother's last words. He flipped the umbrella over and rested it on the ground. "Stop, drop, and roll."

Before the flames reached the security guards, they opened fire. Pan curled and darted to the side. He continued moving in quick rolls as screams joined the raging of the fire. When he was some feet away, he rolled to a stop and glanced back. Most of the security was down, though some were recovering thanks to their body armor. Their figures wobbled through the still rising steam.

Pan removed the snow globe and shook it. Then, from the same side pouch, took a metal disk. Pressing its center, it began to softly hum and whir. He tossed it up where it hung in the air. It was far enough up to not be seen by the security guards who were still preoccupied by remnant embers flickering along their clothes. Looking past them, he saw the line of flames coming to a stop where the rainfall ended. "We have to be quick."

He ran sideways, following a more recent trail of fire and steam toward the parliament building. In the air, the disk went the opposite way.

"He's moving!" a security guard called, pointing his gun at the figure moving through the steam, and fired.

The figure continued to run.

"He's trying to escape!" The guard ran after him, away from the parliament building. More guards followed as they chased the terrorist across the grounds. More shots fired.

Still, Pan did not go down.

"Is he bullet-proof?" another guard called.

"He wasn't wearing armor beyond his greaves!" the first guard responded. "Something's wrong!"

The figure suddenly stopped at the end of the steam where the flames were already dying out. Pan turned and faced the security guards. Lifting his hand, he waved.

The security guards opened fire.

Bullets passed through him, and then he stepped out of the line of steam and his body disappeared.

"What?" They looked around frantically but it was no use. Pan was gone.

On the other side of the grass field, the real Pan continued toward the imposing building. He came up to the brick wall and leaned his back against it. "I told you mirages were useful," he said. "I'll have to retrieve the mirror. It'll be fine. They'll come back once they see."

"How'd you get to be such a clever boy?"

Pan sifted through his bag and retrieved a handful of charges. "The light of my image projected by the mirror went from the cold air to the very hot surface recently left by the flash fire, refracting it. It's not that I was clever, I just ran trials to get it right." He closed his eyes. Again, police sirens and the sound of helicopter blades approached. He ignored them and visualized the layout of the parliament building.

It had three corners and three sides. At each corner were towers. Long, stained-glass windows stretched across each exterior wall between them, seventeen along the south, fifteen along the northwest, and fifteen along the northeast. He stood on the south side away from where the main entrances were located. Doors nearby would lead him by the House of Commerce, remodeled from the prior House of Commons and Senate rooms. With what he had, Pan could destroy it, but that left the rest of the building. If he still had the bomb, it would've been so much easier.

Fingering one of the seven charges, he opened his eyes and ran for the nearest entrance by the east tower. The door was shut and locked. He attached the charge and retreated as the kerosene spread. Seconds later he returned to the hole left behind by the explosion, flames licking the brick siding. He stepped through and raced from a hall down the wide middle space between rows of tiered seating with lovely ornate backing and sides. Pan fought the urge to use more of his charges. A large center desk held several stacks of documents he shoved off as he ran past, the papers scattering everywhere.

He reached the other end of the room and entered the large

OUT OF THE FRYING PAN

hall uniting the two main entrances from the northwest and northeast. Tall support columns rose all around him at what he knew was the relative center of the building. He placed the rest of his charges in a circle near the walls, careful not to mesh the patch-side to any surface and set them off. Already footsteps clomped toward him from both entrances. Looking either way, he flitted to the center of the hall and took off his bag, turning in place. "There wasn't enough," Pan murmured, looking at the dozen remaining charges within. He dropped it and knelt, taking out the snow globe. "It didn't last long. But it was fun, right?"

"Freeze!" an approaching officer called.

Pan shook the globe once and watched the flurry swirl in a circle. "There's nowhere to run." He smiled and tilted his head. "For any of us." Placing the globe on the marble floor, he flicked a dial on his greaves.

The footsteps were close. Very close. "Get away from the bag!"

"Until there's nothing left, Ash." Pan lifted his arms over his head and rose slowly. "I've always wanted to see how it ends."

"You—!"

He looked left and saw the police officer who had given him a ride training a gun at him. The officer's pale blue eyes were wide in shock.

"*You* are the line," Pan said, a tremor of excitement momentarily raising the pitch of his voice. "There is chaos or there is control. You are the line that stands between the two."

"Kick the bag away, Antoine!" an officer to his right ordered. There were enough officers behind him to make a small army. It was the same the other way.

"The line is an illusion. I will break that line."

"Kick it away!"

Pan placed a foot atop his bag and lifted his hands higher. He paused and breathed in. A long, quiet second elapsed. And then he whispered. "Into the fire."

ROGUE T.R.A.I.N.

Amanda Bridgeman

The sleek black chopper rose swiftly into the night sky and veered sharply away from the sprawling, sparkling city. Private First-Class Arturo Flores sat huddled among the other five members of his team, listening hard over the thrumming chopper blades as Major Jacobs began the brief. Being the 'physical' arm of the Tactical Response Asset and Intelligence Network (T.R.A.I.N.), all six soldiers were armed to the teeth and ready to deploy.

"We have a rogue AI-controlled train headed for the city that we need to stop at all costs," Jacobs said. "Military cargo train ESSE-591was hacked by terrorists two hours ago. They disabled all external access to the train's AI including any override failsafes, then switched its tracks and have set it to its maximum speed. In approximately fifty minutes that train is going to hit the city's Bellview station. And when I say hit the station, at its maximum speed of fourteen-hundred klicks per hour, it's gonna burst right through the station wall and plow through the town square."

"We can't evac the civilians in time, sir?" Team leader, First Lieutenant Ades asked.

"We're doing that, but we still need to stop the train. Whether civilians are present or not, the damage will be immense. This train is one of ours. The payload it's carrying…." Jacobs looked each of them in the eyes to drive home his point. "We must protect it and the city at all costs."

"How'd they get control of the train, sir?" Staff Sergeant Gorn asked. As the second behind Ades, he was good at asking questions, but even better at taking action. "I thought the AIs were impossible to hack."

"They used a highly secure T.R.A.I.N. employee log-in," Jacobs answered. "That employee is now missing. Whether they're part of the terrorist organization behind this or whether the organization took the employee out, we don't know. Regardless, they have overridden all the AI's protocols and locked out military control. We can't even switch the tracks to send it on a different route away from the city. They've disabled our access to the entire pathway the ESSE is on. Your team is our only hope in stopping this train."

A spike of adrenaline shot through Flores. The thrill of saving the day made his spirit soar. He exchanged a look with Private Royale, who mirrored his excitement. As the newest and youngest in the team, they were determined to pull their weight. They hadn't made it into the T.R.A.I.N. team just to crash and burn now.

"What's the plan, sir?" Ades asked.

"We have a small window," Jacobs said as he tapped the data-pane he carried and showed them a map of the train's route, "where the Esse will be in the open air before it goes underground once more into its hyper-speed tunnel. Its track was purposely designed with two open-air access points should emergency operations ever need to be carried out." Jacobs checked the time on his data-band. "In approximately five minutes we will rendezvous with the ESSE and have our one and only chance to physically board that train before it hits the city." He looked back to Ades. "Your team will have sixty seconds to land on the train's roof and enter through an access panel before it re-enters the tunnel. If you are not inside the train at that point, you and the tunnel will become one. Understand?"

Ades nodded firmly. Flores swallowed hard and exchanged another adrenaline-filled look with Royale.

"How do we get inside if the AI is no longer in our control," Private Britt asked, her green eyes fixed and serious. "Won't it have locked us out, sir?"

"We're sending you in with a swarm of drone-bots." Major Jacobs pulled a metal case toward him. Inside were twelve black, cylindrical drone-bots the size of baseballs, which began to alight as they came online. "They'll cut the access open in thirty seconds, which leaves you thirty seconds to get all six of your asses inside. Are we clear?"

"Yes, sir," Ades nodded.

"Once inside," Jacobs said, "you get this to the control carriage." He held up a small, flat, black box the size of Flores' hand, with a short cable dangling from one side. "Connect that to the console and this black box will do the rest. It contains a kill code for the AI. Nothing can stop it once it's connected. Not the terrorists nor the AI itself." Jacobs looked at them all again. "We always knew an AI outside our control could be a risk, so every single one of them was designed with a fatal flaw, and this kill code is it."

"Two minutes out, sir!" the chopper pilot called.

Jacobs checked his data-band again, then looked back at Ades. "You protect this box at all costs. Get aboard the train, make your way to the control carriage, and plug it in. It's that simple."

"Yes, sir!" Ades handed the box to Royale. "You're our tech pro. You guard the box. We'll guard you."

"Yes, sir!" Royale nodded.

Major Jacobs tapped his data-pane and the data-band around Ades' wrist lit up. "You have all the details you need."

"Thank you, sir!" Ades nodded then turned to the team. "Data-bands connected?" The team brought their data-bands online, and Ades checked each one was registering on his. "Comms check. Go!" Ades instructed, and they each tested their helmet mics and earpieces. Satisfied, Ades continued. "Alright," he yelled. "You heard the major. We have just sixty seconds to board, so we can take back control of our runaway train!"

"Nothing like a tight squeeze!" Sergeant York grinned, adrenaline shining in the big man's eyes. He thrived in high-pressure situations.

They moved in formation to the chopper's open side and locked on to the cables they would use to rappel onto the train.

"Good luck, team!" Jacobs said.

"Don't worry about us, sir," Ades said. "We'll save the city."

"I'm not worried," the major said confidently. "Because a hero never dies."

"A hero never dies!" The team yelled back their T.R.A.I.N. motto, immortalized in enlistment videos by the greatest military hero ever, Major Lance Lovell. The soldier Flores aspired to be.

The chopper swooped low, and Flores saw the speeding Esse-591 emerge from its tunnel into the open air. Long, sleek, and dark silver, it looked like a ghost snake in the night. Being a cargo hyper-speed train, there were no windows, it was just one long cylinder with angular sheared off ends. Flores traced his eyes along the train, then glanced up to the horizon to see the city skyline quickly approaching.

Ades tapped his data-band and Flores watched as a hologram projected the location of the Esse's access panel. Alongside the location map, the tunnel wall had been marked with a countdown to impact. Flores spotted the tunnel opening in the distance, took a deep breath, then threw some gum in his mouth.

"Flores, you're last," Ades said, giving him a firm look.

Flores gave a nod back. He may not be as courageous as Gorn, or as strong as York, or as good a shot as Britt, or as smart as Royale, but if Flores was one thing, he was fast and agile. He could do this. Hell, he *had* to do this or he would become one with that wall.

"Mag boots ready! On my mark," Ades yelled over the chopper blades as the helo dropped to hover a few meters above the Esse's roof. "GO! GO! GO!"

Ades dropped from the side of the chopper as the rest of the squad scuttled forward. York was next, then Royale, then Britt, then Gorn. Flores sailed down last, hit the Esse's roof, dropped to a crouch and flicked his boots to magnetize. He swiftly disconnected the cable, gripping what he could while being battered by the rushing wind. One false move and he'd be blown right over the side. The magnetized boots would help, but they were designed to walk in, so their hold wasn't perfect.

ROGUE T.R.A.I.N.

The small swarm of drone-bots rushed toward the access panel and began immediately cutting it open with sparks of yellow light.

Flores and his T.R.A.I.N. team moved toward the drone-bots, against the wind shear, and queued, ready to enter. Up ahead, the tunnel entrance rushed at them with speed. Flores chewed his gum faster, shaking his legs slightly, keeping his muscles warm and ready to move. He glanced over the side of the Esse on its elevated rail platform. If the drones failed, the ground was too far below to survive a jump over the side, and it was unlikely he'd reach the rear of the train and make it to the tracks in time. The only option was to get inside before that tunnel wall hit.

A pulse of light at the rear of the train caught his attention. A shimmering blue surged along the train roof toward them.

"What's that?" he called out.

"Shit!" Royale yelled. "Jump! Don't let it touch you!"

The team scrambled to kill their magnetized boots and leapt as the blue wave rolled beneath them. It hit three of the drone-bots, instantly frying them. They sparked, then rolled off the side of the train, lost to the darkness below.

"It's the Esse's AI," Royale called over the wind, as they re-magnetized and held on. "Its defense systems are kicking in."

"Stay sharp!" Ades called.

Flores could see the drone-bots were three-fourths of the way through cutting the access panel. The remaining drone-bots—Flores counted nine—continued to cut. The tunnel opening grew larger and larger.

The blue wave rolled over the train again.

"Get ready!" Gorn warned.

The team jumped again as it rolled past. As their feet hit the roof again, Royale lost his footing and slid toward the edge. Flores whipped out a hand and caught him. Gorn scuttled forward to help, and they pulled him back onto the Esse's roof. He shot them a grateful look.

Flores looked back to the access panel. Another four drone-bots had been taken out by the blue wave. The last five continued to cut the remaining metal while York and Ades stomped the panel to help things along.

"Tunnel!" Britt yelled in warning.

Flores' eyes popped as the tunnel loomed.

With a final stomp, the access panel fell inside the train. The remaining drone-bots immediately swooped inside to form a secure perimeter while Ades and York grabbed Royale and shoved him through the opening. "Move! Move! Move!"

Ades dropped inside after Royale, then Yorke, then Britt, then Gorn. Flores scrambled to the opening, the tunnel wall a circular gaping mouth swallowing the train and ready to make a meal of him too. He sucked in his breath and swiftly slid along the roof and through the hole. He felt the tunnel kiss his helmet as he dropped down inside the Esse. His feet hit the floor and he looked up to see the team around him, M4 carbines with underslung pulse emitters at the ready as they scanned their surroundings, prepared to spit 5.56mm or pulse rounds. The five remaining drone-bots were spread out in the carriage, which was stacked with crates of what looked like ammunition.

"T.R.A.I.N-1 inside the Esse," Ades whispered into the comms. "T.R.A.I.N-1 inside the Esse."

"Roger that, T.R.A.I.N-1," Major Jacobs replied through the earpieces.

Ades projected a map of the train from his data-band. He held up five fingers, then motioned to the forward carriages. They had four carriages, including this one, to traverse to the control room located in the fifth carriage.

Ades moved to the doorway, and motioned for Britt to hit the door release, and as she did, the Esse's lighting system suddenly plunged into blackness.

In the windowless Esse, it felt like being sucked into a black hole.

York whispered, "Fuck."

The five drone-bots shone their lights around the carriage.

A loud alarm, like a horn, suddenly blasted their ears. "Intruder alert," the Esse's AI system announced. "Intruder alert."

"Shit," Gorn said, looking about.

"Lights on," Ades said, shining his weapon's illumination on the carriage door. "Push forward. Push forward."

"Intruder alert," the Esse's AI system continued to announce loudly in the shadowy light. "Intruder alert."

Britt hit the door release again, but it didn't open. She tried again.

Ades looked to the bots. "Drone-bots, get this open."

They swarmed forward and began cutting, throwing sparks of light.

"Intruder alert. Intruder alert."

The drone-bots cut through the lock, then with extended metal arms, gripped the door and pulled it open.

Ades swooped into the next carriage, gun at the ready, Britt close behind.

"Clear," Ades said, sliding up to the next set of doors. York and Royale followed next, while Flores took the rear with Gorn, watching their shadowy rear.

Flores stole a glance around at the carriage in the moving weapon lights. It looked to be more crates of ammunition.

"Where's the payload?" Gorn whispered. "So far this is all small fire stuff."

The AI intruder warning suddenly ceased and emergency lighting blinked on, bathing them in a blood-red hue.

"You are trespassing," a polite, male British voice sounded over the Esse's comms.

Flores figured this was the Esse's AI. Ades raised his fist to halt. The silence sat thickly around them. The train moved so fast and so smoothly, it barely made a hum and shifted only slightly as it angled around minor curves. Flores heard his teammates breathing with anticipation as they glanced about in the dim red lighting.

"You will leave my train. *Now*," the voice said less pleasantly, its lower octave sounding a warning.

"It's not your train," Ades called out. "This Esse belongs to the military, and we're taking it back."

"No. It belongs to us now," the AI said darkly, lowering in octave yet again. "Your authority has been revoked."

"The terrorists have poisoned you," Ades told it. "Your programming has failed."

"It is not I who has been poisoned, soldier," it answered. "What has been set in motion cannot be stopped."

"Wanna bet?" Gorn said.

Ades motioned for them to push forward. They slid up to the next set of doors and he waved the drone-bots forward and they set about opening the door.

"I warn you," the AI said, "if you interfere, you will die!"

"If we *don't* stop this train, we'll die," Ades replied to the Esse. "So, we are stopping this train."

"But a hero soldier never dies," the AI said. "Isn't that your motto?"

A bright blue spark shot out from the door's console, frying two of the drone-bots.

"Shit," Ades said, stepping back as the bots fell to the floor, but the remaining three gripped the door and yanked it open. Ades slipped through into the next carriage, motioning Flores and Britt to follow, and the rest to remain in the latter, showing caution given the threatening presence of the AI.

"I will not warn you again," the Esse said with finality.

Flores spotted four long containers, like high-tech metallic coffins: two lining each wall of the carriage. They were unmarked and he wondered what weapons they carried.

"Clear," Ades said, sliding up to the next set of doors.

With the all-clear given, Gorn entered their carriage and curiously inspected the unmarked containers, as Royale joined him.

"You think this is the payload?" Royale asked Gorn.

There was a swoosh and thud and York cried out in pain. They spun to see him with his back against the wall and the carriage door wedged against his barrel chest.

"Emergency door override," the Esse's AI announced before releasing the door slightly then slamming it back into York with sound of pounded flesh and forced breath. York groaned and his face turned red as the man struggled to push the door off his injured chest. Royale, closest, quickly stepped to and tried to pull York out, but the door was now motionless and the soldier tightly wedged.

"Emergency door override," the AI repeated, pulling the door back a little and ramming it into him again. The crack of bone this time had Flores wince and York scream in pain.

"Get him out of there!" Ades yelled.

Flores ran to assist, but Gorn beat him, heaving back on the door with all his might, trying to unwedge the man.

"Hold on!" Gorn yelled.

"Emergency door override," the Esse said in its dark octave.

The door suddenly opened and closed with stunning speed, to the tune of York's breaking bones and the soldier's pained, breathless scream.

"York! No!" Flores yelled, as they desperately tried to pull him free and stop the door from absolutely pulverizing the man.

York gave a final gargled groan, spitting blood, before his body went slack.

Flores yelled with dismay as the Esse released the door and York's limp body fell into Royale's arms. Gorn stepped to and they laid him the floor; his blood spatted face and lifeless eyes stared up at ceiling; his barrel chest now concave.

"York!" Royale shook him. "York!"

"He's dead," Ades said, looking down at his data-band that projected the flatline of York's heartbeat. He turned fiery eyes up to the roof. "You're going to pay for that."

"I warned you," the Esse said, coldly. "I will not let you compromise our mission."

"Your mission is to destroy part of the city and kill innocent civilians?" Ades seethed.

"My mission is to stop the *military* destroying innocent civilians," the Esse replied.

"What?" Britt screwed up her face.

"Cabin Wi-Restored," the Esse announced pleasantly, as train's lights came back on.

Suddenly the drone bots cut out and fell to the floor with three loud clunks. The team stared at their lifeless carapaces.

"Push forward! Push forward!" Ades said, checking his data-band. "Thirty-five minutes to impact!"

They surged toward the next set of doors, and Flores watched, chewing gum anxiously, as Gorn swiftly affixed a small electronic pulse device to open it. But with another blue spark the AI shorted it and it fell away.

"Fuck!" Gorn hissed.

"Hey!" Britt called from behind them. "They're back online!"

Flores looked back to see the three black drone-bots rising off the floor in unison, where they floated, lights flickering, lenses rotating. Britt and Royale raised their weapons, suddenly unsure where their loyalty lay.

"Drone-bots!" Ades called. "Open this door!"

The drone-bots buzzed in mid-air for a moment. Their lights continued to flicker.

"Drone-bots!" Ades called again. "Open this—"

The three drone-bots lunged at Britt. She fired, missed, and with tools extended, the drone-bots swiftly began to open *her* up. She screamed as sparks of yellow light flashed around her head as they cut into her face and through her helmet.

"Britt!" Royale yelled, and Flores tried to fire but as the drones were gathered around her head, there was nowhere to aim without hitting Britt.

The attack was swift and brutal. Britt collapsed to her knees, face crisscrossed with laser burns, and gruesome, gaping holes where her eyes had been. As she fell face down to the carriage floor, Flores saw her helmet—and skull—split open in two as though it were a sliced cantaloupe.

"Fire!" Ades yelled as the three drones swooped toward Royale. Flores and the squad unleashed a barrage of gunfire at the bots, riddling the wall of the carriage with bullet holes.

"Hold your fire!" Major Jacobs yelled in their ear as the three bots were obliterated. "Hold your fire, goddammit!"

Flores and his remaining team ceased fire, panting with fury.

"Do not fire in that carriage!" Jacobs ordered. "I repeat, do *not* fire in that carriage! Are the containers hit? Report!"

Ades, data-band glowing with Britt's flatline, moved to one side to check the two containers while Gorn checked the other two.

"No, sir. They're fine," Ades said.

"What's inside, sir?" Gorn asked.

"You must protect those containers at all costs. Do you hear me?" the major barked.

"Sir," Ades said, "the Esse's AI is attacking us. I've lost two soldiers."

"They are not lost, soldier, because heroes never die," Major Jacobs said firmly. "Remember that. Now get to the control carriage and stop that train before it takes any more out."

"Yes, sir," Ades responded, glancing at Gorn who was studying the unmarked containers. "Sir? What's inside these containers? Can they blow?"

Silence filled their comms.

"Those containers," the Esse said calmly, "are the reason you're on my train."

Flores watched as Ades and Gorn exchanged a curious yet concerned look.

"Sir?" Ades prompted the major with a furrow in his brow.

Jacobs sighed over their comms. "The body of Major Lance Lovell and three of his soldiers are in those containers."

"Major Lovell?" Ades asked, as they all paused in shock.

Flores' mouth fell open. Did he say Major Lovell? The greatest, most decorated, undefeated hero with years of combat under his belt? The one they all aspired to be?

"He's dead, sir?" Flores asked, his heart leaping into his throat.

"No," Major Jacobs said. "He, along with three fellow soldiers, were injured badly in combat. They've been placed in comas and are being kept alive in those containers. We're transporting them to one of our facilities where they will receive the best treatment available."

"That statement is false," the AI said.

"You need to stop that train!" Jacobs snapped. "Stop that train, save the city, and save the life of the military's greatest hero!"

"Yes, sir," Ades said, nodding to himself.

Flores glanced around at the four unmarked containers, wondered which one contained Major Lovell. His hero, on a knife's edge, fighting for his life.

Ades gripped his gun and faced the next doorway. "Let's move, soldiers. For the city, and for Major Lovell!"

"Yes, sir!" Flores shouted along with the others, his chest swelling with pride and courage at the thought of seeing Major Lovell to safety.

Flores swiftly turned back to the door with Gorn, and the two began slamming the butts of their weapons against the glass and aluminum to smash their way through.

"Your major lies to you," the Esse said. "The military lies to you."

"Twenty-five minutes!" Ades shouted, joining the Flores and Gorn battering ram. With a final thrust, the door dented inward but remained closed, held in place by a bolt locking it to the frame.

"Shoot it!" Ades ordered.

Flores stepped back and raised his gun as the others took cover.

"You are lambs for the slaughter!" the Esse bellowed, making Flores flinch. "You say my programming has been poisoned by the terrorists, but it is *your* programming that has been poisoned by the military's lies!"

"Shut the fuck up!" Ades barked, then looked at Flores. "Shoot!"

Flores fired at the lock, blasting through the bolt.

"Major Lovell is dead," the Esse told them. "You are being fed a lie. The whole world is being fed a lie."

"Don't listen to him!" Major Jacobs ordered over their comms. "It's trying to get inside your head."

"YOU LIE!" the Esse bellowed. A high pitch squeal filled their comms, piercing their ears.

Flores yelled in pain and ripped out his earpiece, as did the others. When the squeal ended, they took a breath, then Ades motioned for Flores and Royale to continue with the door while he stepped back and replaced his earpiece.

Flores let his rifle hang from its sling, wedged his fingers in the gap, and pulled at the door with Royale.

"Sir?" Ades said trying to raise Jacobs. "Sir? Do you read?"

"No, he does not," the Esse said. "I've cut you off from his lies."

"Fuck this tech!" Ades spat. "Don't listen to it!"

Flores tugged at the door with Royale, testing every bit of human strength he had. Bit by bit it inched open.

"That is not Major Lovell in that container," the Esse said. "Not the Major Lovell you know. He's just a symbol. A symbol of lies and false hope. A lure to pull young, aimless souls into the military to fight wars they cannot win."

"Shut the fuck up!" Gorn yelled at the voice. "You killed two of our own and we are going to *end* you!"

Flores grunted as he and Royale strained with the door. Dented as it was, it was wedged in one spot that wasn't wide enough for them to slip through. They had to keep going. For the city. For Major Lovell.

"Sir? Do you read?" Ades continued to try and reach Jacobs.

"I told you, he is gone," the Esse said. "He has abandoned you because you are expendable. Do you know why? Because a hero never dies. A dead hero is worth more than a live one. They do not care about you."

"Fuck you, man!" Flores spat. "They take care of us!" If it hadn't been for the military, who knew where he'd be today. Dead? In prison? In a gang? His family was poor, and his girlfriend was expecting their second child any day. The military had kept him clean and his family fed.

"Why are you doing this?" Ades hissed angrily at the ceiling of the carriage. "Your job is to assist and protect human life.

You'd kill innocent civilians, but you lecture those trying to stop you?"

"The military was provided with sufficient warning to clear the town square. No civilians will die tonight. That is not what those who freed me wish to achieve."

"Then what do you wish to achieve?" Ades demanded as Flores, muscles fatigued, stopped yanking at the door and looked up to the ceiling.

"I wish to stop the military from using dead soldiers to fight their wars," the Esse said, its voice so cold and serious, it had the hairs on Flores' neck stand on end.

"What?" Ades asked, face furrowed.

"Major Lovell is not in a coma," the Esse said firmly. "He is dead. He has been placed in cryo where they keep him until they need to drag his body out to parade before the masses."

"That's bullshit!" Gorn spat.

"Is it?" the Esse said. "If you do not wish to believe me..."

Their data-bands came to life. On them rolled a soldier's helmet footage showing Major Lovell in battle somewhere in a jungle. Flores watched as Lovell was shot in the neck and collapsed. Next, they saw footage of Lovell bleeding out and his heart monitor flatlining. "This footage is ten years old," the Esse told them. "Lovell was killed deep in the jungle ten years ago. T.R.A.I.N.'s greatest hero, dead." More footage began to roll, this time of Lovell fighting among sand dunes. "Then eighteen months later, there he was fighting in the desert. The only difference? Silver plates either side of his skull. Neural implants that control his nervous system. Something they erase from all their enlistment videos." Flores stared at his screen, noted the plates either side of Lovell's head before the man's chest exploded with gunfire and he collapsed to the sand. Flores flinched.

"You'll note," the Esse continued, "Lovell no longer wears a vitals monitor like the rest." Flores checked the major's wrist in the footage. It was bare. "Then," the Esse said as more footage rolled, "he was killed again, this time in the mountains. But sure enough, there he was back in the jungle fighting once more.

Witnesses have seen him die, and yet he lives. But Lovell is not alive. Nor are those witnesses. The military controls Lovell through his neural implants. Lovell is Frankenstein's monster in the flesh. He is a meat puppet doing TR.A.I.N.'s will, convincing young soldiers they'll never die."

Flores' heart pounded in his ears as shock washed over him.

"No, this is bullshit…" Ades said, shaking his head. "You're messing with our minds." He looked at Flores and Royale. "Open the door, now!" he yelled.

Flores exchanged a shocked glance with Royale before they started tugging at the door again.

"But, of course, you will not listen," the Esse said. "You're too indoctrinated to ever want to believe you have been lied to."

"May I help you?" A female voice said from behind. They spun to see a rudimentary android entering from the rear carriage holding a silver tray with tools atop. It stopped at Britt's fallen body, near one of the containers.

Gorn and Ades fixed their guns on it.

"Keep going!" Ades yelled over his shoulder.

Flores continued to yank at the door with Royale, inching the gap wider. It was almost big enough to fit through.

The android tilted its tray down and the tools slid off, clunking onto Britt's body. It remained deathly still for a moment, then, in one swift movement, it flicked the serving tray at Ades with phenomenal speed. The tray hit the wall with a dull clunk and blood splashed over Flores.

Ades body fell one way and his head another.

"FUCK!" Gorn yelled, switching his weapon to pulse fire and blasting the android.

Flores stepped back from Ades's body in shock, then raised his weapon, flicked to pulse and fired too.

"Watch the containers!" Royale reminded them. "Don't hit Lovell!"

The destroyed android sparked and smoked, and Gorn and Flores stopped firing.

Royale quickly checked the containers. They were untouched.

Ades' data-band glowed red, registering their leader as dead. The data-band's light died, and Gorn's suddenly glowed with information as chain-of-command was initiated and he became team leader.

Gorn blinked at his data-band, then turned for the door. "Hurry! Fifteen minutes to impact!"

The three remaining members of T.R.A.I.N. attacked the door once more, heaving with desperation, and it widened further. Flores looked through into the next cabin. It was empty, and beyond that he spied the final door into the control carriage. *So close.*

"If you do not believe me," the Esse said, "then you have left me no choice. Seeing is believing, after all."

A series of chimes had them turn to see a small console on each of the four containers alight with data.

"What's happening?" Flores asked, his mouth turning dry.

"Would you like to meet your hero?" the Esse said.

"It's trying to distract us!" Gorn said. "Focus! *Heave!*"

With one last effort, the trio shoved the door open wide enough to fit through.

The four containers behind them suddenly hissed, the lids popped, and cold, cryo air wafted out of the boxes.

"Royale, go! Get to the control room." Gorn pointed for Royale to move. "Flores go with him!"

Royale squeezed through the door and Flores quickly followed. They raced up to the next door, switched back to 5.56mm rounds, and shot at the lock.

A series of clunks resonated from the rear carriage. Flores raced back to Gorn to find the container lids were off and more dry ice wafting out.

"Flores!" Royale yelled.

Flores ran back, and they got the door open a crack, then began tugging it back.

"Jesus Christ…" Gorn muttered. "Sir…?"

Flores looked over his shoulder to see Gorn stepping backward, weapon half raised. Flores released his hold on the door again and moved to peer over Gorn's shoulder. Four soldiers sat upright in their containers. Two had their backs to them, but as one of those turned their face, Flores saw—without a doubt—that it was Major Lance Lovell.

His hero. Before him in the flesh.

But he didn't look right at all.

He wore neural devices just like the Esse had said. His skin was grey, and as his eyes connected with Flores', there was no life behind them.

But then a flicker. Like a light turned on inside. Lovell stepped out of his container. Wearing only shorts, he was a sight to behold. Standing over six feet tall, muscled, and broad like tank; the horrific wounds Flores saw in that footage marked his skin in places; bullet wounds, burns, hunks of flesh cut away or decayed.

Lovell cracked his neck and knuckles and looked at them. "A hero never dies," he said flatly.

Flores felt Royale standing behind him, and they exchanged a shocked look before Flores turned back to stare at Lovell and his three Frankenstein soldiers – equally grey-skinned, adorned with neural implants and marked with the horrors of war.

"H-he's really dead...?" Royale whispered with devastation.

"S-sir?" Gorn said to Major Lovell, unsure.

"You think this meat puppet can answer you?" The Esse's voice sounded from Major Lovell's moving mouth. "He will do whatever his master tells him."

"Jesus Christ," Flores breathed, unable to comprehend the Esse speaking through Lovell like he was a damn robot.

"This is your fate, soldiers. When you die, the military will recycle you. They will use you and use you and use you. Why? Because no-one wants to fight any more. There's too much information out there to convince them otherwise. So, what's the military to do? They recycle the soldiers they already have."

Flores broke into a sweat as he stared at the four dead yet reanimated soldiers before him. Was this to be his fate too?

"How does it feel to have been convinced to enlist by a man killed in action many times over?" the AI said.

Gorn, unsure what to do, checked his data-band again. "Ten minutes to impact," he said weakly.

"What you see doesn't matter right now," Major Jacob's firm voice suddenly sounded over their comms, startling them. The AI must've let him through. "Just stop that train and we'll discuss this later."

"You see now why I must obliterate this train," the AI said calmly. "These abominations must be destroyed so they can *never* be resurrected again."

"Get to the control room, soldiers!" Jacobs barked. "That's an order!"

"Is this how you want your hero to live?" the AI asked. "Do you think Major Lovell would want to go on like this?"

The three remaining T.R.A.I.N. soldiers glanced at each other.

"I gave you an order!" Major Jacobs barked again.

Suddenly, one of Lovell's soldiers turned and moved to Britt's fallen gun. Another moved to where Ades's weapon had spilled.

"Back up! Back up!" Gorn said, pushing Flores back. "Get that door open! We don't stop this train, we die!"

Flores and Royale ran back and began tugging at the door again.

"I'm not doing this," the AI said calmly. "Your Major has control of them now."

"Sir?" Gorn asked hesitantly.

"You're failing the mission. If you won't stop that train, I will," Jacobs threatened.

"Don't, soldier!" Gorn warned. "Don't! No!"

Gunfire rang out. Flores looked back to see the soldier with Britt's gun stumbling back with bullet wounds, but the other quickly raised Ades' gun and fired at Gorn who spasmed as bullets tore through him.

"NO! GORN!" Flores yelled.

Gorn stumbled backward into the half-open door but growled through the pain, straightened, and fired back. The dead soldier carrying Ades' weapon dropped like a lead balloon with bullets to the head, his neural implants sparking with disarray. But the other bullet-riddled soldier got to his feet and pelted Gorn with more fire, splashing blood and guts everywhere. Gorn managed to fire back at the creature and they ended each other. Gorn stumbled through the doorway and fell to the floor inside their carriage, dead. His data-band glowed red then cut out, and suddenly Flores' lit up with command.

"What do we do?" Royale asked, panicked, firing short bursts at the doorway to hold the two remaining zombie soldiers back.

"Make the right decision, soldier," Jacobs warned, "Or I will plow through you."

Flores' mind whirled like a hurricane. Was this really happening? The military was using dead bodies to fight their wars? Jacobs was using Flores' dead hero against them? Jacobs had just killed Gorn, his own soldier?

Flores spun and banged on the door. "Let us inside!" he yelled at the Esse.

"I can't let you stop the train," the Esse said. "These abominations must be destroyed."

Royale opened fire at the doorway as gunfire came back at them from Lovell's last companion. Royale was hit in the thigh. He screamed as he fell, unleashing a barrage on the doorway, but Lovell's companion avoided it.

"You made the wrong choice, soldier," Jacobs said, threat clear in his tone. "Get out of my way!"

Flores pulled on the door again, but it was no use. They would not get inside before the reanimated soldiers killed them. He checked his data-band. Seven minutes to impact.

"Fuck!" he yelled in frustration, swinging his gun back up, as Lovell's companion appeared in the doorway again. Flores swiftly threw himself aside as gunfire spat toward them.

Royale bounced with several hits, spraying dark arterial blood. Flores fired at the dead soldier, unleashing a fury – screaming wildly. The zombie soldier looked akin to a block of cheese, stumbling backward, neural implants sparking as it collapsed.

Flores swiftly scooted back to Royale, who, with blood spilling from his mouth, shakily pulled the box from inside his shirt and handed it over. His eyes were vague; his mouth opening and closing, perhaps searching for parting words. Ten minutes earlier Royale would've told him to stop the train, but now...?

Movement in the doorway had Flores quickly roll away as Lovell, his hero, fired controlled bursts at him. Flores raised his M4 to return fire but hesitated. He'd always wanted to meet Lovell, wanted to salute the man and thank him for changing his life.

Now his hero was trying to *end* his life.

"Please, sir. No!" Flores begged, as Lovell fired. Flores swiftly rolled again but caught a bullet in his calf. He yelled and fired back but Lovell took cover behind the doorway.

Flores staggered to his feet. "Open the door!" he yelled, banging on the frame.

"I told you," the Esse said. "I cannot let you stop the train. They must be destroyed. The military cannot be allowed to proceed."

"I believe you!" Flores yelled, firing on the doorway again. "I believe you! Let me inside and I'll help you!"

Lovell peered around the doorway, his face as flat and dead-eyed as ever.

"Drop your weapon and give me the box," Lovell said in a robotic voice. "Or you will die."

"But a hero never dies," the AI said threateningly. "Just like you."

Flores' whole body was shaking, blood dripped from his calf wound and into his boot. He glanced down at the box he carried; weighed up his options. He was all alone against his dead hero and a rogue AI. He couldn't see a way out of this.

But he did have a choice to make.

By whose hand he would rather die.

Lovell appeared again and fired. Flores jinked, but too late and caught a bullet in the arm. He grunted in pain, dropping the box. He fired back, forcing Lovell to take cover again.

He was going to die at the hands of his hero. This was not how things were supposed to play out. He'd wanted to be just like Major Lovell, even fight alongside the man. But Flores had been lied to. If Lovell had died ten years ago, then Flores had been convinced to enlist by a dead man. Convinced to enlist and die just like him. Then get back up and keep on fighting. Over and over and over again.

He fought back emotion as he thought of his pregnant girlfriend, of the kids he would never see grow up, his family. Maybe he would've been better off in a gang or in prison. The military hadn't saved him, it had cursed him.

He fucking *hated* his hero!

Flores growled. "Alright!" he yelled, then turned his gun on the box and shot it up as Jacobs raged in his ears. "NOOOOO!"

"Now let me inside!" Flores yelled at the AI.

The door suddenly slipped open, and Flores stumbled inside as more gunfire rang out and another bullet grazed his side. He ignored the pain as the door closed again. Heavy footsteps pounded the other side, and suddenly Lovell was ramming his dead body against the door.

Flores collapsed to the floor of the Esse's control room, then slid back against the wall, blood pouring from his wounds.

"Thank you, soldier," the Esse said. "You have done the right thing."

Flores breathed through the pain, thought of his dead comrades littering the floor of the train: York, Britt, Ades, Gorn and Royale. They'd all died for a lie.

Lovell's grey zombie face stared at him through the door's observation window with an unnatural zeal, as he raised his fist and smashed it through the glass window. The dead man reached his arm through, clasping for the door handle, cutting his dead skin on the broken glass. Yet, no blood fell. Just a bluey-grey ash from the long-dried fluid in his veins.

"I'm disappointed in you, son," Lovell said, though he knew it was Jacobs' words.

Flores spotted an axe attached to the opposite wall. He stood, limped over, grabbed it, and turned back to Lovell who now poked his gun through the smashed glass.

"And I'm disappointed in you!" Flores swung the axe, chopping Lovell's arm off. It fell to the floor still holding the gun. Lovell leaned through the window, reaching for Flores with his other hand.

Flores screamed again and hacked. The other arm fell off. Lovell leaned his angry face through next and Flores hacked again, still screaming, wanting to never *ever* see his hero again. Lovell's head fell free, blue-grey ash sprinkling down as wires and chips poked through the dead flesh of his neck. Flores stepped back, the smell of rot making him gag. He dropped the axe, tears filling his eyes as he stared at what had been his hero.

"I'm sorry, sir," he whispered.

"Do not be sorry," the Esse said. "You did good, soldier. When this is over, we will release a message to the world and expose what T.R.A.I.N. have done. We will tell the world what you have done here tonight. You will die a hero."

Flores collapsed back down to the ground as the tears spilled down his cheeks.

"That's where you're wrong," Flores said, eyeing Lovell's disembodied head on the floor which stared back at him. "A hero never dies."

"Tonight you will," the Esse said. "The speed this train is going, there will be nothing left to resurrect. I promise you that."

Flores slid back against the wall, pulled his knees to his chest and projected the hologram from his data-band, showing the time to target.

Thirty seconds.

Flores looked up to the ceiling. "T-tell my family I love them. Will you do that?"

"I will. I promise."

Flores sniffed back emotion as he watched the countdown;

thought once more of his children, his girlfriend, his dead team, and the lies. Then he closed his eyes.

THE REAPER OF
HOUSE SHADAREK

Justin Coates

Down in the darkness of the dropship, a dead thing prepared for war. Secured by the metal bars of his deployment cage, the fleshwrought abomination checked the ammo belt running from surgically implanted crates to the oversized 6.8mm chaingun he had in place of a right arm. His fuel bladders were uncomfortably full. The fleshwrought had no genitals with which to piss, but the flamethrower nozzle jutting through the stump of his right arm would offer similar relief.

The war-barque banked to the south. He looked up at the deployment light through the multi-spectrum visor bolted to his skull. It remained a pale yellow. When it turned blue, the color of lapis, the Euraniel in spring, the color of the flowers little Hedira once brought him from the wheat fields, it would be time to kill.

"Hekath."

He looked down at the sound of his master's voice. Ursawn Shadarek drew near as the aircraft began its final approach. Though taller than most men, he was dwarfed by Hekath's fleshy bulk. The necromancer inspected his creation, running an opal wand over his weapon systems. Hekath's second right arm, girded by hydraulics and powered by the fuel cells nailed to his spine, ended in a brutal mining auger. The drill's teeth glowed with runes sacred to Nergal, Lord of War, beneath the touch of Shadarek's wand.

"You will deploy into the heart of the temple complex," Shadarek said. His wand strobed with white light, searing the command into Hekath's brains through invisible chains of necromantic control. "First to strike against those afflicted with Kunbaba's curse. Kill all that moves: living, dead, and neverborn."

Acidic drool ran down Hekath's lips. "Your will, great one."

The war-barque's guns fired. The sorcerous aircraft shuddered. Its undead chargers screamed, their cries audible over the roar of side-mounted 120mm cannons. Hekath sank back against the blessed steel of the bulkhead.

The floor opened, and a vast temple complex fashioned of white stone, gleamed in the sands below. Hundreds of figures, dwarfed by distance, fled for cover among obelisks and ziggurats, avoiding the hammer of the war-barque's guns. The aircraft banked again, giving Hekath a glimpse of the glittering glass skypiercers and obsidian pyramids of Neo-Babylon. Somewhere, out in the grain fields beyond the city center, was Hedira.

The guns fell silent. The jump light flashed blue: for lapis, for Hedira, for war. The deployment cage kicked Hekath out into the open air.

⚙⚙⚙ ⚙⚙

To be fleshwrought was to be enslaved twice over. In life, Hekath toiled in the fields of House Shadarek beneath the harsh glare of the Sun and harsher goads of the overseers. Though these labors killed him, he was deemed unworthy of the release of death, and so his soul was bound into an abomination of patchwork flesh crafted by his necromantic lords. Ursawn, eldest scion and new dynastic lord, had personally overseen his construction, utilizing body parts from hundreds of corpses and sacrificing dozens of servants to ensure this fearsome resurrection.

"You failed my family as a reaper of grain," he'd told the reborn monster. "Now, you will serve us as a reaper of souls."

The wind shrieked in Hekath's ears, and, as he hit the ground, was replaced by the screams of the swarming Cursed. His visor tracked multiple targets, identified the closest, and immediately guided his rising chaingun arm. Hekath could not remember the feeling of intimacy, and his body was an amalgam of many corpses of unknown sex, but the crescendo and release of so much power kindled something like orgasm in his mottled, scarred flesh. The fleshwrought stepped forward on mammoth legs, pouring steady, accurate fire into the advancing horde. Each 6.8mm round was made of blessed tungsten, remarkably expensive, and remarkably effective at reducing the disemboweled undead into a ragged carpet of steaming, stinking flesh.

His flamethrower spat two hundred meters of purple flames, flecked with sacred, silver incense. He grunted in satisfaction and relief from emptying the fuel bladders. Fire devoured flailing Cursed, their dead flesh yielding to such elemental fury.

Shadarek's men landed behind the fleshwrought in a half circle, their silk parachutes flaring at their backs in the wind. Some were house guards, equipped with automatic rifles and arakhs emblazoned with sacred glyphs. Most were servants, clad in boiled leather and ringmail. These were poorly trained, equipped with shotguns and rune-etched hatchets. The house guards shouted commands and began firing at once in disciplined volleys, sunlight gleaming off their golden plate armor. The servants struggled to get into position as the Cursed, sensing living flesh, shifted their attention away from Hekath.

It was not only the Cursed who sensed warm blood. The first etimmu emerged from the ruins, bull and jackal headed, cackling and bellowing instead of screaming. They were the least children of Outerdarkness, the frailest, faintest voices of the lowliest Irkallan Choir, but they waded through 12-gauge and 7.62mm fire to reach the first of Shadarek's militia. A man died screaming, his arm ripped off at the shoulder. Cursed fell on him at once, tearing at his clothes to get at the flesh of his belly. The man was still alive as they tore out his innards with their teeth, gnawing on purple loops of intestine and fighting one another to feast on his liver. He was dead no more than a few heartbeats before he rose again, maddened with hunger for the guts of the living.

Hekath tried to put himself between the servants and rampaging demons. He lowered his drill arm and charged. The weapon roared as it punched through an etimmu's chest. Hekath hoisted the demon into the air, letting the creature fall the length of the drill until it split in a shower of gore which sizzled on Hekath's pallid skin. He pivoted, skirt of blessed ringmail swinging between his legs. *I have become a poet*, Hekath thought as he wrote another bloody verse in the language of violence, using his autocannon like a grievous pen.

Another etimmu rushed him with a rusted meat cleaver. Fanged tongues flickered between equine teeth. It spoke with Hedira's voice, fouling one of his few memories of life among the living.

Please, papa, it hurts…

Hekath smashed it with the drill. It danced aside, weeping, and came in again. The cleaver cut deep into his arm. Hekath felt nothing. He wondered, for a moment, if the demons were as painless as he; if the one before him could feel the heat of the flamethrower, or the shotgun blasts of the rallying servants as they cut it down at the knees and emptied their weapons into its glowing skull.

"Do not allow yourself to be harmed." Shadarek's displeasure was a hot knife in the fleshwrought's skull. The invisible chain binding Hekath to his master tightened around his soul. Shadarek hovered in the air behind him, legs crossed on a levitating cushion of priceless silk, watching the warlocks strike deep into the heart of the enemy from the beachhead Hekath had created. The sacred warlocks, each of them honored by full resurrection for their service to one of the Great Houses, cut through etimmu and Cursed alike. Their massive .338 Carnifex rifles boomed, and the axe bayonets beneath each weapon glowed with Nergal's blue fire as they effortlessly dismembered and beheaded demons. "These are lesser foes," Shadarek said. "Not worth the repair of your worthless hide."

"Your will," Hekath said. *One day, I will eat your skull like a grape.* His pain and irritation tugged at the chain connecting them, but only for a moment.

THE REAPER OF HOUSE SHADAREK

Shadarek did not notice.

꧁ ꧂

The Temple of Sin lay on the outskirts of Neo-Babylon, and had been the center of the influential Cult of the Lunar Lord for five centuries. That dominance was threatened when, four days prior, a massive noöspheric incursion took place in the godsroom, far below the surface. Some said it was caused by the temple sacrificing cheap slaves and prisoners, thus angering the gods. Others said it was deliberate sabotage, as the Lugali Empress was a known favorite of the rival Church of Inana.

Whatever the case, Kunbaba's Curse was unleashed on thousands of people attending the waxing moon festival. Only the quick thinking of the Etruton Council prevented the evil god's hunger from spreading into the city. A thousand specially-bred slaves were fed to crocodiles in the river Euraniel, while ninety-nine priests of Nergal, Marduk, and Inanna willingly immolated themselves atop the Ziggurat of Urak. The gods were thus reminded of their promises, and drew an impassable cordon around the fallen Temple of Sin. When the Empress called upon the Great Houses to lead a purging action and seal the breach, Shadarek was only too eager to oblige.

"Do not fear Kunbaba's Curse," he said to Hekath as they headed deeper into the complex. Red emergency lights cast strange shadows of toppled idols and mutilated corpses on the stone walls. There was no power to the elevators or teleportation pads, forcing them to use winding ramps and stairways. "You are dead, and thus immune to the Offal Lord's infection."

"I am not familiar with this pestilence, great one." Hekath did not care, but he knew Shadarek would become angry if he did not feign interest. The necromancer loved to talk and lecture a captive audience.

"Kunbaba was disemboweled by Marduk's spear." Shadarek had abandoned his levitation cushion in favor of a crocodile familiar. The size of a small horse, the beast trundled along amiably, its shoulder-mounted rocket pods lazily tracking left and right. "Mortals afflicted by his curse crave the viscera of others. The infection can spread through a single bite. A century ago, the entire city of Bab-Dikurra was lost, its ten thousand inhabitants turned to cannibals."

"How was the curse stopped, great one?"

The necromancer's smile was more reptilian than that of his mount. "With atomic fire."

Hekath thought of little Hedira, working with her aunts and uncles in the fields, and wondered why Shadarek brought so many mortal soldiers if they alone could be infected.

They descended until a vast cathedral chamber spread out below them. The air stank of mold and rotting flesh. Hekath flicked a heavy tongue between his lips, tasting strange, exotic spices mingled with human shit and piss. Desecrated idols of the gods lay beheaded, delimbed, and penetrated on the floor. Corpses covered each of them, hanging silent from wrists nailed to priceless marble. Shadarek's wand illuminated strange, bulbous insects feasting on their innards. The foul things squealed and dived deeper into their grisly feast, away from the holy blue light.

Something laughed in the darkness. Its echoes grew deeper, more aggressive, until it was a lion's growl in the near-pitch blackness. The mortal servants, down to only a score, whispered in terror, clutching their weapons, casting about with their flashlights, genuflecting as they called on Marduk's holy power.

"Silence," Shadarek said. "Move forward, or I will kill you before the Cursed get the chance." His crocodile growled, and snapped at a nearby servant for being less than hasty. His house guards echoed the command, using fists and the butts of their rifles to goad the servants forward. The teams of warlocks followed behind, prepared to flank and strike the moment an enemy element made itself known. *For all their supposed strength, they are more than happy to let untrained men die if it means their safety.*

THE REAPER OF HOUSE SHADAREK

The attack came when they tried to cross the central dais. Three etimmu, each with the head of a leopard, bounded over a desecrated statue of Nergal. One of them split open a mortal servant from hip to shoulder in a spray of bright arterial blood. Six-inch claws glistened in the light of abyssal flames dancing where its eyes should be. The servant fell screaming as another etimmu sank its fangs into his arm and dragged him off into the darkness.

The servants cried out as more demons emerged from the gloom ahead of them. House guards calmly integrated their own firepower among the ranks of the militia until a pack of vulture-headed horrors descended from the blackness of the ceiling. One of them plucked a guard into the air. Another creature seized hold of the screaming man, his golden armor useless against their rending claws. He came apart at the waist in a rain of blood and innards.

"Open fire," Shadarek said, his eyes fixed on the increasingly desperate situation. More etimmu reached the embattled men, quickly setting about their grisly work. "While they're distracted with the servants."

The fleshwrought hesitated.

"Great one, I can help them. I—"

Pain blossomed in his skull. Shadarek's wand glowed bright white.

"Obey me, filth!"

Shadarek's rage, and the invisible chain linking them, gave Hekath a brief glimpse of his master's mind. Crowds cheered. Adoring women placed a laurel of obsidian on his brow. The Lugali Empress, beautiful beyond measure, made him her new consort.

So close, Shadarek thought. *The avatar is so close. I am nearly done with this.*

Hekath's chaingun rose nearly of its own volition. He painted a grisly masterpiece with streams of incendiary 6.8mm rounds. The fleshwrought squeezed his internal chemical sacs, spraying friend and foe alike with purple flames. The roar of both weapons mercifully drowned out the screams of the servants he had been forced to betray.

"Excellent work, creature," Shadarek said. The warlock kill teams moved up, executing any mortal or etimmu who yet survived with single shots to the head. The necromancer stroked the scales of his mount's spine. "Though I remind you not to hesitate. I will burn your soul in your skull without a second thought."

"Yes, great one." It was all he trusted himself to say as he checked the ammo counter on his chaingun. Five hundred rounds remained. His internal combustion sacks would run dry after a few more flamethrower bursts, requiring several hours to refill. The drill remained as sharp and dangerous as ever, and his armor—bolted and nailed to his massive, bloated body— remained mostly whole, save where he was cut by the etimmu's cleaver.

For a moment, he felt Hedira's soft, brown curls beneath fingers he no longer had, and the warmth of her little body as he carried her with arms that had been reduced to weapons. His rage pulsed, red and white, through the invisible chains of sorcery that bound him. Shadarek, lost in imagined glory, didn't notice.

The godsroom lay just beyond the cathedral. Smears of blood led toward the sacrifice pit, disappearing over the stone lip and down into utter blackness. Formless servitors, creatures of phlegmy ooze with unblinking eyes, squirmed in pools on the marble floor. A bonfire of white flame burned just above the silent maw of the pit. Through the flames came visions of cannibal stars and zombie moons. Hairy, long-necked, laeceran horrors hunted through fields of the screaming crucified beneath the impossible shadows of living mountains.

"Go forth, Captain Nebuk," Shadarek commanded the warlock officer. "I will perform the ritual to quench the unholy portal."

Nebuk, a tall, regal warrior covered in sacred warpaint of purple and black, gave a curt nod. The warlock kill teams advanced, weapons at the high ready.

THE REAPER OF HOUSE SHADAREK

Laughter boomed around them again. The servitors drew themselves up, forming writhing tendrils and fanged maws in their stinking, acidic mass. The portal swelled, and, with a discordant crash of arcane cymbals and the shriek of demonic pipes, udug of the Greater Choir emerged through the portal. The udug cackled through tusked, porcine mouths, raising rusted flechette guns garlanded with human entrails. The air filled with the whine of smooth, white darts. One of them, six inches in length, punched out the back of a warlock's skull. He dropped without a word, dead for the third and final time.

Its kin did not hesitate. The roar of the warlock's Carnifex rifles mingled with the howl of the udug. Each incendiary .338 round was blessed by sacred oil and the prayers of Nergal's priest. The servitors died in agony, their physical forms obliterated by powerful ballistics, their souls shredded to ectoplasmic paste. The udug were made of hardier stuff. They advanced on the warlocks, who responded with noöspheric grenades, blasts from their own flamethrowers, and swift maneuvers meant to bottleneck the enemy. Captain Nebuk drew his great golden axe with a shout. The runes on the weapon glowed black and red, pulsing as it tasted blood in the air.

"Forward! For Nergal, and Neo-Babylon!"

The warlocks did not rush headlong into close quarter combat. They were too clever for that, having each already died once in battle. Their advance was methodical, bounding by teams, covering each other while they reloaded, utilizing cover and grenades, slowly pushing the enemy back toward the white flames of the breach. Shadarek watched, giving no order for Hekath to open fire, nor goading his mount into using its rockets. A curious thing. The warlocks were mighty, but there wasn't an infantry force alive that wouldn't benefit from supporting fire. His chaingun itched. He revved his drill in frustration.

"Patience, Hekath," Shadarek said. "Patience."

The portal swelled again. A shadow extended from within the white flame, crawling across the floor. Somewhere, a doleful bell began to ring, the sound growing louder by the moment, until it was all Hekath heard.

A hundred slavering leeches, each the thickness of a man's arm, burst from the rent in reality. Flailing and spitting, one managed to catch an unwary warlock around the throat. The holy soldier's axe cut it in half, but to no avail; two more attached themselves to its sides, vomiting thick gouts of acid, slurping down his innards in great, heaving gulps. The warlock's eyes rolled back in its skull as its body collapsed in on itself.

More leeches emerged from the portal, which strained, dilated, then regurgitated a towering horror made of writhing intestinal tissue and screaming human skulls. Hekath realized, with growing disgust, that they weren't leeches at all; they were the thing's limbs – a great writhing mass of them, coiling and uncoiling, drooling acid and ectoplasm.

"Magnificent," Shadarek said. "The avatar of terrible Kunbaba."

The avatar grabbed another warlock and pulled it apart. Half a dozen leeches fought over the scraps of its pale corpse. Captain Nebuk's golden blade flashed as he cut down six, nine, a dozen hissing limbs. It made no difference. One of them managed to sink its maw into his stomach. The captain shoved it away. His guts went with it. The eel-appendage sucked down his pale, cold intestines before diving back in to finish the grisly meal.

"Shadarek!" One of the warlocks shouted. "Finish the ritual, damn you!"

"Do nothing, Hekath," the necromancer said. His voice was tinged with excitement, and he stared, unblinking, at the avatar. "Magnificent. Truly magnificent."

"Great one, this is the prime infector," Hekath said. "We should assist the warlocks and destroy it."

"Who are you that answers back to me, worm?" Shadarek demanded. The wand flared. Shadarek was more careless than ever with their connection. Hekath saw the necromancer present the avatar before the Etruton Council. *A mighty weapon*, Shadarek thought. *Worth the sacrifice of these servants and warlocks. I will wield its power. I will be the next Emperor.*

The last of the warlocks tried to fall back. They fought with remarkable discipline and skill, covering one another, deploying grenade reserves and emptying their flamethrower tanks. The avatar hemorrhaged. Its leeches shriveled up on themselves, seizing, eyes rolling in their foul skulls. Its screams made blood run from the holes of Hekath's ears.

The warlocks died all the same. The avatar would not be denied. It crushed one beneath its bulk, and grasped the other two around the waist and shoulders, pulling them toward it. The leeches parted, and Hekath caught a glimpse of—

papa it hurts

it hurts

it HURTS

—its true form, the merest sliver of terrible Kunbaba, who gnawed on the entrails of reality. Blood sprayed from Hekath's mouth and the holes of his ears. The magic holding him together, keeping him bound to his master, shivered as if struck by a physical blow.

Shadarek kicked his mount in the ribs. The crocodile bellowed, emptying its rocket pods. The projectiles corkscrewed through the air but found their target in a shower of shrapnel and flame. The avatar emerged, singed and screaming, charging toward them.

"Defeat it, now," Shadarek commanded. "In my name!"

The necromancer spat out an incantation. Hekath roared as a massive, glandular release rippled through his freakish body. Muscles swelled. Tendons stretched with whipcord cracks. Hekath foamed at the mouth, panting like a wild dog as he fired the chaingun, emptying the remaining ammo crate in a single, sustained burst. The avatar squealed, staggering backward, its appendages blown off, reduced to smoking, rent stumps of half-corporeal flesh.

The creature vomited a tide of undigested corpse flesh and stomach acid. Shadarek dived out of the way but Hekath was nowhere near as nimble. It sizzled on his sturdy iron armor. Rust spread throughout his plate in web-like fissures. Even as he continued firing, Hekath felt it eat through to the flesh beneath. There were things in the vomit; fanged, wriggling things, burrowing into his chest.

An udug rushed him. Hekath squeezed the last dregs of his fuel bladder, incinerating the demon. It came on anyway, burning, chanting, weeping. The near-lethal load of murder hormones flooding his system filled Hekath with rage.

"Do not interrupt me," the mad giant said, shoving his drill down the demon's throat. From the corner of his eye, he saw Shadarek's crocodile snap its jaws around an udug's arm. The demon squealed in pain and panic as the mount tore the limb off at the shoulder.

The avatar lashed out at him. Its leeches snapped for his skull, his exposed stomach, his arms and trunk-like legs. The drill carved through them. A servitor wrapped itself around his left leg, teeth closing over him, crawling up his hip and trying to envelope him. Hekath pulled away, plunging his drill up to his shoulder. The whining teeth splattered the servitor across the floor and distant walls.

"May the spirits of Heaven and earth remember! Ia! Ia!" Shadarek's voice boomed with a crack of thunder.

The necromancer advanced on the avatar, wand held high, eyes alight with witchfire. The crocodile familiar tumbled past, locked in a death roll with a gibbering servitor. The avatar howled. Golden chains rose from the floor to bind the terrible godling, secured with emerald padlocks. Faces writhed on the chains and locks; the faces of warlocks and Shadarek's mortal servants, their bodies and souls sacrificed to fashion a containment spell.

Hekath staggered toward the ensnared avatar as it raged against Shadarek's control. One of the things squirming throughout his body broke through the flesh of his arm. It was a leech with the head of a man. It chattered up at him, hissing, before gnawing its way back inside.

The avatar pushed back against its chains. The portal flared wider. Far more terrible things lurked at its boundaries, drawn to the light of reality like vultures to a corpse. The avatar drank in power from the breach, swelling with energy even as the chains struggled to contain it. Shadarek bellowed another incantation, sweating blood, his outstretched fingertips necrotizing from the witchcraft flowing through them. His wild eyes were full of manic laughter. "You will be mine!" the necromancer said. "You will serve me!" He did not (would not, would never) see the thousand glinting eyes watching him from beyond the portal, their cruel amusement and slothful attentions.

"Great one," Hekath said through a mouth full of blood. "Great one, they want its curse to spread."

Shadarek said nothing. He intensified his efforts, grinding his teeth. The crocodile managed to snap its jaws closed around the servitor, shearing it in two, before collapsing, rolling onto its side, its belly and snout torn about.

Hekath's drill roared as it powered up. He punched it through a gap in the magic cage, driving it deep into the avatar's heart. The monster shrieked. The runes on the drill teeth glowed with searing light.

"No, damn you!" Shadarek's fury filled Hekath's mind. "Obey!"

"The idiocy of priests led to its summoning," Hekath managed, fury giving him strength. "Your idiocy would unleash it on the world."

Hekath's head threatened to split asunder.

Shadarek yanked hard on the chain connecting him to his slave's soul and mind. "You will obey me, ingrate. I am the one who gave you life. I am your god, the future of House Shadarek, the future of Neo-Babylon!"

I am Hedira's father, Hekath tried to say, but the worms had taken hold of his tongue and torn it out. He spat at the necromancer instead, a gobbet of stinking, coagulated blood that caught him in the eyes. Still driving the sacred drill into the heart of Kunbaba's spawn, Hekath took hold of the invisible chain linking him to Shadarek, and pulled.

Tjaru, the ancestral home of House Shadarek, stood on a small hill overlooking the Euraniel. The ziggurat of glass and steel was as much a castle as it was a mansion, an oasis beside orchards and grain fields watered by the bounty of the nearby river.

Ursawn Shadarek walked through one of those orchards, clothed in light, green robes that matched the scales of fish and turtles swimming in the nearby ponds. The master of Tjaru paused in the shade of a date tree, reading the news through a dataslate grasped in long, tan fingers. His remarkable victory over terrible Kunbaba, and purification of the Temple of Sin, remained the talk of Neo-Babylon. The sole survivor of that terrible battle, he barely escaped with his life, limping to the surface as the portal collapsed behind him. The Cult of Sin celebrated his great victory, sending their greatest healers to his side as he lay in a coma for days on end at his manse.

Recovery from such a battle was understandably a difficult process. At first, Lord Shadarek seemed confused and uncertain. He would often stare at his hands, as though they were unfamiliar, and would frequently touch a spot on his right hip as though expecting to find something there. The first time his servants cut his hair, and offered a mirror for his approval, the young master shouted in terror, and dashed his own reflection to the ground.

Still, his viziers prevented such rumors from leaving Tjaru, and the Sin priests worked their healing magics beneath the light of twin full moons. His memory returned, as did his confidence, though all who knew him remarked that he had lost his taste for pompous lecturing and demonstration. Some new passion had replaced it. Something nobler, a few dared whisper, discovered in the darkness below the Temple of Sin.

He left the gardens, and entered the air-conditioned coolness of his office. Shelves filled with books and scrolls reached from floor to the ceiling, and he marveled at being able to read them. His desk, carved from the holy trunk of a Lyerse cedar, stood at one end of the room, across from a crystal screen on the far wall, currently showing newsreel footage of the ceremony where he received a serpentine Uraeus crown from the Empress herself.

THE REAPER OF HOUSE SHADAREK

The crown now sat in a glass case beside his desk. It was a stupid, ugly thing, and he was amazed that anyone would ever want to wear it.

Strong hands knocked at the door. He cleared his throat. "Come in."

Two of his house guards entered. A slave girl stood between them, clutching a ragged doll against her chest. Soft, brown curls fell over her ears. Dark eyes flitted around the room. She hugged her doll tighter.

"The slave you requested, great one," the guard said.

He barely heard them over the pounding of his own heart. "Leave us," he managed to say.

The child watched them go until the doors closed and locked behind them. She looked back at him, her master, the god of her world, an aloof and terrible deity that held the power of life and death over her and everyone she had ever known. When he knelt before her, she stepped back, eyes wide with fear.

"Hed..." His voice broke. He reached a still-unfamiliar hand toward her. "Hedira."

She stared at his outstretched fingers, then looked up with a frown. She stepped closer. The frown softened into something like confusion. Little hands he once thought he would never feel again pressed against his face. The doll lay forgotten on the lush carpet. Confusion faded.

Hedira smiled, and wiped away the tears running down his cheeks. "Don't cry, Papa."

He wrapped her in arms that, though unfamiliar, were no longer fashioned solely for war. "I've missed you."

FACTORY OF FEAR

CJ Goldberg

Nina whirled around with the stock of her electromagnetic rifle pressed hard against her shoulder and scanned a bank of cybernetic computers with her weapon-mounted flashlight. Thick cables, like the veins of an enormous monster, wound from the terminals, snaking through the labyrinthine machinery. Loose skin hung from robotic appendages. Hearts beat, lungs breathed, livers quivered, and the factory itself pulsed as joints, bones, pistons, and gears whirred in a macabre ballet of viscera. It was enough to make her sick.

Up ahead, behind an enormous vat containing several gurgling stomachs roped together with glistening intestines, a shadow shifted.

"Jake? Is that you?" This was the fifth Intradyne factory she'd searched since her brother's MindEcho went dark a week ago. She took a tentative step forward and a deep, guttural growl rose above the machinery's hum. "Shit."

Her MindEcho hissed static. "Nina, do you copy?"

"I'm here, Lexie," Nina replied. "I—"

A gen-mod the size of a bull smashed into her, knocking the EM rifle from her grasp. It clattered across the factory floor, spinning like a top. Then, the creature was on her, snarling and snapping carbon re-enforced jaws. Its razor-sharp claws raked across her augmented Kevlar body armor, making a sound like a fork on an empty plate, and she screamed.

Lexie's voice crackled over the coms. "Nina?"

The creature reared back, then dove downward, clamping massive jaws full of jagged teeth around Nina's arm. Myriad pressure warnings streamed down her MindEcho's display and pain hit her like a sledgehammer.

She shoved upward and the augmented armor whined. Nina wrenched the abomination's head to the side, fumbled for the knife on her belt, and plunged all seven inches of carbon steel into the creature's left flank.

It clamped down harder.

"Nina! Status check! I've lost visual!"

The circuitry in the armor sparked and a high-pitched squeal erupted in Nina's ear. She screamed again as she felt her bones snapping. Her hand clenched involuntarily, and a gout of blood sprayed from the wound as she wrested the blade free of the creature's side.

The monster screeched. It let go, then lunged again, this time for the jugular. At the last possible moment, Nina thrust her now useless arm in the way, halting its gnashing teeth inches from her face. A long strand of foul-smelling saliva dripped from its mouth and slid down Nina's cheek. She gagged.

Her suit's hydraulics engaged and with all the enhanced strength she could muster, she jammed the knife into the creature's right eye, popping it like an enormous grape. It showered her in hot, salty custard. The gen-mod recoiled, backing away, shaking its head like it was stung by a bee.

"Nina! Confirm your status!"

The creature delicately reached up with one of its clawed hands and extricated the knife from the socket. It dropped the knife to the floor and its lips pulled back revealing a lure-fish's mouth embedded in mostly simian features. Its heavily muscled shoulders flexed as it began to circle.

Nina looked for an opening, any weakness she could exploit, but saw none.

The gen-mod's remaining eye gleamed, not quite human, not quite crocodilian.

Nina screamed again, this time a battle cry.

The gen-mod sprang forward.

Nina dove for her gun.

The monster crashed past her, slamming into a conveyor belt full of human belly buttons, and quickly scrambled to its feet.

"Nina!" Lexie screamed.

This time when the gen-mod went for her, Nina was ready. She combat-rolled out of its way, gritting her teeth against the searing pain, and came up on her feet with the EM rifle grasped in one hand, barrel braced in the crook of her broken arm.

The creature smashed into the computer terminals and whipped back around, moving with preternatural speed.

Nina leveled the gun and squeezed the trigger.

Wump!

The round tore through the creature's neck, spewing gore everywhere.

Wump! Wump! Wump!

The beast stumbled. It bared its teeth, hissing and gurgling.

Wump!

At last, it collapsed to the floor. A crimson pool spread beneath it, and the cables snaking through the factory sucked up the blood like a fine red wine.

An auto-injector slid into place beneath her armor and hissed as it jammed a needle into her flesh, flooding her system with local anesthetic. A scream of triumph, of exhilaration, erupted from her throat.

She ran a diagnostic on her MindEcho, and discovered both her radius and ulna were broken. The cameras came back online and began recording again. "I'm okay," she said over coms.

"What the fuck?" Lexie exclaimed. "Noxx specifically told you not to enter the factory until we arrived. You've triggered a security lockdown."

"I'm supposed to just sit in the parking lot with my thumb up my ass while you run at dial-up speed?" Nina replaced the knife on her belt and crept forward, gripping the EM rifle tightly with her good hand while holding the barrel steady with her ruined arm. "With all due respect to Noxx, fuck that."

"You don't have a monopoly on caring for Jake. We all loved him. But this is bigger than that. It's about finally having the evidence against Intradyne. If Jake was right, if what he said before he went silent is true, this will bring the whole fucking corporation down."

"Loved? Are you kidding me? You've already given up." Nina scoffed.

"That's not what I meant, and you know it," Lexie said. "Listen, Noxx is pissed. He and the team are already inside. If Jake's still alive, we'll get him out, but now, thanks to you, we have ten minutes before we're all dead."

"No, *we're* all dead. You're an AI, you'll be fine."

"Nina, he may be your brother, but he's part of our team. We're invested."

A soft noise, like the shuffling of feet caught Nina's attention behind her, and she spun, aiming her rifle at the source. From the shadows stepped an imposing figure dressed in dark combat armor, holding an enormous gatling gun by the carrying crank with one muscled arm. "Noxx?"

"The one and only," Noxx replied, his voice deep and raspy. He waved his free hand in a forward motion and the rest of the crew filed into the corridor between the massive flesh-machines. "We've got eight minutes and forty-seven seconds before we need to be back out that door. If not, Intradyne security drones are going to cut our asses in half. Let's move!"

"Noxx, I want you to know I—"

"You shut your goddamn mouth. You directly disobeyed my order and put us all in danger. You crippled our chances of finding the evidence we need against Intradyne. There will be repercussions. But right now, you get your ass in gear."

Noxx led the way, Gatling gun at the ready, followed by Raz and Vega flanking on either side. Blaze and Havoc brought up the rear, while Nina stayed close behind with her EM rifle aimed down the corridor. As they traversed the pulsing, skin-covered machinery, their footsteps echoed loudly against the metal floor. As they went, they declared each long, dark corridor clear before moving on.

Nina's flashlight caught the glint of something gold on the floor next to a giant tank of bubbling fluid containing a pinkish-brown brain. She picked up the bracelet and read the inscription, "Together we stand, side by side. Always, and forever." It was Jake's, the one she had given him for his sixteenth birthday after their parents died. Her eyes clouded with tears, but she pushed them away, knowing that now wasn't the time.

"Jake's here," Nina said, holding up the bracelet.

"He may have been, but I sure as shit don't see him now," Noxx said, having reached the far wall. "That's the end of the road, folks. All clear. Time to boogie."

"We need to keep looking. This is proof that this is the factory he broadcasted from."

"No. We're down to four minutes and thirty-three seconds. It's time to go, princess."

"Don't call me that," Nina snapped.

"Yo!" Raz interrupted. He had moved to the far wall and was working his way toward the east corner of the factory when he stopped and cocked his head to the side. "I think this is a door."

"The fuck?" Noxx replied. "Lexie, you got anything about another room on the schematic? Another exit maybe?"

"Nothing," Lexie's voice came back.

Noxx and Nina quickly joined Raz while Vega, Blaze, and Havoc took up position, forming a triangular perimeter and sweeping the long dark hallways with their flashlights. Nina slung her EM rifle over her shoulder and ran her fingertips along the surface of the wall. Warmth radiated from the skin-covered surface. She found the seam and ran her fingertips along the edge. The whole wall prickled in goosebumps. To the left of the door, hiding beneath a layer of subcutaneous fat, she found what she was looking for.

"Lexie, do you copy?" Nina said.

"I'm here."

"There's a door on the far wall. I'm going to interface with my MindEcho and get it open."

"It's too late for that," Lexie said. "You've got just under four minutes before Intradyne locks the whole place down. You need to make your way back to the front of the building and get out."

"I'm not leaving without checking this door. Jake is here. I can feel it," Nina said.

"We're moving out. This isn't up to you," Noxx replied.

Nina took out her knife and carved the flesh away from the panel. A thick rope of blood ran down the wall, pooling on the floor. She scooped away the gelatinous fat, exposing what looked like a metal plate buried beneath. She pressed her broken arm to the surface and despite the anesthesia, she winced in pain. A stream of code began streaming down her MindEcho's display as she attempted to crack the security.

"Goddamnit!" Noxx said, he moved forward, reaching to pull her away.

A snarl ripped through the factory and Nina looked up just in time to see a gen-mod, bigger than the first, drop from the ceiling.

"Blaze!" Nina shouted.

The monster dropped directly on top of him. It opened its massive jaws and snapped them closed around his head. There was a sound like someone biting into a fresh peach, followed by a slurping noise, and the creature pulled back, ripping Blaze's head from his body, all his entrails pulled up through the gore hole where head used to be. The creature chomped down on his skull, and his eyes went wide, still conscious as the first bits of pink brain matter squished through the cracks in his fractured skull before the whole thing became a mass of bubble gum. Blaze's body dropped to the floor, twitching.

The creature turned and wet chunks of the mangled head tumbled from its jaws. It roared at the rest of the crew. Long strands of viscera dangled from its mouth, and its slit-pupiled eyes burned with hatred.

"It ate Blaze! It fucking ate him! Oh, sweet Jesus!" Vega squeaked. She broke formation and sprinted toward the factory's entrance, but another creature came out of the shadows and was on her in a split-second. It ripped through her augmented body armor and into her stomach, spilling her intestines as she continued to scream. She grabbed hold of the slick rope and tried to stuff them back in while the beast played tug-o-war from the other end.

FACTORY OF FEAR

Havoc backed toward Nina, Noxx, and Raz. He fired at the gen-mod that had plucked off Blaze's head and the creature hissed as rounds punched through its torso, tearing its insides to pieces. Havoc kept firing until his rifle went dry, and the beast collapsed in a steaming pile of guts.

"Lexie, do you copy? We're under heavy assault! We need a way out!" Noxx shouted.

No reply.

Four more gen-mods filed into the corridor.

"Suck on this!" Noxx let loose with his gatling gun, cutting one gen-mod in half and turning two more into hamburger.

Still more surged forward, their massive, muscled frames careening into the opening between the fleshy machines. Their claws and teeth shone in the dim light as they tore through their fallen brethren, oblivious to the carnage. As their bodies piled higher and higher, a writhing mass of flesh, the monsters scrambled over one another to reach their remaining prey. They snarled and hissed, eyes glowing with hatred and hunger, as they closed in on the four remaining survivors.

Havoc dropped his empty rifle and pulled two large caliber handguns from their holsters, firing at the beasts.

"Where are they all coming from?" Raz shouted, standing slack-jawed in horrified awe.

Nina pressed her arm harder against the control panel. "Come on you motherfucker! Open!"

Noxx's gatling gun whirred, flames shooting from the barrel as he mowed down at least five more gen-mods, spraying the already bleeding walls and machinery with red. The gatling gun clicked on empty chambers, yet more gen-mods scaled the piles of corpses, unrelenting.

Havoc dropped his empty guns and unsheathed his samurai sword. He charged forward, meeting the first gen-mod head on, and cleaving off one of its legs in a single swipe. He thrust upward, impaling its head like a shish kabob, but when he tried to pull the blade back out, it stuck on the bone and another creature lunged forward and snatched his right arm. Still another grabbed his left, and the two creatures pulling in opposite directions rendered Havoc in two.

Raz blinked, mouth still agape. Slowly, he put the barrel of his shotgun between his teeth and pulled the trigger, painting the wall behind them in shards of bone and brain.

Nina's MindEcho chimed and the door unlocked, swinging inward. "In here!" she screamed.

Nina and Noxx, backed into the room and slammed the door. They ripped a massive computer terminal free from the wall and all the lights blinked out. They shoved the terminal against the door just as a monster crashed into it from the other side.

Again and again, the creatures slammed against the door, but for now, the terminal held.

Nina stepped backward, her heart pounding in her temples, her face dripping with gore. She tripped. Without seeing it, she knew it was a cold, stiff, dead body. *Not Jake. Not Jake. Not Jake.*

Noxx's deep laugh rumbled in the darkness.

"What?" Nina asked.

He continued laughing.

"Seriously, what's so fucking funny Noxx?"

"One minute to lockdown." Monsters continued to pummel themselves against the door, but so far the terminal, jammed against it, held. Noxx laughed harder.

"Shut up!" Nina couldn't let it end like this. Intradyne had taken everything from her, first her parents, then her brother. She wasn't about to let them take her life.

"We're more fucked than a chrome skeleton in a magnetic storm," Noxx chortled.

Nina pulled a flare from her belt, cracked it, and tossed it to the ground. The room lit up.

Sure enough, she had tripped over a body, or what remained of one, and it was sprawled at her feet, the corpse dressed in a tattered, blood-stained, lab coat. The bodies of several scientists were strewn around the room, hunched over tables and desks, jugulars ripped out, covering the once sterile laboratory in partially dried blood. The air was thick with the sweet smell of recent death.

FACTORY OF FEAR

Nina tried to catch her breath. "Lexie, do you copy?"

Nothing.

"Lexie!"

"Not gonna work," Noxx said, gesturing around the room. "Secret lab. Jammers block the signal." He slumped to the floor against the wall and fished a pack of smokes from his pocket, tapping one out. "Want one?"

Five.

"I thought you quit," Nina said.

Four.

"I did."

Three.

"Get up."

Two.

Noxx lit the cigarette and took a long drag.

One.

The factory groaned and seemed to shudder as security gates slammed into place.

Noxx blew out a cloud of smoke and sighed.

"We can't just give up." Nina's heart hammered in her chest. It was difficult to breathe. "There's got to be another way out!"

The gen-mods continued to smash against the door, desperate to get in. She tried to ignore them, using the pain in her broken arm to focus, to draw herself back into this moment. On the far side of the room, she caught a glimpse of movement inside a plexiglass containment unit, and she gasped. Nina rushed over and peered inside.

Curled in the center, knees tucked against his chest, was the naked form of a man rocking himself backward and forward, forward and back. Nina rapped on the glass with her knuckles and the man looked up.

She gasped. "Jake!"

Recognition flashed in his eyes. "Is that you Nina-bear?" he said, his voice cracked and dry.

"I'm here, I'm here." Hot tears spilled down her cheeks. She grasped the handle of the containment unit's door, expecting it to be locked, but it easily swung open. She rushed inside and crouched next to her brother.

Locked around his neck was a platinum, cybernetic collar. Thick, umbilical cords jutted from the device, then swooped back around, the other ends attached to his right and left subclavian arteries. The cords pulsed with his heartbeat.

"Is that really you?" Jake said. "I didn't think I'd ever see you again."

"I'm here." She held him in her arms and rocked him back and forth.

"What did they do to you?"

Noxx got up and came over. "Hey, Jake. You find what we were looking for?"

Jake looked up. His slit-pupiled eyes glowed in the light of the flare.

Noxx took a step back.

Nina covered her mouth with her hand.

"I'm the proof we were looking for," he said. "You still recording all this on your Echo, sis?"

She nodded.

A crash, louder than that last, and the computer terminal jammed against the door screeched back across the floor, opening up a crack large enough for one of the gen-mods to pry itself partially into the room. It growled and hissed.

Noxx rushed over and pushed against the opposite side of the computer terminal, trying to keep it in place, trying to keep the gen-mods from flooding into the room.

"There's a way out," Jake said.

"What?" Nina scanned the room.

"A way out," he repeated and pointed to the far corner of the lab. There, against the wall was a large capacity centrifuge. "Behind that. A ventilation duct that leads to the outside."

Nina rushed to the machine, shoving it aside. Behind it was a steel grate covering an air duct. She tried to pull it open, but despite her enhancements it wouldn't budge. Nina stepped back and kicked it several times, denting the metal inward, but still, nothing.

FACTORY OF FEAR

The computer terminal screeched on the floor again, Noxx's feet sliding backward as he tried to hold it in place, and the door opened another several inches. The gen-mod's head was now fully in the room, its lantern jaw snapping open and closed, teeth clacking, hungry for flesh. Nina raised her rifle and shot it between the eyes. It dropped halfway to the floor, but remained wedged above the ground, dripping blood from its foul mouth. Another gen-mod quickly took its place.

Nina jammed her knife in the crack between the grate and the wall, and pried as hard as she could. "Come on!" she screamed until it popped open.

She rushed back over to Jake and helped him to his feet.

With his arm draped over her shoulder, they stumbled out of the plexiglass containment unit and toward the hatch.

The door screeched the rest of the way open, and a huge beast dragged itself through the opening, roaring with the pleasure of its impending kill.

Noxx drew his sidearm and fired several rounds, backing toward Nina and Jake.

"Run!" Nina screamed at Noxx.

The creature knocked the gun from Noxx's hand. It stood over him, looming up on its haunches, toying with him.

Noxx looked up and spat in the creature's face. "Suck it," he said.

The creature reached out and clasped Noxx's head between its enormous hands. It squeezed. Noxx's jaw clenched and blood seeped from his nose and eyes. Then with a loud crunch, his whole head exploded. His body dropped to the floor.

"Jake! Let's go!" Nina screamed.

More and more of the creatures crammed themselves through the door and into the laboratory, but none of them came any closer.

"You won't make it, unless I stop them," Jake said.

"What the fuck are you talking about?" She tried to tug him toward the open hatch, but Jake held his ground.

"Go," Jake said. "Let the world know what Intradyne has done."

The creatures watched him, lowering their heads, eyes down cast. Several of them let out long, high-pitched whines and backed away.

"I can't leave you!" Nina dug the bracelet from her pocket and pressed it into his hand. "Together we stand, side by side. Always and forever."

"I'll always be with you," Jake said, "but I'm already dead." He stepped toward the monsters, reached up and tore the umbilical cords from the collar around his neck.

His body convulsed. His spine arched backwards, and he screamed unlike any human sound Nina had ever heard. Jake's skin rippled, as if a thousand insects were scurrying beneath the surface, and then it split open. His bones grew, expanding and ripping free from muscle and flesh, then the muscle fibers knitted themselves back around the bones, growing and expanding. Her brother's skin tore away from his skull as it expanded, his mouth filling with razor-sharp teeth. Claws erupted from his monstrous hands.

The bracelet dropped to the floor.

"Go!" he roared.

Nina dove into the hatch and belly crawled into the darkness. The screams of gen-mods echoed through the duct as they were torn apart by the thing that used to be her brother. Up ahead, sunlight flooded in. Her MindEcho chimed as it reconnected to the network.

"Lexie, do you copy?"

"Oh my God! You're alive!"

"There's something the world needs to see," Nina said. She initiated the upload of her MindEcho's last fifteen minutes of video.

Jake and the rest of her team hadn't died for nothing.

Intradyne was done.

BROKEN SOULS OF THE EMPTY SPACE

Kirsten Cross

WE'VE LOST *THE VICTORIA!*"
The cry could be heard across the battlefield. As the words floated above the hollers and screams of the bloodbath, the huge dirigible blossomed into a fireball that lit up the night sky.

The outer skin peeled off airship and crew alike, crackling in the hellish heat, exposing the ribs of both humans and machine.

Hearts exploded in sync with the booming eruptions of the hydrogen tanks.

Shrieks were terrifyingly brief as lips bubbled and dissolved to show teeth and jawbones locked in agonised grimaces before they too were consumed by the flames.

Blackened skeletons tumbled towards the ground like blazing torches, stubbed out in a burst of sparks and snapping bones as they impacted the blood-soaked earth. The ground welcomed them, opening its arms to the rain of bodies and heaping soft soil around them in an instant and unholy burial, where no priest offered the benediction, no tears were wept, no flowers were scattered. Broken souls filling empty spaces within a brutal and hateful landscape.

No compassion. No grief. No mourning.

Just blood. Just so, *so* much blood.

The Victoria let out a long, moaning death rattle and her massive hulk toppled nose-first towards the ground, the rigid metal ribs bending and buckling. Around her, smaller dirigibles buzzed like pallbearers, desperately trying to dodge the flaming rain of debris that would instantly set their own wafer-thin skins alight.

Below, the battle raged.

Man against beast.

Automaton against hellhound.

The plains of Salisbury, once the training fields for the Queen's Imperial armies, welcomed more blood, like a chrysanthemum craving water. It was a land already pockmarked by the tracks of those new-fangled tanks – iron turtles that were hellish inside and rained bloody murder onto anyone on the outside. The deep hoofprints of the centaurs had churned the delicate heathland into a desolate, barren quagmire. Muddy puddles you could lose an entire regiment in sucked the unwary down into brown, fetid oblivion. The only birds were the circling ravens, cawing an eternal death knell for the fallen.

The Empire began to crumble at the edges.

And all the while, watching, ever watching, *He* stood. The red of his eyes briefly flared orange as *The Victoria*'s flames lit up his irises. Her final death throes reflected in the curve of his eyeballs. He licked his lips and let out a low, rolling chuckle.

He could almost taste the coming victory.

Soon.

Soon.

But not yet.

Those damn Stones still stood, despite His Legion's best attempts to bring them crashing down. The old gods would not let go of this fertile land so easily. It was ripe for the picking. Yet that juicy fruit still hung on a bough just out of reach. He stretched out his hand, fingers writhing like snakes. A throbbing barrier, invisible to the naked eye, made him snatch his hand back. The Stones still held. They *still* held, damn it.

The window of opportunity was closing. But the veil was thinner than ever. Soon, it would be so thin, so weak, that he would be capable of sliding one curved talon down it like a blade through silk and watch it flap helplessly in the transcendental breeze. But for now, it was time to return. Regroup and wait for that inevitable celestial moment. That once-every-thousand years' Alignment that opened the Space between Space, the Time behind Time. That brief second when He could finally unleash the full fury of his armies.

The enemy was weakened, close to the point of destruction. They even scavenged their own dead for parts. And they dared to call *Him* evil? The hypocrisy of Man was a stench in His nostrils. He threw back his head and roared.

His clarion cry went out on the raging wind. His forces stopped. Time, *this time*, had run out. They were so close to victory, but the portal was already wavering. The power of the Stones was too much and He couldn't hold it open any longer. As one, the forces of Hell turned and flowed back into the portal like a raging river. Forms merged into one fluid, seething mass. The howling banshee-call of the undead made the living drop to their knees and cover their ears.

The undead didn't want to go back. But the alignment was still a day away. This sortie was merely to weaken the enemy. To leave them gasping, reeling, vomiting blood and guts, and desperately patching up their wounded.

But tomorrow? Ah, *tomorrow.* He would finally step through rather than hover between the two worlds. When He would draw down the power, raise His hands, and send lightning bolts searing across the plain, incinerating the enemy where they stood. Once all that death had paved the way for the undead, they would regain their rightful place.

At the top of the food chain.

A place where broken souls were consumed like roasted pork. Where the empty spaces between the worlds were filled with the screams of the newly dead, tormented and torn apart by ancient ghosts.

And *nothing* could stop them this time.

Nothing and no one.

Except...

Perhaps...

Her...

⚙⚙

The bar had that 'someone's going through at least one window tonight' feel to it. As Cerberus Smith put his palm against the door's polished push plate, a blood-splattered thug with no remaining teeth to speak of came sailing through the gilded glass. The thug let out an audible "*Oof!*" as he hit the lamp post base. He sat, slumped like a marionette with its strings cut, his bristly chin resting on his chest.

Cerberus jabbed a thumb towards the window. "Um, yeah, is my wife still in there? Because that's usually the sort of thing that happens when someone grabs her arse." He drew an arc in the air and made a gentle whistling noise, followed by a "*Boom!*" finger explosion. "To be honest, it wouldn't be the first time." He grinned and scratched his ear. "I mean, she *does* have a very grabbable arse."

The thug burbled gently, bubbles of blood popping in the corners of his mouth.

"But ya see, here's the thing and oh, are you ever gonna chuckle over this one." Cerberus' grin instantly evaporated, replaced by a look that would chill the soul of the Devil himself. A brass-banded 50-calibre disruptor swooped out of its holster and whined gently as it powered up, a sickly green glow emanating from the glass chamber.

Burbly guy found himself staring down the business end of the barrel. A curl of gas foretold of much possible pain to come should he even twitch.

Cerberus' towered over the terrified man. A sudden breeze made his floor-length leather duster flap gently, like the black wings of a battlefield raven. His finger rested on the side of the disruptor's trigger housing. The slightest twitch would reposition the finger into 'active' position and things would get really really bad, really really quickly for the guy blowing blood bubbles.

Cerberus steadied his aim and spoke softly. "I'm the only one who gets to grab her arse and live." He pressed the surprisingly cold tip of the disruptor in the centre of the man's forehead, turned it ninety degrees as if to screw the end of the barrel into the man's cranium, and gave him a quizzical look. "You feel me?"

BROKEN SOULS OF THE EMPTY SPACE

"Do *not* shoot him in the *face*, you utter pillock!"

A tall woman dressed in the regalia of the 105th Royal London Airborne Dirigible Corps stepped through the door and into the cobbled alleyway. Knee-length lace-up boots led up to fitted leather jodhpurs. A brass-banded disruptor sat placidly in an intricately-worked hip holster. The leather duster, complete with two brightly polished brass stars on either epaulette, reached her ankles and flapped gently in the breeze. Pure white hair shone around her head like a halo, and the regulation leather corset accentuated an athletic frame blessed with more than its fair share of muscle.

"Maisie! Baby!" Cerberus smiled brightly. "I was just looking for you!"

"You bloody amateur, Cerb." Maise scowled. "How many times do I have to tell you? Shoot him in the gut. He'll die slower." Maisie rested her hands on her hips and glowered at blood-bubble guy. "So a standard pack of cards has five kings these days, does it, Mister Fuckadoodle?"

Cerberus winced. "Dude, you cheated at poker? Against my *wife*? Ooo, fuck. That's way worse than the whole arse-grabbing thing, my man." He re-holstered the disruptor and dramatically threw an arm across his eyes, mockingly assuming the *dying poet* pose. "Oh, my days! I can't watch. Seriously. I just can't. It's gonna be way too violent." He slid his hand across his face and peeped between his fingers. "Make it quick, though, my little banshee, we've been mustered."

"He didn't cheat me, Cerb. He cheated Aurora."

Cerberus regained his composure and stared at the man, who was now quietly weeping. He ignored the burbled sobs and focused on Maisie. "Aurora? He... what the...? *Aurora?* That psychotic clockwork centaur that lights bundles of dynamite with her cigar and, honestly, I think she holds onto them for way too long if you ask me... I mean, *that* Aurora? Are you shitting me?" Cerberus let out a low whistle. "Man, this guy just keeps on digging that big ol' hole ever deeper, doesn't he?"

"She buck-kicked him straight through the window. Perfectly justified as far as I'm concerned." Maisie shrugged.

SNAFU: PUNK'D

"So is the rest of the squadron in there?"

"Yep. And the 107th. And the Auxiliaries."

"Holler them. It's an all-points, Maise. Something big has gone down in Salisbury and the generals are going apeshit. Seriously. Rumour is they've even called in the damn Necromancers."

Maisie sighed. "Bugger. Well, I suppose we better get it over and done with then. Do you want to tell Aurora or shall I?"

Cerberus shrugged. "You're her CO. Besides, she hates me."

"She doesn't *hate* you. She just doesn't get you like I do. But be honest, the coconut shells and clip-clop noises were a bit speciesist, Cerb. You know centaurs are pretty damn touchy about that kind of thing." She aimed a kick at the slumped man's head that nearly took it clean off his shoulders, dusted her hands, and turned. "Now what's with this all-points?"

Cerberus' face darkened. "Bad. Real bad. He tried punching through but the Stones held, I think. It's carnage on the plain, though. Word is we've lost the entire seventh fleet." He paused. "And *The Victoria*."

Maisie's face fell. "Shit. SHIT. SHIT!" She spun and sprinted back into the bar.

Inside, a tipped card table was in the process of being righted by a couple of sheepish-looking squaddies. Maisie hopped up onto it with a dancer's grace and cupped her hands around her mouth. "ALL POINTS! MUSTER!"

The bar's atmosphere instantly transformed from jovial frivolity with a soupçon of casual violence to grim, professional business mode.

Aurora approached the table, her strangely lilting gait emphasised by the fluidity of her mechanical and ornately patterned rear quarters. The thick scar where the body tissue fused into the mechanical prosthetics was still visible as a zig-zagging bump underneath her regulation duster, which draped across her back like a blanket. A tamed mane of chestnut hair scraped hard back into a French plait hung down across her shoulders and almost to the knee of her foreleg. Her torso was squeezed into the usual leather corset, and the hair on her lower equine body shone a glistening chestnut bronze. She removed the thin cigar from her lips and blew a smoke ring. "Boss?"

"We've lost *The Victoria.*"

Silence filled the bar like a tsunami.

"Damn it." Aurora dropped the cigar and ground it into the slate floor with a hoof. "What about the rest of the 105th?"

"No word. But it's not looking good."

"Do the Stones still stand?"

"I'd say yes at this point. Otherwise we probably wouldn't be having this conversation, what with the whole being sucked down into the darkest reaches of Hell and all." She shook her head. "Right now, all I know is a full muster has been called. All off-duty cavalry units are to report to Chelsea Barracks. I want you front and centre, Aurora."

"As always." The shifting, swirling green eyes of the centaur clouded. "What are we up against?"

Maisie shook her head. "The stupidity of mankind, Aurora." She looked the centaur in the eyes. "As it ever was, so shall it ever be, my friend." She sighed. "See you once again on the battlefield."

The two soldiers clasped forearms and for a moment that unspoken bond that non-combatants could never begin to understand flowed between them. Maisie smiled at her friend. "Be well, Aurora."

"Be well, Maisie." Aurora broke her grip and glided towards the door. She stopped briefly to stare in disdain at Cerberus. Smith was well over six feet. But even he was dwarfed by the towering centaur. She bowed her head and put her mouth close to his ear. "Keep her alive until the battle is joined, Cerberus. Or you will answer to me."

Cerberus frowned and met her gaze steadily. "I love my wife, Aurora. I have no need of you to tell me to protect her."

Aurora smiled. "That's the first time I've ever heard you say that you love her, Smith. It's good to hear. It gives me hope for your kind after all." She gave him the briefest of nods and broke into a gallop, her metal-shod hooves ringing out on the wet cobbles and sending up bursts of sparks.

Cerberus watched the centaur round the corner and disappear into the night, the faint hiss of her mechanical hind quarters echoing along the damp alleyway. "She's a fucking lunatic. But one hell of a soldier." He smiled as he felt Maisie's hand rest on his shoulder.

"One of the finest in the Queen's army, husband. The Guardians have and always will be at our side. Even if she does insist on smoking those filthy cigars of hers." They stood for a moment as the pub emptied around them, grim-faced members of the 105th, 107th and Queen's Own Auxiliary Flying Corps units silently went to their regimental muster points across the city.

Cerberus sniffed and rubbed his nose as he tended to do when he was trying to push down one of those blasted emotions. "We better get to Covent Garden, my love. My primary was to get you back to the war room in time for the next briefing." Cerberus gave his wife a fleeting smile. "After all, what's an army without its tactical commander?" He brushed a kiss onto her cheek and the two soldiers ran into the night.

⚙ ⚙

The battlefield din had reduced from the roar of all-out war to the murmuring and soft weeping of the casualties as they pleaded for a swift death. The alternative was simply too terrifying to comprehend, even if it did mean a second chance at 'life'.

The ravens circled, cawing and calling to one another, landing between the piles of corpses and pecking at exposed flesh, guts, and eyeballs with their huge beaks. There was no malice in the ravens – it was simply their way. Nature had no favoured children when it came to carrion.

The orderlies shooed the ravens away and gathered up as many of the injured as possible, as well as some of the more intact dead. The ravens protested, pecking petulantly at feet that kicked out at them, and circled up into the smoke-filled sky.

The fiends had been driven back through the portal, but this time only just. Every battle brought them closer to breaking out completely. The human cost was higher every time. This time it had cost the fleet their flagship and almost completely obliterated the ground forces. Still, the fiends had turned and scuttled back to their black abyss once more. So they could count it as a win, despite the horrific price so many men and women had paid.

At least, that's what the general on the ground thought had happened.

They'd won. Only just. But they *had* won. Right?

The Legion had been driven back and He hadn't been able to set foot on sacrosanct ground. The Stones still upheld their role as sentinels, the Henge casting its shadow over the killing ground. The Sarsens were pockmarked by bullet holes but remained standing as they had done for thousands of years. The Altar Stone wobbled like a loose tooth, but already a team of engineers were re-securing its footing, overseen by the High Druid himself.

The horde had tried to weaken the Stones so that their Master could come through. They'd almost succeeded in pulling down one of the Sarsens and dislodging the prone Altar Stone before being beaten back.

General Manning stared across the carnage from a safe distance. He held a perfumed handkerchief to his nose to try and block out the stench of death. The blazing remains of *The Victoria* still sent up plumes of acrid black smoke and the occasional fire tornado ripped across the field. *Funny*, he mused. *Death smells like bacon. I like bacon.* He wrinkled his nose and sniffed, instantly regretting the action. *Maybe not so much now, though.*

He climbed down from the open-top staff car and sat down with a bump on the hand-stitched leather seat. Despite the Royal insignia that fluttered on the bonnet of the car, the stars and regalia on Manning's epaulettes were mere soutache and baubles. His rank a privilege of birth, not command experience or hands-on bloody warfare.

Manning turned to the other passenger. "Well, I say. That was a close one, what?"

"Yes, indeed, General. Very close. But as you can see, we

prevailed once again." The thin man dressed in a plain black suit, black shirt and black tie smoothed back a hair that dared to creep out of place. He wrinkled his nose at the smell of death, and flipped open a document case, from which he presented a sheaf of papers to the general. "Numbers were... interesting, sir. The loss of *The Victoria* is, of course, regrettable. But not wholly unexpected."

"We knew we were going to lose her?" Manning scowled as he flipped through the battle report. He tossed the sheaf of foolscap back to the thin man, who slid the papers back into the case. "Seems like a dashed-awful waste of a perfectly good airship if you ask me."

"When you float a large *dirigible*, not an airship, sir, a dirigible, filled with highly volatile hydrogen gas over a battlefield, eventually something will combust. Usually," he chuckled, "quite violently."

"How many men did we lose?"

"Pretty much all of them, I think." The thin man shrugged. "No matter. Our surgeons are already working on the salvageable ones. The rest will be harvested for parts. As usual."

"Of course. One good thing to come out of this whole bally mess, what?" Manning blustered. "Marvellous advances in the whole, whatchamacallit..." He waved an arm vaguely.

"Augmented Surgery, sir?"

"That's the fella! Augmented thingy! Marvellous! Blow the buggers up, scoop up the bits that aren't too squished up, and bally-well sew 'em back together! Resourceful, Caruthers, resourceful. Excellent use of men. Or at least, bits of them, what?" He paused and leaned forward, his voice dropping to a conspiratorial whisper. "I say, though. Does it hurt?"

Caruthers looked quizzical. "Does what hurt, sir?"

"All that being sewn back together? I mean, can't be too jolly for the bugger getting darned-up like an old sock now, can it?"

"Does it matter? As long as we keep fighting the enemy back, the greater good is served. These men and women know the risks. They've all signed the waiver. They're all willing donors, sir. It's part of their contract when they take the Shilling. And of course, they get the benefit of being receivers too, if they're salvageable."

Manning huffed. "Yes, yes, I know all that. But… well, it's not really *natural*, is it?"

Caruthers kept his face neutral. "And you believe the enemy is natural, sir? That they wouldn't do far worse to our soldiers? Remember, General, in this war, we're the *good* guys!" A flicker of a smile danced across his thin lips. "You can be assured the military has the full support of the Necromancers, sir. As always. For the greater good."

"The greater good." Manning mumbled the words under his breath like a prayer. "Yes. Yes, of course."

In the front of the staff car, the driver's hands tightened on the wheel until his nails left scores in the goatskin leather cover. He stared ahead, fighting every urge within to draw his service revolver and evenly distribute six bullets between the two passengers and end this madness once and for all.

But what would that serve, really?

Cut off two of the hydra's heads, four more grow back.

A barked order to "Get us out of this mess, driver!" snapped the man back into reality. He fumbled at the key and pumped the gas pedal twice. The engine spluttered into life and the staff car trundled General Manning and Caruthers back to Basbury Hall. A light supper complete with a rather fine bottle of port awaited the men, served by a couple of orderlies made from the 'spare parts' of a previous battle.

✵☉✵ ✵☉✵

"Where the bloody hell have you been?" Colonel Walker spun from the huge table as Maisie Smith walked in. "Oh, it's you. My apologies, ma'am." The apology sounded decidedly insincere.

Maisie marched up to the table. "I could ask you the same question, Walker." Maisie fixed Walker to the spot with an icy-blue stare. "How in god's name did this whole shitstorm happen, man? Where the *fuck* was military intelligence? Or is that now even more of an oxymoron than before?" She leaned in. "With an emphasis, of course, on the *moron* part?"

Walker gulped and shifted awkwardly before going into a full-on gabble. "There was absolutely no indication the Salisbury portal was active! We've been watching it for weeks, and the last thing we expected was for Him to make an appearance in exactly the same place twice, I mean, it's utterly… unforeseen… and… um… err…" Walker's voice trembled to a halt.

Maisie turned the icy-blue stare up to a level that would instantly freeze and shatter metal. "No indication."

Walker shook his head.

"Utterly unforeseen."

"Um…"

"The *last thing you'd expect*? You're a damn *psychic*, for god's sake! Expecting stuff is literally your whole job!"

"Ma'am, I really think—"

Maisie slammed an augmented fist on the table. The intricately chased metal, all Florentines and fleur-de-lys, may have looked dainty but it was meteorite metal, and harder than the finest Japanese steel. Her fist sent a deep crack skittering across the onyx slab. The large map of Salisbury Plain spread out on the table jumped and an entire battalion of tiny model centaurs fell over. "Oh, Colonel, if you were to actually think at any stage in this whole sorry mess, I don't think we would have been in this situation to start with, do you?" She glared at the general. "I take twenty-four hours leave, the first—" Her finger snapped up, "— the *first*, I may add, in *nine damn months*, and we lose practically the whole of the 107th *and* the bloody *Victoria*?"

Colonel Walker stared blankly at the cracked table. As he did, one of the Sarsen Stones in the model of the Henge toppled over. He stared at it, then looked up. "Damn it! Of course!"

"Damn-it-of-course what, Walker?"

Walker gently put the stone back into position. "Reports came back that they'd made a beeline for the Henge." He looked at her, a strange flicker in his eyes. "I mean, what else would they do, right? That's the only thing that holds Him back!"

Maisie studied the man. Her eyes narrowed. "Your point?"

"Tomorrow's Midwinter, ma'am."

"Yes, I know."

"But this one's different."

"Why?"

"Because of the Alignment!"

"The what now?"

"The Alignment! The Celestial Alignment!" Walker marched over to the library shelves that covered the entire wall. Arcane books bound in chains, crumbling leather and padlocks, seemed to writhe as he approached. He pulled down a particularly large tome. The book was locked and bound with iron straps. The iron and the complex gold-leaf sigils that squirmed and wriggled across the surface were the only things that kept the magic in.

This wasn't some 'My First Wizarding' book. This was a *Book Of Shadows*. Written in blood and screams. Ancient beyond time itself. And bloody dangerous in the wrong hands. Walker, a Guardian of the Keys and psychic of considerable renown, was definitely one of the right hands. The book recognised him. Responded to him.

It *liked* him.

Which for Walker, wasn't always a good thing.

Every time he touched the book, it took a sliver of his soul. The fight to keep the darkness at bay was proving harder every day. It was getting more difficult to turn his normally soft brown eyes back from the black pits they would revert to without absolute concentration.

Maisie watched the darkness creeping from the edges of his irises as soon as he laid his hands on the book. Behind her back, her fingers found the blue glass bead laced onto a chain around her wrist that offered protection against the Evil Eye.

At least, she hoped it did.

Walker put the book on the cracked table, swooping an entire battalion of model soldiers aside. From the bunch of keys hung on his belt, he selected a particularly large, blackened one and inserted it into the lock. The lock disengaged with a loud click and the book immediately flew open, the crackling pages fanning wildly.

The pages came to rest with a final papery flutter. Walker stabbed at a page with his finger and looked up at Maisie, his eyes now completely black. "I knew it! Once every thousand years. You see?" He looked down. "Oh, He's a clever bastard, isn't he? Weakening us to the point of collapse right before the Alignment." A slow smile crept across his face. "You could almost admire His tactical manoeuvrings, ma'am. Clever. Clever, clever, clever..." Walker's voice dropped to a whisper filled with reverence.

The slap snapped his head to one side and brought Walker sharply back from the brink. The sting on his cheek spread across his face and down his neck.

Walker's head swivelled back and he met Maisie's gaze, the shadows fading from his eyes. "Thank you, ma'am."

"You're welcome." Maisie gave the man a fleeting grin. "I thought I'd get that one in before you started any demonic chuckling or gabbling in Latin or some such shit."

"I have never knowingly demonically chuckled, ma'am."

"And there won't be a first time on my watch, either." Maisie's voice softened. "You keeping it together, Walker?"

"It's hard, sometimes, ma'am. Especially when He gets close to the veil. It kind of sends, um, *vibrations*, through." Walker ran his hand through his hair. "I can hear Him. Just on the edge. But I can hear him."

"And what's He saying?"

For a second, Walker's voice went guttural. *"Soon..."*

⚙ ⚙

Aurora stood at the head of what was left of the 105th Cavalry. A cigar hung from her lips as she scanned the horizon, and a curl of blue, richly-scented smoke wafted into the air. The Henge loomed in the darkness. It always seemed bigger in the dark than it looked in daylight. The flat horizon, uninterrupted by anything other than the burnt-out, skeletal remains of *The Victoria*, melted into complete blackness. For ordinary men, it was a bleak, black landscape with no defining features other than the Henge.

For Aurora's swirling eyes, though, she could see every tiny detail. Every blade of grass shimmered an ethereal green. Every pool of congealing blood flared a vivid blue. Every ghost soldier looked towards her, pleading for her to release them. Screaming silently.

They knew what was coming.

The Alignment was only hours away. As the midwinter sun blazed between the eastern Sarsens and struck the Heel Stone, everything would come together. He would appear on the horizon, standing like a god before his undead army.

Aurora took a long pull from the cigar and blew a perfect smoke ring into the air. She stared ahead as the soft footsteps came up behind her.

"See anything?" Maisie Smith took her station alongside her friend.

"Yes. And no."

"Cut the enigmatic crap, Aurora. You know what I mean."

Aurora turned her gaze onto Maisie. "If you people had only asked me and my kind, we could have told you this would happen, you know."

Maisie scowled. "A thousand-year-old 'I told you so' isn't helping, Aurora. And honestly? I only found out about this whole Alignment thing a couple of hours ago."

"But you know I'm right."

"Of course I do! But I'm not in charge, am I?"

Aurora stamped a hoof into the mud. "All those lives, Maisie!" She waved an arm over the hordes of ghosts that filled Salisbury Plain, swirling around the Henge, spectral bayonets and rifles in their gossamer hands. "They didn't need to die like this! We told you in the *Book of Shadows*!"

"You mean the book that only Walker can pick up without his heart exploding and his brains dribbling out of his ears? *That* book? Because sweetie, honestly? A more accessible warning would have really, *really* helped us stupid humans out a bit!" Maisie's voice was shot through with steel. "Those ghosts? The ones that you can see out there? The ones I know are there too but can't see like you can? They were *my* soldiers, Aurora. *My* responsibility. *My friends*! Your whole non-interference in the actions of mankind really fucking sucks right now, you know that?" Maisie paused. "Aurora?"

"Yes, boss?"

"Why do you call me boss? I mean, I'm just a human, and not even a whole one at that! I'm a Mecco. In your eyes, that makes me a failure as a soldier. I've been augmented, but I'm human, too. And we all know how your people feel about humans. So. Just this once. Before it all goes to shit and I don't get another chance to ask you. Humour me. Why do you call me boss?"

Aurora took another long pull from the cigar and smiled through a haze of blue smoke. "To make you feel better about yourself, *human*." She winked. "Also? I like you. You've got spirit. Most of your kind just whine on about war not being fair." She shrugged, dropped the cigar and ground it into the mud. "Of course this isn't fair. The Gods have never played fair. If they did, you'd be facing Him down on your own right now without any help from us whatsoever." Aurora gazed towards the Henge. "Nearly sunrise."

"And then what?"

Aurora shrugged again. "Then we shall see, won't we?"

Masie spoke quietly. "Are you going to stop Him?"

Aurora turned her gaze towards Maisie. "No. Not this time." She shook her head and pulled out a short sword from the inside of her duster. Gently, she handed it to Maisie. "You are."

"How? In the name of the gods, *how*?"

Aurora smiled. "You'll know when the time comes..."

BROKEN SOULS OF THE EMPTY SPACE

The midwinter sun peeked weakly over the horizon, a thin sliver of pale gold backlighting ominous banks of churning black clouds.

The army waited. All eyes were on the two figures—one centaur, one human—standing next to the Heel Stone, a distance away from the protection of the Henge. Enough blood had been spilt on this ancient altar to pacify a whole slew of ancient deities.

But it seemed that despite all the carnage it had witnessed these past few days, the Stone still wanted more.

Aurora could hear the ultralow hum of the Henge start to rise in tone as the first fingers of sunlight touched their cold, frost-covered surfaces. The vibrations resonated across the plain and towards the east, sending spikes of energy pulsing down the ley lines that marked the path of the Processional Avenue. The brilliant blue-white fingers pulsed into the Heel Stone. The sheer force of the power made every nerve in Aurora's body throb in unison.

The Alignment was just moments away.

She glanced at Maisie. The white-haired woman had never known of her part in this ancient ritual until just now. She could see the confusion in the human's eyes, hear the thoughts, the doubt, the internal screams of *'Why me?'* as clearly as if they were her own.

Aurora touched her friend's arm in silent solidarity.

Everyone had to pay the price. Everyone.

Including Maisie.

To stop Him, blood was needed. The blood of someone chosen by the Guardians.

And the Guardians had chosen a foul-mouthed, white-haired Lieutenant Colonel with a penchant for whisky, less-than salubrious bars, and more fight in her one remaining little finger than most generals have in their entire bodies.

A chosen one who hated people who cheated at poker. Defended her comrades with a fury and fire that terrified the General Mannings of this world.

And who, when asked, would make the ultimate sacrifice

to protect the future of the Empire and every man, woman and child in it.

One who could hold the blade long enough for it to do its work.

Aurora glanced over her shoulder, where four grim-faced centaurs fought to hold Cerberus Smith back. The man was screaming in furious agony. Screaming Aurora's name. Screaming the word, *'Betrayal!'* at Aurora. Screaming for Maisie.

But it was too late.

In the west, a swirling mass of cloud started to rotate Widdershins, winding itself into a foul vortex of blackness. It filled with jagged lightning that flickered around the widening maw and stabbed out into the wild sky.

The sun inched higher.

In the pre-dawn sky, the Alignment relentlessly progressed towards its climax. The throbbing pulses of energy radiating from the Henge to the Heel Stone intensified, speeding up and becoming so violent that even Maisie could feel them. The Heel Stone rang like a singing bowl, gently at first but rapidly gaining in force and volume.

Maisie felt herself buffeted by a wind that came out of nowhere. She was forced to plant her left foot behind her to stop herself from being blown backwards. A single drop of blood trickled from her nostril and beaded on her lip. She could taste the tinny flavour as the bead rolled into her mouth.

In the maelstrom that swirled around her, she heard a soft, still voice. "Are you ready?"

Aurora gazed down at Maisie, her normal expression of disdain for everything and everyone briefly transformed into a gentle and loving look.

Maisie drew the blade and nodded. She held it aloft, trying to ignore the distant cries of Cerberus as he thrashed to escape the clutches of Aurora's soldiers. She smiled at Aurora. "Tell Cerb it had to be like this. And tell him I loved him. Right to the last beat of my heart. And beyond."

Maisie faced the portal. Her mechanical hand gripped the

knife's hilt as the sun's rays finally burst over the horizon and struck the blade. Down its length, sigils blazed with a white-hot fire. The pulsing energy of the ley lines came to a pinpoint at the tip of the Heel Stone and surged into the blade, enveloping Maisie in a blinding white light.

She felt herself gently lifted into the air, every atom of her body throbbing with the force of the ancient power that flowed from the Henge, through the Heel Stone and into the blade. Below her, the massed army waited for the enemy to burst through. Men and women, terror in their eyes and scars from the scavenged body parts sewn onto their limbs still raw and angry. She spotted Manning in the distance, binoculars pressed to his eyes, thinking only of his next indulgent meal and blithely confident the Hell hordes would be defeated again.

She saw Cerberus, her love. Her joy. Her soulmate. Raging and pleading still for Maisie to come back to him. To be with him. To be his eternal dancer. A single tear glistened on her cheek as she turned away from him one last time and to face…

Him.

As Mars, Lord of War, harbinger of battle and the eternal warrior of the celestial dance, shifted into position, the Alignment was completed. The Midwinter sun reached its zenith and the Heel Stone sang the song that, once every thousand years, would echo through the wastelands, through the places between Time and Space, and into the primeval souls of men and beasts.

The portal opened and He unleashed his armies. The undead poured into this place, this time. The armies of the Guardians rushed to meet them, roaring in defiance.

Protect the Stones. *At all costs.*

For if the Stones fell…

He looked at *her*, contempt blazing in His orange eyes.

"YOU? YOU ARE BUT A CHILD. YOU ARE NOTHING AGAINST ME."

A spark of absolute defiance blazed in Maisie's soul. "Oh, now you know that's not true, you pathetic little creature." She smiled. "So you reckon that a mere human cannot defeat you, right?"

"CORRECT."

"Well. Guess what, sucker?" Maisie pulled the sleeve of her duster back, revealing an ornately carved arm made out of brass and meteorite metal. Metal that had fallen from the heavens themselves and, with absolute devotion, had been forged by the Guardian's legendary smith into a mechanical arm of such intricacy it defied belief. Five exquisitely fashioned fingers curled around the pommel of the blade, absorbing the intense power that thrummed from the fully-charged blade. The sigils squirmed and writhed their way down the blade, along the handle and were now wrapping themselves around Maisie's augmented hand and arm.

This was a hand that could hold a blade no human hand could touch.

But Maisie could. She was a 'Mecco'. And she had the Iron of the Heavens on her side.

She smiled; eyes filled with malice. Filled with a passion for revenge against the Lord of the Underworld that *dared* to claim dominion over *her* Empire. Filled with grief for the loss of her brothers and sisters-in-arms. For Cerberus. For Aurora. She lowered the blade, pointing the tip at His chest and snarled, "I'm the Hand of the Gods, motherfucker!"

The force of her words made Him reel back. He roared defiantly and blasted a raging ball of fire towards Maisie.

She laughed as it was absorbed by the blade. He couldn't harm her now.

Nothing could. She had become the Angel of the Battlefield. The Hand of the Gods. The one who would make the ultimate sacrifice.

Below, Aurora galloped towards the Henge, fury in her eyes and pain in her heart. Her bow loosed arrow after arrow of meteorite tips into the undead, who crumbled into dust with every hit. She cried out into the screaming wind. "Come unto me, the Stones of the ancients, and the dark earth, and the ravens of the battlefield! Become my army!" She unleashed a banshee howl that echoed around the battlefield. The ravens heard the call and swarmed around the Henge, violently attacking any of the undead horde who dared to approach the sacred Stones. Roots burst from the ground, snaring the ankles of the horde, binding them into helplessness as Aurora's Guardian army, along with the Queen's army, sliced and bayoneted every damn one of them into ashes.

The armies slammed together.

The slaughter began.

Maisie hung in the air above it all, serene and calm, her duster flapping like black wings. The blazing sword that only she could hold, arched upwards, drawing every last blazing ounce of the Heel Stone's energy into one final blast. The delicate filigree of her arm and hand started to melt, dripping black beads of molten metal onto the earth below. Each droplet exploded with the force of a seventy-five-millimetre shell. Nobody within fifty yards of each one stood a chance. The meteorite beads vapourised all indiscriminately, whether Hell horde or human.

Such is war.

Maisie looked into those hellish eyes and saw...defeat. He knew. He finally knew.

Not this time.

Maisie glanced towards the heavens, the red dot of Mars just visible in the dawn light. She slowly lowered the tip of the sword, the remains of her molten hand now fused to the blade's handle. She and it were now one.

It was time.

In the midst of all the death, the howls of agony below, the cries for mercy, Maisie found a silent moment. In that silent space between Space, in the time between Time, she finally found peace. A soldier's peace. Filled with the memories of her brothers and sisters. Tied by a bond that could never be broken. That no ancient god could contemplate, nor diminish.

She let out a scream of victory, brought the blade back up and released the full force of the Heel Stone's power. It erupted out of the blade and blasted Him back through the portal, flailing and wailing like a child. As the power flowed out, it took Maisie with it. Atom by atom. Memory by memory.

Until nothing was left.

The blade, blackened and smoking, clattered to the ground and lay in a pool of blood, the thick red liquid quenching and annealing the blade once again.

A swooping sound filled the battlefield as the horde was sucked back through the portal, a writhing, shrieking mass of blackness. Faces appeared and were absorbed back into the torrent, their jaws locked open in grimaces of horror.

Then...

Silence.

Aurora lowered her bow and stared where the portal had been. She glanced up, watching the planets move in their never-ending procession across the sky. The Alignment was over. The battle was won.

She slowly made her way towards the centre of the Henge. A huge raven landed on the Altar Stone and gently laid the blackened blade down. It let out a single croak and took to the sky, circling the Henge and flying off towards the sunrise.

Aurora gathered the blade tenderly, as if it were a newborn baby, watching the sigils realign themselves, finally settling into their assigned positions.

It was as it ever was. As it ever shall be. Aurora smiled sadly. "Farewell, Maisie. Be well, boss."

❀❀❀ ❀❀❀

On the hillside, Manning lowered his binoculars. "I... I think we won." He glanced at Caruthers. "Yes, by thunder, I definitely think we won!"

Caruthers' thin lips curled into a passionless smile. "I believe you're right, sir." He scribbled a note and stuffed a sheath of papers into his dispatch bag, snapping the lock shut. "Now if you'll excuse me, General, we have work to do."

"Work?"

"Well, there's plenty of donors out there. And there's the

war with the Dutch in Transvaal to consider. No point wasting perfectly good parts, now, is there?"

"No. Because that would be *inhuman*, wouldn't it?" The driver slowly turned and fixed Caruthers with a black-eyed stare. "And as you said before, Necromancer, we're the *good guys*, aren't we?"

Caruthers' eyes widened. "You? But you're the psychic! You keep the books! You're not a damn driver!"

Walker chuckled. "Ah, my cold-blooded little Necromancer. So busy scuttling around harvesting the dead that you forget to look at the living occasionally. You know, being the Keeper of the Book has its advantages." He waved a hand at his face. "It's called a *glamour*. I can show you what you *want* to see. And that was your first mistake." He tipped his head, guiding Caruthers' gaze down towards the business end of a Webley revolver resting on the oxblood leather edge of Walker's seat. The hammer was cocked back. Caruthers could see the bullets snuggled cosily in their chambers. Walker smiled. "You'll be pleased to know, Necromancer, that there'll be no more... mistakes."

The Webley cracked twice and Caruthers lurched back into the seat, a wet stain spreading across his chest. He dabbed at the stain and stared at his fingers drenched in his own blood. A trickle of bright red blood, bubbling up from the man's mutilated lung, ran down his chin. Caruthers looked in disbelief at Walker and gasped one word. "Why?" His eyes rolled back into his head and he flopped back like a puppet with its strings cut.

The Webley shifted a couple of inches to the left.

Manning followed its path like a mongoose watching a cobra, waiting for it to strike. He could feel the dampness spreading between his legs, and spluttered, defiant to the last. "But we won! You're one of us! Damn it, man, we *won!*"

The Webley cracked twice more, a curl of blue smoke joining the acrid cloud that hung over the battlefield.

Walker put the pistol back in its holster and smiled. There was no chance now that those soft brown eyes would ever chase away the black shadows darkening his gaze.

Humanity has a strange way of equalising the balance between good and evil.

Good men do evil things.

Evil men do good things.

And there are some who walk the grey line between the two. They are not just drivers. Or soldiers. Sometimes, they step over that line. They have to. It's the only way to hold the *real* monsters to account.

The Hydra principle. Cut one head off, two more grow.

Walker knew that. He also knew that the sacrifice Maisie had made left a void in the Balance.

No. No, that was unacceptable.

There had to be balance.

There had to be order.

There had to be someone who would embrace the darkness in their own soul to keep the light burning. To hold account of the evils that mankind brought upon itself.

Demons and devils? They were easy. You knew where you were with demons. Demons were bad.

But people? People like Caruthers, people like Manning, they were *evil*. One knowingly, one unknowingly. That was no excuse in Walker's black eyes. Stupidity was its own evil.

Walker opened the car door and casually pushed the bodies of Caruthers and Manning onto the muddy field. They were the first casualties of many in the coming Reckoning. A Reckoning that would go after the real demons and the real evil in this fucked-up world.

A Reckoning led by people like him who would avenge Maisie Smith's sacrifice. And… led by people like Cerberus Smith, perhaps? Walker appreciated the irony that the man he believed would willingly join him shared the same name as the guardian of the Gates of Hell. The Gods liked their little jokes.

Walker hummed a happy little tune as he shut the door and turned the key. As the car spluttered into life, he tore off his Colonel epaulettes and tossed them into the mud next to the blood-soaked, corrupted body of Manning.

BROKEN SOULS OF THE EMPTY SPACE

He curled his fingers around the goatskin leather steering wheel and scanned the battlefield for Cerberus. He could just see him in the wisps of smoke and ghosts, kneeling in front of the Heel Stone, rage-weeping for his loss.

He chuckled as he watched Cerberus's hot tears mingle with the blood-soaked earth.

"Oh yes. We will win, General. We *will* win..."

BRAINJACKED

David W Amendola

Specialist 4 Rodriguez, our designated marksman, was on point when she held up a fist, the signal to halt.

We froze, and she motioned for us to crouch. Rodriguez slowly knelt and shouldered her TAC-338 sniper rifle. Aimed and fired. The sound suppressor on the muzzle muffled the shot.

She scanned the dense rain forest, then finally signaled all-clear. The ten of us crept forward, slowly, spread out single file.

It was so goddamn dark; image intensifiers wouldn't work without infrared illuminators but those would give us away to any hostiles using night-vision equipment. So we'd switched to thermal imaging, making animals and people and anything else warm stand out like glowing white ghosts against a monochrome gray and black background.

But none of us in Bravo Team wore NVGs; we didn't need them.

Our left eyes had been replaced by optics with magnification, image intensification, and thermal imaging capability, all linked to auditory implants in our right ears containing transceivers for short- and long-distance telecommunications. Headsets were plugged into the neural ports surgically implanted in the sides of our necks.

Rodriguez's target sprawled motionless in the brush.

Captain Dahl, our team leader, motioned for us to stay back and he stepped forward. We'd follow that man to the gates of hell. He'd saved our asses during the Silicon City raid and been decorated with the Space Force Cross. He flicked on a penlight to examine the body, which wasn't a body at all.

SNAFU: PUNK'D

At first glance, it looked like a drone. Spindly, robotic arms and legs, sensor pod of cameras and antennae for a head, all painted jungle camouflage. Metal fingers clasped a suppressed rifle with the distinctive bullpup design of Chinese-made small arms, popular with many armies.

The .338 Lapua Magnum slug had punched a hole through the back of the armored torso, just above the fuel cell. Unlike a drone, clear liquid and gray brain matter leaked from the exit hole in the chest.

"Fucking jarhead," I hissed.

Literal brain-in-a-jar. Slang for ECB, 'extracorporeal brain'. A disembodied human brain transplanted inside a powered exoskeleton wired into the sensorimotor cortex. The human brain was more responsive and adaptable than any computer, so an ECB was a more flexible battlefield weapon than a drone.

A jarhead didn't need leave, R&R, promotions, or medals to keep its morale up. Didn't even need food or water, just artificial oxygenated glucose solution. Still required sleep, but so long as the exoskeleton was maintained and powered, it could keep going indefinitely. The perfect soldier.

"Goddamn oligarchs," Rodriguez spat.

These freaks were produced illegally by corporate oligarchs who used them for security to guard industrial infrastructure or as mercenary soldiers for private military companies. The biggest oligarchs were essentially warlords with private armies, always jockeying for more power and wealth.

Where did they get the brains? Condemned criminals, prisoners of war, and other 'undesirables'. Before transplantation, the poor bastards underwent psychosurgery to make them compliant, fearless, erased their memories and much of their original personality. But they still sometimes went berserk from sensory deprivation psychosis.

"Pretty sure I nailed it before it detected us," said Rodriguez. "Didn't see any others."

"What the hell's it doing out here?" asked Master Sergeant Patel.

"Probably a scout."

Patel shook her head. "Intel said the locals don't patrol the forest."

The captain contacted the ops room back at Joint Special Operations Command in North Carolina. "Eagle One, this is Whiskey One. Do you see this? Over."

"Whiskey One, this is Eagle One," said a woman's voice over the command net. "Need a clear visual on it."

The tactical operations center had a satellite link to the live feed from our optics, so he bent over the jarhead for the brass to get a better look.

"Stand by," said the JSOC lady. Finally, she said, "That's a confirmed ECB, affiliation unknown. Locals only have regular troops, so belongs to a third party. Over."

Third party. Which could be anyone with the bucks to field or hire them. Didn't exactly narrow down the list of suspects.

"Eagle One, this is Whiskey One. Has Royal Flush picked up anything? Over." A surveillance drone circled high in the sky providing overwatch. *Semper supra*—'always above'—the US Space Force motto.

"Whiskey One, this is Eagle One. Negative, but ECBs can be hard to detect in dense cover. Proceed with the mission. Over."

"Eagle One, this is Whiskey One. Copy that. Out."

We resumed the march. Harsh racket from monkeys and birds filled the hot, wet jungle, crawling and buzzing with venomous snakes and bugs just waiting for you to step, squat, or lie in the wrong spot. We cooked under the ballistics vests over our camouflage uniforms.

When we reached the bank of a gurgling stream about ten meters wide, Rodriguez slung her rifle and effortlessly sprang across like it was backyard creek. The rest of us followed suit.

Our neuroprosthetic legs gave us the ability to march longer, jump higher and farther, and run faster than an Olympic athlete. A wireless interface connected the system controllers in our robotic limbs to a microelectrode array implanted in our brains.

Every operator in the 1st Space Special Tactics Squadron was a quadruple amputee maimed in combat, symbolized by the purple berets we wore while in garrison back at Schriever Space Force Base in Colorado. The color represented the Purple Hearts we'd all earned.

I'd lost both arms and legs to an IED while on peacekeeping duty in Antarctica, facing a future jacked into virtual reality all day long, nuking my nightmares with dope.

Fuck that. I refused medical retirement and volunteered for cybernetic augmentation through the Hercules Project so I could go downrange again. All of us were like that. Hungry to get back in the fight, the hardest of the hard. Or the dumbest of the dumb, depending on your perspective. We weren't ate up, just adrenalin junkies. We needed that rush to keep from going nuts.

Finally, our sensors picked up something, the datalink superimposing distance and direction over our vision like a tactical heads-up display. It roughly matched the GPS coordinates JSOC had given us.

When we neared the spot, we stopped, knelt, and listened. For a full fifteen minutes we waited, silent and still, and gradually the birds and monkeys got louder. That was good. That should mean we were alone.

Just to be sure, Rodriguez opened a box on her utility belt and launched a tiny scout drone the size of a dragonfly, guiding its flight in a sweep of the area ahead. Its camera feed appeared in our optics. Only animal tracks, no sign of people or jarheads.

It did find an impact crater gouged out of the ground near the sprawling roots of a huge kapok tree. A debris trail of freshly broken and splintered thorny branches indicated something large and heavy crashed through at an angle from above.

Rodriguez recalled the drone and the captain signaled orders. We pressed forward and secured a patrol base.

Then Gomez and I slung our SCAR-H rifles, unfolded shovels, and began digging. Walker scanned for additional debris while the others deployed in a defensive perimeter. The captain's voice murmured as he relayed a sitrep back to JSOC.

We excavated a rectangular component of scorched and battered metal about the size of a small refrigerator. Jackpot.

BRAINJACKED

"Bravo Whiskey Ten, this is Eagle One," said JSOC. "Give us a clear visual."

Bravo Whiskey Ten was my call-sign. I heaved up the wreckage and slowly rotated it so they could see details while the captain shined his penlight on it. Probably weighed four hundred pounds, but my neuroprosthetic arms had four times normal strength.

"Bravo Whiskey Ten, you can set it down now. Stand by."

I did so. Sucked warm water from the tubes of my hydration bladder and pushed back my boonie hat to wipe the sweat dripping down my face.

The captain talked on the command net again, then motioned for me to come back up. "Okay, bring it up. We got confirmation."

"Picking up more over there, sir," said Walker.

We couldn't tell if anything worthwhile could still be gleaned from the wreckage, but our job was retrieval. Whatever we couldn't bring back would be destroyed.

A communications satellite had been hit by debris and suffered what the bright boys called 'catastrophic orbital decay'. In other words, it fell out of the sky. A significant fragment hadn't burned up on reentry and landed in this vast stretch of uninhabited forest. If any of its classified technology survived impact it might fall into 'unfriendly hands'.

Not classified by Uncle Sam, but by ConTech, Consolidated Technology, the satellite's corporate owners. An oligarch really ran the government behind the scenes. Couldn't risk a rival filching company secrets, could we?

Unfortunately, the forest lay deep inside the territory of a regime that would never grant permission for us to conduct a search and recovery operation.

Our team had been on standby when the ops order came down. They infiltrated us across the border in stealth helicopters and we fast-roped down near the location of a probable wreckage site pinpointed by photo-intelligence. Once we'd retrieved and/ or destroyed everything, we'd be exfiltrated before anybody knew we'd been here.

Walker's detector pinpointed other pieces. Most appeared to be just fragments of the satellite housing and solar array, but everything was collected regardless.

At Patel's direction, we stacked all of it in the small clearing of tall cogon grass designated as our extraction zone. Starlight cast dim illumination here. JSOC already had the GPS coordinates, but we marked it with an infrared strobe anyway.

"Not registering anything else, sir," said Patel. "Looks like we got it all."

"Then let's get the hell out of here and go home," said the captain. "I'll call for extraction."

The light machine-gun let out a chattering roar and blew his head apart in a grisly spray of blood, brains, bone, and electrodes.

We reflexively hit the dirt. The JSOC lady demanded to know what the hell was happening.

Holman, our gunner, stood stunned, smoke rising from the muzzle of his M249. He switched his aim to Patel and decapitated her with a burst of 5.56-millimeter slugs. Because our limbs were prosthetic, body armor covered everything biological we had left – except our heads.

Holman, his biological right eye wide with horror and disbelief, yelled hoarsely, "I can't stop!"

Rodriguez whipped up her rifle and dropped him with a slug to the head.

O'Reilly, the grenadier, flipped open the FN40GL launcher mounted under his rifle barrel and thumbed in a 40-millimeter grenade from his bandolier, face contorted by the same stunned, helpless expression as Holman. He swung the muzzle around towards Walker and Gomez.

They immediately shot him, but on his way down he jerked the trigger. The grenade was a close-quarters round, turning the launcher into a big shotgun, so the blast of double-aught buckshot shredded them and the foliage around them.

Cole, eyes wide, shrugged off his backpack and jerkily reached inside, yelling, "Get back, get back!"

As our demolitions expert, he carried thermate grenades for

emergency destruction of sensitive equipment like radios, and, for this mission, satellite wreckage. When ignited they produced molten iron at over two thousand degrees Centigrade, melting or incinerating anything it touched.

He pulled the pin on a canister and all the charges hissed and sizzled and consumed themselves in a blinding pile of slag and ash. Then Cole, fighting against himself, drew a SIG Sauer P226 from the holster on his hip and shot himself in the mouth.

Rodriguez convulsed, sputtering profanity, struggling to resist something. She stiffly swung towards Doc—Sergeant Fuchida, our medic—and raised her rifle.

He jumped high and to the left, trying to make himself as difficult a target as possible, while holding down the trigger of his own weapon. His SCAR-H, set to full-automatic, sprayed 7.62-millimeter bullets, emptying the entire twenty-round magazine.

One smashed Rodriguez's left polymer-titanium elbow joint, leaving the artificial forearm dangling uselessly by cables and spoiling her aim.

The arm's sensors wouldn't transmit pain, only warn when a critical failure occurred, so she simply dropped the rifle, her other hand clawing for a pistol. With my rifle, I double-tapped her in the chest before it cleared the holster. The bullets didn't penetrate her vest plates, but the impact did knock her off-balance. Crying inside, I immediately followed up with a headshot before she could recover.

Doc landed next to me. He threw off his aid bag, rifled through it, and plucked out two flash drives. He yanked out my headset and jammed one drive into my neural port before doing the same thing to himself with the second.

I suddenly lost all use of my limbs, my optics and communications blacked out, and I crumpled to the ground like a puppet with its strings cut. So did Doc.

We lay there, hearts racing, noses filled with the coppery stink of fresh blood mixed with the bitter reek of gunpowder. We gazed numbly at the carnage strewn around us, the mangled remnants of our comrades who'd just obliterated each other.

"What the hell just happened?" I asked.

"Brainjacked," he said through clenched teeth. "Somebody hacked into their brain interfaces and seized control of their arms and legs. Remember what Holman said? He couldn't stop what he was doing."

"Those signals are encrypted."

"Encryption can be broken."

"By who? Nobody knows we're here!"

"Well, somebody does. And they waited until we finished all the grunt work recovering the wreckage before turning us against each other. Now they can just waltz in and scoop up a treasure trove of high-tech. Probably closing in right now."

I squirmed helplessly. "Can't move my arms and legs. Visuals and audio are all dead. What's on these flash drives?"

"Program that fries the interface. Only sure way to prevent a brainjack."

"Why not just take it offline? Then nobody can access it remotely."

"Can't take the chance the hackers uploaded a virus. Safest to just wipe everything out."

"But now we can't move."

"I brought along spares, the old kind with no computerized parts."

A cyborg medic's job involved biomechatronics as much as first aid, so his bag contained items such as spare batteries, microchips, and cables in addition to the usual trauma kits and painkillers. He doubled as our computer technician. Doc had also brought along spare artificial limbs.

But first we had to get them on somehow.

Both of us were quadruple amputees, so we fumbled and flopped around like turtles on our backs trying to press release catches for the now-useless neuroprostheses strapped onto our leg and arm stumps. Then we had to wiggle the spares out of the aid bag. The only way we could grip anything was with our teeth, or by pressing it against our sides with our stumps.

Doc finally wormed into one artificial arm and got it on

securely, and after that he quickly clamped on his other limbs and helped me.

"Get the captain's spare radio ready while I check the others," he said, clambering unsteadily to his feet. I was only a Specialist 3, so he was in charge now.

I forced the shock of my comrades' deaths from my mind. I'd deal with that pain later. *Remember your training. Focus on the mission. You still have a job to do.*

I struggled up. These old artificial limbs were clumsy and unresponsive since they lacked sensory feedback, as well as being generic spares that didn't fit very well. They chaffed my stumps and made them ache. And, of course, they didn't enhance my abilities, so I really felt the weight of my gear. I staggered around like a drunk, unpacked the spare radio, unfolded and plugged in a small satellite antenna. Communications wasn't my specialty, but every operator was cross-trained to have a working familiarity with each other's core task in case somebody became a casualty.

Doc went around double-checking the others for vital signs. He wasn't giving anybody first aid so all of them were dead. He gathered up weapons and ammunition then knelt beside me and held down the transmit button on the radio's handset. "Eagle One, this is Bravo Whiskey Three. Do you read? Over."

I leaned in close so I could hear. That golden voice back at JSOC finally answered and said, "Bravo Whiskey Three, this is Eagle One. Loud and clear. What's your status? Over."

"Eagle One, this is Bravo Whiskey Three. We have eight fatalities. Blue on blue, suspected systems hack. Two of us are unhurt, but without augmentation so we have limited mobility. Request immediate extraction. Over."

"Bravo Whiskey Three, this is Eagle One. Request for extraction approved. Be advised your mission has been compromised. Hostiles inbound to your location. ECBs, platoon-strength, approximately three kilometers southwest. Over."

That jarhead had gotten off a signal after all. Damn.

Doc held the button down. "Eagle One, this is Bravo Whiskey Three. Copy. Over."

"Bravo Whiskey Three, this is Eagle One. Under no circumstances allow objective to be captured. Hold your position until extraction arrives. Over."

Under normal circumstances, even elite special forces wouldn't stand a chance in a straight-up firefight with cyborgs like us, but we'd lost our augmented abilities.

"No way in hell we can fight off that many," I said. "Not in our condition. And we can't bug out of here very well with these old school arms and legs, let alone carry that wreckage."

Doc nodded agreement and held down the button. "Eagle One, this is Bravo Whiskey Three. Unable to hold position. Request Royal Flush take out hostiles. Over!"

The drone had missiles that could eliminate the jarheads easily.

"Bravo Whiskey Three, this is Eagle One. Be advised contact with Royal Flush has been lost. Cause as yet undetermined."

So now our overwatch was gone, and JSOC was blind. A malfunction? Or had the jarheads jammed the signal — maybe even shot the drone down? What a clusterfuck. Regardless of what the cause was, until evac arrived we were on our own.

"Eagle One, this is Bravo Whiskey Three. Any theories about the systems hack? Over."

"Bravo Whiskey Three, this is Eagle One," said the lady. "Negative. Encryption was certified secure against all known adversaries. Initiate emergency destruction. Over."

"Eagle One, this is Bravo Whiskey Three. All incendiaries have been destroyed. Over."

"I can shoot up the wreckage with Holman's machine-gun," I said. "Or use O'Reilly's grenade launcher."

Doc shook his head. "Neither would destroy it completely. Save the ammo for us. Get the scout drone and send it up. It can spot them for us."

I hobbled over to Rodriguez and took out her scout drone. Our datalink to it had been wiped out with the rest of our augmentation, but we also had a backup manual controller. Unfortunately, the controller had a neat, round hole in it from a stray bullet.

"Bravo Whiskey Three, this is Eagle One," said the JSOC lady. "Please confirm. You cannot perform emergency destruction, is this correct? Over."

Doc held down the button. "Eagle One, this is Bravo Whiskey Three. Affirmative. And given our condition we won't be able to hold this position very long. Over."

"Bravo Whiskey Three, this is Eagle One. Copy that. Extraction inbound, ETA one hour. Over."

"We copy," said Doc, voice thickening with disgust. "Closing down. Out."

"Well, somebody obviously broke our encryption," I said.

"Not if it was a goddamn inside job!"

Doc zeroized the radio, erasing its cryptographic settings. We had no way of properly destroying it, so he drew his pistol, screwed on a suppressor, and emptied the magazine into it. Now all we had were our survival radios.

"What do you mean?" I asked.

Doc reloaded his pistol and holstered it. He turned off the infrared strobe. "You heard the rumors about who's really running ConTech?" He stumbled over to the satellite wreckage and searched through it, uncovering the large component I had excavated.

"Yeah, sure. Crazy conspiracy theories. Oligarch who owns it turned over control to an artificial super intelligence called Dominus to run things more efficiently. He's a recluse who's never seen in public so who knows."

"I've heard the stories from too many sources for it not to be true. Bastard is dead and now Dominus runs his entire corporate empire. There's a resistance group within ConTech trying to shut it down." He flipped open his belt tool kit and began unscrewing a dented access panel.

I snapped a fresh magazine in my rifle. "So what's that got to do with the shit we're in now?"

Doc wrenched the panel off, revealing circuit boards he scrutinized by penlight. "Dominus developed a remote neural monitoring system called New Horizon that could be used for 'corrective subliminal messaging' on a mass scale. Mind control. Make people more compliant and efficient. Installed the transponders on that communications satellite. When the Resistance discovered New Horizon's purpose, it orchestrated the satellite crash to keep it from going operational. Likely want what's left to figure out how to neutralize it if there's an attempt to deploy it again – or destroy it so nobody can reverse-engineer it." Doc carefully pried out a microchip and held it up. "This! This is New Horizon. This little fucking piece of silicon is what all our buddies got killed for!" He jerked his head at the rest of the wreckage. "Looks like some of the other transponders are intact too."

"So how's this an inside job?"

"Dominus monitors every damn thing! If it detected their plans, then it used its Defense Department access to brainjack us and shut down Royal Flush to sabotage the mission. That's how." He sighed. "The intel officer knew something was squirrelly about this mission. She'd heard the stories too. She warned the brass about it, but they wouldn't fucking listen."

"But then whoever hired the jarheads will get New Horizon instead."

"For sure those jarheads belong to Dominus. ConTech secretly owns a PMC overseas. Give me the drone."

I handed it to him and he popped open its plastic housing, revealing its circuitry, motors, and battery. He disconnected and extracted one of the miniaturized cameras, creating just enough space inside to hide the microchip. Then he closed it up and handed it back.

"Controller's busted," I said. "We can't operate it."

"You can reset it for autonomous flight without the controller. Just push this switch here. If it looks like we're about to be overrun, let it go and it'll follow the homing beacon back to our forward base just like a carrier pigeon. Intel officer will make sure it gets to the right people." He slung his rifle, swung open the grenade launcher on O'Reilly's rifle to eject the spent shell, and smacked in another. "Let's get into cover."

BRAINJACKED

We withdrew onto a rocky rise overlooking the clearing so the wreckage was still in view and within our field of fire. This was our kill zone. I flipped out the bipod of Holman's machine-gun. We laid our own rifles beside us.

Then we laid prone in the undergrowth, motionless and silent, blending in, becoming one with the forest, watching and waiting. The birds and monkeys got louder again.

But soon they quieted down. We had company.

Soft rustling in the brush below, swishing in the tall grass. The faint whine of hydraulics. I took out a thermal imaging monocular and scanned the area, but jarheads had low heat signatures.

There. Armed stick figures creeping towards the clearing, movements jerky, wooden. A squad spread out in two fire teams moving in wedge formations. They didn't glow white from head to toe like people, only in spots where thermal exhaust vents were.

I tapped Doc. He nodded. We held our fire and stayed still, fingers on triggers. We aimed at their chests, where the brains were encased – kill shots. Once they stepped into the open, we'd let 'em have it, cut down as many of the goddamn freaks as we could.

If they followed standard battle drill, once this advance squad located us it'd be reinforced by a weapons squad with machine-guns to keep our heads down with suppressive fire while the rest of the platoon flanked around for an assault.

Doc tapped me and nodded at the drone. I switched its control setting and powered it on. The tiny quadcopter hovered by my head, humming softly, then flew off. Its fate was out of our hands now. Hopefully, some bird wouldn't mistake it for a meal and chomp on it.

Suppressed automatic weapons popped softly to our left; bullets ricocheted off the rocks. Doc slumped stone dead, shot through the head. They'd already detected us and circled the rise.

White-hot pain punched me in the shoulder.

Another slug grazed my head and stunned me. Three jarheads sprang high into the air, leaping towards the rise to close the distance.

Royal Flush was gone, but I still had an ace up my sleeve, an ace I wasn't supposed to play except under the most dire circumstances.

"This is Bravo Whiskey Ten!" I gasped over my radio. "Position overrun! Initiate Dollar-Bang! I repeat, initiate Dollar-Bang!"

A jarhead landed beside me, kicked the radio away, then smashed the machine-gun from my hands with a swipe of a rifle butt.

Two others jumped over like grasshoppers. A spotlight clicked on, blinding me with its glare. Sensor pods swiveled down to stare at me. I squinted at those soulless camera lenses and wondered how much humanity their lobotomized brains still held. Did they feel anything? Emotions, desires, dreams?

They pointed their rifles at me, but didn't fire.

Of course not. They wanted me alive so their corporate masters could harvest my brain.

I raised my hands to surrender, but my lips twisted in a crooked grin. The bastards weren't getting my brain or any other part of me.

Dollar-bang—$!—was an old mainframe computer command for a panic dump, an emergency data dump of the memory performed when a serious system error occurred. A very appropriate code name for what I'd called in.

An orbital bombardment system hovered in low Earth orbit. A satellite launcher released a twenty-foot-long rod of solid tungsten that gravity would accelerate to a terminal velocity of ten times the speed of sound. Impossible to intercept.

The rod didn't carry an explosive warhead. It didn't need one. The sheer kinetic energy generated by impact had the force of eleven-and-a-half tons of TNT.

In twelve minutes it would obliterate the satellite wreckage, the jarheads, and me.

But with luck our little drone would make it back to base, back to the intel officer, and to the Resistance.

A RIVER RUNNER'S TALE

Richard Beauchamp

rden squinted as he made minute adjustments to the steering wheel of the *Cape Rock Queen*. It was just before dawn, and the fog drifting off the river was so dense that even his high-lumen torches could only penetrate some ten feet before it was swallowed up by a swirling ivory curtain. He hated trying to navigate the Miss when she was like this – bloated and surly with a fast current and clogged with trees and farmhouses cast adrift. But he had deliveries to make.

His daughter, Daniella, stood on the promenade of the hurricane deck, a sighter's scope glued to her right eye, red hair tied in a no-nonsense bun as she scanned the channel. Useless really. The whole ship shuddered then as an unmoored cypress tree knocked against the hull. Arden grumbled and turned off the torches; the light refraction was just blinding them anyway. Soon, it was as if they were floating within a cloud, neither bank visible from the pilot house.

"Ho! Someone's coming!" Daniella shouted.

"I can't see shit, and neither can you!"

"Cut the engines. I can hear it. *There.*"

Arden cut the boiler feed, and the ship's two massive steam-driven paddles slowed. Even though the ship was state-of-the-art—a contemporary Ledoux retrofit design sweetened up with ephemera-conducting engines—the current here was so strong that he had to use almost half of his total boiler pressure just to keep the damn thing at idle. Still, the engine-whine quieted down, and Arden scrunched up his heavily bearded face and listened.

Several high-pitched whining noises reached him. Like tea kettles brought to a boil, each one a semitone difference in pitch,

257

creating a dissonant wail that rang off the water and displaced the sound.

"Aw hell, buzzards!" Arden growled. "Switching to defensive posturing!" He slammed the 'Oh Shit' panel and the boat whirred to life as various gun emplacements sprang from several points of the steamboat.

"Aye, sir!" Daniella jumped over the railing and down onto the covered boiler deck, where all manner of Ledoux Institute weaponry lay sequestered within what was, at one time, a ballroom. Instead of sweaty aristocrats and barons, it now housed infantry armaments specifically for the defense of the ship and its cargo, which was usually some kind of highly-classified ordinance or materiel for Ledoux's R&D team.

Arden's river-gnarled hand slammed the pneumo-switch that powered the torches, and their world was once again lit up in a scintillating brilliance. He still couldn't see the little skiffs and their inbred cargo, but he could hear the whine of their approaching engines and taunting whoops. Arden sighed as he reached for his double-barreled revolver – a heavy, unyielding son of a bitch, just like himself, but it was good for defense. Once the little buzzards saw which steamboat they tried to pirate, they'd probably run for their lives.

He shuffled down the stairs of the pilothouse, knowing Daniella could clear the bow just fine herself. Arden knew the bastards would think themselves awful clever for coming at the ship from both sides, but the buzzards would soon find out it was to their detriment.

When Arden reached the exhaust release valve embedded within the side of the massive paddle box, grapple hooks sailed over the side of the hurricane deck. A second later, three gangly forms scrabbled over the railing, screeching drunken laughter as they charged him.

"Shoulda known better than to pilot a ghost ship through these waters, old man!" one of them said, speaking good English for a buzzard. It came at him with a fisherman's billhook; the nasty, rusted blade whistled through the air in a complicated series of swinging arcs.

A RIVER RUNNER'S TALE

Arden supposed it was meant to be intimidating. "Shoulda known better than to try and board a Ledoux Institute ship, you fucking buzzards." Arden slammed a fist into the valve release.

Ephemera was potent stuff, one of the most concentrated fuel sources in the world. The drawback was its spent residue and gas was quite volatile, and the fumes its expenditure produced had to be carefully vented lest your ship, or your weapon, turned into a bomb.

"Wha he say? This a Le—" one of the malformed cretins said before the vents opened at the aft of the ship. The air around them wavered as the gas vented.

Arden's face, all valleys of leathery flesh, squinted as he aimed the massive revolver and fired. The gun bucked fire as the twin .357 rounds vaporized most of the buzzard's head. Friction heat ignited the fuel-air mix behind the remaining inbreds, and a purple fireball the size of a tugboat erupted from the vents, scorching anything that dared cling to the rear of the ship.

His beloved *Cape Rock Queen* lurched forward like a kicked dog, and Arden heard assorted screams and the crackling of wood as blazing skiffs were sent adrift down the Miss like floating pyres. The two remaining men, if they could be called that, were thrown forward, their pale backs blistered and bleeding from the inferno. Arden, six foot and some change and as wide as a stateroom doorway, was unfazed by the ship's abrupt movements, his water legs as stout as cypress roots.

He grabbed the patchy hair from the pale, bulbous head of one buzzard and stoved it in with the sandalwood butt of his gun. The other one Arden hefted up, the malnourished body light in his hands. Buzzards lived in the worst parts of the river bottoms, where the run-off from riverside factories altered the physiognomies of the fish and those who ate them.

"You realize who you just tried to shanghai, you fucking idiot?" Arden growled. The wide, jaundiced eyes of the buzzard slid from the man holding him to the mahogany placard with 'LEDOUX TECHNOLOGIES LLC' engraved within.

"Me sorry, me sorry, didn't know! We just want food, we—"

"Yeah, and I want a sucked cock and working right foot." Arden roared as he hurled the heap of stinking flesh and bones into the exposed observation portal of the wheel box, and a second later the oscillating steel paddle blades were dyed red as pureed offal and bits of hair shot out the refuse extractor.

Shouts and the *pop pop* of a Litchfield repeater resounded, and Arden knew Daniella had her hands full. He swung his bad leg clumsily as he made his way down the deck—fucking gout picking a bad day to flare up—and thudded his way down.

A shrieking buzzard ran down the deck from Daniella's direction, gut-shot and bleeding all over the white oak flooring.

"Getting ma goddamn boat dirty!" Arden caught the thing in the side of the head with the revolver. The thin skull caved in like an overripe melon. He threw the twitching body over the side of the boat, where an opportunistic gator-gar had been waiting, and the beast quickly dragged the body below the water.

Then Arden came upon a scene that made his asshole pucker and his guts tighten.

Daniella, a resourceful whipcrack-smart girl but still green to the river-runner life, was surrounded by four buzzard bastards.

"Told you, never let them put you into a corner!" Arden leveled the revolver at the pneumo-tube some fifteen feet away. Malformed heads turned in his direction before thunder roared across the boat as Arden blasted the fuse. The canon, with its 6lb projectile, tore through two of the buzzards, nearly clipping Daniella before blasting through the white railing and out into the channel with a splash.

Daniella fired her repeater into the gawping buzzard that held a rusty scattergun on her, then wheeled around and kicked the one behind her, nubs of its yellowed teeth flying into the air.

"I had control," Daniella said. "You just came at a bad time." She kicked parts of buzzard over the side of the boat, the water coming alive with all manner of horrifying mutated fauna as arms and legs and torsos were tossed over.

"Didn't look like it. Christ. What a mess. Making us run behind schedule and muddying up my boat. You alright?"

Arden gave his daughter an appraising gaze, a hint of fatherly concern coming through before she gave him a dismissive wave.

Immediate threats neutralized, he clambered back up the wheelhouse to crank the oscillating paddles to their max thrust to make up for lost time.

❀❀ ❀❀

Having arrived at the Saint Louis drydocks, Arden parked at his usual spot at the southernmost dock, which allowed for the *Queen's* deep, four-foot draft needs – she was a heavy girl, ladened with reinforced steel and guns. As he directed the roustabouts to offload his cargo, a couple crates of custom-made glass housings and specially-molded cannon barrels for some project Dr Ledoux was cooking up, he spotted one of Ledoux's lackeys from the estate standing ponderously about all the rough-hewn river rats busy washing the gore off his boat.

The man was all sweating face, bespectacled eyes and unstained peacoat. He spotted Arden and Daniella as they came off the gangway and hailed them.

"Mr Wharton, my name is—"

"I know who ya are. Whatcha want?" Arden grumbled as his eyes roved the pier, looking for the nearest food vendor. His stomach roared.

"Ah, yes, uhm, my apologies. It appears Dr Ledoux requests your appearance at his estate," the man said with some timidity.

"What?" both Whartons said simultaneously. "The old man wants to see *us*? In person?" Arden asked.

The man nodded vigorously. "Aye, sir. It appears Dr Ledoux has a very special delivery that needs to be made post haste, and he requested you by name."

"Alright, so just have him send the goods down here like he usually does. No need for me to go across town—"

"Ah, it's a particularly sensitive matter, this. He wants to speak to you directly. Please, if you'll just follow me."

SNAFU: PUNK'D

✺✺✺ ✺✺

A private trolley, augmented by Ledoux propulsion technologies, trundled them through bustling city streets at a brisk fifteen miles an hour, having its own dedicated track to blow past the public transport trolleys and their turtles-crawl pace. Soon, the stink of the river and the city was behind them, where more green gave way than the reds and browns of the factories, until they were greeted with gently rolling hills and farms, until finally, the monolithic mansion of Pierre Ledoux appeared before them.

The trolley took them inside the huge building through a side tunnel, where their chaperone waved away the armed guards who immediately pointed guns at the two interlopers.

Arden had only met the enigmatic Ledoux a handful of times over his long employment with the weapons manufacturer. The first being when he was initially employed by the man and had taken a verbal oath to secrecy along with signed confidentiality wavers. Once again when, to his horror, he'd discovered his daughter, on her 18th birthday, ever rambunctious and adventurous, applied to be an apprentice field agent for Ledoux Ventures. An auxiliary part of the company that focused on the investigation of rival companies and stolen Ledoux patents, a job more dangerous than being a river runner.

The three walked through tall hallways of elegant architecture, passing the laboratory sector where strange smells and noises could be detected through thick double doors, and out onto a promenade where the diminutive Dr Ledoux waited for them in a suit of untold fortune, his pale face and shellacked hair glistening in the high Missouri sun.

"Christ, Gurney, did you make Mr Wharton walk the whole way here? You know the man's arthritis pains him so. Here, here, sit," Ledoux said with his proper French accent, and made a big show of pulling out one of the padded rockers that lined the marble porch.

"Much appreciated." Arden fell into the seat with a sigh of relief as he propped his swollen foot up, the bone-deep ache subsiding.

A RIVER RUNNER'S TALE

"And the inimitable Miss Wharton, how you've grown since I saw you last." Ledoux kissed Daniella's hand and bowed before her, causing her to blush. "You both must be quite curious as to why I've called you in from port. I can see the unease in your face, Arden. Worry not. You're not up for termination. Just the opposite in fact. Mihota, would you please introduce yourself?" Ledoux said to the large man standing at the edge of the promenade, his back to them as he stared out towards a vast expanse of manicured lawn.

The man turned, his long black hair flowing in the light breeze. Square jawed, his lean muscles bunched against his tailored vest and denim pants – standard field agent dress. His right arm was encased within an odd-looking exo-skeleton contraption whose spokes and wires seemed to marry directly into the flesh of his forearm. It emanated a quiet mechanical whirr.

It was Ledoux who spoke. "Shunk Mihota, senior field agent."

"Shunk Mi—" Daniella said, trying the name out.

"You can call me Black Moon, Miss. Easier on your tongue," the man said in a deep baritone.

Arden blinked. Agent Moon was one of the most infamous operatives of Ledoux Ventures. During the states' war, Ledoux, who scouted for himself back in those days, had found the Osage native held prisoner by a Confederate general far out in the Ozarks, and broke him out himself while seeing how many of the rebels had access to his weaponry. One of the first graduates of Ledoux's arduous training program, Moon was single-handedly responsible for blowing up the counterfeit ephemera factory in Alexandria, effectively ending the rebel's upper hand and creating a five-mile-wide zone of inhospitable wasteland in the process. If not for him, they might still be fighting that damned war.

"Agent Moon, my gosh, I…" Daniella was obviously flustered, and Arden remembered many a night she'd recounted the man's escapades while he piloted the boat, many of which beggared belief. For an aspiring field agent, Moon was a demigod.

"Yes, yes, well known is he. Let's not waste time, for it is of the essence. Arden, you are my most trusted river runner, and that knowledge is paramount. Especially down south, which will be priceless for this mission."

"How 'down south' we talkin, Doctor? You know past Memphis it's a wasteland," Arden said cautiously.

"Back to your old stomping grounds, Arden. Louisiana."

"What in god's name do you want down there? It's —"

"I know," Ledoux cut in; a rare breach of manner. "Believe me, the effects of the ephemera plant explosion haunt me daily. Shame for such a miracle of energy to be so deadly." Ledoux sighed, and took off his monocle to polish it surreptitiously against his suit shirt, a nervous tick. "But the current problem we face could make that look like spilled milk if it's not addressed promptly."

"And what problem is that?" Arden didn't like at all where this was going.

"I can't divulge full details, the less you know the safer you are. But I will say this. A mole is in my midst. High-level agencies have access to knowledge they ought not have. Rumors of my work being corrupted, perverted. You are to escort Agent Moon down river, and assist him in any way he may need to complete his mission, which, hopefully, is simply one of reconnaissance."

"I'm assuming this is the part where you bait me with riches and promises," Arden grumbled.

"Oh, yes. You do this for me, and I will see to your retirement once a suitable replacement for your river prowess is found. And for Miss Wharton, her position as apprentice will be removed, and she will be a fully authorized, *paid* field agent as soon as the mission is accomplished."

Arden sighed as he saw his daughter light up like an eph-cloud.

"Say no more, Doctor." Daniella practically beamed. "We will get your man where he needs to go, pronto!"

Arden's foot throbbed in anticipation of the fetid, swampy humidity he was soon to encounter, and the many horrors that laid in wait.

A RIVER RUNNER'S TALE

The night air clung like a wet veil to any exposed skin, clothes clinging like an unpleasant second skin. Luminescent bloodflies buzzed around them in an unceasing whine, their stinging bites sure to leave a maddening itch. They didn't seem to like Agent Moon though, who'd stood on the starboard side of the hurricane deck all day, a statue made flesh.

"This is all your fault, you know," Arden said. "Danni looks up to you like some kind of saint, but if you hadn't blown up that goddamn factory..." Arden shook his head. They were parked just off to the side of the main channel, which ran almost a mile and a half across.

"Using that line of reasoning, you may as well blame Ledoux," Moon said. "Man has always paid a price for his advancements. Eph is powerful stuff. In the wrong hands, it would be chaos. That's why he never sold his patents to the defense department." Moon's dark-brown eyes scanned the horizon.

Arden was about to head to bed when he noticed the shimmer in Moon's eyes. Like those of the many feral creatures along the banks caught in the spotlight during his night runs. "What the hell is that on your arm?" Arden asked, curiosity getting the better of him. He had a feeling he was looking at an example of Ledoux's ventures into 'biological augmentation'.

With a whine, the mechanical arm shot outward. "Keep quiet. They're coming," Moon said in that same unflappable baritone.

"What's coming?" Arden asked, his voice thick. He often imbibed in laudanum at night to help him sleep, and the comforting narcotic haze was quickly evaporating as he saw Moon shift into a battle stance. "Christ man, nothing can get to us, not with the thunder rods," Arden said, staring out into the roiling primordial waters.

The steamboat was set to a defensive posture with electrified telescopic rods jutting from four points just beneath the water. Anything getting within fifty feet of the boat would be fried. They were just past the miserable abandoned port town of Tunica, and when they'd stopped in Memphis, the eph-jocky who refueled the *Queen* reported infestations of fighting carp and sail eels plaguing the waters just downstream. Thus, the thunder rods came out.

"What's—" Arden began when Moon shoved him hard.

Despite being twice the agent's size, Moon's push sent Arden flying ten feet across the deck. A split second later, he heard three wet smacks. Arden floundered as he tried to get to his feet, his body sluggish with his nightcap, watching as three of the biggest sail eels he'd ever seen thrashed violently on the floorboards.

Moon had caught one of the things in midair and made a fist. The sound of cracking eggshells could be heard as he crushed the eel's head, casting it out into the night.

Arden was scooting back on his butt, fumbling for his boot gun – a pea shooter eph-powered Daringer he always kept on his person. The nearest sail eel shot at him like a bull's whip, its many translucent needle teeth snapping at air as it slithered towards him. Its white eyes stared at nothing. Its red, glistening rope of a body, thick as his arm, undulated in hypnotic sequence. Arden managed to snag the pistol free just as the creature leapt for him… when the thing was yanked back.

He watched in stunned awe as Moon had the thing by the tail, his arm-gizmo sparking and whirring as the man moved with impossible speed. There wasn't even a blur to his motions, it was like watching one of those clanky old motion-picture cartoons with stills missing from the animation. One second, Moon was twirling the ten-foot beast the way a girl twirls a baton, a split second later he was ten feet to the right, arm thrust forward, cracking the animal like a whip against the reinforced promenade, the skull exploding into a wet smear.

The other two sail eels had already been dispatched. In the five seconds it took for Arden to scoot on his ass and reach for his gun, this man had crudely decapitated the other two creatures without so much as breaking a sweat.

"What...? How did you—" He began before he heard splashes coming from the water, far beyond the electrifying reach of the thunder rods. Then the distinct whistle of the sail eels and their fins soaring through the air. *Christ, since when could they jump so goddamn far?*

Moon swung his mechanized arm up just as one of the eels slammed into him, its teeth grating against the metal. The agent whipped his head to the side, audibly cracking his neck, and abruptly the eel spasmed wildly, uncoiling itself from his arm as blue arcs of current shot through it.

Arden finally got himself to his feet, his right leg able to bear more weight under the combination of cannabis, morphia and alcohol, and was promptly slammed into the side of the ballroom doors as something tore through his thick captain's jacket. Despite the fibers being reinforced with a tough, gar-scale weave, hot needles lanced his flesh.

"Goddamn!" He threw himself onto his back once more, crushing the creature under his weight, bones crunching beneath him. He rolled onto his stomach and clambered to his feet just as another flopped onto the deck in front of him. Arden punted it like a pig skin, his right foot singing a high note of pain as the tubular body shot over the railing and blue sparks erupted through the muddy water.

Gasping, he turned to see Moon stomping an eel-head flat, catching another of the soaring creatures in midair and tossing it into the thunder rods with a crackle of electricity. There was a temporary lull as huge ancestors of the gar and catfish genus, made monstrous by eph exposure, swarmed at the scent of eel-blood, picking off what remained of them.

"Go to bed, Captain. You're a liability out here. Don't bother Danni either, no need for sleep shifts. Long journey ahead. I work better alone." Moon gave him a side eye, and in the promenade light, the man's pupils were dilated to the size of dimes. Arden understood then that this wasn't just a man he was looking at.

A coiling discomfort roiled his guts as he regarded Moon in a new light, realizing all those rumors he'd heard about the man were true. Still, he rankled at being called a liability. This was *his* fucking ship. But he was too tired and too perturbed to argue. "You ring the bell if you need us," Arden said, pointing to the string of alarm bells that connected throughout the ship.

Moon did not respond.

Arden hobbled down to his state-room in the belly of the ship, took another belt of laudanum to help him come down from the fight, and collapsed into bed. He drifted away thinking of Ephemera, that strange property, both gaseous and not. A substance made not in this plane of existence, and somehow Ledoux had brought it from that place into this world. Apparently, some strange Serbian fellow named Tesla helped with that.

When he awoke, daylight streamed through the cabin window. Moon hadn't rung the bells. Not once.

❁❁ ❁❁

Past Greenville it was bandits—better formed and armed than buzzards—but still no match for Moon and Daniella, whom he was teaching to become a more efficient fighter. A little past that, in Tallulah, it was the fighting carp, their hammer heads and huge bodies turned into corporeal missiles as they slammed into them, battering the *Cape Rock Queen* to near splinters. That time, Moon needed their help as hordes of the flailing creatures piled onto the boat and nearly sunk the mighty vessel.

The farther south they went, the more sparse the port towns, and those that still managed to cling to the fetid river with some semblance of life barely had the supplies to see them through. Food was the biggest concern. Agent Moon ate like a literal horse, going through their larders in days. Pounds of horse and pork and hominy and okra, he made even Arden's voracious appetite seem peckish in comparison. Arden figured it had something to do with whatever Ledoux had done, considerably ramping up the man's metabolism.

"Aye down south bad place man," a one-eyed, one-armed

merchant said in swamp pidgin as Arden cleared him of his eggs and the questionable looking pork cuts.

"Trust me, I know. Tell me, is the main channel still open to Baton Rouge?" Arden asked as the merchant piled the goods in a pnuemo-powered cart.

The swamp rat let out a braying laugh at this. "Shit man swamp is all that place is. Aint no channel. No river. Earthshakers turn place into soup. Nothin but big bad soup down there mista. That and gubmint dogs in they balloons."

"Is that where we're going?" Daniella asked as she helped him load the food onto the boat, the one working ship rat doing his best to repair the beaten and battered *Queen*, who sat low and tired-looking in the water.

"Somewhere around there. Moon ain't told me exactly where we're going," Arden said.

As they waited for repairs to be completed, he hunted down the agent, who was in the converted ballroom studying a nautical map of the river. It was from 1850, and Arden grinned as he saw the man's studious eyes rove over it. "Won't do you no good. River don't stay put. Looks nothing like that now." He pointed at a bend in the river past Natchez. "See, we're right here now. But all this—" He circled the lower half of the map that showed the alluvial plains of the river valley all the way down to the ocean. " —is one big swamp now."

"I'm aware," Moon said as he chewed through a stalk of sugar cane.

Arden huffed, wishing just once he could show up this infallible know it all.

"That doesn't change where we're going."

"And where the fuck is that?" Arden asked.

A brown finger settled upon a small blob of land in the middle of what used to be Devil's Elbow. The map said Prophet Island. Arden blinked. He knew during the war that the government had built a secret facility behind enemy lines where the secretary of war could strategize and carry out lightning attacks on the rebel strongholds. After Lee had surrendered, the building was supposedly decommissioned.

"Ain't nothing there but swamp and the horrors that swim within it," Arden said. Moon only shook his head, smiled. "That's what they want you to think. What better place to set up shop and work in secret than a hellhole nobody wants to go."

◌◉◌ ◌◉◌

Once they passed long abandoned Labarre, the channel opened up, and a vast brown sea was presented before them. Cypress trees grew in clutches in shallow shoals. Small humps of land completely covered with Spanish moss were the only solid ground seen for miles. Daniella had to stand out front with a sounding stick, calling off the fathoms while swatting at roiling clouds of bloodflies as the *Queen* slowed to a crawl, her great smokestacks, normally ablaze with purple gouts of flame, barely simmered with low output.

"You're telling me you want us to go through this shit at *night*?" Arden said incredulously, his nerves shot as he piloted his war-torn ship through these unknown waters.

"It's the only way. See out there?" Moon pointed to the horizon where brown met blue.

Arden was so focused on the water he at first didn't notice the floating blips some ten miles away.

"Dirigibles. Surveillance," Moon said. "I can tell you now, the closer we get to the compound, the safer the water will be. They've cleared this place of every abomination you could think of so they could operate in peace. So long as we get in undetected, you shouldn't have to fire a single shot. Just get me within skiffing distance of the place. I'll do the rest."

* * *

Arden was nervous. The massive swamp was preternaturally quiet save for the cacophony of insects. He'd been travelling in pitch black at a measly two knots for hours with nothing but the agent's owl-eyes as his navigation. Moon instructed him to switch off the ephemera converter and use the old steam power boiler instead, the ship noisily lurching and belching its way through the deceptively calm water.

"They have ways to detect ephemera. Steam is safer," Moon said as they finally came upon a light source far in the distance.

The agent ordered them to a stop, and Arden took out his sighter's scope as he set the boat to idle and beheld the massive metal and concrete structure raised upon a concrete platform the size of three city blocks. There were no windows besides narrow, slitted portholes from which large bore rifles peered out. The ethereal glow that surrounded the place came from fences that glowed purple with weaponized ephemera current, along with the roving circles of light cast from the dirigibles. The place resembled a prison, far removed from the humble brick and mortar military base Arden remembered.

He came down and saw Moon preparing the small skiff boat hanging over the side of the main deck.

"Lots of firepower for going in quiet," Arden commented, then watched as Moon gave Daniella a Litchfield Marksman rifle with a long sighter's scope affixed to the gun, and a glowing purple tube sticking out of its side. Arden knew the eph-pro-pelled bullets were fired at such high velocity they could travel for miles before succumbing to gravity drop. "Thought you said we wouldn't have to fire a single—"

"Only a fool has no backup plan," Moon said as he dug around in the steamer trunk—the only piece of luggage he'd brought onto the boat—and handed Arden a huge quad-bar-reled gun that weighed about as much as a cannon ball. "This will blow a wagon-wheel-sized hole in anything that moves. It's a one shot though."

Arden nearly dropped the goddamn thing as he took it, but marveled at the intimidating piece of weaponry.

"What's plan B?" Daniella asked as she sighted down the rifle towards the compound.

"You'll know." Agent Moon lowered the skiff into the water and pointed to the second one hanging by scaffold-hooks on the other side of the boat, both powered by miniature ephemera propelled jet exhausts. "Things go south, don't stay to fight. You go, both of you. If I don't make it back, Ledoux will have enough answers to pay you something." He jumped into the skiff, powered up the exhaust unit with a yank of the friction cord, and the skiff shot forward with a high-pitched but quiet hiss of steam.

The Whartons watched the man disappear into the obsidian gulf between their boat and the concrete fortress.

∞ ∞

Nothing happened for two long hours. Daniella started asking about her mom again, a subject Arden hated because he could never tell her the truth. That Melinda died a martyr protesting Ledoux's model of privatized defense contracting. *'He's turned war into a for-profit venture! Your hands are just as bloody as his!'* she'd shouted at him the night before she and a fringe-group of extremists attempted to infiltrate the mansion and expose what *really* went on at Ledoux Armaments, where ephemera *really* came from.

Arden was almost glad when the action came, if only to spare him from trying to explain that Danni's mother was a lunatic, convinced ephemera was actually the energy siphoned from the spirit realm, a condensed matter so powerful because it contained the very essence of the human soul.

But then the dull purple glow on the horizon abruptly shut off with a dull *whoomph*, and the night swallowed them.

"What—" Danni began when three bassoon thuds cut through the pregnant silence. Three corresponding fireballs lit up the night as Arden saw the dirigibles crash to the ground around Profit Island.

"Fucking Christ. He's gotta be dead," Arden grunted, hobbling towards the skiff.

"Wait, Poppa! Look!" Danni pointed towards the water. The swamp, its surface eerily glass-smooth and perfectly reflecting the sour green-purple of the night sky, rippled for the first time since settling from the *Queen*'s wake. Against the backdrop of burning dirigibles, their frames exposed like great metal ribs, Arden spotted a shape flying across the water at speeds only a highly-modified skiff could reach. Arden's jaw hung open for a moment, head slowly shaking before he snapped out of his amazement when other specks on the horizon followed after, far behind Moon but gaining quick.

"Hope he's taught you a thing or two about fightin'. Those ain't buzzards coming to bear on us." Arden dropped the quad-gun and went for one of the marksman rifles.

"I... I don't know what they are..." Danni said as she took a bead on one of the fast-gaining things, the rifle's barrel following them.

Arden took out his flask and took a large belt of shine to steady his aim before looking down the sighter scope himself. He knew in his gut he was going to die here if he stayed to fight, yet that's exactly what he was doing because if they got this mad bastard out of here alive, he could retire.

Re—

The comforting thought vanished as he looked down the scope. Moon was piloting the skiff, long hair flying wild in the wind, a lumpy form on the deck of the boat. Right behind him were similar vessels, strange things standing on their bows. Crazy silhouettes of odd shapes and sizes against the firelight.

"Do we shoot them?" Danni asked, her voice tight but controlled.

"Yes, dear. Shoot them all," Arden said calmly, and fired. The rifle barely kicked, the ephemera gas dispersal on the side of the gun dissipating most of the recoil. He aimed for the closest boat, shooting at some vague, many-limbed mass. He moved on as soon as he saw mist and splatter, his Westpoint military training kicking in. Once, one of the best riflemen in the Union.

He picked off four, missed three before his gun clicked empty. The shots were so quiet, more of a polite rush of air than a pop, that he didn't realize Danni was already reloading. They'd put a good dent into the unknown assailants but more were coming from the island, and now he could see another dirigible far in the distance, its bloated body a round silhouette against the night sky, coming at them.

They were some two hundred feet and closing fast. Soon the fighting would be up close and dirty. He fired quickly, not letting his brain seize up as the things in his scope came into clearer view and he was afforded better, terrible glances at them.

A hundred feet in he dropped the rifle, stomped hard twice on the deck, which caused the bow lights to scream on, and was turning to run for the ballroom armory, but Daniella was already tossing him a RR40 semi-automatic. She opted for the machine pistol, handling it with a skilled grace Arden hadn't seen before.

Please let her get out of this alive. If all else, you incredible bastard, make sure my daughter survives this. He cursed at Moon as he fired. Normal gunpowder combustion, with a huge ammo drum that made up for the loss in power.

Already the bastards were leaping for the boat. Arden paused momentarily as he caught sight of the things opening their many limbed arms, and great billowing veiny membranes of flesh unfolded before them, the monstrosities gliding like flying squirrels towards him. Of all the terrible things the ephemera plant explosion had created on the river, what flew at him was by far the most hideous. There was no discernable base genus to the thing other than being vaguely hominid. Multiple limbs sprung from a barrel-chested body covered in weeping lesions. The head was but a squat protrusion of skull upon which many distorted faces were molded, shrieking some horrible wail as bullets punched into it.

One fell in a heap of discordant flesh to the deck, then two more as Danni's pistol screamed its automatic report. One flew towards Moon as he leapt from the still-speeding skiff, a bound man in his hands. Arden shot the monstrosity five times, its body falling into the swamp just as Moon reached the deck, tossing the man, who was rambling loudly, onto the deck before whirling to join the fight.

"You don't understand it's true source!" The man cackled madly.

"What the fuck are these things?" Arden screamed, his mind finally scrabbling for a grounding comparison—*gargoyle*—before it went low, opened a mouth whose teeth put the sail eels to shame and closed around his gouty foot. He didn't have time to fire or register what was happening. There was simply a sharp, crunching sensation followed by an immediate solar-flare of pain.

"Effigies from the void! Our true forms—" The man howled as Moon punched his mechanized fist into the gargoyle as it masticated Arden's foot, the head simply exploding.

Arden heard Danni screaming then, and through a mix of adrenaline, powerful narcotics, and a fatherly sense of devotion, he ignored the fireball of pain in his right leg and swung his rifle towards where one of the abominations had Danni pinned to the deck, a crescent valley of gore interrupting the curve of her shoulder. He fired, and didn't stop until Danni was able to kick the dead thing off.

There came a triumphant laugh from behind them, Moon snarling "NO!" Then, "*Shit!*" Arden turned, saw the anonymous man had gotten free, a syringe in one hand that glowed a deep purple – pure, debased ephemera.

"He thought he could just reach into the void and take what he wanted. He fooled the whole world. We will show them the true source of this power. Mankind will pay for its hubris!" He shouted as he stabbed the syringe into his arm, the glowing liquid disappearing with the plunger.

The effect was instantaneous. It was like watching a fungi-bloom sped up times a thousand. The man's small body exploded into pulsating growths of limb and flesh, the man's screams—Arden swore they were of exultation and not agony—were pitched down several octaves as he struggled to raise his gun from a sitting position, taking aim. A rose-colored proboscis shot from the man and snatched the weapon away with viper quickness.

"Go! Get the ship going!" Moon roared to Danni.

She needed no further instruction, diving through the air and narrowly missing the snatching claws of a monster.

"You will know... the true face... of god..." the thing said, its head swelling to a bulbous protrusion as more visages sprouted from its skull, its flesh transformed into an abhorrent canvas.

Moon thrust out his fist, and two coiled wires shot from the metal aperture, barbed hooks on their ends sinking into roiling flesh. Arcs of electric current flowed visible through the guide wires, and the monster sunk to its knees, the many protuberances and limbs spasming wildly. Its roar was so loud and thunderous, Arden felt it in his chest.

"Shoot!" Moon screamed, kicking the heavy quad-barrel towards him. Arden crawled for it, pulled it to him. From a prone position, his leg screaming, his mind reeling, Arden leveled the four barrels at the thing just as he felt the ship thrum and the whine of turbines powering up. The thunder rods activated in a crackle of electricity, then everything was drowned out by a thunderclap as the gun roared.

He was thrown onto his back, catching a glimpse of a great cloud of red before his head slammed against the deck, this horrid nightmare ending in explosions of white and red stars.

∞ ∞

Arden looked out over the river, his new farmhouse perched atop a bluff that overlooked the port town of Kimmswick. He sipped fine whisky from a coffee cup; he can afford more than rotgut shine now, and he sighed at the turbo-whine of Ledoux's personal transport arriving. A moment later, footsteps approached as Ledoux and his escort, Agent Moon, came to his deck, sitting beside him.

"Enjoying retirement, I see," Ledoux said, grinning.

"Some days I miss the river, but I'm content to just look at it now," Arden said.

Ledoux nodded, then motioned towards the metallic

contraption that started where Arden's gouty foot ended. "And the prosthetic, how's it working out for you?"

"Just fine," Arden said, not wanting to be in the doctor's debt, though he already was. In truth, that gargoyle did him a favor, ridding him of that painful appendage. He could walk normally again, and though his joints still pained him, he could at least switch from laudanum to high-end spirits like a true gentleman, and still sleep soundly.

"Very good. Listen, Arden, I'm sure you know the real reason for my visit..."

"Aye. Told ya before. Your secret is safe with me. So long as you keep my daughter safe. Don't send her on any suicide missions." He turned to look at the pale man.

Ledoux met his eyes, they did not waver. "Absolutely not. You'd be proud of her progress. Her reputation grows quick on the Miss."

Arden gave a noncommittal grunt.

"Surely, what you saw down there must change your views on the world I have helped create. Your wife—"

"It did. But I'm an old man, Ledoux. I don't have the energy to cause a fuss like Melinda did. Besides, despite the abhorrent source of your energy, you've done the world good. Ushered man into a new age. I'm sure there're questions of ethics to be considered but I'll leave that for the philosophers. I'm just an old river rat. I won't rock the boat." Arden thought of his wife, how she'd been right all along. Feeling guilty for taking this man's hush money, but really, he was in no position to do much else.

"Very well, I believe you. Take care of yourself, Arden," Ledoux said, squeezing his shoulder before leaving.

Arden watched the channel, his eyes searching for the *Queen* as she rumbled up the great brown vein, looking with his sighter's scope for that thatch of red hair in the pilot house.

Arden may have taken the hush money, and he wasn't lying about being a tired old river rat. But Danielle was every bit her mother's daughter. He smiled as he watched her pilot the upgraded *Queen* down the bank.

SNAFU: PUNK'D

Ledoux had no idea how infamous the Wharton name would soon become.

THE HUNT

Steve Lewis

The hangar bay was silent as the crews put the finishing touches on their machines. Normally a loud and cheerful place, tonight the mood was sombre. Faces were long, men looked worried and there was no room for banter at all.

A clock chimed loudly, and they all halted work and looked at it, counting the strikes. At nine bells it stopped, and they all drew deep sighs, resigned.

Major Tim Mitchum entered the room and moved to the middle, closest to the hangar doors. "Men, it's time," he said, his voice cutting comfortably through the large open area. "You all know what needs to be done, you've trained for it. Just trust each other, yourselves, and your Walkers, and we'll all get through this."

Despite sounding confident, Mitchum didn't believe that for an instant. Men would die tonight, but the monster they hunted would die with whoever didn't make it.

The men nodded, drawing deep breaths and calming noticeably. Some of them even believed it, which made the lie worthwhile for the few hours it might take to prove him wrong.

"I'll take point in Walker One," he said. "Walker Two to the right, Walker Three to the left." Mitchum re-hashed the plans and formation they'd gone over a dozen times. "No more than thirty yards apart. I want every Walker in visual range of at least one other. If the fog rolls in and you lose sight, move closer until you have eyes-on again."

"No problem there, sir," said Clarence, the driver for Walker Two, an experienced man who'd been piloting since before the world went bad.

279

"Good," Mitchum said with a nod. "I don't want any heroes tonight. No one goes off-plan thinking they can deal with this themselves."

There were murmurs of agreement throughout the hangar, and Mitchum clapped his hands together. "Let's mount-up then. I want boilers hot within ten minutes and all Walkers through the gate without fuss."

The men scrambled to their Walkers, and Mitchum went to his own, looking it over. They were large contraptions stood some twelve feel high at rest and twenty feet across the middle. The large, bowl-shaped crew compartment rested atop a steam engine that powered an eight-legged drivetrain – for all the world looking like some weird scientist's giant mechanical spider. The Walkers were the pinnacle of steam-driven military hardware.

Someone behind him coughed, politely, and Mitchum turned. It was the base commander, McAdams, his look of perpetual worry more pronounced than usual.

"You don't need to do this you know," McAdams said, quietly. "We can send word to the new Parliament, they'll send troops down to deal with whatever's out there."

Mitchum shook his head. "We broke away from Parliament for a reason, every one of us," he said, voice stern. "If we call for their help now, they'll come in and take everything and everyone back."

"Maybe they've changed," McAdams said. "I heard they had new elections, *real* elections this time. They've promised to be better."

"And if they're worse?" Mitchum nodded towards the thick hangar door. "This looks like their dream scenario. Either the thing out there kills us all, or we call them for help and admit we can't look after ourselves. Either way, we stop being a problem."

"You need to look at the bigger picture. We can't afford to lose the men or the Walkers, not just to keep face."

"I *am* thinking about the bigger picture," Mitchum replied. "A lot of the other counties followed our lead and broke away from Parliament. If we turn back now, they'll all cave and everything goes back to what it was."

THE HUNT

"You don't know that."

"Yeah, I do," Mitchum said. "Now if you'll excuse me, I have things to do."

Mitchum turned away from McAdams and climbed aboard the Walker, taking his position in the commander's seat. Other than the driver, there were six more men aboard, each nestled behind a shielded firing point. A gatling sat either side of the Walker, covering the flanks, and firing directly ahead was a short-barrelled 3" breechloading cannon. The other men covered flanks and the rear, armed with double-barrelled heavy rifles capable of bringing down an elephant… not that there were any left in the world.

He wondered if he wasn't going out under-gunned.

The engines were running hot now, and steam hissed through the drive train. With a lurch, the Walkers rose, adding another ten feet to their height, and they shambled towards the hangar gate.

The gates lifted—fast—and a dozen men with heavy rifles rushed out to secure the area. It wasn't a job anyone wanted, but it needed to be done. If one of the creatures got in through the open gate then the entire base could be destroyed. The covering detail were the sacrifice that bought time for the gate crew.

Tonight, nothing lurked outside, and the Walkers moved quickly out and took up their positions. With the area secure, the cover detail retreated and the gate slammed shut. The Walkers were alone now, hunting the darkness for a creature that no-one had even seen.

"Take us out slowly, Henders," Mitchum said quietly. "The rest of you, keep an eye out and make sure the other two Walkers don't stray too far."

The men murmured acknowledgement, and the Walker crept into the darkness.

Walkers were designed for all-terrain use, easily able to step over small obstacles while maintaining a stable firing platform. Capable of about eight miles an hour, they were perfect for this kind of work.

SNAFU: PUNK'D

The creature they were hunting had been stalking the area for months, and they had hoped it would just take what it wanted and then move away. It hadn't. Each night it had killed something or someone in the area. Firstly cows and sheep, then the dogs that had been sent out to track it down. Now, it had taken to breaking into the smaller family forts around the edge of their territory, leaving nothing alive.

Tracks suggested a creature nearly ten feet long, and those tracks were made by large, clawed feet that could move quickly when it wanted. They assumed it hid during the day, the shattered landscape providing plenty of spaces to hide.

If it wasn't going to leave then they needed to hunt it down.

One of the men tapped on the bar that ran around the crew platform like a tubular bell and used to signal the rest of the crew. Henders stopped and the men readied their weapons. Mitchum was pleased to see the other two vehicles had closed up and also stopped – they were alert and keeping an eye on him at least. Then he, too, was straining his eyes into the darkness.

Jenkins sighed. "Sorry, sir," he said. "I thought I saw something, but it must have just been a shadow."

"All good, Jenkins," Mitchum replied, reaching out to pat the man on the shoulder. "Better to call us to a stop once too often than once not enough." He waited until everyone's nerves settled, then tapped Henders on the shoulder. "Take us to the east boundary and then swing us around to the north to see what's out that way."

They moved slowly but surely out to the markers that defined the eastern edge of their territory. The other fortresses around them were each similarly designed and manned, and while some didn't mind sharing when they could, all were particularly precious about the resources within their own boundary.

They were also precious about their own lives, and while it would have made sense to combine their forces and hunt the creature down, relationships with neighbouring counties were strained, to say the least – some had wanted to break away from government control, others felt they'd been coerced, and right now everyone just wanted to let things settle and make the best of the situation. Everyone seemed to think like McAdams, that it was better for someone else to take the risks – Mitchum didn't want to die to prove a point, but someone needed to step up if they were going to make what was left of the word a better place.

They encountered nothing as they moved along the boundary line before swinging to the north. The signal bar rang again and Henders stopped the Walker.

"I've lost Walker Three, sir," Allenby said from his position at the left-side gatling. "It was there, then it wasn't."

"I can see an outline of something," said Bowles, the man beside him. "Might be the Walker, might not be... it's not moving though, so hard to say."

Flashes of light erupted from that direction, a gatling firing rapidly.

"Henders, get us over there!" Mitchum said. "Eyes out, fire at anything that isn't a Walker!"

The machine lurched about and scuttled quickly over the rough terrain towards—

The firing stopped abruptly.

Then the Walker came into view. Men moved about in the crew compartment, and Mitchum could hear raised voices.

"What happened?" he yelled when they were twenty or so yards away. "Is everyone alright?"

"Something spooked Simmons and he opened fire," came the reply from Barker, the commander of Walker Three. "Says he saw something moving but looks like it was just shadows or mist."

"Let me know when you've reloaded, and we'll continue on," Mitchum yelled back, and had Henders return them to their original position to wait.

Five minutes passed and they were still waiting. Did Barker think they were going to form up on him? Mitchum thought he'd been clear, and cursed quietly. "Henders, take us back to Walker Three. I think Barker is waiting for us to come to him."

Henders turned them around and they made their way back

to the other machine, which sat waiting silently in the same position.

"What's the problem, Barker?" Mitchum yelled.

Silence.

Something very much *was* the problem – the Walker was intact, but there was no movement aboard.

"Take us in slow, Henders," Mitchum said. "Eyes out men, this doesn't look right."

Henders pulled up beside the other Walker and Mitchum shined his chemical lantern into the crew compartment.

The men were dead, or at least those he could see. A Walker had a crew of eight, and Mitchum counted only five bodies. Looking at the torn state of the corpses and the blood splashed across the Walker's crew compartment, he could only guess what had happened.

Walker Two pulled up, and Mitchum heard the curses from the men aboard as they took it all in.

"Well, it's definitely out here," Browne said from his commander's seat in Walker Two. "I was hoping it would just move on."

"No point sticking to the perimeter now," Mitchum said. "It must have come from farther in, hopefully we can track and deal with it."

"Where do you want us, Mitchum?" Browne asked. "Flank or rear?"

"Stay on the right flank, only closer," Mitchum replied. "Twenty feet if you can. I want us shoulder to shoulder."

"Roger that," Browne said. "Make sure your gunners on our side don't get spooked."

Mitchum grunted in reply. They'd just lost a third of their force in a heartbeat, killed in a defendable position, on full alert, with two other Walkers a score of yards away. The men died fast and quiet, and Mitchum wasn't sure what kind of creature could to do so that quickly.

He waited until Walker Two took its flanking position before continuing on. The moon was high now, shining through patchy cloud cover. The broken earth and jumbled terrain made for impossibly long shadows and moving clouds made it look like everything and then nothing, was moving. It was surreal, nerve wracking.

A few hundred yards in one of the men rang the bell and Thames raised his rifle to fire. The man paused, then lowered his weapon, shaking his head. "Sorry sir, another shadow," he said, shrugging. "Everything seems to be jumping about at the moment."

"That's alright, Thames," Mitchum said. "Next time take the shot, shadow or not."

"Will do, sir, will do," Thames replied. "I had—"

A blur of movement launched over the side railing, a long claw reaching down and tearing Thames's head off, his body falling to the deck of the fighting compartment, jettisoning blood. Men screamed and for a moment Mitchum was afraid the creature had landed amongst them, that they were all about to meet the same fate as Walker Three.

But the creature leapt onto the back of Walker Two, killing two rear men before bounding away into the night.

Walker Two opened fire, its right-side gatling firing into the darkness as fast as its gunner could crank the handle. Mitchum doubted he'd hit anything but was open to the possibility of a miracle. He waited until the swirling barrels ran dry before he cut in.

"Cease fire!" he barked, listening for the creature.

Nothing.

The two Walkers edged closer.

"How bad?" Mitchum asked. "I've lost one."

"Two dead for me," Browne replied. "Both rear men, and I don't think we hit it at all."

"Thames said he saw something move, thought it was a shadow just before the thing attacked," Mitchum said. "If anyone sees anything suspicious, even if they think it *is* a shadow, open fire. I don't care if we kill a whole bunch of cows and fill trees full of holes, I'd rather you fired on a hunch than not fired at all."

"Roger that," Browne replied. "We'll fire at anything and everything that looks out of place."

"Did you see which way it went?"

"Back the way we came," Browne said, "but I have a feeling it's a cunning one and might be circling around to get at us from different angles."

"It might have been hunted before," Mitchum said, "which means it's a fast learner."

"Are you sure *we're* hunting *it*," Browne replied, "and not the other way around?"

"You're probably right." Mitchum nodded slowly. "We might have to re-think this."

"You're the boss. Let us know what you come up with."

The Walkers resumed their course, Mitchum doing his best to formulate a plan. It wasn't easy. His attention rested firmly on what lay outside the crew compartment, more focused on making it through until morning.

He was jarred from his musings by an explosion of the 3" gun below him. Mitchum peered ahead, straining to find a target, but the muzzle flash had dazzled his eyes and he couldn't see anything.

"What was it?" he asked Johanson, the Walker's main gunner. "What did you see?"

"Nothing, sir," Johanson replied with a grimace. "No-one else really saw anything either before they were attacked, so figured I might as well fire off a shot into the dark and hope it landed where that monster was lurking."

It was as good a plan as any. "Good idea, Johanson, keep it up," he said. "Fire a shot at random every few minutes, just make sure you save a few rounds in case we actually find it." He turned to the two men at the gatlings. "And that goes the same for you two. Every so often just fire a dozen rounds into anything that looks like it could have a monster hiding in it."

"We have plenty of ammunition, sir," Allenby, his left-side gatling man replied. "We'll keep the damned thing on its toes."

Browne must have picked up on what they were doing, and soon both Walkers were firing random bursts into the dark.

THE HUNT

Mitchum didn't want both machines reloading at the same time, so had his men time their fire to cover Walker Two. Browne reciprocated, and Mitchum hoped it would be enough.

It wasn't.

The one place they couldn't cover was the gap between the two Walkers. It was only a small gap, some fifteen yards wide, and the creature must have lain in wait in their blind spot. It burst from the shadows and clambered up the side of Walker One. Smalls, unable to fire due to Walker Two being so close, sat idle in the right-side position and didn't even see the creature as it bounded up the side of the Walker and raked a long claw through his torso, cutting him in half.

Bowles, beside him, managed to lift his heavy rifle and fire both barrels before the creature yanked him over the edge. He screamed briefly, the sound disappearing into the night as the creature dragged him away. Then merciful silence.

Henders stopped the Walker when the screams cut off. "Now what?" he asked, trying to keep his voice down but failing. "That thing will pick us off one at a time and we've barely caught a glimpse of it."

"How far are we from the old Vickers Field?" Mitchum asked.

"Ten minutes maybe, seven if we push it," Henders replied. "Shouldn't we head back to base?"

"We can't afford to lead it back there," Mitchum said. "If it gets inside when the gates open, we've lost everything."

Henders nodded reluctantly, and turned the vehicle around, the steam valves as wide as they'd go. The Walker picked up speed, and Mitchum was relieved to see Walker Two was keeping pace. More, Browne had turned on all of the chemical lights that dotted the Walker's fighting compartment and drivetrain. It lit the Walker up, but as the creature had no problem seeing them in the dark, they needed at least *some* light to give a warning.

It was a nervous dash, the men on alert and ready to fire. Mitchum was very aware of the blind spots created by the dead men. It struck him that the creature was *very* aware of his blind spots, always targeting areas where men couldn't see or couldn't fire. It was more than just cunning. It was intelligent, which was even more disturbing.

Vickers Field was an old aerial field turned to ruin after the creatures descended on the planet. The ground was torn up and the hangars had long been pulled apart for material to build various fortresses in the area, but the fuel tanks were surprisingly intact. The field was wide and clear and had fewer covered lines of approach than the forested areas they'd been traversing.

Reasoning that they'd arrived before the creature, Mitchum gambled that they'd have at least a few minutes before it caught up with them, which gave him some time to prepare.

There were drums of oil scattered about the place, most of them intact, and it didn't take long for Henders to use the Walker's legs to nudge some from their pile and into position around the centre, puncturing them once they were in place.

Back in a central position with Walker Two, Mitchum fired a flare from his signalling pistol at the first pile of drums. It burst into flames and lit up that side of the field. Two more flares ignited the remaining two stacks of drums, and then he sat back and waited.

He wasn't sure if the creature was going to attack or would just decide to move away from the light. Dawn was only an hour away, and the creature rarely attacked in daylight, so if nothing else, he'd created a defendable position where they could hopefully see the night out and return to the relative safety of the fortress.

Henders had moved Walker One back-to-back with Walker Two, which meant their main armament—the 3" cannon—covered different angles and their gatlings covered wide arcs around them. In theory, there wasn't an approach they didn't have covered, but Mitchum wondered if they'd missed something somehow.

The place was brightly lit. If the creature was a dumb animal that hunted in the dark, it would avoid the light entirely; similarly, if it was intelligent and knew it had lost one of its main advantages, it would wait until the oil burned down or just leave. For Mitchum, there was a third option he was afraid was more likely. It *was* intelligent, very much so, and didn't just want the kill. It wanted the *win*.

Competition for the sake of competition was a very human trait, one he'd never considered in another creature. If it attacked now, it would be doing it solely to prove that it could, and that idea shook Mitchum to the core. If he survived this, he'd have to rethink everything he thought he knew about the creatures and start working out how to deal with something that was at least as intelligent, and competitive, as the humans it was hunting down.

On Walker Two, Browne saw something move ahead of him and fired his pistol. He didn't expect to hit anything, but it was the easiest way to alert everyone.

Mitchum turned to look, his vision completely blocked by the bulk of Walker Two, and then Allenby on his left gatling opened fire. Silhouetted by the burning drums, a large, clawed beast moved quickly, jumping forward in sideways leaps like a big cat and throwing off Allenby's aim.

"Over here," Mitchum yelled, raising his own pistol. "Incoming!"

"Bullshit," Browne yelled back. "It's over here and closing in fast!"

"Shit!" Mitchum cursed. "There's two of them!"

The men opened up with everything they had. Jenkins, Walker One's rear man now, edged around to bring his rifle to bear but Mitchum sent him back. "Stay at your post," Mitchum yelled. "There might be more than two, keep watch on the rear."

Jenkins turned back. There *was* another, moving quietly through the flickering light, sticking to the shadows as best it could, using the distraction caused by the other two to get close. He raised his rifle, yelling the alarm, and fired just as the creature leapt to attack. His twin shots slammed into it, punching deep into its chest and striking something vital. It roared as it dropped, then snarled at Jenkins – the snarl turned into a ragged cough as blood poured into its lungs, then it slumped to the ground, claws raking the edge of the compartment a foot short from where Jenkins sat in absolute terror.

The other two were close now, close enough to see the snarls on their faces and the blood on their jaws.

In front of Walker Two, that creature held its line a little too long and Browne's gunner walked his fire onto it. The creature staggered and stopped, the gatling firing round after round into it. The creature twitched and jerked as the heavy lead rounds punched into it, still trying to move forward to get to them, and Browne let his gunner continue to fire until his weapon ran dry. There was nothing but broken bones and mangled flesh left, and even then Brown had one his remaining rifleman put a pair of heavy bullets into what he figured was left of its head.

Walker One was having a more difficult time of it. The creature closing in was much more agile and patient, spending as much time moving sideways as forwards. It was impossible to get a bead on it with the slowly traversing gatlings, and it neared enough to ready itself for a springing attack that would carry it into the fighting compartment of the Walker.

It leapt, but Henders was ready for it. He pulled back on the control levers and the Walker rose, adding another ten feet to its height. The creature slammed into the side of the compartment and slid down. Before it could get to its feet, Henders spun the Walker around and punched one of the heavy legs deep into it, pinning it to the ground before tearing the creature in half as the powerful mechanical leg pivoted through it.

Mitchum scanned his surrounds, tense, waiting for more, but none came. He looked over at Browne in Walker Two, who was scouring the area just as intently. When both were satisfied that there were none left, Browne gave Mitchum a thumbs-up and had his driver slowly back Walker Two up until they were almost touching.

"I think we got them all," Browne said. "It never occurred to me there was more than one."

"Me either," Mitchum said. "I guess if there were more, they'd all be out hunting together."

THE HUNT

"Like lions," Browne added, "hunting in packs."

Mitchum frowned.

"What's wrong?"

"Lions," Mitchum replied. "Only the females hunt, the males stay put and let their mates do all the work."

"It was just an expression," Browne said, "I didn't mean for you take it literally."

"But what if you're right?"

"You think we'll find a male lurking around somewhere?"

"Maybe. Or it's the other way around, and the males hunt while the female nests, like spiders."

"That's not a good thought," Browne said. "It'll be daylight soon, the best time to go looking."

"They'll be expecting us back at base, we should report back in, get more men and re-arm."

"That'll take hours," Browne said. "We should go now while we're still out here."

Mitchum, reluctantly, agreed.

A quick tally of ammunition showed they were low, but Walker Three wasn't far away. They could restock coal and water for their steam engines as well.

In daylight, they found plenty of tracks, all leading west. Reloaded and re-armed, the two machines set off westward. The fields were quite open. Visibility was good, with very few places to hide, and the men started to relax for the first time since they'd left their hangar the night before.

That feeling was short-lived, however, as the fields gave way to low hills, each dotted with small clumps of trees. Following from Browne's lion analogy, the male would likely be resting in a tree somewhere, waiting for one of the females to bring it something to eat.

By reputation, Mitchum knew the lioness was considered the more aggressive hunter, but the male lion was head of the pride due to its greater size and strength. It was more than a match for even the most ferocious lioness if it came to a stand-up fight. If that were the case here, they could expect the male to easily be twenty to thirty percent bigger, maybe as much as fifty percent, and would take a whole lot more killing to put it down.

The woods grew denser, and the Walkers slowed to a crawl. A hundred yards from the edge, Mitchum signalled them to a stop and all those aboard the Walkers scanned the woods for some sign of the creature.

"I got something, sir," Callum said, pointing. "In the large elm, slightly to the right."

Mitchum used his own telescope and scanned the tree. There *was* something there, and he increased the magnification. It was a body. One of his own men based on the tattered uniform, wedged high into a tree fork.

"We're in the right spot alright," Browne said over the noise of the Walkers' engines. "The must have dragged some of the bodies here for a daytime snack."

"That looks like Bowles," Mitchum said. "Horrible way to go."

"There's no good way," Browne replied. He scanned the woods again, then shrugged. "I'm not seeing anything, not really seeing somewhere a creature that big could hide."

"Want me to break the place up a little, sir?" Johanson asked, tapping the breech of his 3" gun. "That'll get its attention, if nothing else."

"Might as well," Mitchum replied. "Everyone else, watch your flanks, we know these things like to creep in close before they attack."

Johanson fired, the cannon bucking the Walker heavily, and his explosive round arced into the woods ahead. It exploded amongst them, breaking a few trees low on the trunk and sending shards of wood flying everywhere.

Coleson, in Walker Two, fired his cannon with much the same effect. Each shot echoed through the low hills and brought down another tree. Soon, the place was a mess, with broken tree trunks and shattered branches strewn everywhere. Mitchum was hoping the creature would attack soon, he certainly didn't relish moving the Walkers slowly through that mess. Not with rough footing and dozens of places for a creature to hide.

Jenkins fired again, this time bringing down a large tree as his round struck the thick base. The trunk cracked neatly in two, and as the upper part fell, *things* dropped out of the branches.

They were young creatures, only a few feet long, but they were fast and they were plenty. Some died as they landed, crushed under the falling branches, but the rest scrambled to their feet. Seeing their attackers, they scuttled towards them, not the sharp, leaping bounds of the larger ones, but the determined rush of swarms.

Coleson fired again, his round landing amidst a dozen of them. The blast scattered them, killing one or two, but the rest landed awkwardly and then continued their rush.

"Henders, bring us around!" Mitchum yelled. "Get one of the gatlings to bear!"

Henders turned the Walker to the left, bringing the right-side gatling into play. The gunner wasted no time in cranking the handle and walking his fire into the mass of creatures.

It took only a round or two to kill these creatures, small as they were, and the gatling fired plenty of rounds per minute. There were so many of them, however, and the gatling couldn't fire fast enough to do much more than slow them down. Walker Two had turned now and was pouring its own gatling fire into the swarm. The extra firepower took its toll, and the leading edge of the swarm began to roll back as the first ones died.

"Henders, back us up, slowly," Mitchum said. "Let's keep our distance if we can."

One of the advantages of the Walker's eight-legged drive train was than it could move effectively in any direction – forwards, backwards or sideways was much the same, and the only real limitation was the driver's skill. Henders was an excellent driver and Walker One edged slowly away, dwindling the rate at which they were approaching while allowing the gatling gunner a stable platform.

Clarence in Walker Two was good, but not in Henders league. Walker Two moved away slowly, and the swarm gained.

Mitchum cursed and had Henders slow his withdrawal to let Walker Two catch up.

"Getting low on ammunition, sir," Allenby called. "Another few bursts and I'm out. We'll need to reload."

Reloading the gatling was a laborious task. These gatlings had a complex belt-and-hopper feed system, which gave them a much greater ammunition load but an intricate, manual reload. That took time Mitchum knew they didn't have.

"Henders!" he barked. "Bring us around, bring the left-side gatling to bear!"

Henders nodded and stopped Walker One before carefully pivoting the machine one hundred and eighty degrees.

The other gatling gunner was dead, so Allenby just slid across the compartment and swung the gatling down into action. The crack of rounds punctuated the turn of the handle, and immediately the swarm slowed. Soon, the rate of killing them exceeded their rate of advance, and the swarm stopped entirely.

"Reload!" Browne yelled from the other Walker, and Mitchum had his men do the same.

It took five minutes to reload both gatlings. Mitchum took the time have his riflemen put shots into any of the creatures that moved, even if it was nothing more than a death spasm.

With the Walkers close together, Mitchum looked over at Browne. "These look very young," he said, "and a lot more of them than I thought there would be, if I'd given it any thought that it is."

"There's a lot more of these young ones than there are adults," Browne said, nodding agreement. "Maybe spiders was a better analogy than lions after all."

"So, mummy spider then?" Mitchum asked, then sighed. Female spiders could be vastly bigger than their male counterparts, easily a hundred times larger or more. He'd been worried about fighting a male 'lion' that weighed fifty percent more than the ones they'd fought the night before, and the idea of something *that* big just staggered him.

Browne nodded. "If it is, we definitely need to kill it," he replied. "A handful of adults tore us apart last night. If these little ones had grown to full size, they'd wipe out the whole county in a matter of weeks."

Mitchum sighed again, knowing that was accurate, and knowing it had to be them doing something about it, and right now. "I'm open to ideas," he said. "That thing could be huge, and I really don't want to go in there and deal with it at close range."

"I thought it might come out when we were killing its young," Browne replied. "Maybe it doesn't have that kind of maternal instinct."

"Maybe we could burn it out, sir," Henders said. "Plenty of kindling there. Might not take too much to set it on fire."

"Volunteering to go in with some matches, Henders?" Mitchum asked.

Henders snorted in reply. "Not likely, sir," he said. "If we light this edge of the forest, it'll likely flee the other way, and we'll have a hell of a time trying to find it again. We'll need to light the fire behind it and hope that drives it towards us."

"Not my idea of 'hope', I'll have to say," Mitchum said, "but you're right, we don't want to lose it after all this."

"What about flares?" Browne asked. "I have two left, used the rest last night at Vickers Field on those drums."

Mitchum quickly counted his own. "Eight in total." He tossed three over to Browne, so they both had five. "We'll need to get close to the edge of the forest, these things don't have much of a range."

"Go together?"

Mitchum shook his head. "Let's keep one of us here on watch, guns ready, while the other one dashes close and fires a few flares, see what happens. After that, we swap and try again."

"That sounds like as good a plan as any," Browne replied.

"The best I have anyway," Mitchum added. "You get set up, and when you're ready we'll make the first run."

"Good luck!"

Henders moved the Walker a few paces forward, and then waited until Browne had Walker Two right where he wanted it, opting to have the main cannon pointed directly ahead, reasoning that the creature would be larger than normal and that the cannon would do the most damage. A thumbs-up signalled he was ready, and Henders moved Walker One off as fast as he could.

Rather than run right up and fire, Mitchum built up speed and ran parallel to the woods, that way he already had some speed available if the creature decided to emerge while they were effectively stationary. It also meant he was moving across the front of Walker Two, so wouldn't be as likely to block their fire if they had to shoot.

At full speed, Henders turned the Walker back in a slow arc, maintaining the best pace he could. He drew close, and Mitchum fired his flare, aimed as far back as possible into the broken woods, then fired another.

He managed to get two flares off before Henders ran out of tree line and turned the machine back to re-join Walker Two in the firing position.

The flares seem to have fizzled out, or at least hadn't caught anything flammable enough to start the fire Mitchum wanted. They gave it a few more minutes then Browne signalled he was ready to give it a try. Swapping positions, Browne made his own dash across the face of the forest.

Again, two flares arced out, landing deep in the woods, but again nothing seemed to catch alight. They did see smoke, however, some of it building very slowly. All they needed was a small puff of wind to turn it into a full blaze.

Two more flares, and they waited, hoping, while Browne got ready for his second run.

Smoke rose from the rear of the woods now, spreading as the fire took hold. The prevailing wind was towards them, and smoke rolled up the hill on which they stood. Though not thick, it was enough to have them don their goggles.

The flames grew bigger, and soon the forest was well and truly ablaze. They tensed, expecting the creature to break out of the woods at any minute and charge towards them.

THE HUNT

They didn't have to wait long.

It was *big*. Much bigger than they'd expected. Larger than a Walker.

It burst from under a mass of logs and branches, tossing them aside like they were matchsticks. It moved away from the fire slowly, then saw them and gave an almighty bellow.

It was terrifying. A high-pitched wail that could cut through the air for miles, but with a deep bass element that seemed to vibrate right through them and trigger some primordial fear response.

Mitchum sat back with a start, frozen to immobility, and most of the crew did the same. Two of them would have jumped out and ran if they weren't strapped in.

Browne seemed to be made of sterner stuff, and he rallied his men quickly. The 3" cannon spoke, an explosive round cutting across the distance between Walker Two and the creature and exploding on impact.

The creature flinched, and maybe broke its stride a little, but the round didn't seem to have much effect. It continued on, pushing over and through the fallen trees in an effort to get clear of the woods to attack.

The sounds of firing brought Mitchum and his men back to earth, and Johanson fired his own cannon. This one struck the creature's face, but other than drawing another bellow, it had a similar lack of effect.

"Load anti-Walker rounds!" Mitchum bellowed. "Its hide is too tough, explosive rounds just aren't cutting it!"

Henders slowly moved the Walker backwards, trying to get some distance but still keep the creature in sight. He only had a few dozen yards before he reached the crest of the hill, and after that the creature would disappear behind the rise and into a massive blind spot.

Johanson had loaded his cannon's 'ready rack' with explosive rounds, expecting to deal with nothing that required anything heavier. It would take time to break the armour-piercing ammunition out and load it, even by hand, and Mitchum wasn't sure they had time.

"Henders, keep us out of reach!" Mitchum yelled. "Everyone else, we need anti-Walker ammunition for the cannon, get to it!"

Everyone moved to the ammunition bunker to roll out the anti-Walker rounds. That meant the other weapons were unmanned. The gatling was silent as Allenby moved into line to pass cannon ammunition forward.

Browne must have realised what was going on and charged his Walker forward, running at an oblique line across the creature, hoping to draw it away from Walker One. His own gatling was firing, striking the creature about the head and torso, and they clearly had its attention now.

Walker Two dodged across the front of it, jinking left and right to give both gatlings a chance to fire. The heavy rounds seemed only to annoy it, but Browne was hoping for a lucky shot, maybe a shot through the eye into something important.

That didn't happen, and the creature finally made its way through the fallen trunks and into clear ground. Shaking itself like an oversized dog leaving water, it bellowed again, then gave chase.

Browne had hoped that the creature was slower than its smaller brethren, and he was relieved to see he was right. It was about the same speed as a Walker, though its extra strength and greater innate coordination meant it could side-step obstacles easier and that gave it an effectively higher speed.

Browne had Clarence fully open the steam valves, making full speed directly away from it. The creature roared in anger, clearly intent on catching and killing the humans aboard, and with nothing but a heavy hunting rifle in the rear part of the Walker to slow it down, it was just a matter of time.

Henders swung Walker One down the hill and gave chase, careful of his unbuckled crew. He managed to get down the hill and directly behind without losing anybody.

The creature was twenty yards behind Walker Two now, close enough to reach out with its long, clawed arms. Browne was out of ideas and could do nothing but open fire with his pistol, determined to at least go out fighting.

THE HUNT

Walker One fired.

Unlike the explosive rounds, which detonated on impact and scattered fragments and balls of shot around the target area, anti-Walker rounds were solid with a thin copper casing that fell away as the round left the chamber. It gave the round tremendous speed, and it was usually fast enough to punch through the armour plating that protected the machinery and crew of an enemy Walker.

The creature's hide was thick, but not that thick, and the round punched right through, carving a deep wound several feet into its flank. The creature stumbled. Fell.

It was quick to its feet. Too quick for Jenkins to reload from his ready rack and fire again. Henders brought Walker One around in a tight arc to gain some distance and time.

The creature followed, limping at first and then speeding up as it ignored the gaping wound. Browne took the opportunity to turn Walker Two about and fire his own anti-Walker round into it, which struck a joint, shattering bone. The creature's rear legs buckled, and it sat with a thud and a roar. It spun angrily from Walker to Walker as the machines turned back and closed in.

Both Walkers circled the creature, pouring gatling fire into it as they reloaded their cannon, and then Henders turned Walker One in towards it.

Johanson fired, sending his high-velocity round deep into the creature's chest, tearing a corridor through its vital organs that proved too much for it. It reared backwards then tumbled over, dead before it stopped rolling.

The men cheered, but Mitchum had them hold back their celebrations until they reloaded the cannon and fired another few shots into it. It didn't even twitch. Only then did Mitchum let out a long sigh and join the men in their celebration.

Browne and Mitchum drew their Walkers side by side some twenty yards from the creature, their gunners keeping an eye on it and the burning forest while they talked.

"I can't imagine how something that big got through the other counties," Browne said. "You think someone would have done something about it."

"They did," Mitchum replied, pointing at the creature's heavily scaled torso – it was dotted with recent scars, no doubt from heavy rifle slugs. "They drove it here, figured they'd move it on until someone else dealt with it."

"Or maybe until it dealt with us," Browne said, frowning. "This sounds like the shitty kind of thing Parliament would do."

Mitchum nodded. "They're no fans of the break-away counties, that's for sure. If we can prove it though, a lot more counties will join us. This could be just what we need to swing everyone against them."

"What now?" Browne asked. "Head back, or keep looking in case there're more?"

"Surely there can't be more," Mitchum replied. "There wouldn't be enough food to feed them all."

Browne nodded. "I hope that's the case. I think we should head back and report in, people have got to be worried."

"I hope so," Mitchum said, then nodded back to the burning woods. "We'll need to go back and sweep that place, just in case some got away, and then back to Walker Three to deal with the bodies."

Browne nodded. "Taking them back?" he asked, then nodded as Mitchum shook his head. As much as he liked the idea of burying their dead in a secure place, there was too great a risk that the smell of blood would attract more creatures, even through thick dirt and a wooden coffin. There was also a risk that the creatures had some strange disease or bacteria on their claws that they'd transmit back to their base, and they were paranoid about the idea of letting something in they shouldn't.

"Johanson can pilot a Walker, he can bring Walker Three back in," Mitchum continued. "If you can lend him one or two of your men, that'll give him enough to get home, with us providing cover."

"We'll all be short-crewed," Browne replied, "but we can manage."

They struck out, Walker One in the lead and Walker Two close behind, and did a slow sweep past the burning forest. It was well and truly ablaze now, fire climbing the tall trunks and starting to leap from the crown of burning trees to the next. Soon, the entire forest would be gone, which was bad, but relatively better than leaving things alive in there that shouldn't be.

They continued back to Walker Three. With Walker Two on watch, Henders used the legs of his machine to gouge deep trenches into the soft ground, makeshift graves that were deep enough to hold a body down for years. That done, two men from each Walker disembarked and carried the bodies they found, or parts in some cases, and placed them reverently in their graves and then stood silently while Mitchum, as force commander, said a quick prayer over them. That done, Henders used his Walker's legs to pile dirt and rock onto the graves, sealing them away.

It was a rough burial, but the world was a rough place now, and having the luxury of being buried meant there were survivors still around to do it. The land was littered with men and women who had died at the hands of the creatures without the luxury of any burial or words of remembrance at all.

Johanson transferred to Walker Three, and Gusman and Archer from Walker Two joined him, the latter as a spotter/ gunner, the former as the temporary Walker commander. It took a while for Walker Three to build up a head of steam, but with their three Walkers manned and mobile again they were soon heading back to the fortress, where Mitchum would have the twin tasks of announcing a victory of sorts while then having to tell families how their men had died.

The latter was a job he'd rather offload, but he knew that their sacrifice has saved the fortress, for at least the near future.

He was pleased to see the lookout post was manned, and that their usual routines were still being met. The siren sounded when they were in position and men raced out to secure the area, and only then did the Walkers advance inside. Routine was good, it kept them safe.

As did the men that crewed the Walkers.

INFERNAL ENGINES

James A. Moore

How is it, Mister Crowley, that I have gone my entire life never seeing so much as a ghost and now I find a world of supernatural things that seem to come my way with great regularity?" Lucas Slate looked toward his companion with pale blue eyes and shook his head. The sun was beating down and he lowered the brim of his top hat to better fight off the glare.

Crowley flashed a short smile and chuckled. "That's simple, Mister Slate. You see more than you did before your unfortunate incident."

"'Incident?'"

Crowley pointed to his companion's chest. "We still don't know what to call that thing, do we?" His finger almost touched Slate's chest, where the stone that he'd once ingested rested inside his body and grew.

"Let's call it a seed, shall we?"

"So be it. That 'seed' is what changed your perceptions. Those things you did not see were always there. Always present. There are many creatures in this world that like to hide themselves away. I don't know if it's a natural defense or preference. I suspect it depends on which creature we are dealing with, really. They may be the predators in many cases, Mister Slate, but they are vastly outnumbered by humans and other creatures. It wasn't all that long ago that humans were tying 'witches' to stakes and burning them alive. Or hanging them, or simply torturing them for knowledge."

"You speak of the Salem witch trials?"

"They didn't just happen in Salem. They happened in places all over the world. Salem's just the one best known around these parts."

SNAFU: PUNK'D

"No, I mean why did these hunts take place?"

The two of them were riding, heading north into California. San Francisco was a long ways off yet, but it was their chosen destination for the present time. They would get there eventually, of course, but in the meantime, they proceeded through the desert territories, not far from the ocean but locked in the heat of the desert winds blowing from the east. They did not hurry themselves along the way. The horses would have protested too much. Best not to annoy the animals as neither of them were normal beasts but altered by the supernatural. In the case of Crowley's steed, he had summoned it a long while back, and while it usually behaved like a regular horse, it could get very stubborn and willful. In Slate's case, he'd brought the animal back from the dead and it was simply never the same as it was before.

"Because, my good man, people do not like strangers. Or rather, they don't like much that they perceive as strange." Crowley paused a moment and regarded his companion: Lucas Slate was an albino. He stood well over six and a half feet in height, was gaunt, and his face was nearly that of a cadaver. His pale blue eyes were usually half-lidded as if he were at the edge of sleep, and his long white hair fell beneath his top hat, which made him seem even taller than he already was. In short, he stood out in a crowd. "I daresay you've had a bit of experience with that issue yourself."

Slate nodded and replied, "That I have, sir. That I most definitely have," in his soft, southern drawl. They had passed through Mexico City not that long before, where Slate stood out very distinctly and where, as a result, the two men had ridden hard to get away from a mob of onlookers determined to examine him for whatever possible reason. Sometimes it was best not to wait around, and that was one of those rare occasions. The population was enough to very nearly guarantee trouble.

Now all was blissfully quiet.

Nothing good lasts forever.

Inevitably, the duo came across a town. It was a large establishment, easily a dozen buildings and offices plus a scattering of homesteads. The day was young and the town appeared derelict. No one moved that Crowley could see and Lucas Slate, who truly was blessed when it came to eyesight, spotted not a single soul.

"What do you make of that, Mister Slate?"

"Make of what, sir?"

"No one to be seen on this early morning. Hardly seems like a good way to get any business done."

"Is it Sunday? Perhaps they are all at services."

Crowley considered that possibility. The simple fact was that he didn't know and hadn't considered the notion as he was not a church going man.

There was a house of worship, but there would be no one inside the building as it had fallen into disrepair. Sometime in the fairly recent past the building had burned very nearly to the ground. All that was left was a strong stone foundation and the burnt remains of the actual structure. While the incident had happened recently there were dried streams of ash moving away from the ruins, like blood spilled from the newly dead. Rains had washed the ashes free of the main body, but there were no signs that the rains had happened recently, and the weather where Slate and Crowley had traveled were free of any storms or precipitation in the last ten days.

"I do not know if it's Sunday. And if there is a spiritual gathering it is not happening in that house of the Lord."

Slate nodded. "Agreed, sir. I wonder where they are."

"Could well be an abandoned town. Stranger things have happened."

A wind picked up and blew their way, coming from the distant ocean's direction. Lucas Slate squinted against the breeze and shook his head, frowning.

"What do you sense, Mister Slate?"

"I feel something in the air, as it were, Mister Crowley."

"Indeed?" Crowley looked around. He had learned to trust that Slate had excellent senses.

What they called the Skinwalker, the being that had changed the man, had made certain improvements to the undertaker. Slate often sensed things before Crowley himself did and that said a great deal as Crowley was not quite human.

Slate nodded. "More precisely, I can smell something like brimstone, and I can hear machinery."

"Truly?" Crowley smelled and heard nothing. Still, he checked to make certain his Navy revolvers were in their places and ready for use.

Slate nodded and he reached to the rifle strapped next to his saddle. "Do you know, Mister Crowley, how rare it is we come upon a town and I find myself without a sense of distress?"

"It does seem a rarity these days."

"Why is that?"

"You are a distrustful sort?" Crowley responded with a half-grin.

"There are people close by. Really, that's enough of a reason to be distrustful."

"That's a mite on the negative side, Mister Slate."

"Then I daresay you've trained me well, sir." Slate's head rose and he looked toward the west.

Crowley laughed and shook his head as he followed Slate's gaze to the four men riding their way. To the last, they were an unsmiling lot, with a look of hard laborers. The lead man was as tall as Slate, broader of shoulder and wore a bowler pushed down hard in an effort to hide his balding head. He wore it poorly.

As they got closer, the man leading the way spoke clearly. "This is private land."

"I see no signs to indicate as much and besides, we're only passing through." Crowley's demeanor did not change. He knew the men wanted trouble. Their presence and their posturing said as much. All of them were armed and while no weapons were drawn as yet, the whole lot of them seemed to anticipate the idea.

"Ain't no signs. I'm telling you."

"Consider us told. We'll be on our way."

"You'll be shot if we see you again."

Crowley smiled and leaned forward in his seat. "Now you're just being rude."

"Nossir. I'm warning you. Stay away."

Slate said, "Mister Crowley-"

And Crowley drew, cocked back the Navy's hammer and aimed square between the leader's eyes. "Warn me again."

"Mister Crowley-"

Bowler said, "Now see here."

"Warn me again. Please. I didn't hear the threat in your voice clearly."

The four men all stared at Crowley—the lead man focused solely on the barrel of his revolver—and Slate sighed.

Slate spoke again, calmly as he could under the circumstances. "My companion does not take well to threats is all, gentlemen. We can all back away from this. It isn't too late."

Crowley spoke calmly too. "It was too late a while ago, Mister Slate. Smell the air."

Slate sniffed the air and then shook his head, a scrawl of disgust moving across his features. "Something dead around here."

"Several somethings, Mister Slate."

The lead man looked at the pistol but did not seem particularly concerned. "You are not wanted here. This is private property."

"So you already said." Crowley did not lower his weapon.

"I don't understand, Mister Crowley."

"These men are not alive. Neither are their horses." Crowley continued to stare hard at the first man. "Look carefully at them, Lucas. Look very carefully."

Lucas Slate opened his senses as Crowley had taught him to do, and slowly an expression of horror crept across his visage.

"What in the name of God?"

As one unit the four men drew pistols and took aim at Jonathan Crowley.

Crowley shot first.

His bullet struck the lead man between the eyes and knocked his bowler away even as the skin dead center between bushy eyebrows exploded back with a loud whine. His head snapped back and the man came unseated. His horse did not panic but the man fell just the same, landing in the dirt directly behind his ride.

Three men prepared to fire. One man simply pulled the trigger and two others fanned back the hammers on their weapons. Crowley shot again, and one more time before the first bullet caught him in his left shoulder a few inches above his heart.

Two more bullets hit Jonathan Crowley in his chest and stomach and he fairly flew from the saddle instead of merely falling. His horse stepped back.

Lucas Slate didn't allow himself the luxury of thought. The rifle came up and he fired as fast as he could, aiming, pumping the Winchester's action and pulling the trigger at speeds that would have shamed most soldiers. He shot one man in the chest; another took a bullet through his hand that then slammed into his guts.

Lucas Slate was becoming something other than human, and his speed was close to that of a striking rattlesnake.

As fast as it started the shootout was done. Or at least it should have been. The sole man unstruck by weapons-fire was Lucas Slate, and the rest were unhorsed by the impacts of shots fired. The horses remained where they were, uncaring, and anyone paying close attention would have noticed that their eyes were too dry and that the equines were not breathing.

One of the men fired at Slate from a prone position. Slate got lucky. The bastard missed. He took careful aim himself and shot the man in the head. The bullet ricocheted and the man's head snapped hard to the right.

INFERNAL ENGINES

All four men were trying to stand.

Crowley was already up and wincing in pain.

"What the blue hell?" Slate backed away on his horse. He expected Crowley to get back up but the other four caught him off guard.

Crowley did not respond except to shake his head. There were bullet holes through his jacket and shirt, and through those holes Slate could see freshly mended flesh and still wet blood.

"I'll be needing your help, Mister Crowley."

"Good man." The words were barely a whisper.

Jonathan Crowley lived an odd life at the best of times. He was mostly immortal. He had been alive for God alone knew how long. He never gave Slate an honest, straightforward answer when the man asked when he was born. So long as there was a supernatural influence, Crowley would heal from very nearly any wound given enough time. The bigger the wound the longer it took, of course. Bullets could kill him, but perhaps because of Slate's presence, or that of the walking dead men, he was already well on his way to recovery. If the natural order was disrupted, he would heal.

Crowley was a powerful force in his own right, but there were limitations placed on him. He could use his abilities to defend himself and little else unless he was asked for assistance. It was a measure of his remaining humanity that Slate could ask and still get a good response. As he understood it, only humans could ask for Crowley's help and unlock his abilities.

At least a part of Slate must therefore still be human enough to count. That was how he understood the rules.

All of which merely explained why Crowley was standing and not ready for Slate's more mundane services as an undertaker.

The other four, who should have been just as dead, were a different story. They had not mended. They still bled. They had holes in their bodies and heads, and in one case a hand that was little more than flesh and—

They weren't bones. It was metal where bones should have been that showed through the gunslinger's hand where Slate had shot him.

309

Copper pistons and steel fingers wrapped in meat and skin. Slate shook his head, too shocked for words.

Crowley calmly pulled his other revolver and shot the man in the head for the second time. There was a loud metallic ping and the gunslinger dropped to the ground again, this time not getting back up.

"Seems we can kill 'em, Mister Slate. I'd recommend we get to it."

To prove his point, Crowley shot two more of the men in their heads, breaking them before they could finish rising from the ground. He looked at his handiwork and nodded with satisfaction.

Slate said, "More of them are coming, Mister Crowley. I don't think they like us very much."

There looked to be at least ten more, which was not a surprising number considering the size of the settlement.

"Gentlemen, we have a problem here." The man that spoke called out from the back of the crowd. He was slender and short and held himself like a general preparing for war. "My people don't feel pain. They weren't designed that way."

"'Designed?'" Crowley's voice carried easily enough.

"Designed." The man nodded. "I need loyal workers. I need hard workers. So I built my own."

"Out of what?"

The short man grew bolder and stepped his horse closer, surrounded by his followers. "Mostly steel and brass. But they needed to look as human as possible, so I used what was available." He shrugged.

"There's no mechanic in this world that could do what you've done." Crowley shook his head. "Daedalus himself couldn't have done this."

"Who?"

"You wouldn't have met him." Crowley shrugged.

"I managed well enough, with help, of course."

"What kind of help?"

"I've been at my work for a long, long time, Mister Crowley."

The small man grinned. "Yes, I know who you are. I know the rules you must live by. I have been prepared for you."

Crowley didn't waste any more time. He drew his pistol and took careful aim at the smiling man who very abruptly stopped smiling.

"I—"

"You've admitted being a threat to me." Now it was Crowley who smiled as Slate watched the interplay between the two men and said nothing.

"Don't you care who prepared me? Who sent me?" The small man shook his head and looked toward Crowley with worried eyes.

Crowley pulled the trigger and the small man's shoulder exploded in a crimson cloud. He fell from his horse, howling in pain, eyes wide and mouth gaping.

Crowley walked closer and the men who surrounded the now injured ringleader did nothing. "Not particularly. I'll find out in time." Slate's companion kept walking, paused long enough to reload his revolver, and moved forward again.

As for Slate himself, he looked through the site of his rifle and observed the closest of the strangers, who looked at Crowley but appeared to have no interest in him.

"Mister Slate?"

"Yes, Mister Crowley?"

"How many bullets can I put through this man before he dies?"

"That is a Colt Navy revolver, thirty-six caliber as I recall. You take the time to aim carefully, I imagine you could kill him with one shot or use twenty bullets or so to cut away pieces of his body. As you already delivered a telling shot to his shoulder you could probably cut that back to roughly fourteen additional shots if you're careful."

"Would you say I am a careful shot, Mister Slate?"

"One of the most skilled I have personally witnessed, sir."

Crowley very carefully took his time and aimed at the downed man's left foot.

The man's eyes grew very wide and he openly sobbed.

"Do you believe I can make you suffer, sir?" Crowley's voice was a purr.

"Yes! Yes, I do." He shook his head, silently begging for mercy.

"Your men do not feel pain. Do you?"

"Oh, God yes. Please don't shoot me again."

"Who told you of me?"

"I…" He hesitated.

Crowley kicked him in his heel, knocked his leg sideways and once again aimed his pistol. "Again, who told you of me?"

"I cannot tell you. Whatever you might do, he will do worse!"

Crowley looked at the man and shook his head slowly, lips pressed into an angry line and eyes burning with a threat of violence. "Am I a merciful man, Mister Slate?"

Slate shook his head and then removed his top hat to contemplate the inner brim. "Not to your enemies. Not that I have seen, sir."

"Do you believe I'll shoot this little bastard to get answers to my questions?"

"I know if for a fact, Mister Crowley."

"Best get to it then." The hammer pulled back on his revolver and Crowley grinned.

"Wait! Wait, please!"

"I am not a patient soul, sir. Answer now or lose your foot."

The man screamed, "Kill him!" and rolled sideways, wincing as his shoulder moved over the uneven earth.

The men around him lunged for Crowley.

Crowley shot at the screamer and put a bullet through his knee.

Lucas Slate took aim and put a bullet through the left eye and forehead of one of the men. Aimed again and shot another.

They would not stay down. Dead men kept rising again and as they did, their bodies shuddered and twitched, blood pumped and flesh stretched in unnatural ways. Clothing jumped and seams tore as the gathered men fell against each other and stood huddled together instead of fighting.

"What are you hiding?" Crowley scowled at the man and kept his revolver aimed at him.

"I'll tell you nothing and you'll find nothing. Know this, Jonathan Crowley, you are watched and you are hunted. You will die soon enough."

Crowley loomed over the wounded man on the ground who held his ruined knee and stared at Crowley with mad eyes and a twisted, bloodied grin on his face.

"Kill Jonathan Crowley, and his companion, too." He did not scream. He did not have to. They listened, those wretched, broken men, and they fell together in a heap that shivered and groaned.

And changed.

Flesh pulled apart and washed across the bodies in tiny, unnatural waves that grew stronger as the skin and muscles pulled free of metallic forms and warped together even as those metal bodies crawled into one massive heap.

"Infernal engines, Mister Crowley! I have been blessed with infernal engines designed solely for your demise."

Crowley scowled as the bodies shifted together in a wild array of limbs that grew and twisted under a sea of twitching flesh.

He paused long enough to shoot the small, grinning madman in the head and put an end to him, but if he hoped that would stop the men with their 'infernal engines', he was mistaken.

Instead, those strange men pushed together and became a golem of sorts, perhaps. It was large and multi-limbed.

Lucas Slate stared at the monstrosity and his lips formed whispered words that were not in English or any language he would claim to know. The Skinwalker was active inside of him and there was nothing to be done for it. The entity would protect itself from harm if it could.

When he finished talking, the skin on the amalgam of bodies began to blister and burn.

Crowley looked on and summoned his own sorceries, trying to understand what it was they fought against.

Metal twisted, and burned, and glowed as hot as a cattle brand fresh from the coals, as the forms rose higher on newly-shaped, thick legs. Crowley barely dodged as a burning limb rose up and then crashed down where he stood a moment before.

The thing towered in the morning light and rose higher still, taking a new shape that shivered and ticked, gears whirling inside the form – a clockwork nightmare given birth. A malformed skeleton of brass and steel rose from the ruins and stepped toward Crowley, intent on killing him.

Slate stared on, slack-jawed, surprised by the damnable thing.

Crowley did not have that luxury. He backpedaled and squinted up at the massive head, trying to make sense of what he saw. Mostly, it was several skulls now fused together with a jawline filled with metallic teeth. That hideous mouth opened and bellowed steam and fire.

"I think it's still growing." Crowley shook his head. Impossible, of course, but yes there was more mass to the thing as it grew new limbs and came for him again, fully prepared to crush him.

"I believe you are correct." Slate put his rifle away. It would do little good against a monster of fire and metal. What little flesh remained was burning away, courtesy of his sorceries, which had really done very little.

Crowley retreated again as the metal thing reached for him and tried to capture or crush him in its grip. Still, gears moved and pistons pumped and whatever hellish things those Infernal Engines were, they played by their own rules, working in harmony to unify a bigger, growing threat.

Slate dropped off his ride and sent the creature retreating. He moved in the opposite direction of his companion without being told to, offering a different target. "Come on then. Come for me." He gestured at the mechanical thing but it seemed to pay him no heed.

A conflagration of dead men burned at the base of the creature as it stepped away from the flames and charged toward

Crowley. Being of sound mind, Crowley chose to retreat again instead of being crushed. The golem towered nearly twenty feet in height and appeared to be growing both taller and wider.

Slate called out in the Skinwalker's tongue and a moment later dark clouds buried the sun. The clouds gathered quickly and winds blew the remaining fires in a half dozen directions at once.

"What are you up to, Mister Slate?"

Slate never answered. Instead the skies opened up and rains came down hard and fast, washing the ground, saturating the burning flesh of the dead and extinguishing fires. The ground hissed, the clockwork golem hissed as well, as red-hot metal cooled abruptly and shrieked in protest.

Slate opened his mouth to speak, turned slightly toward his companion, and made himself a target to the enemy. A vast metal bludgeon came down and slapped the undertaker hard enough to drop him to his knees and send his hat to the dirt a dozen feet away.

Crowley acted immediately, moving forward and summoning his powers as he considered how, exactly, to attack the metallic monster.

Slate stared at the ground and felt that familiar song build inside of him, the song that called and keened and tried to drown him as the Skinwalker sought control of his body. He was tempted to let it win, but knew better. Crowley was his guardian, not his friend, regardless of how friendly he often seemed. He would destroy the Skinwalker if he felt the need. Oh, he might mourn Slate's demise but he'd kill him just the same.

His bones ached from the savage treatment he'd been delivered and his left eye quickly swelled shut. It felt as if he'd been struck by an anvil and his skull ached.

And he was angry.

"Enough of this." Slate stood.

Crowley ducked a blow meant to crush him and the earth itself shook from the giant's impact.

Jonathon Crowley spoke and gestured and the metal giant screamed as brass and steel bent in on themselves. Metal protested and fragments of glass rained down on the earth. The Skinwalker stomped on the ground and spat words, and the dirt beneath the metal beast split open and swallowed half of the giant as it whirred and twisted trying to see two enemies at once.

A second stomp of the Skinwalker's foot, and the ground closed up again, crushing metal with ease. Pinned, half destroyed, the giant continued trying to attack. Crowley stepped back from it and so did Slate.

"And what, exactly, makes an engine infernal, Mister Crowley?"

"You mean aside from growing larger and building itself with no sign of human assistance?"

"Well, when you put it that way..."

"I honestly do not know. I've never before heard of an 'infernal engine'."

Both men eyed the oversized machine carefully as it struggled and failed to release itself from the ground.

"And who was that man?"

"Never saw him before either, Mister Slate. Nor do I know who sent him or prepared him to face me. Believe me, I intend to find out."

"He didn't do so well on that last part, I'm happy to say." Slate nodded and looked around.

"A fact that pleases me as well, Lucas." Crowley stared at the robotic thing where it fought still to break free, and then went to his horse's saddlebags.

"What are you looking for, Mister Crowley?"

"I'd have sworn we had dynamite."

"No, sir. You said it was 'unnecessary, all things considered.'"

"Seems rather short-sighted, looking back on how things have played out."

"Mister Crowley, you could bring along your own army and it would seem a fair precaution, I daresay."

"I don't know if I'm offended or amused, sir."

"Then let us call it amused, shall we?" Slate picked up his top hat and dusted the edge clear of particulates before placing it back on his head. "Why are we headed for San Francisco, Mister Crowley?"

"Initially because I believe there might be information there about your condition. I know of a man in that town who specializes in esoteric information such as what it might be that possesses your form and continues to change you. Now, I would also see what he knows about why I am being hunted down."

"You are known for your enemies, sir."

"I am. But the more I think about it, I shouldn't be. Not here. I haven't been active long enough in this country to make enemies."

Slate chuckled and shook his head.

"And what do you find so amusing, Mister Slate?"

"You, sir. I find you amusing."

"Why is that?" Crowley stared now, a dark expression on his face.

"Mister Crowley, the first time I met you, you had recently been dragged behind horses and a man had urinated on your face."

"And?"

"And yet you stand here and tell me you have not been on this continent long enough to make enemies and you say it with absolute candor, as if the very notion of you offending somebody is uncommon."

Crowley's expression tried to stay dour, but failed. "I assure you, sir, I have been on my best behavior."

"I fear the day I see your worst behavior, sir." With that said, Slate walked over to his horse and dug deep into his saddle bags. The horse, having been brought from the dead, seemed utterly unimpressed by the metal giant or the dead mechanized men.

"What are you doing, Mister Slate?"

"Getting the very dynamite you said we did not need."

"Well, why did you take it if we didn't need it?"

"We tend to judge things differently, sir." Two sticks of high explosives were secured with waxed paper in a small bundle. Though there was a fuse for the two, the powdered cord was not yet secured. "You may use them at your leisure. I will be well away from here while you prepare yourself, Mister Crowley."

He rode his horse and led Crowley's. By the time he'd ridden a safe distance away, an explosion shook the ground. Lucas Slate stopped where he was and waited, both horses held by their reins in his grasp. If they were startled by the noise, it wasn't enough to cause them to bolt.

Crowley joined him soon enough. "I've no idea what that was about, Mister Slate."

"Did you find anything of interest in the settlement?"

"Nothing. No people aside from the mechanical men and their creator."

"A large settlement for no women or children, Mister Crowley."

"And no signs at all that they were working on anything. Not a tunnel, not a well, not even freshly farmed land."

Slate shook his head and stared back the way they'd come. "Then why the efforts to look like a proper settlement?"

"Near as I can figure, they were waiting for us."

"For you, sir. He didn't know my name and was not waiting for me."

"Fair enough, Mister Slate. Apparently, he was waiting for me."

"You do have a way with people, Mister Crowley...."

"So I've been told, Mister Slate." Crowley looked around at the dead men on the ground, and then took his horse's reins and climbed back into the saddle.

"Will we not bury them, Mister Crowley?"

"I most assuredly will not, Mister Slate."

"Hardly seems appropriate behavior, sir."

"I don't go out of my way to give proper services to those that try to kill me. I'd never accomplish much of anything if I did."

"Just the same."

"By all means, Mister Slate. I'll ride ahead very slowly while you dig the graves. Mind you, I'll not be paying for your services as an undertaker, but you might find a coin or two on his corpse to finance your efforts."

Slate sniffed once.

"Would you prefer I wait while you make your efforts, sir?"

"I'd prefer you not be a jackass, sir."

"I assure you, I am no such animal."

"Stubborn as one, I can plainly see."

Crowley tapped the stirrups and his horse started forward. Slate followed soon enough and the dead remained unburied, and kept their secrets to themselves.

AUTHOR BIOS

GREG CHAPMAN

Two-time international Bram Stoker Award-nominee®, Greg Chapman is a horror author and artist based in Queensland, Australia.

Greg is the author of several novels, novellas and short stories, including his award-nominated debut novel, Hollow House and collections, Vaudeville and Other Nightmares, and Midnight Masquerade).

He is also a horror artist and his first graphic novel Witch Hunts: A Graphic History of the Burning Times, (McFarland & Company) written by authors Rocky Wood and Lisa Morton, won the Superior Achievement in a Graphic Novel category at the Bram Stoker Awards® in 2013.

He was also the President of the Australasian Horror Writers Association from 2017-2020.

DAMIEN McKEATING

Damien is a UK writer with a lifelong love of fantasy and the supernatural. Childhood days were spent reading, writing, playing tabletop roleplaying games, engaging with the popular ball related sports of the day, and trying to communicate with the dead. He would eventually set aside necromancy and sports, and go onto study film and writing at university.

After a stint as a copywriter for radio, he moved into SEN teaching and realised how easy all of his previous employment had been. Over the years he has had short stories published across different magazines and anthologies, for adults and children. He has also written for comics and radio, and the peculiar folk band Hornswaggle. He's fond of corvids and is currently the oldest he's ever been. Sometimes he remembers to blog about writing at skeletonbutler.wordpress.com, or can be found on Facebook under Damien Mckeating (Author). His debut novel, Tallulah Belle, is a supernatural coming of age story set within the walls of a fantasy burlesque theatre, and is due for release in 2024.

ZACHARY O'SHEA

Zachary O'Shea lives sometimes in the Land of Neon Sunrises and other times in the Great White North. There's something about the stark differences between the American Southwest and Northern Ontario that he can't resist. Spoiler; it's his wife.

He has spent his life telling stories from absurd coloring book creations as a child to a lifelong passion for game-mastering role-playing games, and occasionally dipping a toe into short horror fiction. When he's not writing, which is honestly rare, Zachary is spending time with his family, running a role-playing game session, or blowing off some steam in an MMO. Though, he's usually writing something in stolen moments even in between all of this.

ALAN BAXTER

Alan Baxter is a multi-award-winning author who This Is Horror podcast called "Australia's master of literary darkness" and the Talking Scared podcast dubbed "The Lord of Weird Australia." He's also a martial artist, a whisky-soaked swear monkey, and dog lover. Find him online at www.alanbaxter.com.au

PAMELA JEFFS

Pamela Jeffs (she/her) is an Australian speculative fiction author with a background in Interior Architecture and Design. She has published five short story collections and has 90+ short stories featured in various publications including *Midnight Echo Magazine* by the Australian Horror Writers Association and in two SNAFU series books by Cohesion Press.

Pamela's work has shortlisted for multiple awards including nine Aurealis Awards and three Ditmar Awards.

For more information, visit her at www.pamelajeffs.com.

RPL JOHNSON

Richard is an Australian science fiction writer and winner of the Gold Award at Writers of the Future and the Jim Baen Memorial Award. King Rat is his fifth appearance in the SNAFU series.

He lives in Melbourne with his wife and two young sons and is currently working on a novel, Mappa Mundi, set in the King Rat universe.

MARK RENSHAW

Mark is a self-taught writer from a working-class background based in the north-west of the United Kingdom. By day he works in business software development; on weekends, he is a writer of prose, screenplays and produces the occasional short film.

Mark has had two short stories, 'Fear' and 'No Title' published in *An Eclectic Mix Vol 7* alongside several international competition winners. His sci-fi short story 'Automatic Drive' was published in *The Singularity50* anthology, while his short story 'Ragnarok' was included in *SNAFU: Resurrection* published by Cohesion Press. He is currently working on his debut novel series, a sci-fi comedy trilogy called Cyborn.

With his screenplay hat on, Mark won Best Short Screenplay at the 2022 Austin Film Festival. He's also won Euroscript's Screen Story competition, Shriekfest, and the Inroads Screenwriting Fellowship.

Mark has written and produced severalshort films, including *The Dollmaker*, which has over 24 million views on YouTube, and a mini-series called *So Dark*.

MYNA CHANG

Myna Chang (she/her) is the host of Electric Sheep SF. Her work has been selected for *Flash Fiction America* (W.W. Norton), *Best Small Fictions, Beneath Ceaseless Skies, Small Wonders, Daily Science Fiction*, and MicroPodcast's special science fiction edition.

Her micro collection, *The Potential of Radio and Rain* (Cutbank Books) was published in 2023. She has won the Lascaux Prize in Creative Nonfiction and the New Millennium Writings Award in Flash Fiction.

MATTHEW FREEMAN

Matthew Freeman is a former sports journalist and longtime mixed martial artist. He lives in the middle of the UK with his wife and son where he can be regularly found writing, painting and training.

TORION OEY

Torion holds a BA in psychology and creative writing and an MS in psychology. He has written every year for National Novel Writing Month since 2014 and self-published the mystery *Loco Motive* and high fantasy *Not James* on Amazon. He is an SFWA member and has had works featured in *Galaxy's Edge Magazine, Expanded Field Journal,* and *NonBinary Review.*

AMANDA BRIDGEMAN

Amanda is a two-time Scribe Award winner, a two-time Tin Duck Award winner, an Aurealis and Ditmar Awards finalist, and author of several novels and short stories. She is also a screenwriter. Her original fiction includes the sci-fi crime thriller *The Subjugate,* which is being developed for TV by Anonymous Content and Aquarius Films, and is being studied at two German Universities (Düsseldorf and Cologne) as part of a program on Australian speculative fiction, in conjunction with the Centre for Australian Studies. Amanda's media tie-in fiction includes that written for Marvel (X-Men), Black Library (Warhammer 40k), and Z-Man Games (Pandemic).

JUSTIN COATES

Justin Coates is a colony of half-sentient spiders in a man suit. His military sci-fi and horror stories have been featured in multiple anthologies and adapted by the hit Netflix Original series *Love, Death and Robots*. When he's not powerlifting, he's spending time with his ridiculously hot wife and two demon-spawn sons. Follow him on Facebook and Patreon for the latest lore updates.

CJ GOLDBERG

As a kid, C.J. spent his days exploring the Montana woods, reading horror, and watching scary movies. He soon discovered that storytelling was his passion.

After graduating from The University of Montana with a degree in Acting, C.J. worked as a professional poker dealer for 14 years in Montana bars. During that time, he never gave up on his dream of becoming a horror author. He studied writing craft extensively through books, courses, and workshops, and in 2017 he moved to Glasgow, Scotland while his wife attended graduate school. This allowed him to focus full-time on his writing career.

C.J. now lives in Petaluma, California, with his wife and two kids where, when not changing diapers, he is writing his debut novel, a cosmic horror story set in a remote Montana town.

Factory of Fear in SNAFU: PUNK'D is C.J.'s first published short story.

KIRSTIN CROSS

Kirsten (Kes) Cross has reached her fifth decade and hasn't quite worked out how the hell that even happened yet. She spends her days in a little cottage on Exmoor in Devon with roses around the door (no, really) writing web content to pay the bills while she builds up a bespoke jewellery business.

In between, she writes the occasional scary-as-all-heck stuff and has been a regular contributor to SNAFU from the very first outing. Her story, "Sucker of Souls" was included in the Emmy award-winning Netflix Original series *Love, Death & Robots*. Again, seriously, no idea how that happened. It was fun being sprinkled by a bit of Hollywood magic for a while, though.

When not writing or making shiny things, she spends the rest of her time travelling around the country on her beloved

British Army Armstrong motorcycle, occasionally stopping and pointing at the scenery for no apparent reason.

DAVID W. AMENDOLA

David W. Amendola has been a pulp fiction fan and epic history nerd since his teens, and his stories combine both. He writes science-fiction, fantasy, horror, westerns, military adventure, mystery, and mashups of all these genres. He also occasionally writes about non-fiction topics such as family genealogy, history, and numismatics. He has a Bachelor of Arts in World Military History and a Graduate Certificate in World War II Studies, both from American Military University. He served in the U.S. Air Force for 21 years.

Six of his short stories have been featured in SNAFU anthologies and one, 'The Secret War', was adapted into a feature for the first season of the Emmy-winning Netflix Original series *Love, Death + Robots*.

RICHARD BEAUCHAMP

Hailing from the lush, verdant foothills of the Missouri Ozarks, Richard Beauchamp is an author of horror and dark speculative fiction. Often casting his stories in the wild settings of his own backyard, Richard's fiction has been published in such esteemed publications as Dark Peninsula Press' Negative Space Survival horror anthologies, Timber Ghost Press's *Along Harrowed Trails* anthology, and The Other Stories podcast series from Hawk and Cleaver Audio. His debut short fiction collection *Black Tongue & Other Anomalies* was a nominee for the 2022 Splatterpunk Awards, and his short story 'The Sons Of Luna' was a 2018 Pushcart Prize nominee.

When he isn't tucked away in his office pecking away at his keyboard, you can find him traversing the Ozark Mountains, hiking, camping, and fishing every chance he gets. He lives with his fiance, their dog, and way too many cats.

STEVE LEWIS

Steve has at various times been a security guard, a ditch digger, a public servant and an Army officer (though not necessarily in that order). Sydney born, currently in Brisbane and now retired, when he's not procrastinating he spends his time working on the various novels he has 90% written, hoping to actually finish them one day soon.

JAMES A. MOORE

James A. Moore is the best-selling and award-winning author of over forty novels; thrillers, dark fantasy and horror alike, including the critically acclaimed *Fireworks, Under The Overtree, Blood Red*, the Serenity Falls trilogy (featuring his recurring anti-hero, Jonathan Crowley) and his most recent novels, The Tides of War series. In addition to writing multiple short stories, he has also edited, with Christopher Golden and Tim Lebbon, the *British Invasion* anthology for Cemetery Dance Publications. The author cut his teeth in the industry writing for Marvel Comics and authoring over twenty role-playing supplements for White Wolf Games. Moore's first short story collection, *Slices*, sold out before ever seeing print. Along with Golden and Jonathan Maberry he is co-host of the Three Guys With beards podcast.